ALSO BY E.E. 1

SHADOW OF THE BROTHERHOOD

SHADOW OF THE BROTHERHOOD

THE GATEWAY TRACKERS

BOOK 10

E.E. HOLMES

FAIRHAVEN PRESS

Fairhaven Press

Townsend, MA

www.eeholmes.com

ISBN 978-1-956656-15-2 (Paperback edition)

ISBN 978-1-956656-14-5 (Digital edition)

Publisher's note: This is a work of fiction. Names, characters, places and incidents are either the product of the author's imagination or are used fictitiously.

Cover design by James T. Egan of Bookfly Design LLC

Author photography by Cydney Scott Photography

For Oliver, warmer of laps, stealer of treats, happy tap-dancer extraordinaire. You are so very missed.

Life is not a dream. Careful! Careful! Careful!
We fall down the stairs in order to eat the moist earth
or we climb to the knife edge of the snow with the voices of the dead dahlias.
But forgetfulness does not exist, dreams do not exist;
flesh exists. Kisses tie our mouths
in a thicket of new veins,
and whoever his pain pains will feel that pain forever
and whoever is afraid of death will carry it on his shoulders.

Federico García Lorca

PROLOGUE

He could not stay; that much was certain.

In the liminal space between materializing and vanishing, Alasdair waited, pondering. Surely, they would be looking for him. It was no longer safe for him in Edinburgh.

He had not come to this moment of calm consideration easily. The thought of abandoning his Collection was almost enough to break him. His rage burned through him, razing every other thought into ash. All of that time, all of that work, *wasted*. For a moment, in the blazing power of it, he nearly lost his head. Only by exerting a most painful self-control did he prevent himself from storming back into the place that had been half-prison, half-workshop. Only by the very tips of his fingers did he cling to his common sense. The Walker and the others were clever—now that they had discovered his experiment, they would not leave it unguarded. He was sure, even now, that they were fortifying the place against him, to ensure he could not access it again.

He spared hardly a passing thought for Danica MacLeod. The woman was, after all, an imbecile—a useful imbecile, but an imbecile nonetheless; and she had now outlived her usefulness. What happened to her next, he did not care in the least. She had meddled in Castings far beyond her comprehension, and now she would pay a price for it. Alasdair even managed a smile, considering that she might suffer even a fraction of what he had endured at the hands of Clan Rìoghalachd. Every Durupinen deserved to taste that pain, and he had had no pity for her as he listened to her agonized screams echoing through the labyrinthine passages as he escaped.

He could not stay. He must flee, and at once. But where?

He stilled himself, and in his stillness, the answer floated calmly to the surface of his mind. There was one other place where seeds of his work may have taken root, where the modern world had risen up like a beast; and yet the core of his beliefs had been protected, safely cocooned against the storm of relentless progress. A place where tradition and loyalty still meant something.

It had been centuries. Could he even find the way through this ugly and altered world and, if he did, would anything remain for him there?

He had no choice but to find out.

1

AFTERMATH

"I still say we should have burned it all."

The words were Hannah's, and they repeated as they broke into ghostly echoes around the cavernous room in which we now stood.

"You know why we can't do that," I replied, reaching out to give her cold little hand a squeeze.

"Sure, *logically* I do," Hannah said, her teeth gritted against the anger. "Emotionally, though?"

I nodded. "I get it, I promise. And when we're done with it, I promise to hand you the blowtorch myself."

It would be an easy promise to keep, I thought, and a shudder of horror jolted down my spine as we surveyed the room's contents. It was the result of ten days' worth of excavation, extraction, and organization of the contents of MacLeod Close and the underground *priosún*. It was truly staggering to see, now that it was all laid out in front of us, just how much of Alasdair's possessions and work had been squirreled away beneath the streets of the city. It was an apt metaphor for the dark and sordid tale that Clan Rìoghalachd had been hiding in its past.

We'd arrived in Edinburgh only a few weeks previously to answer the distress call of Clarissa MacLeod, head of Clan Rìoghalachd, and one of the most powerful women in the Durupinen world. The newly restored Geatgrima in Edinburgh was behaving strangely, and Clarissa, who was furious about the

Reckoning, decided to make it the Trackers' problem—and therefore, *my* problem—to solve; I was, after all, the scapegoat for the whole of the Northern Clans when it came to the Reckoning and its subsequent fallout. She stonewalled us from the moment we arrived, giving us as much trouble as possible, probably hoping we would have no choice but to reverse the Reckoning and restore the Gateways to the Durupinen bloodlines. Unfortunately for her, the Geatgrima had been restored successfully—it was Clarissa's own sister, Danica, whose interference was causing spirits to vanish as they attempted to Cross.

The restoration of the Gateway had had one unexpected consequence in Edinburgh—it had interfered with Castings in their *príosún,* and therefore released their oldest and most dangerous prisoner: Alasdair MacLeod. In life, Alasdair had been a Caomhnóir whose fear of death and quest to conquer it led him to join forces with the Necromancers. But his experiments quickly became too twisted and extreme even for that notoriously evil cult, and soon he was murdering people in the darkened closes of Edinburgh to steal their souls and use them in his demented quest for immortality. Alasdair was eventually caught and imprisoned, but not before he earned himself the moniker "The Collector," a name as feared in the streets of Edinburgh as Jack the Ripper was in the squalid corners of Victorian London.

Danica discovered Alasdair, newly freed, and joined him in the resurrection of his vile life's work. Danica somehow convinced herself that she could use Alasdair's research to help Clarissa reclaim the powers of the Gateway. Instead, she'd nearly killed her sister and helped to create "The Collection," an abomination of writhing, trapped, and dismembered souls that we hoped somehow to reverse—and thus the quest to clean out Alasdair's underground lair of everything we might find useful.

A warehouse-like storage room had been cleaned out in Canongate Collective, one of Clan Rìoghalachd's many properties, and had now become the holding area for everything that could be salvaged. Clan Rìoghalachd had provided a veritable army of manpower to help complete the task, which was a welcome change from the obstruction we'd been met with on our arrival in Edinburgh. Maybe they were afraid of more Council retribution if they didn't give us their full cooperation—after all, Celeste had already handed down several sanctions. But I thought, just maybe, they now genuinely wanted to help. After all, Alasdair was their own personal Frankenstein's monster, a horror they had created and then tried to hide from the world. Helping to track him down would be only the first step in beginning to make amends to the untold numbers of his victims.

As if to emphasize this point, there was a soft knock on the door and Maeve MacLeod poked her head inside.

"Hello. I came to see if... *wow.*" Her mouth fell open as she took in the full contents of the room.

"Come on in, Maeve," I told her, and though I gestured for her to enter, she hung back in the doorway, shifting anxiously from foot to foot.

"I... didn't realize there'd be so much," she murmured, hand tensed on the doorknob as if she half-hoped to flee. "He was really hiding all of this under the city?"

"Yup. A whole deluded life's work, buried for centuries. It would be kind of cool if it wasn't so ghoulish," I said.

"I only hope we can do some good with it," Hannah replied, more to herself than to anyone else.

Maeve took a tentative step inside, closing the door behind her. "I promised my mother I'd check in on your progress. She's anxious to know if there's anything else she can do."

"Tell your mother she has enough to be anxious about and that she should take it easy and focus her energy on getting well," I replied.

Maeve smiled tightly as she ran her fingers through the boldly pink locks of her hair. "Do you honestly think I haven't tried? I'm sure you could infer this from your brief acquaintance with my mother, but she doesn't exactly excel at taking it easy."

I returned the strained smile. "Yeah, I could have guessed that. How is she doing?"

Maeve shrugged. Her makeup didn't quite succeed at hiding the deep purple shadows under her eyes. "I imagine she'd be doing better if she'd let the other members of the clan take the reins for a bit; but, as I said, it's not in her nature. She's already turned her hospital room into a makeshift office. The doctors were furious at first, but they learned pretty quickly that resistance is futile."

I shook my head. "Leave it to Clarissa MacLeod to treat a near-fatal stabbing like a minor inconvenience."

Maeve nodded, sighing. "She also doesn't seem to realize that she can't simply bully her body into healing more quickly. She was gobsmacked to learn they wouldn't just load her up with painkillers and let her get on with it."

"Doesn't she have a punctured lung?" Hannah asked, incredulous.

"Yes, but as she informed her nurse only yesterday, 'it was just the one hole, and it's been stitched up now, so what's all the fuss?'" Maeve said, adopting a credible imitation of her mother's commanding tone. "Honestly, and the woman thinks *I'm* impossible."

"I don't suppose the subject of Reilly has come up at all?" I asked, referring to Maeve's clandestine relationship with a Caomhnóir on her security detail.

Maeve made a face. "It's hardly the moment. The woman just survived a knife to the chest. I don't need to add to the drama by plunging a metaphorical one into her back."

I laughed. "Fair point. Just remember, it isn't illegal anymore."

Maeve pressed her lips into a grim smile. "Small comfort."

"What about Danica?" Hannah asked. The mention of the name seemed to suck all the air from the room. Maeve's face twitched with tension as she pulled in a shuddering breath.

"They've mostly had to sedate her. Every time they try to wean her off the sedatives, she becomes so hysterical that she can't be questioned or reasoned with. Two days ago, she demanded paper and a pen so that she could write an apology. They wouldn't give her the pen, of course—afraid she might do herself harm with it. But they gave her some crayons to appease her. So far, she still won't answer any of their questions, but has written more than two hundred pages worth of explanation and apology to my mother, most of it so scattered and rambling that they can barely make any sense of it. She was still trying to scribble a few more sentences on the back when they finally took it away from her."

"Wow," I muttered under my breath. "Does your mother know?"

Maeve laughed. The sound was rather hollow. "Oh, she knows, but she's too outraged at Danica to humor her right now. We'll see what happens as she heals, but for the moment, my mother's refusing to speak to Danica or read the novel-length apology." Maeve swung her backpack around to the front so she could unzip it, and pulled out a stack of paper tied together with twine. I could see the bright red crayon scrawl that covered the top page. "She has, however, tasked me with delivering the apology to you. She thought there might be information in it that could help the investigation."

I reached out and took the slightly crumpled bundle. "Thanks. We'll uh... add it to the list of documents to be examined by—" But before I could finish my sentence, Hannah snatched the papers from my hand, plopped herself cross-legged on the rug, and began untying the twine.

Maeve caught my eye, and I leaned forward, lowering my voice. "This whole situation has her really upset. She's desperate to do something to help—especially with the Collection."

"I understand," Maeve replied, her voice full of that familiar combination of awe and horror that the Collection inspired in everyone unfortunate enough to know of its existence.

At that moment, Finn and Savvy strode into the room, Finn slamming the door behind him.

"All right, you lot?" Savvy said by way of greeting, and though she was speaking to us, her wary gaze was still following Finn.

"I'm just giving Maeve an update so she can let Clarissa know how the investigation is going." I turned to Finn, who was violently tugging off his rain gear and tossing it into a nearby corner. "So, this might be a stupid question, judging from the literal cartoon storm cloud over your head, but how did it go?" I asked.

Finn didn't even look up as he worked his feet out of his rain boots. "Smashing," he growled.

I traded glances with Savvy, who gave a rueful smile. "That well, huh?" I pressed.

"We found nothing," Finn replied before Savvy could open her mouth. "Absolutely nothing. Not the slightest whisper of him anywhere, not a sighting or an encounter."

"We must've interviewed every spirit in this city," Savvy confirmed, stifling a yawn with the back of her hand. "They all know him, of course, but they all swear they've not seen hide nor hair of him in days."

"And you believe them?" I asked.

Savvy shrugged. "What reason would they have to lie?"

"They're only confirming what we already suspected," Finn interjected. "You remember that foul energy he exudes, don't you?"

I nodded. Remember it? I had to stifle a gag just thinking about it. That numbing, brutal cold, accompanied by the rotting, sulfurous stench? Yeah, I wouldn't forget that in a hurry.

"If he was lurking somewhere, we'd be able to track him by that energy alone. But there, again, not a bloody trace unless, of course, he's found a way to mask it," Finn growled.

I didn't want to say it out loud, but I'd never expected them to find Alasdair still in the city. I felt in my bones that Alasdair had left Edinburgh. First of all, he'd be a fool to stay, knowing that every available Caomhnóir in the Northern Clans would be searching for him. Then there was the fact that he hadn't exactly endeared himself to the other spirits haunting these ancient streets. There wasn't a ghost for miles who didn't fear an encounter with The Collector, as he'd been known, even in life. Alasdair might have been mad, but he wasn't stupid; he'd have gotten as far from Edinburgh as he possibly could. The challenge now was to figure out where he would go.

"Is it possible he's left the city?" Maeve asked, voicing my conclusion.

"Yes, it's possible. Probable, even," Finn admitted, the words scraping out through his clenched teeth. "But we don't want to assume, so we're combing every inch of it anyway."

"His only reason to stay is his research, and we've taken possession of it," Hannah said. "He must realize by now that he can't get near a page of it. We've put up every Ward and protective Casting we can find, and there are Caomhnóir posted at every door, window, and mousehole twenty-four hours a day."

"That's what I've been saying. He's done a bunk!" Savvy exclaimed, then she caught Finn's foreboding expression and quickly cleared her throat. "What I mean is, it might be time to uh... widen the search parameters, as it were."

Finn dropped his head into his hands with a groan. I gave the others a tight smile and went over to join him. He was still sitting on a bench, surrounded by a jumble of dripping, sodden outerwear.

I sunk onto the seat beside him. "Hey."

He sighed, rubbing his hands over his unshaven face. "Hey, yourself."

"You've got to stop this," I said, my voice gentle.

"Stop looking for that bastard? Not bloody likely," Finn snapped.

"That's not what I mean. Of course we're going to keep looking for him," I said, slipping my hand through the crook of his arm and pulling him a little closer to me. "I know you're not going to rest until you find him, and neither am I."

Finn frowned. "Then, what are you—?"

"You need to stop blaming yourself, Finn," I said. "It's not your fault that Alasdair escaped."

Finn laughed humorlessly. "You may want to review the footage on that one, Ballard. I'd say it's pretty damn clear cut whose fault it was."

"Finn, you were trying to save Clarissa's life!" I reminded him. "You were the only one standing close enough to realize what was happening."

The moment flashed into my memory, razor-sharp. Alasdair, lunging and snarling inside the circle Finn had trapped him in; Danica, desperately trying to show Clarissa what the Collection could do; Clarissa, knocking candles from her sister's hands, shrieking that she didn't care, that Danica must stop. And then the moment Danica's hand found the hilt of the knife, the way she snatched it up, possessed with a sudden, manic fury...

It was over in a moment. There was nothing anyone could have done.

"And so not only did I lose my hold on Alasdair, but I didn't even manage to stop Danica from stabbing her own sister in the chest," Finn said. "Maybe if I'd been able to knock the knife away it would have been worth it, but I didn't even manage that."

"Clarissa's okay. She's going to recover."

"No thanks to me," Finn said.

"At least you tried to do something!" I cried, feeling my own temper flare now. "What about the rest of us? We just stood there, watching!"

"You and Milo were both trapped in cells," Finn argued. "There was nothing you could have done!"

"What about Catriona?" I pointed out. "She was standing right there, too! Why aren't you blaming her?"

Finn shook his head mulishly as he fumbled for a reply. "That's not... it wasn't..."

"Exactly. It wasn't. It wasn't her fault, and it wasn't yours. It was a dangerous, impossible situation that we were lucky to get out of alive; but we did, and now we keep going. I am with you, Finn, every step of the way, but not without calling you on your bullshit. And blaming yourself for any of this? It's definitely bullshit."

Finn looked up at me. His mouth twitched just a tiny bit at the corner.

"Bullshit," I whispered again, before planting a tiny kiss on the end of his nose.

He sighed in defeat. "Fine. I won't blame myself anymore."

"Good."

"Out loud."

I punched him none-too-gently in the arm, but apparently my punches were pathetic because he didn't even have the decency to wince before he grinned at me.

"Watch it, Carey," I grumbled at him.

He saluted and then jumped to his feet as Milo came sailing through the closed door, looking disgruntled.

"Look, I don't want to make generalizations about the Caomhnóir around here, especially when so many of them are *very* pleasant to look at, but how many times am I going to have to go nine rounds with some jumped-up security guard before they remember that I have clearance to come in here?" Milo's whole form vibrated with indignation, and he looked like he was experiencing his own paranormal earthquake.

"They stopped you again?" Hannah asked.

"Mais oui!" Milo said. "I've had to explain the exception to the Wards every time there's a shift change, and that's only after they try to Banish me. Is there not a memo we could distribute? Should I have it printed on a t-shirt? How do we solve this before I go full-out poltergeist on the night shift?"

Finn shook his head. "Sorry, Milo. Leadership's been a bit shaky with Clarissa in the hospital. It seems no one wants to risk her wrath, and so every order is getting second guessed." Finn caught Maeve's eye and his face contracted into an apologetic grimace. "Sorry, Maeve. No offense meant."

Maeve shrugged. "Oh, none taken, I assure you. My mother's reputation for terrorizing her subordinates is well-earned. Her own mother used to call her 'the dragon.'"

"I'll have another word with the head Caomhnóir and get this sorted, Milo," Finn promised.

"Thanks. Not to put something else on your plate, but a diva likes to know her name's on the VIP list, even if she comes bearing bad news."

"No joy, then?" Finn asked.

"Apologies, sweetness, but not a trace," Milo said, and his expression turned as dark as Finn's. "I think I've talked to every spirit in this city, and they all say the same thing: there's been no sign of him in days. They're all thrilled about it, mind you," he added. "In fact, I had one spirit today start shouting at me that I was stirring things up, and to leave well enough alone. It's been a terrifying few months for them."

Savvy nodded. "Too true. Imagine having to fear for your life when you're already dead. Seems like overkill, if you'll pardon the pun."

"Exactly," Milo agreed with a shudder. "And speaking of Alasdair's unfortunate victims, where are we with cleaning out his cave of horrors?"

"The last of the artifacts and research were excavated this morning," I told him, "And they've just brought it all up. We were about to give Maeve the grand tour."

I felt a pull on the hem of my sweater and looked down to see Hannah tugging on it like a small child. I squatted down beside her.

"What's up?" I asked her, dropping my voice as she put a finger to her lips.

"Are we sure we should be showing Maeve what we've found? Are we sure we should be showing anyone?" Hannah murmured into my ear. She was watching Maeve through narrowed eyes as Maeve peered down at the nearest table of artifacts.

"She's only here so she can report back to her mother," I told her. "It's not as though we're going to let her sit down for hours and study this stuff."

Hannah ran a hand over her face—she was looking paler than usual, and exhausted as well. "I know, I know. I just... I can't help but feel like all of this is a mistake." She gestured helplessly around at the contents of the room. "Who's to say someone won't turn around and use this information for the evil it was intended for?"

"Hannah, we're being careful," I said. "Everything has been carefully cataloged and recorded. And the only people who are going to be allowed to study it will be trusted scholars and Scribes."

"Alasdair was a trusted Caomhnóir before he devolved into that... that *thing*," Hannah countered, still shaking her head mutinously. "These ideas... they're too dangerous, too monstrous to expose people to!"

"Look, I understand why you're worried," I said. "And you're right. It is dangerous. But there's a big difference between theory and practice. It's hard to imagine anyone being anything but horrified at Alasdair's work. Still, even if someone felt a spark of inspiration, all we would have to do is walk them under this building and make them stand in front of the Collection, and that spark would fizzle and die."

Hannah bit her lip. I hadn't convinced her.

"It's just... there are so many Durupinen out there—and Caomhnóir, too, of course—who are pissed at the way things have changed since the Reckoning. Like... really pissed. Clarissa and Danica are only the tip of the iceberg. Danica didn't see lunacy in Alasdair's work. She saw potential. Who's to say another desperate person won't do the same?"

I couldn't reassure her because I had the same worries. You couldn't rock the boat as much as we had over the last few years without being hyper-aware of the sharks circling in the water. What we needed was more people we could trust.

"Okay, how about this? What if I get on the phone with Flavia and get her down here?" I suggested.

Hannah perked up. "Flavia?"

"Who better? She's probably the most brilliant Durupinen scholar of the last century, but more importantly, we trust her implicitly." And though I'd said it just to appease her, the more I thought about it, the more I realized how much better I'd feel to have Flavia as a part of the team. She'd been right by our side during some of the most harrowing moments of the last few years, and she had a wealth of obscure knowledge that could be invaluable. In fact, I was surprised I hadn't thought of it earlier.

"Do you think she'd agree? It's an awfully gruesome task to volunteer for," Hannah said.

"Gruesome, but uncharted—and what scholar wouldn't take the chance to break new ground like this? Besides, if I know Flavia, she won't be able to say no after she finds out about the Collection. She'll be as horrified as we are."

Hannah nodded along, and I could see she was caving. I swooped in and took advantage of the moment.

"Keeping and studying this work is too important to understanding the Collection. Without it, we don't have a prayer of helping those spirits." *If they aren't beyond our help already*, I added silently to myself.

I watched as Hannah's tensed-up shoulders slowly lowered themselves from the vicinity of her ears. She took a deep breath. "Okay. You're right. We use it to reverse the Collection, and then we destroy it. Don't tell Kiernan I said that, though," she added, suddenly wide-eyed. "He doesn't believe in destroying documentation of anything, no matter how gruesome it is."

It may have been the only thing they'd ever disagreed about since they started dating. Kiernan was too devoted a scholar to ever concede that there were some historical documents better left undiscovered and unstudied. However, he'd understood Hannah's trepidation, and so he had promised to keep his research team very small and carefully vetted. No photocopies or photographs of any kind were allowed—not a single piece of Alasdair's work was to be replicated or documented in any way that could spread its influence. He was firmly of the opinion that we should leave it up to Celeste, High Priestess of the Northern Clans, to decide what should be done with the research after we'd finished with it. Hannah thought it was better to burn the whole lot to ash and ask for forgiveness later. I wasn't sure who was right, so I just nodded to placate Hannah, and she returned to feverishly poring over Danica's disjointed ramblings.

I joined Finn and Maeve as they worked their way around the tables, eyes roaming over dusty journals, moth-eaten cloaks, and rusty daggers. I spotted the objects that had been taken from Alasdair's living victims, the ones he had murdered in the darkened closes of the city all those years ago. Each one was a gruesome trophy of a crime, but they were more than that. He had used them one by one to trap the soul as it escaped the body he'd just killed. As I looked at them, I felt the rage rise in me, bubbling up and over.

We had to catch this sick bastard.

2

NIGHT TERRORS

The hallway was long, dark, and made of pale, crumbling stone. There were carvings along the walls. My brain cataloged them as I ran by.

A long-haired woman holding a chalice and a wand.

A circle of animals—they looked like pigs or wild boar.

A boat with a man in it, crossing a river of flame.

I tore my eyes away from them and began to run. Torches burning in brackets flashed past me like orange blurs. I lost my footing on the uneven floor, but I couldn't stop, not now. I had to catch him.

Ahead of me, a figure in a dark cloak sprinted for the far end of the corridor where it ended in an arched wooden door. My heart was thudding in my ears, pounding out a rhythm, a mantra that kept me running even as my breath burned like fire in my lungs.

Don't. Let. Him. Get. Away.

But I was too slow. Too far behind. My legs seemed to weigh a thousand pounds, sinking through the floor, slowing me down like a patch of quicksand.

The cloaked figure had nearly reached the door. I let out a shriek of frustration and heard an answering cackle below me. I looked down, distracted momentarily from my quarry.

Skeletal hands had gotten hold of my legs, snatching at them, hindering my progress. And not just hands. Arms. Legs. Wasted, grinning, fleshless faces, mouths gaping in that maniacal laughter that now echoed around me as I struggled in vain against them.

"Let me go!" I shouted in desperation.

But the faces laughed louder. The hands began to drag me back, to pull me down.

"No," they shrieked. "He's come for us at last. We must stop you."

I tumbled to the ground. I had just a glimpse of the hooded figure disappearing through the door before a bitterly cold and slimy hand clamped down over my mouth.

My scream burst from me as I wrenched myself free from the clutches of both the creature that held me and the dream itself. In fact, my escape was so complete that I launched myself out of the bed and landed with a painful thump on the floor, a bedsheet still wrapped around my ankle.

"Ow."

"Jess! Bloody hell! Are you all right?" Finn's sleep-slurred voice called for me as he fumbled for the lamp on the bedside table. I sat untangling myself in the pale-yellow light, cursing profusely.

"Yeah, I'm okay. Just a nightmare," I said, aggravated to hear the way my voice trembled. "You'd think I'd be immune to them by now, but here I am, shaking and crying like a preschooler."

"Don't be daft. Can I get you something?"

"I don't... a glass of water, maybe."

"Nonsense. A nice cup of chamomile tea to put you back to sleep, that's what you need." He rolled over and glanced at the clock. "Actually, it's just gone five. I've got to be up in twenty minutes anyway. How about some coffee instead?"

"Now you're speaking my language, Carey."

"Right, then. Coffee it is." He was out of the bed and across the room in a single bound.

I didn't follow him right away, choosing instead to take a few deep breaths and allow my limbs to stop trembling. It had been a long time since I'd experienced such a visceral dream, and I still felt a bit disoriented. I stared around the little bedroom, taking stock of my surroundings to steady myself. The curtains were drawn back from the tall windows, revealing a smattering of wispy clouds scuttling lazily across a brightening sky. I clambered carefully to my feet, testing my legs to make sure they'd stopped shaking before crossing to the nearest window.

We'd been moved from our hotel to a rented flat just off the Royal Mile, in yet another building owned by the MacLeods—seriously, these people owned half the city—along with the rest of the Trackers and Caomhnóir still working the case.

I felt a strange sensation in my head, a sort of buzzing, prodding sensation as Hannah tested the connection.

"Jess? You okay?" Her voice in my head was more thought than sound, like a comforting whisper from my subconscious.

"I'm fine."

"I thought... did you just have a nightmare?"

"Yeah. I'm okay, I promise. It was just... vivid. Go back to sleep. I'll pop up to see you at a more human hour, okay?" Hannah and Kiernan were staying in the flat just above ours. It was good to know she was just above me; but then again, thanks to our connection, she was never far away.

"'Kay," she mumbled, and the connection closed again, gently, like rising water closing over my head.

I slid my feet into my slippers and shuffled out into the main living area, where the sitting room blended seamlessly into the kitchen. Finn was standing at the counter, watching the coffee dribble down into the pot. He looked up at the sound of my entrance and smiled. His dark hair was sleep-tousled, and his jawline sported a dark shadow of unshaven stubble.

"Have I ever told you how unbearably sexy you are when you first wake up?" I asked him.

"Am I?" he chuckled, "or do I just appear that way because it's before 6 AM and I'm making you coffee?"

"Hmm, good point. I'll have to investigate." I crossed the room and hopped up onto the counter, wrapping my arms around his neck and kissing him gently. I smacked my lips and pretended to consider.

"Nope, definitely sexy, coffee or no coffee."

"Glad to hear it." His smile faded as he poured out a cup of coffee and doctored it for me. He handed it to me and gestured toward the couch. "Now, about that dream."

I steeled myself with a scalding sip before launching into a description of what I'd experienced in my dream. Finn listened to every word, a frown marring his otherwise perfect face.

"Do you think it was a spirit-induced dream?" he asked when I'd talked myself out.

"I'm not sure. I... I was definitely myself. I can usually tell when a spirit is trying to show me things through their own eyes, and this didn't feel like that."

"Did you recognize the place? You mentioned torches. Could it have been somewhere down in the buried closes?"

I shook my head. "I don't think so. It was definitely old, but it didn't have quite the same derelict appearance. Down in the closes, everything's rotting and falling apart. This place wasn't quite like that."

"Any place else you've been before? After all, we've experienced more than our share of old, creepy buildings, wouldn't you say?"

I had to agree, but though we both wracked our brains for the next few minutes, I couldn't jog my memory. I had to conclude that I'd never seen the place in real life, wherever it was.

"And the figure you were chasing? Did you recognize them?"

"It could have been anybody. Although," I squeezed my eyes shut, conjuring an image of the figure, "I think it may have been a man. Something about the build..."

"So if it's not a place you've been before, maybe it's a place you'll be in the future," Finn said, rubbing his chin. "Which means we could be dealing with a Seer vision."

I groaned. "God, I hope not. I have no desire to relive any single part of that dream, especially if I can't just wake up from it. But..." I touched a finger to my mouth. I'd been drinking hot coffee for several minutes now, and yet I could still feel the aching cold of that hand on my mouth.

Finn gave me a long, hard look and then jumped up from the couch. He disappeared into the bedroom for a few minutes, and then emerged holding one of my sketchbooks and my pencil case. He thrust them out toward me.

"Draw it. Every detail you can recall before it starts to fade," he demanded.

I sighed and handed him my mug. "Fine. But I'm gonna need a refill."

I was still finishing up an hour later when there was a soft knock on the door, and it opened a crack.

"Finn?" Hannah's voice was tentative.

"Come on in, Hannah," I called, setting down my pencil and rubbing at my neck where it ached from leaning over my sketchbook for too long. "Finn's in the shower."

"Oh, Jess!" Hannah slipped through the door and pulled it shut behind her. "I didn't think you'd be awake yet, because... well..."

"Because I still have the sleep patterns of a teenager?" I smirked. "I couldn't fall back to sleep after that nightmare, so I just got up with Finn instead."

"It was a bad one, huh?"

"Actually, we're trying to figure out if it might be a good one."

Hannah's nose crinkled in confusion. "Huh?"

Suddenly, Milo's voice sounded through the connection, humming with energy. "Doth mine spectral connection deceive me, or is Jessica Beyonce Ballard awake and functioning before 7 AM?

"Since when is my middle name Beyonce?" I inquired.

"Since her latest single's been stuck in my head all night," Milo announced. "Where are you?"

"My flat. Hannah's here too."

He gasped. "Quality girl time without me? Unacceptable! Hang on, manifesting..."

A moment later, Milo sailed through the wall and drifted to rest on the couch between us. "There, that's better. Now what are we discussing at this ungodly hour? It must be important. Your maid-of-honor look, I'm assuming? Playlist for the DJ?"

I held up the drawing I'd just completed. Milo's eyes widened.

"Ew! What fresh hell is this? I hope it's not the new wedding aesthetic because even I can't work with that gothic mess."

I explained my dream to Hannah and Milo as succinctly as I could, and they listened with increasingly serious expressions.

"I was just telling Hannah that we should consider the possibility that this is a Seer vision, not just a nightmare."

Milo leaned in, gazing intently at my depiction of the twisted mass of ghoulish figures restraining me. "Why can't you ever See pleasant things?" he muttered.

I shrugged. "I don't suppose this place looks familiar to either of you?"

They both shook their heads.

"What are those markings on the wall?" Hannah asked, pointing.

"That's the weirdest part," I admitted, and turned the page to where I had drawn each carving in greater detail. Milo stared at me, and I rolled my eyes. "Okay, okay, the seething mass of zombie-like creatures is probably the weirdest part, for normal people. But these are a close second."

"How strange," Hannah murmured. They both leaned over me as we examined them, causing one side of my body to feel warm while the other tingled with cold. "It almost seems to tell a story, doesn't it? Almost like hieroglyphics?"

I tried to follow the markings like words on a page, but I just couldn't make sense of them.

"Weird," I murmured. "Well, at least I can stop torturing myself trying to recognize the place. I've definitely never seen anything like this outside of a museum exhibit."

"Hmm. Do you mind if I show it to Kiernan?" Hannah asked. "If it's anything to do with Durupinen or Necromancer magic, he'll find it."

"Knock yourself out," I told her, tossing the sketchbook into her lap and getting up for another cup of coffee.

"More importantly, do you think the dream had anything to do with Alasdair?" Milo asked.

I took my time responding, thinking it over. None of the faces of the writhing figures had been Alasdair's, I was sure of that. And the figure running ahead of me had definitely been living; I could hear the heavy footfalls as he sprinted ahead of me. But there was something—the intense cold, and the almost-memory of a smell that burned my nose...

"I think so," I said finally, "but I'm just not sure how."

At that moment, Finn appeared in the doorway, wearing only a towel.

"How did it... oh, hi, Hannah. Milo. I didn't hear you come in," he said, completely unfazed. He'd grown used to our trio of codependency by now.

Milo made a growling sound and then turned to me, eyebrows waggling. "Seriously, girl, why have you not locked that down yet? I'm in my wedding dress era, you know."

I just rolled my eyes at him.

"Hi, Finn. I see you're hitting the gym," Milo called to Finn, wolf-whistling for good measure.

Finn grinned. "Cheers for noticing, mate!"

Milo sighed. "Always 'mate.' Never 'ghost boyfriend of my dreams.' So disappointing."

"Jess! It's so good to hear your voice! It's been forever!"

I smiled at the genuine delight in Flavia's voice on the other end of the phone, savoring it all the more knowing I'd shortly wipe all delight from the conversation when she understood why I'd called.

Hannah and Milo had left, and it was still pretty early for a phone call, but I knew Flavia would be awake. Unlike me, she had always been an early riser, perhaps a result of living all her life in a Traveler Durupinen caravan, where everyone was up with the sun. I'd given up on sleep for the present—every time I nodded off, my mind teemed with unsettling dreams about Alasdair. It seemed safer to keep my eyes open for the time being.

"I know, it's been too long. Sorry, I suck at keeping in touch," I replied.

Flavia laughed. "Please, Jess. Everyone sucks at keeping in touch. It's part of being a functional adult."

"Excuse me, but I'm going to have to stop you right there. We all know I am neither functional, nor an adult," I insisted.

Flavia laughed. "If you say so. So, what's going on?" She sighed a knowing sigh. "Usually, we just communicate in a bi-weekly exchange of memes, so I don't suppose this phone call is just going to be a cozy catch-up, is it?"

"Unfortunately, no. I need your help, and no meme in the world could cover it," I admitted; and without further ado, launched into the full story of Alasdair.

Flavia was an ideal audience, gasping at all the right moments and peppering my pauses with exclamations and carefully curated curses. In fact, I would have actually enjoyed telling her the story if it weren't all so disturbing.

"That's... I never... what the actual *hell*?" she whispered as I finished.

"I know. It's a lot," I said, agreeing with her honest, if inarticulate sentiment. After all, sometimes there really are no words.

"And this Collection monstrosity... it's still there, under the city?"

"Mm-hmm. We can't leave it there, Flavia. We have to find a way to undo it," I said.

"Of course! And I hope you're calling me to help you!" Flavia exclaimed.

I smiled in spite of myself. "Yes. That's exactly why I'm calling. Clan Rìoghalachd and the Trackers are working on this, but we have to be careful. This research in the wrong hands... well, we're already dealing with that fallout, and I'm trying to avoid making it any worse. We need people we can trust, people who won't be tempted to follow in Alasdair's footsteps."

"Tempted? The only feeling I seem to be able to register right now is nausea," Flavia said, her tone dripping with disgust.

"Oh, believe me, I concur, but Hannah's worried. I promised her I'd assemble a team we could trust to handle the research carefully and ethically. How soon can you be here?"

"Hmm. Well, I've got a research project I'm working on, but I can bring my notes with me and finish up on the train. I might be able to get there by Wednesday."

I felt my anxiety loosen its hold on my muscles as I sank into the chair with relief. That was only two days away. "Thank you, Flavia. Seriously, you're saving my life here. There's no other Scribe I would want on this job."

"Well, you're in luck because there's no job I'd rather devote my considerable talents to," she replied, a laugh in her voice. "So let me arrange things here, and I'll text you as soon as I have a better idea of when I'll be arriving in Edinburgh. I'm assuming the Trackers have some accommodations I can crash in?"

"Absolutely. We've got you covered. Catriona's still here overseeing things, so I'll speak to her, and get a contract drawn up for you, so you can get paid."

"Jess, that's not why I agreed to—"

"I know," I cut her off, "but I know what your time and talent are worth. Besides, the Northern Clans are rolling in money. Let them finance your nerd habits for a while."

Flavia laughed again. "Okay, then. Look for my text. I'll see you soon."

I ended the call. The crushing weight of the situation with Alasdair had been sitting squarely on my chest for weeks, but now it seemed to have lessened just a little. Help was on the way.

3

SEARCHING

By the time I stumbled into the Collective an hour later, there was already a flurry of activity. A few bleary-eyed Scribes were shuffling past me for the door, having spent the night cataloging and organizing every item we had pulled up from MacLeod Close and the old *priosún*. The day shift had begun, and Catriona was walking among the Scribes who were seated at the various workstations that had been set up since the previous day, all bent over an assortment of artifacts and documents, clicking away on laptops, and scribbling in notebooks. In the far corner, a sort of archeological research area had been set up, where Trackers donning gloves and goggles were meticulously cleaning and restoring items for further study. I watched in fascination for a few moments while a woman, her nose barely an inch from the table, used a moistened cotton swab to wipe the grime from the crevices of a ceremonial dagger with a wickedly curved blade and a silver handle. I repressed a shudder. If Danica had reached for that blade instead of the shorter one within her reach, Clarissa never would have survived.

"Jess!"

I looked up, startled out of my somewhat grotesque reverie by Catriona, who was walking toward me with a satisfied expression on her face. "Well, what do you think?"

I blinked. "Of what?"

Catriona gestured around her. "Of what? All of this! Fifteen Scribes came in overnight, and another dozen Trackers as well to aid in the efforts. Not too shabby, if I do say so myself."

I bit my lip. "Were they all vetted, like we discussed?"

Catriona smiled smugly. "What do you take me for? Impeccable references, every one of them. And they've all signed contracts agreeing to the parameters we've set. No discussing their work outside of the team, no work is to leave the room, and no devices of any kind that haven't been issued directly to them by the Trackers can be used. I reckon that's the best we can do, don't you?"

I nodded in agreement. "I've got one addition for you. I think she'll be invaluable." And I handed her Flavia's resume.

"Ah yes, the Traveler Scribe," Catriona said, giving the paper a cursory read-through. She let out a low whistle. "Yeah, I'd say she'll do. And she agreed?"

"She's on the next train, pending your approval," I said.

Catriona nodded. "I'll put through the paperwork. Tell her she's hired, will you?"

"I'll let her know."

"Excellent. Sorted," Catriona took a deep breath, and then her face fell just a little. "Bloody hell, I hope this all comes to something useful. I can't fathom having to tell the rest of the Council that we can't fix that Collection monstrosity. Celeste wants to come see it, you know."

My mouth fell open. "She wants to come to Edinburgh?"

Catriona nodded, her expression grim. "I've managed to convince her to stay put for now, but if this drags on too long, I won't be able to keep her from coming to see it for herself."

"And that's bad?"

"Well, it's not good. If we can't handle the situation, she'll be tempted to bring it to the International High Council. I really don't want to hand this over to that lot if we can help it."

"Why not? They must have a lot more resources they could throw at it?"

"The more people who know about it, the more dangerous this all becomes," Catriona said, echoing Hannah's sentiments. "What if they decide they want to understand it better? To study it and test its capabilities rather than simply unmake it? What then?"

I bit my lip. I had to admit that I would like to spare Celeste the full knowledge of the Collection, but I hadn't considered that she might involve the International High Council. My only experience with Havre des Gardiennes, the highest seat of Durupinen power, had not exactly inspired my confidence in our most powerful leaders. Nowhere in the world should the true mission of the Durupinen have been more revered, and instead, our International High Priestess had been in league with the Necromancers. If it was true that power corrupts, then Havre des Gardiennes was rotten to the core.

"No, you're right," I told Catriona. "The closer to the chest we can keep this, the better."

She nodded. "Glad we're in agreement on that, at least. Oh, I almost forgot. Your sister wants you in the archive."

"Thanks. I was wondering where she was. I expected to see her here." I turned to go and then stopped, hand on the doorknob. "Hey, Cat?"

"Mm?" came Catriona's distracted reply as she turned her attention back to Flavia's resume.

"I'm really glad you're here. Thanks for staying."

Predictably, Cat rolled her eyes. "You make it sound like a personal favor. I'm not here to hold your hand, Ballard. I'm here because, like most missions I send you on, you cocked this one up beyond repair." Her mouth twitched. "But you're welcome, I suppose."

I grinned and left the room. Classic Cat.

When I arrived in the archive, it was to find Hannah and Kiernan surrounded by stacks of books. They looked up as I entered, breaking up what had looked to be a very serious conversation.

"Hey, you two lovebirds. Everything okay?" I asked.

Hannah sighed and slammed the cover closed on the book she was reading, causing Kiernan to flinch slightly. He treated books the way most people treated teacup puppies.

"Oh, everything's just peachy," Hannah snapped, with a level of sarcasm usually only achieved by the other half of the womb-duo.

Kiernan gave me a tight, apologetic smile. "We've run up against a bit of a wall in our research into Alasdair's life."

"A bit of a wall? Try a complete dead end. A literal vacuum of information," Hannah added. "We've gone through everything that might have even a passing reference to Alasdair, including everything that Kiernan brought with him from Skye, and still, nothing. It's like he never existed."

I turned my disappointed gaze on Kiernan. "Really? Nothing?"

"Not a word," he said, sounding personally offended that thorough research had failed him. "And it's not for lack of documentation. Clan Rìoghalachd is one of our oldest and most influential clans in this part of the world. I have to conclude that the lack of information on Alasdair is intentional."

"Meaning?"

"Meaning that they erased him from their histories at Skye as thoroughly as they erased him from the archive here," Kiernan said. "Hannah told me about all the pages that had been cut out of the books here."

"You're telling me that people have torn pages from the books housed at Skye as well?" I asked, horrified. The Skye Archive was like our own library of Alexandria. Everything that could be learned about the Northern Clans was housed there. Those texts were considered sacred, revered even. I couldn't imagine anyone defacing one and getting away with it.

"Not exactly," Kiernan said. "Take a look at this one, for instance. These are Caomhnóir graduation records. This page, where Alasdair ought to be, has been badly water damaged. The ink's faded to almost nothing. And here..." He searched for a moment before carefully extracting another book from the pile. "This book documents the legal cases brought before the individual Clan Councils. Back then, large clans were allowed to form their own councils to handle issues that arose among their own members. It was abused too frequently and was eventually abolished, but in Alasdair's time, the Clan Council would have decided his fate."

"Another conveniently located water spill?" I guessed, my heart sinking.

"A rogue candle, it would seem," Kiernan replied dryly. "All very innocent, I'm sure, but it's burned clean through the paper, and the wax has obliterated the text. Even scraping it away doesn't help."

I groaned. I knew that Clan Rìoghalachd had gone to great lengths to obscure Alasdair and his crimes from Durupinen history, but this was obsessive. Would it really have been so bad for the rest of the Northern Clans to be made aware of what had happened? I almost voiced the question aloud but then considered the matter for a moment. I thought of the competitive nature of clan politics and the constant struggle for power and prestige. I thought of the lengths I'd seen people go to with my own eyes to neutralize perceived threats to their own power, and I knew: yes, in the eyes of Clan Rìoghalachd, there could be nothing worse than to bear the shame and attendant consequences of Alasdair's transgressions.

Kiernan watched the conclusion form on my face with grim satisfaction. "So you see, not only have they destroyed priceless artifacts for our historical record, but they've sabotaged any chance we might have had of gaining any insights about Alasdair himself."

"He has to have gone somewhere familiar—somewhere he feels comfortable and safe," Hannah said, rubbing at her temples. "He's on the run. He's in spirit form, and so he's going to feel pulled toward places he frequented in life."

"But most of those places won't be safe," I told her. "With the entire city on alert looking for him, he's going to be hard-pressed to find a place he won't be discovered. That's why I've been telling Finn I think we should expand the search beyond the city, but he doesn't want to admit that Alasdair might have gotten that far."

"If only Danica hadn't torn out those pages," Hannah groaned, dropping her head onto her folded arms.

A thought occurred to me. "She removed them, yes. But... did she destroy them?" I asked. "What if she didn't? What if she kept them or hid them somewhere?"

Hannah's head shot up from the tabletop. "Oh my God! Has anyone searched her rooms at MacLeod Manor? Or her office?"

"Her office has most certainly been searched. I saw them at it right after she was arrested," Kiernan said. "But I don't know about her rooms at the manor."

Hannah turned a frantic face on me. "Jess?"

But my phone was already out of my pocket and halfway to my ear. "I'm on it."

Finn picked up after barely two rings.

"Jess, everything okay?"

I didn't waste time on pleasantries. "Finn, do you know if Danica's rooms at MacLeod Manor have been searched?"

"I... I don't know. Why?"

"Because it just occurred to me that she may not have destroyed the documents she stole from the archive. What if she just hid them somewhere?"

Finn swore. "I'm not sure. The Clan Rìoghalachd Caomhnóir have been handling that end of things. I'll have to see who I can—"

"Don't bother. Just meet me over there, okay?"

"I can't right now. I'm right in the middle of—"

"Okay, can you send Savvy?"

"She's on patrol right now. I'll send Rana over to meet you."

"Okay, perfect. I'm on my way there now."

I ended the call and turned to see Hannah on her feet. "I'm coming too," she said.

"No, you should stay here," I told her.

"But—"

"Hannah, we have to divide and conquer. Stay here and help Kiernan go through the rest of these books and documents, okay? I'll stay in touch and let you know as soon as I find something."

Hannah sank back into her seat. "Okay. Be careful over there, Jess. I know Clarissa's not out of the hospital yet, but a lot of the MacLeods are still pretty protective of their privacy. They may give you trouble."

"Then I'll just have to give them a little trouble back, won't I?" I said, smiling my sweetest smile.

I had the satisfaction of seeing Hannah crack a genuine, if somewhat anxious, smile in return before I closed the door.

MacLeod Manor resembled nothing more than a fortress. Stony-faced Caomhnóir, each one with the approximate build and demeanor of a mountain gorilla, lined the perimeter of the property. The two posted at the gatehouse spent so long checking our Tracker credentials that it was clear they were looking for an excuse to deny us entry. It was only when I casually suggested calling Catriona to sort it out that they relented and opened the gates.

"They're a bit intense, this lot, aren't they?" Rana remarked as we parked the car.

"Just a bit," I agreed. "Although I suppose I'd be a bit intense too if I had to answer to Clarissa MacLeod."

The door opened as we approached. Evidently, the guards at the gate radioed up to the house because they were ready for us.

"Good morning, Ms. Ballard, Caomhnóir Patel. How can I be of service to you today?" The smile on the man's face did not reach his eyes, and there was a coldness to his polite words.

"We need to see Danica's rooms, please," I told him.

The man frowned. "Miss Danica is not presently available."

Oh, so it was still Miss Danica, even after she betrayed the entire clan? Interesting. I managed not to voice this aloud and instead replied, "I know that. We need to search her rooms as part of the investigation."

The frown curdled into a puckered knot. "I'm not sure I can allow that."

"And you are?"

"MacDowell, miss. The MacLeod family butler."

"Well, Mr. MacDowell, these are extenuating circumstances, and what you will and won't allow really doesn't concern me."

Behind me, Rana stifled a snort.

MacDowell, meanwhile, had his nose in the air and was now looking down its rather crooked bridge at me. "I shall have to confer with the mistress of the house."

"You do that," I muttered, pushing past him. "And we'll get started."

"I really don't—"

I whirled around, all semblance of patience gone. "Look, Jeeves, there is a lunatic ghost on the loose who has already corrupted one MacLeod sister and landed the other one in the hospital on the brink of death. I can see that rules and decorum are literally your entire personality, but you're going to have to get that stick out of your ass and point us in the right direction so we can do our jobs and find this spirit before he does something else that will besmirch this clan for a century, got it? Now are you going to show us where Ms. Danica's rooms are, or should we just start kicking down random doors?"

I watched with relish as the man's face turned purple with indignation. I felt Rana tense behind me, prepared in case he might lash out, but I simply waited patiently, looking him in the eye as his resolve crumbled.

"I shall still be checking with the mistress," was his feeble rejoinder as he turned on his heel and led us up the staircase.

"Quite the diplomat, aren't you?" Rana whispered to me.

"Yes, it's the secret to my universal popularity," I told her with a grin.

The longer I did this Tracker thing, the less tolerance I had for petty bullshit.

It was a good thing I didn't have to carry out my threat of kicking down random doors because I would have had a very sore foot. MacLeod Manor had more rooms than most hotels I'd stayed in. Finally, however, after traversing what felt like a mile of corridors, MacDowell stopped in front of a door and opened it with a brass key from the ring he wore at his waist. Rana thanked him (I didn't bother), and we stepped inside.

Danica's suite comprised a large sitting room, a bedroom, a dressing room that doubled as a walk-in closet, and a palatial bathroom complete with a clawfoot soaking tub. It was all elegantly furnished and absurdly messy. It was the kind of room I'd expect to belong to a spoiled teenager, not a grown woman who ran her own business. The closet looked like someone had let a rampaging toddler loose in it, with clothes tossed all over the floor, piled onto chaises and chairs, and even draped over the massive full-length mirror that hung in the corner. Piles of books and towers of boxes teetered everywhere; most of the boxes had been torn open with tissue paper and bubble wrap strewn around them.

"Ah, bollocks," Rana said as she surveyed the mess. "It's going to take us forever to sort through all of this."

For the next several hours, we searched Danica's rooms. After the first hour, we discovered there was a pattern to the chaos, at least. The boxes were all full of home accents for her interior design business, so we largely ignored them. The books that Rana and I tackled enthusiastically were not the kind of books that were likely to be helpful. I'd hoped for old family tomes swiped from the archive, but mostly what I found was a large collection of self-help books and piles of mass-market romance novels. I picked up one of the self-help books and turned it over to read the cover.

"'How Not To Be Invisible: A Guide to Self-Assertion.' Yikes. Apparently, Danica tried a few other methods of getting her sister's attention before she resorted to stabbing her."

"They're all like that, the whole lot," Rana said, beginning to pile them up. "'Finding Your Voice.' 'Ignored No Longer.' 'A Beginner's Guide to Speaking Up.' Bloody hell."

We gathered all the books and stacked them over with the boxes to clear a path to the desk. The drawers contained more chaos, crammed full of paper clips and organizers, measuring tapes, and fabric swatches. We thumbed hopefully through the planners and journals but came up empty—everything Danica had scrawled in them related to work or family events.

"Oi, look at this, then. Apparently, Danica's been appealing to higher authorities," Rana said, and she handed me a folded letter that had been stuffed between the pages of a datebook.

It was a letter she wrote—but apparently never sent—to Havre des Gardiennes. The date in the top corner meant she had written it only a few months after the Reckoning. I scanned through it, mouth open.

To the International High Council,

My name is Danica MacLeod of Clan Rioghalachd. I am writing on behalf of my sister, Clarissa MacLeod, who has been inconsolable over the loss of our Gateway. I understand that there have been many meetings and resolutions carried in the months since the Reckoning, but still nothing has been done to restore the Gateways to their rightful place—in the Durupinen bloodlines. This cannot continue.

The Gateway was the one connection between my sister and me that could not be severed or ignored. We were as one because we were two parts of the same whole. Now we have been cleaved from each other, and I have had to watch as she has drifted farther and farther from me. This cannot be borne.

How can the Gateways be safe, scattered in piles of old rocks? It was much better when they could be hidden within our clans. Clarissa is beside herself, and I can't bear to see her so angry and sad. Even if you can't restore all the Gateways, couldn't you just restore ours? I was told that there would be catastrophic effects if the Gateways were not returned to the Geatgrimas, but surely it would do no harm to hold on to just one? It would make Clarissa so happy, and we would be connected again, the way we were meant to be. Clarissa is very important and influential, you know, and she is not used to having her orders refused..."

"It just keeps going and going!" I muttered, flipping through the rest of the letter, which continued on the fronts and backs of three more sheets of paper, becoming more rambling and less coherent as it went.

Rana, who had been reading over my shoulder, shook her head with a snort of disgust. "If we'd seen this when we first arrived, we'd have known that she was off her rocker."

"It's too bad she didn't send it," I said, setting the letter aside. "It's a minefield of red flags."

Our search continued fruitlessly through the desk, the bedside tables, and the drawers of the dressers and vanity table. It wasn't until we were tits-deep in her disaster of a closet that we finally found something to make all our efforts worthwhile.

"'Ello, 'ello, 'ello! What's this, then?" Rana suddenly cried, pulling a shoebox down from one of the top shelves.

I waded my way through the sea of discarded clothing to reach her. "What is it?! Is it the missing pages?"

"No, but... just have a look!"

She held out the box to me, and we both sank to the floor to examine it. Inside was a silk-wrapped item; long, thin, and remarkably heavy for its size. I lifted it from the box and carefully unwound the fabric, which slid through my fingers like water.

I now held a ceremonial dagger in my hand, with a wickedly curved blade and an ornately carved handle. The blade itself was gruesomely stained.

"Is that..." Rana began, swallowing hard.

"Yeah, I think so," I answered. The dried, rusty-red smears were hard to misinterpret.

"What's that on the handle?" she asked, shifting herself next to me to get a better view.

I hadn't yet been able to tear my eyes from what was probably centuries-old gore, but I did so now to examine the handle. It took only one glance for my heart to begin pounding in my chest.

"Holy shit," I muttered.

"What?" Rana asked.

The handle had a carving of a figure—a woman—with a cup in one hand and a long thin object in the other, like a stick or a wand. And I'd seen it before.

"I... I know these markings."

"How?" Rana gasped. "Where did you see them?"

"I don't know."

Rana's face fell. "You don't know?"

"Sorry, I mean I saw them in a dream last night—only it might not have been a normal dream. It might have been a Seer vision."

"Blimey, Sav told me you were a Seer, but I'd forgotten. And you Saw this knife?"

"No, I Saw a hallway, and this was one of the images carved into the walls!" I turned the blade over carefully in my now shaking hands and experienced a secondary jolt of surprise. "And this symbol here, on the very bottom of the handle! This was carved into the door at the end of the hall!"

"That's... is that good?" Rana asked, bouncing up and down on her knees, unsure whether she should be excited or not.

"I'm not sure—but this can't be a coincidence. Whatever my vision meant, this dagger is connected to it somehow. Is there anything left in that box?"

Rana tipped it over, shaking her head. "Nothing."

I swore. I mean, I hadn't expected a handwritten note explaining the dagger's origins, but still.

Rana jumped to her feet. "So, what do we do now? Take it back to the Collective? Maybe the Scribes can—"

"No. The longer we spend getting bogged down in obscure research, the more time Alasdair has to wreak havoc. We have to go straight to the source."

I jumped to my feet and Rana followed, stumbling a little in the sea of garments in which we now stood.

"The source?"

"Yup." I re-bundled the dagger gingerly in its silken wrappings and put it back into the shoebox, which I tucked under my arm. "I'm done allowing this investigation to run its course. Interested in taking a drive with me?"

Rana shrugged. "I reckon so, but where are we going?"

"Oh, I think it's high time to pay a visit to Danica MacLeod."

4

INTERVIEW

"Um, Jess? I'm not entirely sure we should be doing this."

Rana spoke these words from the passenger seat of our rental car as I maneuvered my way through the traffic toward the MacLeod Medical Center. I didn't hear her at first because I was muttering, "Right is left and left is right," under my breath as I tried to overcome my American driving instincts. When she repeated her words, I merely shrugged.

"Oh, I'm not sure either. That's why we're not asking anyone's permission," I said.

"You don't think they'll turn us away at the doors?" Rana asked.

"Possible, but I'm guessing probably not with these credentials." I patted my jacket—my Tracker ID was tucked in the inside breast pocket. "But if we run into any resistance, I've got Cat on speed dial."

MacLeod Medical Center was a state-of-the-art medical facility on the outskirts of Edinburgh, funded almost entirely by the MacLeod family and reputed to be one of the better hospitals this side of the Atlantic. Somehow, I wasn't surprised that the MacLeod name was on a hospital; it was on several dozen buildings in the city, including a museum, a theater, and a library. One of the perks of funding a hospital, as it turns out, was keeping a wing of it for your own private use, allowing the MacLeods on-demand medical care as well as the privacy and authority to run things however they damn well pleased. Another was having a convenient place to lock up your sister when she tried to murder you.

We already had access to this special private wing of the hospital because Clarissa was recuperating there, and we had been there to visit her, though she wasn't conscious at the time. With official visitor badges in hand, we would at least be able to get through the doors. After that? Well, I was used to winging it.

Finn being Finn, I knew he would loathe the idea of us going to see Danica. His overprotective streak was legendary. So when I called him to let him know where we were headed next, his reaction was predictably manic.

"Jess, that woman stabbed her own sister in the chest. What could possibly possess you to enter a room with her?" Finn growled into the phone.

"Finn, she's locked up in a psych ward. They won't even let her have a pen. She's disarmed, okay? And anyway, I have Rana with me."

"I'm meeting you over there," he declared.

"No, you're not. You have a meeting with Catriona and the head of the Rìoghalachd Caomhnóir in an hour, remember?"

"I'll put it off."

"No, you won't. That doesn't make sense, Finn. You're the three leaders on this mission; you can't just blow it off. Look, if you're worried, send another Caomhnóir over to meet us. Find the biggest, burliest brute you can and stuff him in a car over to MacLeod Hospital, okay?"

Finn sighed, defeated by logic. "Fine. Sav just got off patrol. I'll send her over to meet you—burliness aside, there's frankly no one I'd rather have beside me in a bar fight."

Rana heard this and started snorting with laughter. I, for one, thought he had a point. I'd been in enough tight spots with Savvy to appreciate that she was tough as nails.

Meanwhile, Finn was still lecturing me. "But be smart, please. Don't get within striking distance, and don't provoke her. Remember, as far as she's concerned, this whole situation is your fault. You triggered the Reckoning. You made Clarissa miserable, and then you foiled her plan to fix it all. You are Public Enemy Number One in her eyes, and if she's going to lash out again, it will undoubtedly be at you."

"Fair point. I'll give her space, and I'll keep Rana and Sav close, okay?"

He grunted and hung up. It was as close to agreement as I could have hoped for, so I considered it a win.

When we pulled into the visitors' parking garage, Savvy was already there, standing by the elevators. The fact that she beat us there from the center of the city meant she had broken every conceivable traffic law at least twice. I took a moment to appreciate the way Savvy's face lit up when she saw Rana. Seeing the independent, utterly carefree Savvy smitten with someone was an experience I was sure I'd never have. We took the elevators to the top floor, where a middle-aged woman in a crisply starched uniform greeted us in an equally starched voice.

"Good afternoon. How can I help you today?"

I glanced at my watch. Jeez, was it afternoon already? Time flew when you were on a panicked manhunt for a murderous ghost.

"Uh, yeah, we're here to see Danica MacLeod," I said.

Predictably, the woman's face pinched up into a disapproving expression. "Oh, I'm sorry, but that won't be possible. Ms. MacLeod is not allowed any visitors at this time."

"Apologies, I should have clarified," I said and, extracting my ID from my pocket, placed it on the desk and slid it toward the woman. "We're not here for a social call. We have to ask Ms. MacLeod some questions pertinent to the events that landed her here. We have clearance and permission as three of the lead Trackers and Caomhnóir on this case. I'm happy to get some Council members or the High Priestess of the Northern Clans on the line if you insist on continuing to hold us up. Your call."

I smiled sweetly as the color drained from the woman's face. She squirmed in her seat, clearly flustered.

"No, that won't be... I just need to check... just give me a moment, please," she snapped, as though I was rushing her. Muttering mutinously under her breath, she scanned our IDs and printed out new visitor badges for us. She handed them over to us with a sour expression on her face. "Room 712."

"Thanks so much. You're a real brick," Savvy said with a dazzling grin. The woman narrowed her eyes and pursed her lips, but decorum prevented her from saying whatever retort she was chewing on. She took out her annoyance on the button that opened the doors into the closed ward.

"So, fill me in on why we're here?" Savvy said. "Did you find something at MacLeod Manor, then? Finn was a bit... well... clipped when he rang me."

As we walked down the long hallway toward room 712, we quickly gave Savvy the details of the knife we'd found, and I explained its connection to my dream.

"So, not a normal dream, then," Savvy concluded.

"Nope. It's definitely some sort of Seer vision. I'm not sure what it means yet, but the dagger is connected somehow. Danica had the dagger and obviously knew it was important because she kept it hidden away. We need to find out where she got it and what the markings on it mean."

"You haven't brought it with you, have you?" Savvy asked, looking suddenly wary. "There's no way I'm letting that woman near another pointy object, especially within reach of you."

"I appreciate the almost Finn-like paranoia, Sav, but I'm not an idiot. The dagger is locked in the trunk of the car. I took some pictures of it, though, in case we need to jog her memory about exactly what it looks like."

Even if we hadn't been told Danica's room number, there could be no doubt where she was being held. Two barrel-chested Caomhnóir stood guard in front of the door at the very end of the hall. The taller of the two checked our passes and our IDs for good measure. Then he muttered something to his companion in which the words "bloody females" and "infiltrating our ranks" were decidedly clear.

I turned to give a warning look to Savvy, but it was Rana who looked red-faced and ready to pounce. She caught my eye and relaxed her shoulders. Savvy was trying to smother a grin. It was clear she would have loved nothing more than to unleash her girlfriend on these unsuspecting lugs, and watch them pay dearly for underestimating her. I wouldn't have minded watching that myself. Hell, if we weren't in such a rush to speak to Danica, I'd have made popcorn; but instead, we stood quietly by like the boring, responsible adults we were supposed to be, and waited for the guards to unlock the door.

"You're on your own in there," one of them grunted. "We're only here to make sure she doesn't get out. Don't go crying to us if you can't han—"

"Yeah, yeah, keep it in your pants, mate, no one gives a shit," Savvy sighed in exasperation, pushing past the man, and opening the door.

My mouth fell open. It had only been ten days since I'd confronted Danica MacLeod in the underbelly of the city, but the change that had been wrought in her since then was startling. Her face was pinched, her cheeks hollow. Her hair was lank and dull, hanging in snake-like tendrils around her face. Her usual wardrobe of colorful caftans and butterfly clips had been swapped out for a dull blue set of pajamas that looked like scrubs, from which her wasted wrists and ankles jutted like scarecrow limbs. How could she have deteriorated so dramatically in less than two weeks? Then I spotted the tray of food and the paper cup of water sitting on her bedside table, completely untouched. Maybe she was on a hunger strike.

She didn't look up as we came in, but remained absorbed in her task, which involved a stack of paper and a pile of half-used crayon stumps. When she heard the door shut behind us, she gave an exasperated sigh.

"Stop pestering me! I didn't eat it, and I'm not going to eat it, so just take it away. Haven't you listened to a word I've said? I'm not eating anything at all until you bring me to Clarissa."

I cleared my throat. "Danica?"

Danica froze like a wild animal scenting a predator. Her hand clutching its purple crayon hovered, trembling, above the crumpled pile of paper. She lifted her head slowly until her eyes met mine, and I took an involuntary step backward. Behind me, I heard Savvy whisper, "Bloody bollocking *hell*."

Danica's eyes were huge and sunken in her face, her pupils practically swallowing the irises so that they looked almost entirely black. The shadows under them could have been scribbled on with the same purple crayon in her hand, and there was a manic light shining from them that raised goosebumps on my arms.

"You," she replied in a strangled whisper. Her face twisted into a hateful leer —an expression I could never have imagined on her features only a few weeks ago—and I felt Savvy and Rana both tense beside me. Savvy actually took half a step between us, but Danica didn't move. She simply glared at me a moment more and returned to her frantic writing. "Go away. You've already ruined enough," she muttered.

"I need to talk to you," I told her, still hovering near the door.

"I have nothing to say to you. All of my words are for Clarissa, now," Danica replied snappishly, though her voice faltered and cracked when she spoke her sister's name. Then she continued to mutter under her breath, the words almost unintelligible, but I caught a few phrases, including, "...can't ignore me forever..." and "...*make* her listen..."

"Danica?"

But she had absorbed herself again in her task and was studiously ignoring me.

"Danica, I need to ask you some questions."

Danica gave no reply except to shift her weight so that she was now sitting with her back completely to me.

I looked at Rana and Savvy, both of whom were looking very tense and uncomfortable.

"Now what?" I muttered.

"What have they done to her?" Rana whispered.

"Drugged her out of her gourd, most likely," Savvy said, sounding disturbed. "Not that she needed drugs for that, mind. Fairly well out of her gourd already, wasn't she?"

"But she looks ill," Rana pressed.

"You'd look ill too if you almost murdered someone and then didn't eat anything for almost a fortnight," Savvy pointed out.

"What do you want to do, Jess?" Rana asked.

I bit my lip, watching Danica as she scribbled feverishly on her paper. I certainly hadn't come all this way to simply give up. There was too much at stake. I needed to try a new tactic—simply asking questions wasn't going to get me anywhere, I could see that plainly enough already. She wasn't going to cooperate with me just because I asked her to. It was time for a little subterfuge. After all, Danica had lied her ass off in her misguided quest to reverse the Reckoning. I could lie a bit, too, if it would help to repair some of the damage she'd caused.

I tossed a wink to Savvy and Rana before heaving a dramatic sigh. "Oh well. She's not talking. I guess we'll just have to go back and tell Clarissa we can't help her."

Danica's head snapped up with an audible cracking noise. "What about Clarissa?"

I pretended not to have heard her. "Let's go. She'll be disappointed, but—"

"Stop, STOP!" Danica shrieked, scrambling unsteadily to her feet, and flinging herself across the room toward me. Rana and Savvy leaped into action, throwing themselves between me and Danica and restraining her arms behind her back.

"No! Ow! I didn't... let *go!* I only... I wasn't going to hurt her!" Danica cried.

"Yeah, well, seeing as you're in here for shanking your own sister, you might see why we're not prepared to take your word on that, mate," Savvy grunted as Danica struggled against her hold.

For a woman weakened by self-imposed starvation, she put up an impressive struggle, but Rana and Savvy managed to wrest her into a sitting position on the edge of her bed.

"Fly at her again and I'll string you up by your ankles, yeah?" Savvy panted, stepping cautiously back from Danica.

"I won't, I promise," Danica said meekly, folding her hands in her lap like an obedient schoolgirl. "Please, I only want to know what she was saying about Clarissa. Have you really seen her?"

"I just came from her room," I lied.

"How... how is she?" Danica's voice shot up an octave in her anxiety.

"She'll be disappointed you can't help her," I said with a heavy sigh.

"But I can help her! That is, I... I want to! That's all I ever wanted!" Danica cried. She half rose from the bed again, but Savvy growled at her, and she quickly sat down again. "It's all I ever wanted," Danica repeated in a whisper.

I felt a tiny spark of pity for the woman, but then the Collection flashed into my mind and quickly snuffed it out.

"Danica, Clarissa needs my help. We have to find Alasdair," I said.

Danica's face folded into a frown of aggravation. "You can't honestly believe you're the first person to ask me that?" she snapped, folding her wasted arms over her chest. "I've told every Caomhnóir and Tracker who's come in here. I don't know where he is. He vanished after... after..." Her owlish eyes filled up with tears that spilled down over her chapped and reddened cheeks as she no doubt recalled her attack on her sister.

"I realize that, Danica. But just because you don't know where he's gone doesn't mean you don't know anything helpful," I said, taking a tentative step forward. When she neither lunged nor hissed at me, I ventured another. "Could I ask you a few other questions? For Clarissa?"

"Did she really send you here?" Danica asked, eyes narrowed.

"Of course she did."

"How do I know that's true? Clarissa doesn't even like you. She called you a thorn in her side," Danica pushed.

It was all I could do not to roll my eyes at the irony of being called a thorn in Clarissa's side by the woman who literally stabbed her. I swallowed my snarky reply, however.

"Honestly, she still doesn't like me," I said. "But we're working toward the same goal now, which is tracking down Alasdair, so she has put those feelings aside."

"She could have come and asked me herself if she wanted to know. She knows I'd do anything in the world for her," Danica pouted.

It took every ounce of strength I had to swallow the incredulous laugh that bubbled up at these words. Instead, I adopted a somber expression. "Her condition is too serious for her to come see you, Danica. She's recovering from a very high-risk surgery. She's in the ICU, hooked up to at least half a dozen machines. Surely you know that."

Danica clapped her hands over her ears and started rocking back and forth. "No, no, no, I'm sorry, I know, it's my fault, and I'm sorry. I'm sorry, I'm—"

"Danica, STOP!" I shouted. The sound startled her into silence. I had to take a very slow, deep breath before I could continue. I threw a quick look over my shoulder to make sure the guards posted outside weren't about to come barging in, but then I remembered they had no intention of rescuing us if something went wrong. "Look, no offense, but your apologies are meaningless without some action behind them. Do you want Clarissa to forgive you or not?"

Danica nodded, her eyes still streaming.

"Then stop wasting your time on empty words!" I cried, gesturing at the pathetic pile of scribbled ravings that littered the floor. "Let me ask you this: what is the most important thing in the world to Clarissa?"

Danica didn't even hesitate; the answer was on her lips at once. "Clan Rìoghalachd's reputation and power."

"Okay, well, thanks to you and Alasdair, that's all in tatters right now. You can't undo Clarissa's injuries, but you might be able to repair the rest of the damage if we can just find Alasdair. Now, will you answer my questions or not?"

"If... if I can. But I need you to do something for me as well."

I crossed my arms. "Danica, you really aren't in a position to bargain here."

"I only want you to deliver my apology to Clarissa. That's all. Please, just give these to her and make sure she reads them!" Danica scrambled off the bed and dropped to her knees on the floor, gathering up the papers she'd been working so frantically on when we'd entered. She started toward me, but Savvy shouted.

"Oi! I'll take those!"

Danica flinched but only hesitated a moment before thrusting the messy pile into Savvy's arms. Then she turned to me. "You'll do it? You'll take it to her?"

I nodded. I was fairly certain Clarissa would toss them straight in the rubbish bin, but that wasn't my problem now, was it?

"Okay, then," Danica said, settling back on the bed again. "What do you want to know?"

"Well, I know that when you first learned of Alasdair, you did your best to hide his existence. That meant removing all trace of him from the books in the archive," I said.

Danica nodded. "I had to protect his identity."

Savvy made a derisive huffing sound. I shot her a warning look and Rana elbowed her in the ribs. We needed answers, and we wouldn't get them if we angered or offended Danica.

"Right, but what did you do with the pages you tore from the books?" I asked. "Did you destroy them or just hide them away somewhere?"

Danica hesitated. "Clarissa wants to know?"

"She needs to know, Danica. It's crucial."

Danica bit her lip. "I burned them," she whispered.

I was prepared for it, but it was still a blow. I swallowed the curse I longed to hurl at her and kept my voice neutral instead.

"Okay."

"Clarissa will be mad, won't she?"

"Not if you keep cooperating, no," I said, changing tacks. "But the pages you burned, you must have read them first, right?"

Danica nodded slowly.

"Okay!" I said, smiling. "That's good! So, you might be able to recall some of what you read?"

Danica squirmed a little. "I've always been a bit of a numpty when it comes to names and dates and the like. But I... I can try, if it will make Clarissa happy."

"We're trying to figure out where Alasdair would have gone to hide," I explained. "We think he's left the city."

"You mean you've driven him out of the city," Danica muttered, her expression darkening.

I refused to take the bait. "He's cunning, Danica, you know that. Clever. He wouldn't stay here when he knows we're scouring every inch of Edinburgh for him. He'll have found somewhere else to hide out, someplace safe."

Danica made a strange jerky motion, half-shrug, half-shudder. "I've told you, he never—"

"Somewhere he knew when he was alive," I pressed on, talking over her. "Someplace he felt comfortable. Spirits are drawn to the places they knew in life. You're the only person who knows anything about his life. Can you think of a place he might have gone back to?"

Danica frowned in silent concentration for a few moments before shaking her head hopelessly. "I... I don't know. I can't think, I... he lived all his life in Edinburgh."

I clenched my hands into fists to vent my frustration so I wouldn't spring forward and shake the woman violently by the shoulders. Instead, I took my phone from my pocket, pulled up the photo I'd taken of the knife, and held it out so that she could see it. "Danica, what's this?"

Danica swallowed hard. "Where did you find that?"

"You know where we found it. Right where you hid it, in the top of your closet," I said, more sharply than I intended. This woman was trying every last ounce of my patience. Rana must have picked up on it because she caught my eye and mouthed the words, "Calm down."

"Yes, I... I never thought anyone would..." Danica was now muttering, hardly able to look directly at the photo, probably because it reminded her of what she'd done to Clarissa with a similar weapon.

"Where did this come from, Danica? Where did you find it?" I asked.

Danica squirmed again. It was like watching a small child trying to worm their way out of trouble. "We have a collection of artifacts in the basement at MacLeod Manor. I took it from one of the cases."

"Was it Alasdair's?"

"Yes."

"How do you know?"

"It was cataloged in the evidence at his trial. It was the one item they took off him when they finally caught him. He... he used it in his research."

"You mean he used it to murder people," I replied sharply. I might be walking on eggshells with this woman. Still, I wasn't about to tolerate euphemisms like "research" when we were actually talking about the serial, ritualistic killing of actual human beings.

Danica only nodded. Maybe she had sensed the edge of anger in my voice, but she didn't dare reply out loud.

"Why did you hide it?"

"For the same reason I burned all the records of his life. I didn't want anyone to remember that he had existed."

"Did you notice the markings on it?"

Danica nodded, and my heart began to thrum with anticipation.

"Do you know what they mean?"

"No," Danica said, looking almost scared to admit it. "I... there was no mention of them in the documentation. I never really paid them much mind."

I felt my hopes sink. Another dead end.

But Rana wasn't ready to give up. "Why did you keep it? Why not destroy it, like every other reminder of him?"

Danica's eyes went wide. "Oh, he told me not to!"

"Who? Alasdair?" I asked.

"Oh, yes. He said he would need it one day when he regained his body, and I was to keep it safe!"

"Why? What's so special about it?" I asked.

"He said it was all he took away with him when he left Kingshurst."

I froze. A strange and unknowable something inside me was setting off alarm bells.

"What's Kingshurst?"

"Kingshurst University," Danica said, and even as she did, her eyes grew wide. "Oh, my! I forgot," she whispered. "Alasdair did leave Edinburgh. He attended Kingshurst as a young man."

"Blimey," Sav whispered, and I whirled on her.

"What? You've heard of it?"

Savvy shrugged. "Who hasn't? One of the top universities in the UK, innit? Right up there with Oxford and Cambridge."

"Kingshurst." The word rolled off my tongue too easily, as though I knew it already, though I'd be willing to swear I'd never heard it before. I looked at Savvy and Rana, who were both staring blankly at me. I stood up.

"We need to find out everything we can about Kingshurst."

5

LONG LIVE THE QUEEN

Danica was shrieking at us as we left the room, hounding us with desperate pleas about Clarissa and her apology, but I wasn't listening. My head was buzzing with this new piece of information, the name of a place that meant nothing to me now, and yet meant something very important to that enigmatic Seer part of my brain. It was like experiencing déjà vu before the fact—an unsettling feeling, but one I'd grown unwillingly accustomed to.

"What's going on?" I heard Rana whisper to Savvy as we pushed past the bewildered-looking guards outside Danica's room.

"Not sure. Probably some Seer shit. Just roll with it," Savvy muttered back. They both kept silent pace with me, Savvy's arms still full of Danica's crumpled pile of apologies as I charged down the hallway. I broke into a jog, ignoring the stares of the medical personnel, and finally skidded to a halt outside of Clarissa's room on the other end of the ward.

Pippa, Clarissa's personal assistant, was sitting in a chair just outside the door. She looked up in alarm as I stopped, panting, in front of her.

"Jess! Good gracious! What is it? What's wrong?" Her words tumbled out over each other as she jumped to her feet, her clipboard and pen sliding from her lap and clattering to the floor.

"Hi Pippa," I gasped. Even in my haste, I noticed how pale she was, and how her usually flawlessly put-together appearance was now looking a bit frayed around the edges. Her hair was coming loose from her ponytail, and her clothes were wrinkled, as though she'd slept in them. "Sorry to startle you, but I need to see Clarissa. It's urgent."

"I can see that it's urgent," Pippa replied, pressing a hand to her heart. "Is it something I can help you with? It's important to disturb Clarissa as little as poss—"

"I know that, and I wouldn't ask if it wasn't incredibly important. I'll be very quick."

Pippa pressed her lips into a thin line, looking for a moment like a stern school mistress who was about to rap my knuckles with a ruler. "Very well. I will let you in, but you must compose yourself first. If you burst in there in such an agitated state, you'll alarm her, and I can't have that, not when her health is so fragile. She nearly died, you know."

"I know," I said, and I meant it. Danica's assault on her sister was a moment I had relived, with sickening clarity, many times since I'd witnessed it, and would dearly have loved to forget. "Sorry. I definitely don't want to set her back. I'll be calm. Cross my heart."

Pippa turned her steely gaze on Rana and Savvy, who were quick to reassure her that they, too, would be on their best behavior. Finally, still looking like she was doing this against her better judgment, Pippa turned to the door behind her and gently eased it open.

Clarissa lay propped up in the bed centered on the back wall, hooked up to a vast collection of beeping, whirring machines. She looked strangely frail and tiny for a woman whom I knew to be a terrifying force of nature in her daily life. Someone had pulled a rolling table over to the bed, and a laptop, notebook, and cell phone lay scattered on top of it. Clarissa had a pair of reading glasses slipping down the end of her nose as she dozed, snoring softly. Pippa threw me a silent look of frustration, and I shrugged apologetically. I didn't want to wake the woman either, but this was an emergency.

Pippa reached a tentative hand out toward Clarissa and touched her gently on the shoulder. Clarissa started as though someone had sounded an air horn, and her glasses slid off her face into her lap.

"What? Who's—oh, Pippa, it's you. Blast it, did I nod off again? Get me the nurse. I want them to cut back on these painkil—oh!" Clarissa started as she noticed the rest of us standing behind Pippa. Her hands fluttered uselessly around her blankets and tubes as though trying to cover up something indecent. Her cheeks flushed as she said, "I didn't realize we had visitors."

"I know, that's why I woke you," Pippa said. "And I wouldn't have allowed them in without clearing it with you first, but Jessica insisted it was an emergency." She turned a fiercely protective gaze on me as though to say, *and it had better be an emergency.*

"We're so sorry to burst in on you like this, Clarissa. How are you feeling?" I asked in a far gentler tone than I'd ever used in her presence before.

"I'm fi—recovering," Clarissa said, because as determined as she may be, no stretch of the imagination could suggest that she was anywhere close to fine. "Although I can't get anything done because these blasted doctors insist on pumping me full of drugs, and I can't get a decent cup of coffee. In fact, I'm not even allowed a terrible cup of coffee."

"I'm guessing you've never been forced to slow down a day in your life, huh?" I asked, not quite smothering a grin.

"Last year, she organized and hosted a multi-million dollar fundraiser while she had the flu and double pneumonia," Pippa muttered under her breath.

"And raised a record-breaking amount, I might add," Clarissa replied, and I was actually happy to hear a shadow of the familiar snap in her voice. It was the first moment since the attack that I felt certain she would make a full recovery.

"Well, we won't keep you. We know you have hospital staff to terrorize," I said, ignoring Savvy's smothered snort of laughter from behind me. "We have what I think might be an important piece of information about Alasdair, and we hoped you might be able to help us shed some light on it."

Clarissa looked suddenly alert, despite being no doubt pumped full of sedatives. "I see. Well, let's have it, then."

"Well, we just came from Danica's room—"

"You've seen Danica? You've spoken to her?" Clarissa's expression became strangely wooden.

"Yes?"

The word came out like a question because I suddenly remembered that Danica wasn't supposed to have visitors, which meant I was possibly about to upset a very fragile woman. Beside me, Rana cleared her throat and shifted uncomfortably. But instead of erupting in anger, Clarissa's voice became rather small as she asked, "How is she?"

The question pulled me up short. For a moment, I wasn't sure how truthful I should be, but then I decided that lying probably wouldn't do anyone any good in the long run.

"She's safe," I said, still choosing my words carefully. "They've made sure she can't hurt herself or anyone else. But she is singularly fixated on seeing you and making sure that you know how sorry she is."

Clarissa let out a sigh that made her whole form crumple and seemed to age her twenty years in a matter of seconds. "Yes, I imagine so. I must admit I was too angry with her to indulge her requests when I first came into recovery. They say she isn't eating. Is that so?"

"That's what she told me."

Clarissa snorted. "Stupid woman. That's nonsense. How am I supposed to forgive a corpse?"

"So, you do forgive her, then?" I asked. The question popped out of my mouth rather than staying safely and silently in my head like I'd intended.

Clarissa didn't answer at first. Her gaze had fallen on the tall windows, and she was looking out over the city like she expected to find the answer to the question somewhere among the bustling roads and busy sidewalks. "I hadn't intended to. Looking at it logically, how can you forgive someone who tries to kill you? I was furious. I wanted to punish her. I still want to punish her. But some of the fire has burned out of the feeling. It's hard to stay angry at Danica. She's just so damned devoted to me. Always has been. She's followed me like a shadow since the day she learned to toddle about her own two wee legs."

I didn't reply, struck silent by the tenderness that had crept into Clarissa's voice. It was odd to think of her as a child, but even more so as a person from whom tenderness could be extracted. I'd have thought that well dried up long ago, if indeed it had ever existed at all.

"I know she didn't mean it," Clarissa continued, almost to herself, "but her devotion has always been fanatical, and I've done nothing to curb it. It was good, I thought, that she was so utterly besotted with me. Made it easier for me. What I ought to have done was push her out of the nest and made her learn to fly on her own. What chance did she have against the manipulations of that monster? I made her what she is, and now I'm paying for it." Clarissa cleared her throat and wiped a traitorous tear from her eye before it could sully her cheek.

No one spoke. Pippa looked close to tears, never having heard Clarissa open up in such a vulnerable way before. The moment was short-lived, however. Clarissa recovered herself, and I watched the armor snap back into place—it was easy to recognize, given how often I'd hidden behind my own.

"You said you had something to tell me about Alasdair. Has he been located?" Clarissa demanded.

The sharp return to interrogation startled me, but I answered. "No. We're fairly sure he's left Edinburgh, but I found something today that might give us a lead as to where to look next. Can you tell me if you've heard of a place called Kingshurst University?"

Clarissa coughed out an incredulous laugh that made her wince. "Heard of it? The MacLeod name is on at least a dozen of the buildings."

"Excuse me?"

"Fairhaven isn't the only university in the world with ties to the Durupinen, you know," Clarissa said. "Except while Fairhaven only masquerades as a normal university, Kingshurst really is a top-rated educational institution."

"I don't understand," I said. Savvy and Rana were looking bewildered as well.

"In order to maintain our level of influence and power in the wider world, we must be trained in more than Castings and runes. It was fairly early on in our clan's history that we decided we must be able to mold and shape an institution to fit our needs. Thus, we began donating generously to a fledgling university and, as a result, have been able to tailor it to our needs. Nearly every MacLeod has graduated from Kingshurst, including myself. Maeve is attending now."

Of course. Why hadn't I assumed the MacLeods basically owned a world-class university? I was standing at that moment in the private world-class hospital they'd built.

"So, the students are all Durupinen and Caomhnóir?" I asked.

"Hardly. We make up only a tiny fraction of the student and faculty population there. But we're able to maintain tightened security there that keeps our clan members safe, along with any other Durupinen from around the world who choose to attend. We have a world-class faculty and top programs in all major fields of study, from medicine to business to engineering. A Kingshurst education, along with the network of Durupinen connections, is a golden ticket in this world."

"Danica told us that Alasdair attended Kingshurst," I said eagerly. This lead was sounding increasingly promising.

"I must admit I know little of him other than the nature of his most heinous crimes, but that is very likely. Even hundreds of years ago, clan members were encouraged to pursue higher education so that they could make their marks on the world. I regret, of course, that Alasdair's mark is much more of a stain," Clarissa said, her lip curling with disgust.

"Well, we think he may have returned there. We've been trying to find links to places that would have been significant for him in life, and Danica helped us understand this one because of this artifact." I pulled out my phone and pulled up the photo of the dagger. Clarissa adjusted her glasses and peered down at it, frowning.

"Hmmm. I don't think I've seen it bef—wait. Isn't that the dagger from our artifact collection at the Manor? The one used to commit the Collector murders?"

"Yes," I said eagerly. "Can you tell me anything else about it? About the markings on it, perhaps?"

Clarissa leaned forward to examine the dagger more closely, wincing again. After a moment, she shook her head. "I'm sorry, but as we tried so hard to bury that particular chapter in our history, I really can't tell you much other than the fact that it belonged to him. Did Danica tell you it was connected to Kingshurst somehow?"

"Yes," I said, my heart sinking. "I was hoping you might know how."

"I'm sorry, but I don't. And believe me, if I knew, I would tell you. We may not have been aligned in our goals when you arrived here, Miss Ballard, but I assure you we are now. I want that monster of a ghost captured and punished for what he's done to our reputation."

It was all I could do not to roll my eyes. Of course. She wanted revenge for herself, not for the spirits currently trapped in dismembered misery beneath the city at this very moment. Still, we had a lead, and now we knew it was one worth following. That would have to be enough for now.

"Thank you, Clarissa. We won't take up any more of your time." I stood to leave, but Savvy stepped forward.

"Ms. MacLeod," she said, in a strangely quiet voice. "We told Danica we'd deliver this to you. I can't make you read it, but I've got to keep my word." And she set the jumbled heap of desperate apologies on the table beside the laptop.

Clarissa stared at it for a moment, then sighed and nodded. "I suppose I'd best respond to her somehow. I don't want the fool starving herself to death."

Back out in the hallway, Rana turned to Savvy.

"That was unusually...sympathetic of you, Sav," she said.

Savvy shrugged, looking almost churlish. "I dunno. I'm not saying Clarissa deserved to get stabbed, but Alasdair didn't make Danica what she is. Clarissa did that."

It was a quiet drive back to our lodgings.

6

FIELD TRIP

"Oh, my God, I can't believe you caved."

We'd opened the door to Hannah and Kiernan's flat to find Hannah standing on a stool in the middle of the room draped in a shimmering white fabric that pooled on the floor around her like quicksilver while Milo flitted around her, an overexcited butterfly with a tape measure and a fanatical gleam in his eye.

Hannah's expression was just shy of shooting actual lasers as she glared at me. There were three large sketches propped up on easels around her showing three different wedding dresses.

"What can I say, I should let myself get kidnapped by a murderous ghost more often!" Milo sang. Then, when Hannah turned her glare on him, he added quickly, "I jest, sweetness, I jest! No more kidnapping for me. Hostage chic is decidedly not my vibe."

"Kidnapping is all wrong," I agreed. "It was diva-napping, if anything."

Milo snorted in amusement, but Hannah was still dishing out Queen Victoria levels of "we are not amused." I sobered up my expression.

"Well, we've got news that might just make you happy enough to let Milo throw in a fourth dress," I said.

Hannah whipped her head around so fast she nearly toppled off her stool. "Really? What is it?"

"Wait, are you serious?" Milo muttered out of the side of his mouth. "Because I've got this jumpsuit design that is—"

Hannah silenced him with a look before turning back to me. "Well?"

As succinctly as I could, I explained the day's events. "Which means we now have a real lead to follow. Well, real, if you count the extremely tenuous connection between this dagger and my dream as real," I hedged.

"Of course it's real!" Hannah cried. "It was part of a Seer—OUCH!" She spun around. "Will you watch it with those pins?"

"Do you want to look saggy on your wedding day? Stop moving!" Milo snapped back. "It's hard enough to manipulate these pins using spirit energy without you writhing all over the place!"

"So, what's next?" Hannah asked, choosing to ignore Milo's sass in favor of not getting stabbed again.

"Where's Kiernan? I want to see if he can dig up any student records from Kingshurst, just to make sure."

"I kicked him out," Milo said. "The groom isn't allowed to see the bride in one of her trio of wedding dresses, even if it is still only a bolt of fabric."

"I'll text him," Hannah said wearily, pulling her phone from the only pocket that wasn't obscured yet by Milo's confection-in-progress.

At that moment, Finn walked in the door, looking more hopeful than I'd seen him in days. I'd called him before we'd even left the hospital to fill him in. He stopped short when he saw Hannah.

"Am I interrupting something?"

"Yes," said Milo.

"No," said Hannah.

"Right, then," said Finn, crossing the room to kiss me. "Have you told them?"

"Yes. We're just discussing what to do next. I was saying we should get Kiernan to double-check the school records and gather any information he can find about Alasdair's time there."

"I reckon that's a good place to start," Finn agreed, sitting down to pull off his boots. "Not that I expect him to have any luck, given how thoroughly the MacLeods have destroyed all traces of him. And then?"

"Well, assuming Kiernan can confirm that Alasdair was a student there, I think we need to go to Kingshurst and investigate. Where is Kingshurst, anyway?"

"On the Isle of Skye, on the outskirts of the town of Dunvegan," Finn said at once. "Clan MacLeod has an ancient castle seat there."

I shuddered. My time on the Isle of Skye had been some of the most traumatizing in a long string of traumatizing events. "Well, at least if we track down Alasdair, we know there's a good prison nearby," I joked weakly.

"Skye Príosún is too good for that monster," Finn growled.

"How do we investigate without drawing attention to ourselves?" Hannah asked, biting anxiously at her lip. "If we go charging in there with an army of Caomhnóir, we're going to tip Alasdair off, assuming he's actually there."

"We don't need an army of Caomhnóir," Finn said. "The campus is already crawling with them, both students and campus security. I was almost assigned to a post there after Ileana betrayed us to the Council, but they shipped me out to the príosún instead."

"Wouldn't it be, like... wildly stupid for Alasdair to go there, then?" Milo asked, pausing in his pinning. "If the place is crawling with Caomhnóir like you say, wouldn't it be too risky?"

"He's desperate," Finn said. "I'd be willing to bet he'd take the chance that no one would uncover his connection to Kingshurst. After all, Danica burned all his personal records. That said, he'll be well aware of the dangers and will probably lay low."

"Maybe we try an undercover operation!" Savvy said enthusiastically, emerging from her room where she had been changing into sweatpants. "We could pose as students there for a spot of research!"

"No one's going to believe we're undergrads, Sav," I said.

"Aw, come on, sure they will! Every actor on the telly who plays a teenager is nearly thirty!" Savvy cried.

"This is real life, Sav, not Gossip Girls," I laughed.

"Kingshurst is crawling with post-graduate scholars, actually," Finn said. "Doctoral students, researchers, you name it. I think we can blend in as long as we're careful."

"And we don't all need to stay on campus," Hannah said, and I heard the same spark of excitement in her voice. "Kiernan still has his big research project at the Skye Archive. We could make our home base there, and we'll have access to all the resources and research we could possibly need!"

"How far is the príosún from Kingshurst?" I asked.

"Barely half an hour," Finn said. "It's a brilliant idea, Hannah."

Hannah smiled for what might have been the first time since Alasdair disappeared. The sight of it filled me with a cautious but powerful burst of optimism. We were finally getting somewhere.

"What if we—"

"Hannah, stand *still!*" Milo cried out in exasperation. He stamped his foot impatiently, but the power of the gesture was lost since it made no sound at all. "Seriously, people, there is an artist at work here! Can we please respect the process?"

"Sorry, Milo," Hannah said, pocketing her phone and submitting once again to her sartorial fate.

"This is going to take careful planning," Finn said, pacing the room now, sans boots. "We'll need to make the proper connections at Kingshurst and have our cover stories well in place."

"Maeve might be able to help us with that," I said, remembering my conversation with Clarissa. "She's a current student there, and she's likely to be returning to campus soon now that her mother is recovering well."

"Well, then, we'll have to talk to Catriona and get this stage of the operation approved," Finn said, pulling out his phone. "Brilliant job, everyone." He reached out and snatched my hand, pressing it to his lips.

"And you. Well done, you."

"I hope I'm not wrong about this," I said, voicing my doubts out loud. "We're putting an awful lot of pressure on a tenuous connection between a dream and a hunch."

"Jessica Ballard, you need to have more faith in yourself," Finn said, reaching for my other hand and holding them both tightly. He searched out my eyes until I finally looked at him. "It's mind-boggling that you don't know it by now, but you have extraordinary instincts. Your gifts rarely lead you astray. Of course, they lead you into danger more often than I'd like, but then if I had my way, I would wrap you in bubble wrap, so you mustn't mind me."

"Yeah, the bubble wrap thing doesn't sound very comfortable, honestly," I said, cracking a smile.

"My point is, trust yourself, love. We all trust you."

"What if I'm wrong?"

Finn shrugged. "Then you're wrong. Everyone's wrong sometimes. But this is the best lead we've got, and we'd be fools not to follow it. So, full steam ahead, I say."

"When the two of you are done being unbearably cute over there, I have a suggestion," Milo said.

I felt the heat rushing to my face, and I pulled my hands out of Finn's and thrust them rather grumpily into my pockets. "It better not involve me acting as a human dress form for bridal gown number 2," I said.

"Of course not," Milo said, rolling his eyes. "What good would that do? You and Hannah aren't even close to the same size. I meant I have a suggestion about Kingshurst."

"Oh! Okay, let's hear it," I said.

Milo released his energy hold on the fabric he was draping. "I think we can all agree that Alasdair has a very unique energy. And by unique, I mean utterly repulsive and gag-inducing."

"Agreed," I conceded.

"Then if he's been anywhere near Kingshurst in his spirit form, we'll know it. All we'll have to do is walk the campus and do a little exploring. If we pick up on his energy, then we can set up the whole sting operation or whatever. If not, we go back to the drawing board."

I blinked. "Oh my God. That's... genius."

"No need to sound quite so surprised," Milo grumbled.

"No, she's right, Milo, you're brilliant!" Finn said, firing up with enthusiasm. He was like a hunting dog scenting a fox, animated with barely restrained energy. "If Alasdair is at Kingshurst, we don't want to spook him by showing up en masse. Best I go on ahead and scout it out. Then if there's any trace of him, I can send for the rest of you."

"Don't be ridiculous, Finn," Milo scoffed. "I can get there much faster and sense him better than the rest of you. I'll just manifest and—"

"No!" Hannah's voice was shrill with panic. "No, Milo! Absolutely not!"

"Hannah, it'll be f—"

"Milo, so help me God, if the word 'fine' escapes your lips right now, I will show up to my wedding wearing a garbage bag!" she shrieked.

Milo froze, eyes wide, then slowly raised his hands like she was pointing a weapon at him.

"I know you are a capable, self-reliant spirit guide, but I cannot handle it. It almost destroyed me when you went missing. If anything happened to you after we've only just gotten you back, I will not survive it. Do I make myself clear?" Hannah's voice was so fierce, so raw with emotion, that Milo flinched with nearly every word.

"How about this, then," Finn said in his most soothing tones, moving slowly toward Hannah like she was a skittish animal. "Milo and I will go together—and stay together. Think of it as a little light reconnaissance, yeah? I'll gather the sensory clues, Milo will gather the spirit ones, and we'll have a complete picture. If we think it's worth further investigation, we all pack up and head to Skye."

Hannah opened her mouth to object, but Finn forestalled her. "Now, Hannah. Surely you trust me to keep Milo safe, don't you? I won't let him out of my sight, cross my heart."

Hannah's face twitched as she tried to find something to reasonably object to in this plan. Finally, her shoulders sagged, and she nodded. "Of course I do." It was obvious she wanted to keep Milo in bubble wrap as badly as Finn wanted to do the same to me. If Milo and I didn't start being a bit less reckless with our independent investigating, we'd both wind up under house arrest.

"Excellent. If everyone's on board, I'll start making the arrangements. With any luck, we'll be approved and ready to head out in the morning."

"The sooner the better, as far as I'm concerned," Milo said, his voice quiet and fierce. I knew he feared Alasdair—hell, we all did—but his righteous indignation for the spirits still trapped below burned a hundred times brighter. In fact, everywhere I looked, a face alight with grim determination looked back at me.

If Alasdair was smart, he'd realize just how formidable an enemy he'd made in me and my friends. But if he didn't know already, he was sure as hell about to find out.

I woke early the next morning—not by choice, obviously—to find that Finn and Milo had already set out, a fact I gleaned from the note left in the refrigerator for me stuck to the side of an extra-large iced latte.

Didn't want to wake you—you looked so beautiful. Will keep you posted in real time if you keep the Connection open.

xx Finn

I snorted. I knew full well what I looked like when I slept, and it was far from beautiful—slightly feral and twitching with nightmares, more like. Bless his lying heart. I gratefully took the coffee, though, threw an oversized cardigan on over my pajamas, and walked up the stairs to Hannah and Kiernan's flat. As I'd suspected, Hannah was already awake. Kiernan waved to me from the kitchen, where he stood in a pair of plaid pajama pants and a t-shirt in front of the stove.

"Hey, Jess. Have you eaten? I'm doing a full English to keep everyone's strength up," Kiernan said. His eyes were heavy behind his glasses, but he had the usual gentle smile on his face.

"That would be awesome, thanks, Kiernan," I said, plopping down next to Hannah on the sofa. "He can cook, too? Looks like you hit the fiancé lottery!"

Hannah managed a ghost of a smile and then returned to staring moodily at the cup of herbal tea steaming in her hands.

"Do you know what time they left?" I asked. "Finn didn't—"

"Four o'clock. Did you sleep?"

One glance at the purple rings under her eyes, and I knew why she was asking me. She'd clearly been awake most of the night.

"Uh, yeah. Yeah, I slept."

"Slept" was probably too mild a word to describe my night's activities, which included tossing, turning, and falling headfirst into dream after disturbing dream, all of them involving Alasdair chasing me around a campus that looked suspiciously like St. Matt's. The dreams would always end the same way: pursuing a hooded figure down that same mysterious hallway, my progress impeded by the snatching ghostly hands of a wasted horde of spirits. I wondered, somewhat wistfully, what normal people dreamed of. At this point, I'd give almost anything to have a boring dream about grocery shopping or missing the bus to school.

"What are you looking at?" I asked, scooching closer to Hannah, and resting my chin on her shoulder so that I could get a better look at the notebook resting in her lap.

"It's a list of catering options that Karen sent me in her weekly wedding email," Hannah sighed.

"There's a weekly wedding email?" I asked.

"Oh, yes. I told her not to include you on it. No reason for both of us to suffer," Hannah said, chuckling softly.

I kissed her on the head. "As much as I appreciate the gesture, you should just forward it to me with the subject line 'I CANNOT EVEN,' and let me deal with it. You've got too much on your plate without this added stress."

"I would have agreed with you a couple of weeks ago, but honestly, right now, I welcome it. It's a relief to distract myself with lists of passed hors d' oeuvres," she said. "What do you think? Kiernan already picked his favorites."

I scanned the list and my jaw dropped. "Mini grilled cheeses with a shot glass of tomato soup? Lobster roll sliders? Holy shit, Milo's going to need to put an elastic waistband on my bridesmaid dress."

"I said the same about my tux," Kiernan called from the kitchen. "If our wedding has to be a spectacle, I at least intend to stuff my face through the whole thing."

"Are you really okay about this wedding?" I asked Hannah. "Seriously, I think Karen would back off if you asked her to. And Milo, too, for that matter, if you told them you were really unhappy about it."

But Hannah shook her head, and she smiled a genuine smile. "I've decided to relax and let them have their fun. It makes them happy, and everyone will have a great time. And in spite of it all, I'll get exactly what I want. Everyone wins." And she looked up at Kiernan, their eyes locking in one of those looks that often passed between them, a look of such genuine, unfiltered adoration that I got a lump in my throat. No one—literally no one—deserved a happily ever after more than my sister. I cleared my throat, blinking back the evidence of my emotions, and hoping neither of them noticed it.

"Well, that's cute, but the offer stands. I'll have a car revving in the driveway on the morning of, in case you want to hightail it to city hall."

Hannah laughed just as Kiernan announced breakfast was ready.

We were halfway through our food when the Connection broke wide open, and Milo's voice sang through like birdsong. "Are you both there? Hannah, tell Jess to wake her ass up. We're pulling through the gates of Kingshurst!"

"My ass is awake, thank you very much, as is the rest of me," I grumbled.

"Oh! Hey! Sorry, it's before noon, so I figured—"

But Hannah cut him off before we could start bickering in earnest. "Is Finn there with you?" she asked, her voice already trembling with anxiety.

"No, I'm driving a vehicle by myself. I got some confused looks from passing motorists, but at least if I get pulled over for speeding, I won't be—"

"Okay, okay, I get it. Stupid question," Hannah thought hastily. "Just... stick together, okay?"

"Hannah, you may not believe this, but I would also like to avoid getting ghostnapped again, okay? I promise I'm not going to do anything reckless. You can see all my thoughts right now. Am I about to go rogue?"

I reached out into Milo's thoughts just as Hannah did the same. They were pliable, offering no resistance as Milo chose to allow us in further. I found only caution and concern as my consciousness melted through his like a hot knife through butter. I knew Hannah sensed the very same, and watched as her shoulders relaxed and her breathing calmed to a slow, steady rhythm.

"You didn't have to do that," she said, both in our heads and out loud. "But thank you."

"I don't have any secrets from you, sweetness," Milo said. "You know that. Now, concentrate! We just need to park, and then we're going to start investigating."

Hannah and I sat, eyes closed, hands held to increase the strength of the bond between us. When we were first in the grips of the Prophecy, and Hannah had been taken by the Necromancers, Milo and I had accidentally discovered that we could see, hear, and experience everything Hannah did if Milo used my body while I was still in it. Hannah and I couldn't quite achieve the same level of clarity with Milo's activities, as we couldn't exactly inhabit the same body. However, by focusing together, we could arrive at something very like it. Milo's thoughts unfurled in real time in our heads, and our senses tried to fill in the blanks, almost like having a dream of what Milo was experiencing.

They stopped at the guard house to sign in and gain admittance. Milo noted the guard's pointed glance at him, and we all realized at once that the guard himself was a Caomhnóir. They pulled up a long drive that swooped around and closed in on itself. They parked along its curve and got out of the car. I imagined in front of me a sprawling campus as I manifested Milo's thoughts in my mind's eye. Buildings sprang up right in front of me, Milo's observations splashed across the blank canvas of my mind. I saw craggy great trees standing like ancient sentinels on the grassy lawns, and yellow stone paths snaking through the grass. I saw fifteenth-century stone edifices adorned with gothic arches and crowned with turrets, rotundas, and towers that reached into the blue sky above. It was, I realized, a place in which ghosts would seem more at home than modern living people—a place where modernity itself was the anachronism.

"Jess, don't forget to breathe," Hannah whispered, and the air whooshed out of me at the reminder.

"Right. Breathe. Can't concentrate if I'm unconscious, can I?" I murmured, taking a few deep breaths, and trying to settle myself into a regular breathing pattern as I sank into concentration again. It was easy to forget to breathe when sunken so deep into the thoughts of someone for whom breathing was no longer a consideration.

"What's happening?" came Kiernan's anxious whisper. I opened one eye to see him hovering over Hannah's shoulder, bouncing on the balls of his feet.

"Nothing yet—they're just walking across the campus. We'll let you know, I promise," Hannah said.

Although I couldn't actually hear Finn, I felt his words drop into my head as Milo listened to them. "We should head for Old Campus, behind the second set of gates," he told Milo. "That's the part of the college that would have been standing when Alasdair went to school here, so that's likely to be where he'd return to."

"If the hallway I saw in my vision is on that campus somewhere, it's definitely in a very old building," I said. I felt Milo pass the information on to Finn.

"My thoughts exactly," he replied.

We sensed their passage past several modern additions to the campus, buildings that blighted the place's history—the architectural equivalent of drawing a mustache onto the Mona Lisa with a Sharpie. As an art student, I couldn't stop cringing. There was also a constant chill that seeped through the Connection, a chill that flourished despite the warmth of an unusually sunny day. The reason for this soon became clear.

"Spirits," Milo confirmed what we'd all sensed. "The place is positively crawling with them, but only in Old Campus. Huh. I wonder why that is?"

"It'll be the Wards, I expect," Finn said. "Old Campus is only for clan students, so spirits can roam more freely there."

"Well then why can I walk through this New Campus area?" Milo asked.

"You're a spirit guide, Bound to a Durupinen bloodline. You're an exception," Finn said.

"It's true. I am exceptional," Milo cooed.

At last, they passed through a set of iron gates covered in elaborate curling grillwork and arrived at a courtyard frozen in time. Crumbled stone pillars and gnarled and ancient trees thrust up at the deep blue sky. Buildings of warm, yellow sandstone worn to smoothness and throttled with creeping ivy stood proudly among beds of sunshiny primroses, ling heather, and wild orchids.

As Milo reached out to connect with the spirits wandering this area of the campus, we connected as well. There was a peace here. These spirits belonged to this place, and it belonged to them—endemic, like the native flora nestled into the numerous garden beds. The spirits were here because it felt like home to them, not because they were lost or trapped or wandering aimlessly. I wasn't sure whether to be reassured or disappointed. On the one hand, the spirits weren't unsettled by Alasdair's possible presence. He had not yet done anything to disquiet or disturb them. On the other hand, that could mean that we'd been mistaken, and that he hadn't come to Kingshurst at all.

The thought flitted through the Connection before I could get a proper hold of it, but Milo caught it and cradled it in his own replying thought. "Don't jump to conclusions. Alasdair is smart. He knows he can't draw attention to himself here, with so many Durupinen and Caomhnóir among the students and staff. If he's here, he'll be laying low, planning his next move."

For a few minutes, they walked the perimeter of the courtyard, and I knew, though I couldn't hear his thoughts, that Finn was making a mental map of the area, making note of the layout and the exits, and committing it all to memory. It was part of his training, a crucial first step to feeling safe and prepared in any new location. Milo, meanwhile, was straining every spirit sense he had for some trace of Alasdair's foul energy. If any place could hold onto him, it was this place: a place trapped in time, built of memory, and mortared together with whispers of the past.

"Nothing?" I felt Hannah's half-desperate question drop into my head like a drop of water into a bucket.

"Not yet," Milo said. "Be patient."

We waited as Finn and Milo circled one building after another, following the winding paths through cloisters and small courtyards. At last, they gave up on the grounds and decided to enter the buildings themselves, although they were hardly buildings plural. They were all connected to each other in some way, sometimes with a pointed gothic archway, sometimes with a covered walkway or an iron fence. It was like the buildings were clinging to each other, standing together, united against the relentless marching on of time around them.

They started at one end and began to wander through. Finn's booted footsteps echoed inside my head, the only sound in an otherwise silent place. The vaulted ceilings and lack of carpeting magnified the sound. The cold was even more prevalent here than it had been back in the grounds—a deeper, mustier cold, the kind that wormed its way into your bones and chilled you from the inside out. It made Milo stop in his tracks as he probed at it, searching.

"I... I don't think that's him... but it's... similar. Jess, Hannah, do you feel that?"

"Yes," Hannah breathed. "You're right. There's something off about it, but I don't recognize it."

"I think it's just... like... *really* old spirit energy. Like some of these ghosts have been here so long they've sort of... petrified," Milo said. "I've come across it before at Fairhaven, and in London, too."

"Let's keep going," Finn said, his words filtering through Milo's consciousness.

They continued through the first building—a small, circular structure with a vaulted ceiling and arched niches set with busts of stern-looking men and women—and into a long hallway lined with stained glass windows and hung with monstrous black iron chandeliers. They'd barely gone halfway down it when Milo stopped again.

"Hang on..." he muttered. The cold was deepening, and something in the atmosphere had shifted slightly. I could feel a slight vibration in the air, a buzz of something trying to be sensed—or perhaps something *scared* to be sensed. Milo floated forward, and I felt Hannah stiffen, but his reassurance drifted through to her. "Finn is right beside me, ready to Expel at the first sign of trouble."

Hannah let out a whimper but said nothing else.

Milo continued to drift forward, every particle of his concentration on the energy they had detected. It was so faint that, at first, he doubted himself. He wanted Alasdair to be here, he hoped for it, and that's why he thought he...

No.

No, no, no.

He was not imagining it. There it was, the faintest whiff of decay. I recognized it, even filtered through Milo's thoughts.

"He's been here," Milo whispered.

"Then get out of there!" came Hannah's hysterical reply reverberating like feedback through my head, and also through the room as the words burst from her mouth.

"What? What's happening?" cried Kiernan.

"They've scented him! He's there, Alasdair's th—"

"No, no, it's okay," Milo reassured her. "He's not here now, I'm sure of it. It's a faint trail, barely lingering. I'm not sure it would have lingered at all if there weren't so much other spirit energy in this place to cling to. But it's him. I know it's him!"

"How do we know that's not old energy? After all, he's been there before," Hannah wondered.

"Not as a spirit, though," Milo reminded her. "He was caught in Edinburgh and died in the príosún there. He was trapped there until just a few months ago when Danica found him. Besides, his trail faded quickly from his old haunts in Edinburgh—he was here recently, within the last day or two, I'd say."

Milo's thoughts were taut with excitement, his words strumming them in a raucous melody.

"Right, well, we've got what we came for. There's no reason to proceed any further, not without back-up," Finn said; and though his outward demeanor was calm, we could all sense the vibrations of agitation beneath. "Get yourselves packed and get Catriona on the phone. I want all the arrangements made before we get back to Edinburgh. We can't afford to waste any time. Just because he's been here recently doesn't necessarily mean he'll linger."

If I knew Finn, I knew it took every bit of his determination to call off the hunt. He'd been so singularly obsessed with finding Alasdair that I half expected him to just charge on through, caution and proper planning be damned. But he knew how important it was not to screw up this chance—maybe our only chance—to stop Alasdair. His commitment to seeing it through overpowered his protective instincts. I was so proud of him, even more so because I knew that if I had been there with him, I probably would not have possessed that kind of self-control. I'd have tracked down that scent like a deranged bloodhound.

"Yes, you would have." Hannah's response to my thought twanged like a sour note.

"Sorry," I said, out loud this time.

"We're turning around now," Finn said firmly. I pulled back from the Connection, my head spinning as I tried to readjust to reality. Hannah remained stubbornly integrated into Milo's thoughts until he and Finn had gotten back into the car and driven out of Kingshurst's gates. She refocused on the room to find me pacing.

I didn't know how to feel. Elated? That was too positive a name for the emotion now roiling through me. Relief? That was definitely part of it. We may not have located the exact corridor from my dream, but the tenuous link between the vision, the dagger, and Alasdair had turned out to be real.

Alasdair had fled to Kingshurst. And we would soon be right on his tail.

7

BURNING

"You're bloody *joking*."

I stood for a moment and just enjoyed the gobsmacked expression on Catriona's face. It was so rare for her to express anything but boredom or mild disdain that I couldn't help but allow myself the pleasure of having made her jaw hit the floor.

"I am not, in fact, bloody joking," I said when she'd recovered. "Finn and Milo are on their way back as we speak."

"And they're sure—*absolutely* sure—that it was him?" Cat asked.

"One hundred percent. You've experienced that energy. Do you honestly think there could be any mistaking it?"

"Jess, I've had to come to terms with at least half a dozen previously impossible things since arriving in Edinburgh. I'm not taking any chances."

"Well, Hannah and I both experienced it too, through our Connection with Milo, and there's no mistake. Alasdair is at Kingshurst, or has been recently, at any rate."

Cat nodded. Evidently, that was good enough for her. "Well, then. There's not a moment to lose, is there?" She sat on the corner of one of the work tables in our makeshift museum at the Collective. "What's next?"

I blinked. "I kind of thought you'd be telling me."

Cat snorted. "Like you'd listen."

I grinned. "Fair enough."

"Look, just tell me what you need. I spoke to Finn last night before he set out, so I've got a rudimentary plan in place, but we'll need to finalize the details."

"Have we sorted out who's coming, for a start?" I asked.

"When I learned a trip to Kingshurst may be in the works, I took the liberty of contacting Maeve MacLeod."

I blinked in surprise. "Maeve? Really?"

Cat cocked an eyebrow. "Yes, really. She's a current student and would therefore be an excellent choice to bring into the loop. After what happened to her mother and her aunt, she's chomping at the bit for a way to help."

"Ah, she's just a kid," I groaned. "I don't want to get her mixed up in this."

"Jess, she *is* mixed up in this. This is a MacLeod catastrophe from start to finish," Cat pointed out.

"I had mentioned her to Finn, it's true, but I kind of thought she could just give us some intel on the place. I don't want to put her in any danger."

"And I don't intend to. I'm not putting her on the investigative team, per se. I'm just asking her to be a sort of guide—someone who can show you around campus without drawing attention to you. If you're led everywhere by a pack of burly security Caomhnóir, you'll stick out like a sore thumb."

I sighed. "Yeah, okay, fair enough. And speaking of Caomhnóir, who's going to be coming?"

Cat nodded. "We've got Patel, Todd, and Carey; that's your usual crew. But I'd feel better if we had a fourth to round it out, although there are lots of Caomhnóir on site we could enlist if needed."

"Why don't we use Reilly Bell?" I suggested on sudden inspiration.

Catriona frowned, as though trying to place the name. "He's not one of ours. Bell. He's one of the Clan Rìoghalachd lads, isn't he? Tall, wiry, bit of a babyface?"

"That's him."

"Sort of an odd choice. He struck me as a bit of a pup compared to some of the others on their security roster. Why him?"

"He and Maeve are a couple, covertly. This would be a great chance to—"

"Ah, come on, Jess. I'm not a sodding matchmaker!" Cat groaned. "We can't afford to cock up this mission over a spot of star-crossed lover's drama."

"Don't be ridiculous. Finn will keep him in line. And besides, if he can distinguish himself on this mission, he might worm his way onto Clarissa's good side. Maybe she'll soften her stance on Caomhnóir and Durupinen relationships."

Cat snorted. "It's frankly adorable that you still think Clarissa MacLeod might have a good side."

"Come on, Cat, it's worth a try, isn't it? Look, check his record, and talk to his superiors. If he doesn't seem like a good fit, then find someone else. But give the kid a chance."

This was an ace in the hole. I might have been giving too much credit to Clarissa for having a good side, but I definitely didn't underestimate her commitment to security, especially for her own family. Reilly would never have been assigned to Maeve's detail in the first place if he wasn't one of the most promising Caomhnóir on the roster. Clarissa would have seen to that personally.

Catriona gave a long-suffering sigh, and I smothered a smile, recognizing the sound of her relenting. "Fine, we'll give him a go."

"Thanks," I said, knowing that if I crowed over it, she'd just change her mind. "Now, what about when we get there? Are we going to be completely undercover? Is there anyone there we can trust?"

Catriona frowned. "It's going to be tough to keep your presence a secret, frankly." She leaned in and adopted a stage whisper. "I'm not sure if you're aware of this, but you have a bit of a reputation in the Durupinen world for being, at best, a shit-stirrer and, at worst, a traitor of the highest order."

I smiled blandly. "You don't say."

Cat straightened up, sighing. "My point is we should probably limit the people you interact with to a small circle. The smaller, the better. I'll talk to Clarissa to see who she thinks might be our best chance at a contact there, besides Maeve, of course. As I said, I only want to involve her peripherally."

"It would help if our contact had some knowledge about the history of the college and the buildings, that kind of thing. We're going to concentrate our efforts on Old Campus and any documentation we can dig up about activity when Alasdair would have been a student there."

"Hmm. Yes, that's a good point. If I'm not mistaken, Kingshurst has its own historian in charge of preservation and the like. I'll start there."

"What are the chances that historian is a member of Clan Rìoghalachd who hates me with a passion, and therefore refuses to help us?" I asked dryly.

I expected Cat to crack a joke at my expense, but it was a mark of how serious the situation was that she instead risked more frown lines to contemplate the question. "Well, as to the first point, it's almost definitely going to be a member of Clan Rìoghalachd. Clarissa will have seen to that. Kingshurst is one of the many pet projects she prefers to micromanage. And if they toe the clan line, as they will doubtless do, they may be less than fond of you."

"Super."

"But as to refusing to help us, I can't see how that's possible. As unlikely as it seemed at the outset of this mission, you and Clarissa are on the same side now, at least temporarily. She wants nothing more than to save face and catch Alasdair, and therefore I rather expect the rest of Clan Rìoghalachd to be falling over themselves to make sure that happens. Even Danica, in her twisted way, was simply trying to serve the queen, as it were."

I nodded, feeling the tension in my stomach ease just a bit. Unpopular though I may be, Cat was right. We'd likely get all the help we needed, and then some, if Clarissa was pushing for it.

"Speaking of help, didn't I approve a request to bring a Scribe here that you wanted to have on the case?"

I full-on smacked myself in the forehead. "Oh my God, I completely forgot! I asked Flavia to rearrange her entire life to come to my aid, and now I'm leaving!"

"Do you think she'd be willing to go to Skye instead?" Catriona asked. "I'm not sure what else we'll be able to discover from all this," she waved her arm at the roomful of artifacts from beneath the city, "and she might prove more useful to you within a few miles of Kingshurst."

"That's a great idea, Cat, thanks," I said. "I'll call her now and see if I can set it up."

"Good. Keep me posted. I'm off to see what I can arrange for contacts and accommodations at Kingshurst. Let's have the whole team meet here in..." she consulted her watch, "three hours? That should give Finn and Milo enough time to get back from Kingshurst and give me a chance to bring Reilly Bell on board. Can you let the others know?"

"Sure," I said, pulling out my phone to start texting.

Savvy and Rana got back to me at once—Rana with a long text full of logistical questions, and Savvy with a single thumbs-up emoji. Kiernan confirmed as well, but Hannah didn't respond. I was about to call her when Kiernan texted again.

Hannah probably won't see this text. There's no way she's got mobile service.

Why? I texted back. *Where did she go?*

I watched the three little dots appear and reappear a few times before Kiernan's reply finally popped up.

Down there. To say a sort of goodbye, I suppose. I offered to come with her, but she wanted to be alone.

My heart sank. Of course. I should have known.

Luckily, I no longer had to lower myself down through an actual sewer to get to the long-buried *príosún*. Since we discovered Alasdair and Danica's secret lair, Catriona had overseen a complete excavation of the site. It could now be reached via a recently uncovered staircase, narrow and winding to the point of inducing claustrophobia in even the most intrepid of travelers, but surprisingly sturdy. I eased my way down it now, hands pressed against the rough crags and crevices of the stone walls for support. With Alasdair gone, the air was less foul than it had been; but the musty dampness of ages still clung to my skin, and seeped into my lungs. Everything was soft, rotted, and decaying in the dark, lit only by naked bulbs suspended from orange industrial extension cords that snaked along the floor and coiled into corners like serpents ready to spring.

It felt like traversing the underside of a grave. I shuddered.

The staircase opened into a short corridor that ended at a doorway—its door had been so old it had fallen to pieces when the Caomhnóir who found it tried to pry it open. It now lay in a little dusty heap of shards on the floor beside the doorway that gaped like a silently screaming mouth into the nightmare beyond.

Hannah stood in front of the Collection, her slender hands balled tightly into fists as she gazed up at it. I was a little ashamed that I hadn't been back down here since I'd emerged in Walker form to reclaim my body. I hadn't admitted to myself that I was avoiding it, but maybe I was.

Okay, I definitely was. And standing beside my sister, lifting my eyes to the Collection, I was reminded all too clearly why.

It wasn't only the Collection's appearance, though that would certainly have been enough. The whole of it pulsed, expanding and contracting like a diseased organ; and in its depths, I could see the hands and feet and faces and drifting hair and contorted limbs of dozens of spirits, all trapped in a seething mass of misery. But worse than the sight of it were the waves of terror and pain and confusion that rolled off it and crashed over me, a storm of spirit energy that threatened to drown me. I took a moment to brace myself against it, to conquer the urge to run from it before I cleared my throat to speak. Hannah, perhaps having already acclimated herself to the horror of it all, beat me to it.

"Did Kiernan tell you I was down here?"

"Kind of," I admitted. "Sorry. He said you wanted to be alone, but—"

"No, it's okay. I'm glad you're here. Besides, there's no being alone down here."

Silence washed over us for a moment. I fumbled for her hand and pried her fingers open so that I could lace mine through. She allowed it.

"I tried to Call them."

This was enough to pull my gaze from the Collection.

"You what?"

"I tried to Call them," she repeated. "The spirits in the Collection. I thought maybe I could free them that way."

"By yourself?"

"Yes."

I could barely breathe. The Collection was an experiment—a monstrosity that broke every rule we'd ever been taught about the spirit world. No one knew how to undo it, least of all us.

"Hannah, that... could have been dangerous," I said, endeavoring to keep my tone gentle even as I reprimanded her.

She just waved her other hand impatiently, batting my admonishment away like an irksome fly. "It doesn't matter. I had to try."

"It would have mattered to me—and a lot of other people—if something had happened to you," I said.

She shrugged, and I gave up. Her actions had been reckless—the kind of shit I'd be likely to pull, leaving Hannah to scold me for the unruly toddler I could sometimes be. To switch positions now—me, acting like the sensible one while she took uncalculated risks—was nothing short of disorientating. But she was clearly okay, so what was the point of harping on it now? I decided to let it go and try to get some details instead.

"So... what happened?"

She swallowed hard. "Nothing. I couldn't connect with them, not really. I reached out for their individual lights to gather them into me, but there was nothing to grab hold of. I could feel a faint aching wish to come to me, but it was as though someone took the impulse, crushed it to powder, and then scattered it like sand. It was impossible to gather the pieces. Again and again, I reached out, and again and again I came back empty-handed."

I swallowed hard against a huge lump of misery that swelled in my throat as she spoke. "I'm sorry, Hannah."

"The worst part is that they *know*, Jess," she whispered. "They know they're broken. They can feel the absence of every missing piece, every jagged edge. It would be one thing if he'd taken their sentience, but this..." She shook her head, which in turn shook loose the tears that had been glimmering in her eyes. I watched them roll down her cheeks, tremble on her chin, and then splash to the floor.

I hardly knew what to say. All I wanted in the world was to tell her that I would fix it, but I couldn't fix it, not yet. Hell, I didn't even know if it *was* fixable. Could the damage Alasdair had wrought even be undone? He had embarked on his mad quest for immortality with no regard for the people he murdered or the spirits he collected as a result. To him, they had been no more than objects to be broken up for scrap, stripped of the parts he needed, and then discarded like garbage. It was hard to fathom anyone who had grown up in the Durupinen world could think of spirits in such a way, but I'd given up trying to fathom Alasdair's kind of evil. He may have been a human once, but the monster that remained was anything but.

"We can't let him escape, Jess," Hannah said when I failed to fill the quiet stretching out between us. "We have to catch him, and we have to make him reverse this. There must be a way. There *must* be."

"We won't let him escape," I said softly. I couldn't promise the Collection would be reversed, but I could promise this. The sight of the Collection filled my sister with inexpressible sorrow, but it filled me with something that flared red and angry.

We stood in silence for a long time, sorrow and rage burning side by side.

8

BACK TO SCHOOL

The rest of the afternoon and evening was a whirlwind of preparations for our trip to Kingshurst. We all shared the same urgency—the determination that we ready ourselves as quickly as possible to ensure that Alasdair didn't have a chance to slip through our fingers yet again. I'd rarely seen Finn so unsettled. He seemed hardly able to still his body. Every time he sat down, he was up again within minutes, pacing or re-checking orders or cataloging Casting supplies. I knew it had damn near killed him to turn around and call off the hunt at Kingshurst that morning. I was anxious too, of course, but there was a deep part of me—the Seer part of me—that knew that we were on the right path. Alasdair was at Kingshurst—or at the very least, the key to catching him was.

Hannah, on the other hand, had turned to something resembling a pale marble statue of herself. While Finn seemed unable to sit still, Hannah's stress had turned her to stone. Kiernan bustled around her, doing what he could to keep her calm by ensuring everything for our journey was ready. When he could find nothing else to double or triple-check, he heaved out a stack of relevant reading material and dove in, eager to find some small snippet of information that might be of use to us when we arrived. His anxious glances at Hannah were so frequent, however, that it seemed he could hardly be making any progress. Savvy and Rana stopped by the apartment to check in, but they didn't stay long —the tension was unbearable and made Savvy jumpy and irritable.

Only Milo seemed able to be truly productive, throwing himself headlong into his designs for Hannah's dresses. I could hear him shut away in the bedroom, cursing and celebrating quietly to himself through the trial and error process of creation. I tried to steal a peek, but he used his pent-up energy to slam the door right in my face. I almost lost a finger, but I let him be. I knew he needed the distraction as well—after all, he'd spent more time with the horror that was Alasdair than any of the rest of us had, and therefore had more to forget.

As for me, I stayed awake for as long as I could, but finally surrendered to sleep after nodding off over a cup of lukewarm tea and spilling it all over myself. As if it was merely waiting for me to close my eyes properly, the dream began the moment my head hit the pillow.

There was the cloaked figure, darkness fluttering out behind it as though the person was draped in shadow, or thick smoke, rather than fabric. I followed at a distance, not wanting to be seen. We stood at opposite ends of a courtyard—it was exactly as I envisioned the courtyard within the gates of Old Campus, with careful flower beds and austere trees. And yet, as the figure moved through the grass, everything around it began to shrivel, darken, and die. The blossoms wilted, the petals drifted to the ground like ash. The tree branches curled in against the aged trunks like wounded limbs as the leaves upon them shivered to the ground. A trail of frost lay in the figure's wake, as though winter fell where it tread.

The frozen grass crunched under my foot, betraying my presence. I froze, and ahead of me, the figure froze too, listening.

The figure whirled to stare at me, and I woke up gasping.

"Jess? Are you all right, love?" Finn's voice was gentle.

"Yeah." I panted, brushing cold sweat from my forehead with a shaking hand. "Yeah, I... it's okay."

"The vision again?" His voice was layered with concern for me, but eagerness, too.

"Sort of. I was still following that hooded figure, but we were in the courtyard of Old Campus this time. And everything in its path sort of... died as he touched it."

Finn nodded as he rubbed some warmth back into my shoulder. "And you're sure it was Kingshurst?"

I nodded. I may not have seen the place with my own eyes yet, but I knew it all the same. Milo's impressions had been like a sketch in my head, allowing me to fill in the details, and yet providing the outline. I had no doubt I would recognize it when I set foot there later that day.

Finn nodded, and I saw the spark of confidence kindle in his eyes. He was willing to accept my dream as a sign that we were headed to the right place. "Well, your wake-up was well timed. The alarm's just gone off."

"Already?" I shook my head like a wet dog, trying to shake the clinging vestiges of the dream from my body. "I... it feels like I just fell asleep."

"Dreams are strange like that," he said.

"And Seer visions are even stranger," I muttered.

A van waited for us outside, a sleek gray ten-passenger model that looked more like a small RV or bus than a van. I spotted Reilly Bell in the driver's seat. He gave me a friendly nod, and I wondered how much he knew about why he'd been chosen for this mission. Somehow, I didn't think Catriona would drop any hints that his love life was a factor. I opened the door to the van and caught the quickest glimpse of Maeve before she launched herself forward and flung her arms around me in a violent hug.

"What the—" I choked.

"You did this, I know you did! Don't deny it. Thank you!" she murmured in my ear before pulling back to reveal a broad grin.

I winked at her. "I have no idea what you're talking about," I insisted.

Maeve's grin dropped into a deadly serious expression. "Of course not," she said solemnly, and then returned the wink.

Savvy was grumbling about the length of the journey.

"I just get so bloody bored on long car rides," she groaned, her leg bouncing like an elementary school kid trying to sit still at a desk. "Surely the MacLeods have a fleet of helicopters and private planes we could have taken?"

Maeve smiled sheepishly. "We do, actually," she admitted.

"Clarissa offered, but Catriona thought this method of travel would draw less attention," Finn said. "We're trying to stay under the radar, remember?"

"Ah, come on, it's not like we'd land it on the roof of the school or some such nonsense," Sav whined.

"No, but we'd have to arrange ground transport to pick us up, which would have alerted more people to our presence," Finn said with galling patience. He looked at Sav's grumpy face and grinned broadly. "Ah, chin up, Todd. If we manage to catch Alasdair, we can take a chopper home, all right?"

"Have fun with that. I'll stick to the van," I said. Thanks to my crippling aviophobia, I was more than happy that our travel arrangements didn't include air travel of any kind.

I dozed fitfully through most of the journey to Skye, the cloaked figure popping up here and there in the scattered patchwork of my dreams. When at last we pulled into view of the *príosún*, I was stiff and numb, and my brain felt like a wrung sponge. I was grateful to get out and stretch my legs, even if the sight of the *príosún* itself filled me with dread. That dread must have splashed itself across my face, because I felt a small cold hand slip into mine, and turned to see Hannah beside me.

"Are you all right?"

"Yeah, I'll be fine. Just... reliving all those warm fuzzy Skye Príosún memories," I said.

"Hey, look on the bright side. You don't even have to go in. Me, on the other hand..." She gave a delicate shiver as she gazed up at the imposing stone façade of the place, which looked every inch the medieval fortress as it was originally designed to be.

"You don't have to stay here either, you know," I told her. "You can come to Kingshurst with us."

Hannah shook her head. "I know, but I'll be of much more use here. Necromancer magic was the basis of Alasdair's experiments, and Skye has the biggest collection of Necromancer writings. That means I have the best chance of figuring out how to unmake the Collection if I'm here. And besides, Kiernan will be with me, and I'll be linked to you through the Connection."

I suppressed a smile. She was repeating all the placating things I'd been saying to her for the last twenty-four hours as we'd prepared for this trip. It sounded like she had finally convinced herself, although now that we were facing the moment of parting, the idea of separating was filling me with dread. Luckily, Kiernan came along to stand beside us just then, and I missed my window to chicken out and beg her to come with me to Kingshurst.

Several Caomhnóir came jogging down to meet the van. After a hurried conversation, we all helped extricate Kiernan and Hannah's bags from the others, along with boxes and boxes of Alasdair's notes and artifacts. We hadn't brought the whole collection—the Scribes back at the Collective still had plenty to keep them busy—but nearly all of the writings had made the journey. Kiernan and Hannah would be joined shortly by Flavia, who would aid them in their efforts. I'd worried that asking Flavia to change her plans and come to Skye instead would turn out to be a deal breaker, but Flavia had been thrilled. After all, access to Skye archive was every Scribe's wildest dream, and Flavia had never yet had the chance.

A woman emerged from the massive doors of the fortress, a clipboard in her hand and an enthusiastic expression on her round, cheerful face. She hurried to meet us, her long skirt whipping around in the cliffside breeze.

"Ms. Ballard and Ms. Ballard, I presume?" she said, looking us both over with keen interest. "Polly Keener, a pleasure, a pleasure. I've heard so much about you!"

"All of it glowing, no doubt," I said with a sarcastic smile.

Polly's smile widened, crinkling her brown eyes. "Glowing, perhaps not, but all of it simply *fascinating*." I guessed she was probably in her mid-to-late 50s, with fading brown hair shot through with silver, piled up on top of her head in a very messy bun held together with pencils. She was wearing an oversized cardigan comprising brightly colored granny squares, which I had a feeling she probably knitted herself.

"You're the head Scribe here, isn't that right?" Kiernan asked, holding out his hand and grabbing Polly's enthusiastically. "Kiernan Worthington, Apprentice Scribe from Fairhaven."

"Ah, yes, Mr. Worthington, I've heard about you as well!" Polly said, turning her smile on him.

Kiernan's face fell. "Oh," he said softly, but Polly only laughed.

"Don't worry, young man, I hold none of those traditional views. Happy to have another keen mind on the job, doesn't matter who it belongs to," Polly said, winking.

Kiernan's smile bloomed once more, and he continued to look at Polly as though she was some kind of celebrity as she went on.

"I've got an office set aside for you in the archive, as well as living quarters in the Scribes' wing. I assure you it's much cozier than the rest of the building. Once you've gotten settled, if there's anything else you need, you just let me know, and I'll make sure it's seen to at once." Her broad smile faltered, and she leaned forward, dropping her voice. "I understand we have rather a serious situation on our hands back in Edinburgh. I hope you find what you need here, and my staff is ready and waiting to assist in any way they can."

Hannah's shoulders had been relaxing by degrees through the whole conversation, and when she finally spoke to Polly, she was able to return her smile without affectation. "We truly appreciate that, Ms. Keener."

Polly waved aside the formality impatiently. "Now, now, no need for that.

Everyone here just calls me plain old Polly, and I'd prefer if you do the same. And I must tell you, I'm all aflutter having you here. I'm not sure if you know this, but I'm the official historian of Clan Sassanaigh!"

I blinked. "I had no idea we had an official historian. Is that, like... a standard thing?" A clan historian sounded like the pretentious kind of status symbol our grandmother would have ensured we had, back in her day.

Polly beamed. "I wouldn't say it's standard, no, certainly not; but for a clan like yours, with so much important history..." She leaned toward us, eyes shining. "I don't suppose I could bother you to answer some questions for me?"

Hannah stepped in. "Jess isn't staying—she has to go on ahead to Kingshurst. But I'm sure we can find some time to chat over a cup of tea, Ms. Kee—"

"Polly, my dear, just plain Polly," she insisted.

Hannah returned her smile. "Polly, then. And please, it's Jess and Hannah."

Whether Hannah was actually looking forward to being grilled by this woman, or whether she was simply trying to get on her good side, I couldn't tell; but Polly lapped it up. "Oh, we'll be thick as thieves in no time, I'm sure of it. But don't you fret, I won't interfere with your research, and I know time is of the essence. Has the other Scribe come with you, the Traveler?" She said the word with an air of fascination, and I was guessing she'd never met a Traveler Durupinen in person.

"No, but she should be along by this evening, I expect," I told her.

"Jolly good!" Polly replied, sounding almost as excited about meeting Flavia as she was to meet us, and I made a mental note to text Flavia and warn her that she was likely about to be bombarded with questions.

"Well, I won't keep you. It sounds like you still have more urgent things to be getting along with. If you'll follow me, I'll get you settled," Polly chirped, before turning on her heel and bouncing back toward the *príosún* doors.

"She seems... caffeinated," Milo said. "You'd better be careful, sweetness, or she'll be penning the first Durupinen bestseller." He drew words in the air in front of him, like a theater marquee: "Misunderstood: The Untold Story of the Ballard Twins."

"Thankfully, I think the code of secrecy will prevent anything quite that mortifying," Hannah said, trying to smile. But her anxiety was ramping up at the moment of parting, and it was with a little squeal of distress that she flung herself on Milo in what would have been a lung-collapsing hug to anyone who still had functioning organs. "If you let anything happen to yourself, I will find a way to bring you back to life just so I can kill you again."

Milo rolled his eyes. "As if I'd take that risk. You'd wear something off the rack without me."

Hannah frowned severely. "The *clearance* rack," she clarified, thereby constructing a far more effective threat.

Milo gulped. Then it was my turn to get hug-throttled.

"I need those ribs," I gasped.

"I love you. Be careful, please."

"I always am," I said, which was definitely the wrong answer. Hannah pulled back from me, eyes narrowed.

"*I'll* make sure she's careful," Finn said, stepping in.

Hannah turned her narrowed eyes on him instead. "You'd better. She does a better job of playing the part, but I'm actually the scary twin, you know."

Finn smiled and clicked his heels together, giving a little bow. "Duly noted."

"Hannah, they'll be all right. Polly is waiting. They can look after themselves," Kiernan said mildly.

Sighing, Hannah took his hand, and I watched as the *priosún* swallowed them both up.

I was too distracted with nerves to appreciate how beautiful the scenery was between the *priosún* and Kingshurst. The road wound through the craggy, wild, untamed countryside, giving glimpses of sea and cliff, flower-strewn meadow, and misty moor. I'd have to marvel at it all another day. Alasdair's evil loomed too large in my mind, tainting this scenic journey just like it had tainted everything else he'd ever touched. Finally, the road crested, and we were descending into a little valley.

"That's Kingshurst there, below us. We're nearly there," Reilly announced.

"Saints be praised," Savvy muttered, repressing a belch. She'd been looking a little green since we'd started driving again.

"Seems like it ought to have a cloud of doom hovering over it, doesn't it?" Maeve murmured, "knowing who's waiting for us there?"

"Or a sign," Rana agreed, nodding. "Like from the Wizard of Oz. 'I'd turn back if I were you.'"

"No turning back now," Finn said. No one answered, mostly because we were trying to wrangle our nerves under control; and Savvy, more likely because she was trying not to vomit.

We pulled up to the elaborate wrought iron gates marking the main entrance to the campus, and Finn had a brief conversation with the guards before procuring a parking pass to hang on the rearview mirror, and a manila envelope full of keys, IDs, and instructions. It was a supremely strange experience, driving into a place I'd never been before, and yet knowing exactly what it looked like. The tension in the car was like a living thing breathing down our necks.

He was here, somewhere. And we weren't going to leave until we found him.

Maeve showed Reilly where to go, and we parked in front of the first in a line of square, brick buildings that I soon figured out were the dormitories. Students milled in and out, all too wrapped up in their own worries and thoughts and conversations to pay us any attention. Finn handed out the IDs which identified each of us as a graduate student. Catriona had considered giving us false names just to keep us under the radar, but in the end, she decided it wasn't worth the trouble. There were certainly people who knew who I was, and pretending to be someone else would probably draw more attention than it would deter. The dormitory they put us up in was separate from the undergraduate housing, and set up more like small apartments than regular dorm rooms.

"They've put you in the apartment across from mine," Maeve told us, checking the room numbers on the sheet. "Come on, I'll show you."

"Hang on," I said. "But you're an undergrad, aren't you?"

Maeve grinned a little wickedly. "Well, yes, but being a MacLeod has its perks, and first choice of housing is one of them." I'm not sure what my face looked like, but Maeve's expression turned a bit defensive. "Hey, just because I mostly hate my mother doesn't mean I won't use the family name for all it's worth."

I put my hands up in surrender. "Hey, no judgment!" I said. After all, being a member of Clan Sassanaigh had had its upsides, even with all the baggage.

We carried our bags up to the top floor, where there was one long hallway with apartment units on either side. Maeve stopped at the first door on the left, put her key in the lock, and pushed it open.

"Ladies, this is you!" she said, gesturing us inside. "Reilly and Finn are meant to be right next door, but I certainly won't snitch if you decide to reconfigure the sleeping arrangements." She winked, and I felt the heat rising up my cheeks as I caught Finn's eye and grinned.

We followed her into a neat and clean little flat. It comprised one large, central room that was a sort of open-concept living room, dining room, and kitchen. On the left side of the kitchen were two doors, both leading to good-sized double bedrooms. On the right side were two more doors, one leading to a third double bedroom, and the last one to a bathroom. At the far end of the main room were several large windows that looked down on the quad below. The furniture had the nondescript, utilitarian look I'd come to expect from institutional furniture; but the place was spacious, meticulously clean, and smelled slightly of bleach and air freshener.

"The dining hall is in the building next door, but you can have groceries delivered from town if you'd prefer," Maeve said. "The IDs will get you into the dining hall and the rest of the buildings on campus that require swipe card entry, which is basically all of New Campus, as well as a few of the more exclusive buildings on Old Campus. And because all Durupinen-related studies and materials are located in Old Campus, only Durupinen and Caomhnóir students are allowed access. It helps maintain secrecy while also allowing the college to expand its offerings and programs to non-clan students."

"It seems a bit risky," Rana said, frowning. "It's hard enough keeping up the pretense to the outside world that Fairhaven is a normal university, and that's without admitting non-clan students. Aren't they afraid the other students will figure out that something's up? Where does the code of secrecy fit into all this?"

Maeve shrugged. "I imagine that's why they keep Old and New Campus so separate from each other. Even the Wards are set to keep spirit activity restricted to Old Campus, and with Caomhnóir disguised as campus security, they're able to keep a close watch on things to make sure secrecy is maintained. And as far as my mother is concerned, this is the way to keep the clans in power—not just in our own world, but in the outside world as well, by making a degree from Kingshurst a coveted achievement in any field."

"And just so we're clear, as a spirit guide, I've got free rein of both sections of the campus?" Milo asked, raising his hand like we were sitting in class.

"Absolutely," Maeve said.

"But the Wards should prevent Alasdair from moving around New Campus, right?" Finn asked.

"Aye, unless someone screws around with them," Maeve confirmed, nodding. "But the Caomhnóir check them regularly, so it's a fair bet he'll be somewhere on Old Campus with the rest of the ghosts, if he's here."

Finn gave a grim nod. This information confirmed what he and Milo had already discovered on their first visit. We'd assumed Alasdair would gravitate toward Old Campus because it was familiar to him—old stomping grounds and all that—but now it was clear that the Wards themselves would prevent him from stalking New Campus as well. There was something oddly comforting about that—at least we'd be safe in our beds, and the non-Durupinen students would be safe as well, as long as they didn't wander where they shouldn't.

"Maeve? I thought I heard your voice! What are you doing back?"

We all turned to see a girl standing in the doorway to the apartment, which we had forgotten to shut behind us. She was tall and curvy, with sleek dark hair parted in two shiny curtains on either side of a pale, heart-shaped face.

"Grace!" Maeve cried, trotting to the door, and throwing her arm around the girl in a quick hug. "I'm sorry, I should have texted. They moved my mother out of the ICU, and she didn't want me to miss any more classes."

"So, she's going to be okay, then? Your mom?" Grace asked, even as her eyes darted curiously over to the rest of us.

"Aye, she'll be just fine," Maeve said, bravely attempting a smile. "Back to terrorizing me in no time, I'd imagine."

Grace darted another glance at us, and then raised her eyebrows at Maeve. Maeve took the hint.

"Oh, right, sorry. This is Grace Cameron, my roommate. Grace, this is Finn Carey, Savannah Todd, Rana Patel, and Jess Ballard. They're all here doing some uh... research work for my mother."

This was the cover we'd all agreed was in the best interest of the mission. Using Clarissa's clout would give us a lot of access on campus. If we said we were here from the Trackers office, there would be a lot more questions.

Grace hadn't gotten this memo, however. At the sound of my name, her eyebrows had flown right up into her bangs, and she zeroed in on me with unsettling intensity. "Jess Ballard? *The* Jess Ballard?"

"Guilty," I said, attempting a smile, but it slid off my face as soon as I managed to hoist it there. Grace's eyes narrowed at me, and she crossed her arms defensively over her chest.

"A Ballard working for Clarissa MacLeod? How the hell did that happen?" she asked bluntly. Beside her, Maeve's cheeks flamed pink.

"I...am not really sure," I replied. "Just lucky, I guess."

"She hates you, you know," Grace said with the same measured bluntness. "Positively loathes you." She cocked her head to one side, as though interested to see how the words would affect me. Luckily, I had enough experience with privileged clan princesses looking down their noses at me, that I was able to smile blandly back at her.

"I did sort of catch that vibe, yeah," I replied. "What can I say, I just endear myself to people, generally."

Grace continued to look at me appraisingly with her wide, dark eyes, until Maeve cleared her throat and broke the awkward pause.

"Grace, I'll meet you over at the apartment in a minute, okay?" she said, in a falsely cheery tone.

Grace glared at Maeve, turned on her heel, hair swinging, and stalked back down the hallway. Maeve watched her go, and then turned back to us sheepishly.

"Sorry about that. Grace's clan is a lot like ours—none too pleased when the Reckoning came to pass. You're not likely to find many fans here at Kingshurst."

I shrugged. "Well, luckily for me, I'm not here to join a sorority. You can go, Maeve. It's fine. We can figure things out."

Maeve bit her lip. "Text me if you need anything, okay?"

"We will, thanks," I said easily, and she left with a parting smile. The truth was that I had no intention of texting her at all if I could help it. It was bad enough that she was back on campus with Alasdair here. I didn't want her any more involved with our investigation than was absolutely necessary. I didn't need any more guilt about a MacLeod getting hurt on my watch.

"Ew," Milo said, wrinkling his nose. "What was her problem, anyway?"

"Grace? Probably another Council brat bitter about her perceived loss of status," I said, rolling my eyes.

Milo's expression lit up. "What was her last name? Cameron? That explains it. There's a Dominique Cameron on the Council now. She's all buddy-buddy with Geraldine Porter, and I've heard she and Marion summer together in the Cotswolds."

I tried not to dive too deeply into Council politics these days, but the name Dominique Cameron sounded vaguely familiar from Milo's breathless recounting of Council meeting drama. And Geraldine Porter was Aisling's mom, the ringleader of last winter's witchcraft scheme to restore the Gateways to the Durupinen bloodlines. Well, if those were the families Grace was palling around with, it was no wonder the girl looked at me like I was some kind of insect she longed to squash beneath her shoe.

By this time, the sun was starting to sink below the horizon. It had been a long day of travel, and by the time we had all unpacked and reconvened in the living room of the flat, the exhaustion was clearly etched into our faces. Even Milo was manifesting paler than usual.

"Now what?" I asked.

"As much as I hate to lose any more time, we need to wait for daylight before we venture onto Old Campus," Finn said grudgingly. "We know Alasdair can't reach us here on New Campus, and I don't think a few hours will make much difference. In the morning, we're meeting with our contacts here to begin the investigation in earnest."

"Who are these contacts?" Savvy asked, looking wary. "Because reception's already less than warm, innit?"

"There are three campus historians in residence," Finn said, picking up the envelope from where he'd discarded it on the coffee table, and pulling out the file inside. "Damien Brightwell, he's the head of the department, and an expert on all things Kingshurst. His assistants are Gareth Cadwalader and Aoife O'Malley. Catriona has arranged with them that we will be conducting our investigation out of the MacLeod Archive Building, which is where their offices are. They will be giving us access to anything that might help us predict Alasdair's movements on campus."

"If he's even here," Rana said.

"Oh, he's here," Milo said quietly. "There was no mistaking it."

"But if he realizes we're here, won't he just take off again?" Rana asked, biting her lip.

"I don't think so, somehow," Milo said. We all turned to look at him. "When you're a spirit, you're drawn to the places you knew in life. It's like you've got an internal map, and an undeniable impulse to retread your own footsteps. It's a little different for me, obviously. I'm Bound to Hannah, and so her pull is stronger for me than any particular place or memory. But I can still feel it, too— that tug toward the places I knew. The longer you're dead, your hold on who you used to be kind of... slips away bit by bit, and for some ghosts, it's only by walking in their own paths that they can hold on to it at all."

No one answered. We'd all learned about this phenomenon in Apprentice and Novitiate training, but that had been academic. It was very different hearing someone you loved talk about experiencing it for themself.

"Danica told you that Alasdair was very disoriented when he first emerged from the *príosún*," Milo went on. "It was only when she got him talking about his past, his experiments, and his goals, that he seemed to regain a sense of himself. And when they went back to MacLeod Close, that was when he really woke up again—became more than just a shadow of his former self. The sense of place reconnected him to himself. If she'd never gone down and spoken to him, never tried to help him... I imagine he would have simply wandered Edinburgh, lost and confused. After all, the city has changed so much since his time, it probably felt like he'd never even been there before. But the Close was like a time capsule—left untouched for centuries. It would have been like coming home again, déjà vu solidifying at last into actual memory. When he found the Close, he found himself."

We all took a moment to absorb this before Milo went on.

"Then we discovered what they were doing, and he had to flee. But his sense of self, his sense of purpose, was so tied to that place, I'm not sure if he could have held onto it if he simply wandered. And so, he obeyed the pull of another place, one almost as important to him as Edinburgh was. He came back to Kingshurst. And since Old Campus has been well preserved, he's going to feel safe there. I think he's more likely to go to ground than flee, even if he finds out we've followed him here. He will still feel safer here than anywhere else."

"Well, that's all the better for us," Finn said. "Because I don't want to chase this bastard all over the damn planet. I want to end this here."

He looked at all of us in turn, and one by one we each nodded; and each nod was like a solemn vow.

We would end this nightmare at Kingshurst, no matter what it cost.

9

REUNION

Exhaustion alone should have meant a deep and untroubled night's sleep, but Seer visions don't care how tired you are, and so my slumber was a restless one, peppered with disturbing and confusing images I could barely string together into anything coherent; although there was one image that popped up over and over again, and that was of a black-cloaked figure. Sometimes it would simply be standing there, watching. Other times I would be chasing it through the campus or back down that passageway. I never managed to get close enough to see their face. They never spoke or tried to interact with me in any way. It was just... there. Haunting my dreams.

I dragged myself out of bed after the tenth time I started awake, deciding to give up on sleep altogether, and arm myself for the day with caffeine instead. Who needed sleep when you could just buzz off chemicals all day, right? I shuffled out to the little kitchenette of our flat, and though there was a single-cup coffee maker sitting on the counter, there was no coffee to be found. I sighed and returned to the bedroom, trading my sweatpants for a pair of jeans, and throwing a sweatshirt on over my ratty oversized sleep t-shirt.

"I'm going to the dining hall for coffee," I whispered to Finn, who blinked bemusedly at me for a few seconds before he was awake enough to answer. "You want me to bring you one?"

"Huh? What?" He was looking around him like he'd completely forgotten where we were.

"The dining hall. Coffee. You can just nod or shake your head if your brain isn't ready for words yet," I said, laughing. Usually, I was the one who had a hard time waking up, but between the travel and the stress, Finn was off his morning game as well.

He mumbled something in which the words "coffee" and "please" were audible, so I took it for a yes and headed out the door.

The morning was brisk and a little foggy. I didn't pass a soul, living or dead, on the very quick walk to the dining hall—which made sense, once I remembered it was Saturday and there wouldn't be any classes that morning. I wondered, stifling a yawn as I walked through the door to the cafeteria, if my body would ever adjust to an adultier schedule, or if I'd just fight the urge to sleep till noon forever, like a perpetual teenager.

There was a smattering of people in the dining hall eating breakfast. Most of them looked like faculty members, aside from a small knot of girls who were wearing matching uniforms, which meant they'd probably come from an early morning practice for some team or other. I made my way to the coffee counter and found they were well-stocked with to-go cups, trays, and packets of sweeteners and creamers, so I decided to grab coffee for Rana and Savvy as well. Knowing the apartment had not a crumb of food in it yet, I also raided a nearby basket of pastries, stacking up scones and muffins and a rogue bagel into a little tower between the cardboard coffee cups. Then I lifted my tray, balanced it carefully in my hands, and headed back out the way I had come. A girl breezed through the lefthand door just as I was coming out of the righthand one, and my tray wobbled. One of the cups tilted and I swore under my breath, trying to right it. I set it down on a low stone wall just as the door swung shut behind me, muffling the voice that called after me so that I almost didn't hear it.

"Jess? Oh my *goodness!* Jessica Ballard!"

Like an idiot, I turned at the sound of my name, despite the fact that I was supposed to be keeping a low profile at Kingshurst. All I could do was let out a yelp as a windswept cloud of jet-black hair flew through the door at me, and temporarily obscured my vision. The owner of said hair slammed directly into me, enveloping me in a hug so violent that, at first, I mistook it for an actual assault.

"What are you—" I began, wondering if Grace Cameron had indeed decided to murder me; but my attacker was now squealing with delight, rather than shouting at me.

"What in the world are you doing here of all places? Are you here to surprise me? Oh, I can't believe it's you, it's been ages!" shrieked the voice in my ear.

My heart, pounding a moment before, skipped a beat. I knew that voice. I knew this hug. I even knew the familiar smell of the hair still clinging to my face. I extracted myself from her grasp and held her out at arm's length so that I could see her glowing face.

"Tia!"

It was impossible. Tia Vezga, my college roommate and best friend, was beaming at me, her cheeks flushed with pleasure, her face split in a brilliant smile.

"What the... why are you... *how?!*" was the closest I could come to constructing a complete sentence.

Her smile drooped just a little. "You didn't know I was here?" Then she narrowed her eyes. "Do you even read the emails I send you?"

"I..." Okay, so keeping up to date on email was not exactly my strong suit, even when I wasn't on a cross-country hunt for a murderous ghost. "I'm sorry, it's been a little crazy the past couple of weeks," I said. "But seriously, what are you doing here?"

"Well, *as I told you in my last email,*" she said, whacking me lightly on the arm, "I accepted a short research fellowship here. Kingshurst has one of the most cutting-edge medical research programs on the continent! The work they're doing with stem cells is just..." She stopped abruptly and narrowed her eyes at me again, suddenly tense with suspicion. "But what are you doing here, if it's not to see me?"

I dropped my voice. "Durupinen stuff. I'm trying to fly under the radar, actually."

Tia dropped her voice to match my hushed tones. "What kind of Durupinen stuff?"

I glanced around as the knot of teammates emerged from the dining hall behind us, chatting and laughing together. "Why don't we find a quieter spot to chat? It's only going to get busier here as people come down to breakfast," I said. "Speaking of which, do you want to grab something? Weren't you on your way in to eat?"

Tia rolled her eyes. "Yes, before I was understandably distracted by the sudden appearance of my long-lost bestie! I'll eat later, for goodness sake. Come on, there's a nice little courtyard over here, behind this wall. It's usually pretty quiet. Follow me."

I picked up my tray, and she led me down a walkway around the side of the dining hall. Together, we sat down on a wooden bench nestled under a statue of a man working at a desk with a quill. I wondered briefly who he was, and if he was connected to the Durupinen in any way, before Tia took my hands and pulled my attention back to her.

"I know you. You only get involved in Durupinen stuff when you have no other choice, which means whatever brought you here must be serious."

I bit my lip. Most of the time, it was wonderful to have a best friend who knew me so well, and had such empathy and intuition. But at moments like this, it was very inconvenient because the same emotional intelligence that made Tia such a great friend also made her a flawless bullshit detector. I wasn't going to be able to pass this coincidence off as a pleasurable little jaunt, that was for sure.

"Okay, yes. You're right," I said with a reluctant sigh. "I'm here on a Tracker mission."

Tia frowned. "I thought you quit the Trackers?"

"I was re-recruited," I said. "Catriona, for all her lack of social skills, can be very persuasive."

"I suppose this is what you meant when you texted me, 'We have a lot to catch up on.' You know, from most people, that's an innocuous comment. I should have known."

"Yeah, sorry, my news dumps are more dramatic than most," I said with a wry smile.

"Well, I know you didn't do it for the money, so that means..." Tia's eyes went wide. "Oh, no. What is it? Is it... are there... *Necromancers*?" She was panicking and I knew why. It was only a couple of years ago that she had been targeted by a Necromancer who managed to disguise himself as the perfect boyfriend. It had been Tia's first tentative step into the dating world since our college friend Sam had broken her heart, and she'd barely escaped with her life. The worst part was that she'd been the target because of her proximity to me. She'd never admitted that I carried any of the blame for that, but naturally, I'd never forgive myself for it. Since then, as far as she'd chosen to share with me, she hadn't ventured back into the cesspool that was dating in the modern world, choosing instead to focus on her increasingly impressive medical research resume.

"Tia, calm down," I said, as soothingly as I could manage. "I'm here on the tail of a rogue ghost, not a Necromancer." *A ghost so evil that even the*

Necromancers he befriended thought his ideas went too far, I added in my head; but there was absolutely no reason to alarm her unnecessarily, at least not yet.

"Well, that's a relief," Tia said, expelling a shaky breath.

"Tia, does your work here ever take you onto Old Campus?" I asked. I knew what the answer should be, but I needed to make absolutely sure.

Tia shook her head. "No. I've never even been through that second set of gates. It's all a bit... morbid through there," she said with a delicate little shudder. "I think the only students who take classes in there are some of the history and architecture students, and I suppose some of the art students as well. You can't even get into the older buildings without the proper permissions and a special I.D."

I reached into my sweatshirt and tugged out my lanyard. "You mean one of these I.D.s?" I asked.

'That's the one. But why...?"

"Okay, so the truth is that this campus has Durupinen ties. It's practically owned by a powerful Scottish clan. You may have noticed the name MacLeod on several of the buildings."

Tia's mouth fell open. "*Those* MacLeods are Durupinen?! You're joking!"

I shrugged. "What can I say? We're everywhere."

"I can't believe it! I'm here on a MacLeod Fellowship! Are you telling me Durupinen money is funding my research?!"

"Sounds like it," I said.

Tia just shook her head, laughing incredulously. Then suddenly, she choked off the laugh and looked up at me, eyes narrowed again. "You didn't have anything to do with this, did you? Me getting the fellowship? I did earn it myself, didn't I?"

I raised both hands in immediate surrender. "Tia, I'm as shocked to find you here as you are to find me. You got here on your own merit, not because of your Durupinen connections. Cross my heart."

Tia held my gaze with a hard, searching look before she seemed to accept I was telling the truth. Then her face crumpled back into lines of worry. "So what's happening with this rogue ghost, Jess? Whatever it is, it must be pretty bad."

I sighed. "Yeah. It's pretty bad," I said, and launched into a reluctant account of Alasdair and my time in Edinburgh. It wasn't an overly detailed account by any means, and I completely left out all mention of the Collection— there was no need to traumatize the girl; and let's face it, Alasdair's history was disturbing enough without highlighting his most recent crimes. When I had finished, Tia's usually glowing, warm complexion had turned sallow.

"And you're sure he's here?" Tia asked, when she had found her voice.

"All we know for sure is that he *was* here," I hedged. "He's left traces—he's got a distinctively unpleasant energy. But wherever he is, he'll be laying low and trying to avoid detection. We believe he's hiding out somewhere on Old Campus. The rest of the campus is heavily Warded, so we're concentrating our search specifically through that second set of gates."

"Hmm, you said he's been dead for centuries, right? Then I suppose it makes sense that he'd return to Old Campus. I'm sure it's the only part of Kingshurst he recognizes from his time here," Tia said.

"Tia, I'm only telling you this to put you on your guard, not to drag you into anything. The last thing I want to do is ruin your time here," I said, as the familiar guilt started seeping in.

"Nonsense," Tia snapped. "You're not ruining anything. It's this Alasdair who's complicated things, not you. None of this is your fault."

I pressed my lips together over the long list of reasons why this was absolutely my fault. She wouldn't let me say them anyway.

"So. How can I help?" Tia asked.

A single bark of laughter burst from my lips. "Help? You can help by keeping yourself safe!"

"But—"

"That means staying as far from Old Campus as you can, and never walking alone at night. Also, I'm assigning you a Caomhnóir."

Tia crossed her arms, looking mutinous. "I don't need security, Jess."

"Yes, you do, and if you'd had even a single encounter with the nightmare that is Alasdair, you'd be begging for it," I said. "If you have a Caomhnóir nearby, there will always be someone who can sense him, which means you'll never be in danger. In fact..." I felt the lightbulb go off in my own head. "In fact, I think I've got the perfect person for the job!"

Tia frowned. "Jess, I've met enough Caomhnóir to know I don't want one following me around like an overgrown guard dog, no offense to Finn or Savvy."

"Oh, I don't think you'll mind this security assignment at all," I said, a grin spreading slowly over my face. "And he's decidedly not a Caomhnóir."

"Jess, you're a genius!" Hannah said, her voice ringing happily through the Connection.

"Every now and then."

I'd only been back in the flat long enough to set the coffees down and flop onto the couch when I'd opened the Connection, found Hannah waiting, and filled her in about the unexpected Tia complication. She was gobsmacked, of course, but she brightened at once when I told her my plan for dealing with it. Her euphoria was short-lived, however, as her doubts began to skitter across the Connection like nagging little insects.

"But do you think he'll go for it," she worried, "or will he think this is just a way to keep him out of danger? He can be awfully petty when he thinks someone is underestimating him."

"There's only one way to find out. Hey, spirit guide, you there? We need your infallible wisdom." I reached out into the Connection, feeling for Milo's presence.

At once, he popped into our heads, answering the summons. "Ooh, I like that. Infallible wisdom. I demand to be summoned exactly like that from now on."

"Where are you right now?" I asked. "You'd better not be anywhere near Old Campus without backup."

I could basically hear his eyes rolling. "Of course I'm not. I haven't even ventured within ten yards of the gates. I've been investigating the Ward situation. They definitely aren't perfect. I found a couple of areas that aren't totally fortified, probably students messing with them, or sloppy Casting work. I'll make sure to let Finn know exactly where the problems are, so he can get them all shored up. Also, I've been testing the limits of where I can go. Maeve was right. As a spirit guide, I seem to have free reign, including in and out of all the buildings."

"That was a great idea," I said. "The better we understand the lay of the land around here, the better."

"Obvi. Hang on, I'm right outside the dorm." And with that, Milo floated right through the wall, and came to rest several feet above the couch. "Now, back it up a little because I thought I heard someone say the word petty, and that's the battle cry of my people. What are we getting petty about?"

"Before we get to that, I have news for you. You might want to sit down for this."

Milo glanced down at the sofa, and then back up at me again, smirking. "Very funny. Now, what is it?"

"Tia's here."

The news sent a shimmering shudder right through him. "Tia?! Here?! Oh my Gucci, WHY?!"

I explained about the fellowship and the medical research program, but Milo seemed only to be half-listening.

"Well, you need to tell her to leave!" he cried. "Tell her to pack her bags and find a new research program!"

"I can't do that, Milo. It's too good of an opportunity. You know Tia, she'd never just pack up and leave."

"I know that, so that's why you've got to make her!" Milo said, crossing his arms. "It's bad enough we got her mixed up with that psycho Charlie. We can't throw Alasdair into her path, too!"

"My thoughts exactly," I said, "which is why I want you to protect her."

Milo blinked. "Huh?"

"She needs someone with her, someone who can sense if Alasdair is nearby. But we can't stick her with a Caomhnóir, it'll be obvious that she has security; and even they couldn't protect her all the time. You can go places they can't. You can keep an eye on her without drawing attention to yourself."

"And of course, you can always stay in touch with us through the Connection, so you'll always know what's happening in real time," Hannah added hastily.

Milo narrowed his eyes. "Why does this feel like the Tracker equivalent of telling me to go wait in the car?"

"No, dragging you back to Skye Príosún with me and Kiernan would be the equivalent of telling you to wait in the car," Hannah said. "This way, you're right on site if anything happens, and you're keeping someone we all love safe."

Milo was tapping his foot and chewing the inside of his lip, looking thoughtful.

"Well?" Hannah asked.

"Hang on, I'm trying to think of a reason why this is a bad idea," Milo grumbled.

"Well, good luck with that because it's a brilliant idea," I said loftily. "Won't you feel better knowing Tia's okay? Because you sense Alasdair better than anyone, which means he won't be getting anywhere near her. And don't forget, we've got the Connection. If we make sure it stays open, you'll always only be a second away from the action."

Hannah's displeasure at this zinged through the Connection, which made Milo look just a little more placated.

"Think about it, Milo. Why do we want to catch Alasdair in the first place?"

Milo considered for a moment, and then nodded. "To stop him from hurting anyone else."

I didn't reply. I simply let his words sink in. He sighed and raised his hands in defeat.

"Okay, you're right. I'll feel better if Tia's safe. But no big showdown with Alasdair without me, you got it? When we take him down—and I do mean *when*, none of this 'if' bullshit—I'm a part of it."

"Deal," I said, and though I felt Hannah's frustration surge through the Connection, she didn't argue. What was the point? She wanted to take Alasdair down as badly as the rest of us.

"Good," I said with a sigh. That's all settled. Now all we have to do is tell the others."

"You're *joking!*"

Finn was staring at me, tousle-haired and open-mouthed over his cardboard cup of coffee.

"Can you think of anything less funny?" I asked with a snort.

"Not much, no," Finn said, taking a sip.

"What are the bloody odds of that?" Savvy chimed in as she doctored her coffee heavily with cream and sugar.

"With my luck?" I muttered.

"Well, I think you've handled that little complication beautifully," Finn said, giving me a satisfied nod of approval.

"Why, because it keeps me out of the way?" Milo grumbled.

"No, because I know you will be a flawless protector, and with the rest of us concentrating our efforts on Old Campus, having someone to keep an eye on New Campus will be invaluable. It covers all possible bases at once. You already proved the Wards could be an area of weakness," Finn said, in such a practical tone that it was impossible to argue with him; and the last of Milo's lingering frostiness toward the plan vanished.

Finn looked at his watch. "Blast it all. We should really head over to Old Campus now. We have our first meeting with the campus historian in a quarter of an hour, and it will take nearly that long just to walk over there."

We said goodbye to Milo, who floated off to meet up with Tia. She wouldn't be able to see him for the time being, but I had promised when we parted ways that morning that I would meet up with her later so that I could perform a Melding on her. We'd done it before, so that she could communicate with Milo back when she first moved to London. It would be important for the two of them to be able to communicate if he was going to be keeping her safe.

While the others downed the rest of their coffee and Savvy crammed a scone into her mouth whole, I retreated to the bedroom, pulled my backpack out from under the bed, and checked the contents carefully: my sketchbook, containing the drawings I'd done of my Seer visions, and Alasdair's knife, still wrapped carefully in the black silk wrappings we'd found it in at the top of Danica's closet. I zipped it back up and slung it over my shoulder, praying that, at last, we were on our way to getting some concrete answers.

10

DISCOVERIES

Being back on a college campus was... weird.

"Were we really that young in college? Because I definitely remember feeling older than these kids look," I muttered, watching another group of kids pass us.

Savvy gave them an appraising glance and nodded. "Fetuses, the lot of them."

I turned to Finn. "Do you—" But I swallowed the rest of the question. Finn had stopped walking and was staring down the path ahead of us.

The gates of Old Campus stood before us like iron arms wrapped protectively around a forgotten wrinkle in time. I shivered.

Finn turned on me. "Do you feel something?"

But I shook my head. "No. I think I'm just... anticipating it."

"Right. Well, no time like the present," Finn said, taking a deep breath to steel himself. "Everyone be on high alert, now. We can't afford to let our guard down, not for a moment."

With those reassuring words, we approached the gates. There was a tiny guard house there, half buried in a hedge, and the Caomhnóir leaning out of it frowned at our credentials one by one, head bobbing up and down repeatedly as he confirmed our faces matched the ones on the IDs.

"Get on with it, mate," Savvy muttered under her breath, but I was actually kind of relieved to see that security was so thorough. That meant no innocent kids wandering onto Old Campus who shouldn't be there.

When we were finally cleared for access, the guard opened the gates for us, and we stepped through. The air within the gates was measurably cooler than the air outside them, and the goosebumps had not even finished rising on my skin before I figured out why.

Spirits, just like Milo said. All of Kingshurst's spirit energy was contained here.

It was like being back at Fairhaven. Kingshurst had an entire invisible population within these walls—milling around, passing through buildings and shrubs, and strolling down walkways. Most of them had been there for centuries, judging by their outdated attire. There was also a certain quality to their movement, almost like watching people move through water. There was no hurry, no drive or purpose to their steps as they glided along. They were simply re-treading their own steps, lost in memory. It was at once peaceful and a bit melancholy to watch. Still, at least none of them were running and screaming in fear. Alasdair, wherever he was, had not yet disturbed their tranquil monotony. I couldn't decide if I was relieved or frustrated that I could detect no immediate sign of him.

We crossed to the north corner of Old Campus, walking toward the Kingshurst Historical Center. As it came into view, Finn slowed his steps, his expression suddenly alert and tense.

"What is it, Finn?" I whispered as I came up alongside him. "Did you see something? Sense something?"

He shook his head slowly. "No, nothing like that. I'm sorry to alarm you, it's just... that's where we caught just the slightest hint of Alasdair's energy when Milo and I first came here."

He raised a hand and pointed to the building now looming up in front of us at the end of the path. It was actually buildings, plural; four structures that had been connected to each other by covered walkways, like the cloisters at Fairhaven, with columns on one side and open Gothic archways on the other. The buildings were laid out in a rectangle, with the cloisters running between them, connecting them, and enclosing at their center a grassy courtyard, which I could just catch a glimpse of through the nearest cloister. The Kingshurst Historical Center was the smallest of these buildings, and set the furthest from where we stood, at the far side of the courtyard.

We'd all frozen at Finn's words, each of us listening hard, eyes scanning the scene before us, every sense on high alert. I found it difficult to tune out the energy of all the other spirits around us as I searched for some hint of the one energy that mattered. But if Alasdair was here now, he was well hidden. I could sense no trace of him.

"I'm not getting 'im now, mate," Savvy said at last, voicing the conclusion we'd all come to.

"Neither am I. Let's be on alert nevertheless," Finn said, and we started forward again. We followed the walkway up to the front steps of the nearest building, letting Finn lead. We moved deliberately past the steps to the entrance of the cloister and entered it. Ivy crept up the sides, wrapping its greedy emerald tendrils around the colonnades, and digging intrusive fingers into the cracks in the stonework. We passed a couple of students walking in the other direction. They gave us curious looks, one tugging the other closer to whisper in her ear. I felt them looking back over their shoulders at us, but I didn't bother to turn and return the stare. I was too busy trying to pick up on what Finn and Milo had sensed when they were last here; but traces of Alasdair's passage through this place had already faded away. I turned to take in the courtyard, and gasped.

A Geatgrima. There was a Geatgrima in the courtyard.

How the hell hadn't I sensed it? Now that I was looking at it, the Gateway's energy was almost overpowering, seeping its way under my skin and singing in my blood, reminding me of when I used to be one of its homes. It was hard to describe the feeling I got now whenever I was near a newly restored Geatgrima. It wasn't a sad feeling, though it might have been something akin to it—a longing maybe, or even something like homesickness. But also, there was a contented shine to that feeling, a sense that all was as it should be. I wished that the discontented among the Durupinen felt that way—maybe they would if they could set their anger, resentment, and pride aside for long enough to let the feeling manifest. Then maybe this pointless struggle against the natural order of things could stop, and we could all get back to the heart of our calling.

Helping lost souls. Guiding them. Taking them home.

We reached the end of the cloister, and Finn used his ID to swipe into the Historical Center. The card reader looked so out of place on the ancient stone façade—an anachronistic blemish on the otherwise beautiful complexion of the place. He held the door open for us, and we filed in, finding ourselves in a room that looked like a converted church. The ceiling arched high above our heads, held aloft by great stone pillars. Stained glass windows were set high into the walls, throwing jewel-bright patches of light onto the rows of long wooden work tables that would have looked more at home laid with a medieval banquet than the modern desk lamps that had been set at intervals along them. The walls below the stained glass windows were lined with towering bookshelves, complete with rolling ladders and two wrought iron spiral staircases leading to the upper level, where more bookshelves could be seen in the shadowy recesses of the gallery above.

I took all of this in for about five seconds before a tiny figure came hurrying toward us.

"Hello. You're the group from Fairhaven, are you not?" The young woman had an almost birdlike appearance, delicate and yet sharp in her movements, with a heavy dark braid of hair curled over her shoulder, and a narrow face overwhelmed by a pair of tortoiseshell glasses and the wide brown eyes magnified behind them. She shook a slender, long-fingered hand free from the sleeve of her baggy blue sweater, and each of us shook it in turn. I was slightly taken aback by how cold it was, but then again, the room had a definite chill.

"I'm Aoife O'Malley, one of the apprentice historians here at the center," she said, withdrawing her hand from mine and tucking it back into her sleeve. Her eyes lingered on me a little longer than the others, bright with curiosity. "Mr. Brightwell asked me to come meet you and take you along to his office, where we can speak more privately."

She was still looking at me when she said it, so I cleared my throat to reply. "Thank you. We'd appreciate that."

She nodded once and waved us along, shoes clicking on the highly polished floors. Perhaps half a dozen students were scattered throughout the room, heads bent over their work. Only one bothered to look up as we went by, and he returned his attention to his book again almost at once.

Aoife led us down the central aisle of the room, then turned sharply to the right and took us along the last row of bookshelves to a glossy paneled door. She gave three sharp knocks and then waited.

"Come in," came the voice from the room beyond.

Aoife twisted the handle and pushed the door wide, ushering us inside. The room was much bigger than I had been anticipating when she said she was going to bring us to someone's office. The room was narrow but long, running almost the full length of the building, with a row of tall arched windows along the back wall, and large wooden desks placed at intervals beneath them. The wall opposite the windows was, predictably, obscured entirely by built-in bookshelves, as well as drawers and shelves crammed with all manner of artifacts, from statues to artwork to ceremonial items.

"Flavia and Kiernan would have a full-blown nerd meltdown in here," I muttered to myself as Savvy stifled a sneeze.

I glanced at her. "Too dusty for you?"

"Probably just my allergy to schoolwork rearing its ugly head," Sav replied with a wink. Rana smothered a smile.

A man was hurrying toward us now, looking every inch the quintessential librarian, from the meticulously groomed combover to the round silver glasses perched on the end of his long nose, to the paisley bowtie peeking out above his sweater vest.

"Damien Brightwell, head historian at Kingshurst. Delighted, delighted," he said, nodding at each of us. "Or, perhaps delighted is not quite the correct sentiment, given the nature of your visit."

Finn returned Damien's nervous smile. "We appreciate it all the same. And we apologize for crashing your workspace. Hopefully, our stay will be a short one."

Damien's lips tightened, and he nodded in a way that seemed to say he hoped so, too, though it would be rude to say so out loud. He ushered us over to a desk near the back of the room, where a second, younger man was half-buried in manuscripts.

"This is Gareth Cadwalader, my second in command, as it were. Gareth," he repeated the name more loudly, and Gareth started, looking up from his work in some bewilderment.

"What? Oh, I say, terribly sorry, I was rather caught up," Gareth said, blinking up at us like a mole poking its head out of its burrow and being assaulted by the sunlight. He rubbed at his watery blue eyes and stood up, looking more than a little miffed that we had interrupted him in his journey down whatever historical rabbit hole he'd been plumbing.

"These are our guests from Fairhaven," Damien said, raising his eyebrows like a parent reminding an unruly kid about the talk they'd just had.

Gareth attempted to play along by smiling at us, but it was forced at best. "Yes, of course. I'm glad to meet you all."

We went down the line, making the introductions again, though each successive name seemed to fluster Gareth more and more, first meeting two female Caomhnóir, then meeting me, the walking-talking destruction of the Durupinen status quo. By the time he had shaken all of our hands, he looked quite flustered. His eyes kept darting to his pile of research, no doubt eager to return to it.

"Please, everyone have a seat," Damien said, gesturing toward a wooden work table flanked on two sides by long benches. "Aoife, see what you can scrounge up for tea, will you?"

Aoife, who had been about to sit as well, blinked at Damien and then, coloring slightly, mumbled her assent and hurried off. Gareth returned to his place at his desk, looking relieved to no longer have to engage directly with us, and bent his head of frizzy strawberry blonde hair back over his work.

"Now," Damien said when we were all sitting. "I spoke with Clarissa MacLeod regarding your visit, and I reviewed the file sent over from the Trackers." He tapped a finger against the file folder he had placed on the table in front of him. "I understand that you are on the trail of a rogue ghost, is that correct?"

"That's right," I said, answering before Finn could. "Alasdair MacLeod."

Damien nodded. "You'll forgive me, but there seems to be very little documentation of him, which is rather unusual for the MacLeod family. Their records are, generally speaking, widely and meticulously kept."

"Yeah, well, it makes a little more sense if you consider that Clarissa is more interested in keeping up appearances than she is in keeping meticulous records," I said with a wry smile.

Damien seemed to be trying to decide how offended he should look. After all, Clarissa was basically his boss, and people who answered to Clarissa were usually sycophants—or at least had to give the appearance of it. Finn threw me a quick wide-eyed look that said, "Tread carefully!" and it was only through impeccable self-control that I didn't stick my tongue out at him.

Finn took the lead now, adopting a diplomatic tone. "What Jess means is Alasdair's crimes were so horrific that Clan Rìoghalachd did their best to keep them from being too widely known. It was clan pride more than anything else. They didn't see the harm in keeping it quiet since he had been caught and dealt with."

"Quite so," Damien said, his face relaxing again.

"But, due to circumstances they could not have foreseen," Finn went on, "Alasdair is at large once more, and the MacLeods' eagerness to erase him from history has left us with very little to go on. One of the few scraps of information we have is that he was once a student at Kingshurst. We're hoping you can help us learn more about his time here, given your almost encyclopedic knowledge of this place, along with your vast collection of resources. The more we can understand about his time here, the better chance we will have of tracking him down before he can hurt anyone else."

It was masterfully executed, I had to admit. Just the right combination of ego stroking and urgency, none of it overdone. I really shouldn't have been surprised. Finn had spent his life navigating the minefield of living in the same clan as Marion and Peyton. It would have been a matter of absolute survival to understand those complex dynamics and hierarchies. I knew I ought to be better at it all by now too, but the main obstacle in my way seemed to be, as always, a complete inability to give a shit.

Damien was preening now, and I refocused my attention on him. "Well, Clarissa has certainly sent you to the right place. When you say that you want to learn about his time here, what exactly did you have in mind?"

Finn looked to me. "It's hard to tell what would be useful," I said. "Any personal student records you might have on him, of course, but I'm not sure if they kept records back then the way they do now. But if there's any mention of him in articles or journals from the years he attended, that would be a start. We're trying to uncover what might have been important to him—how and where he spent his time."

Damien tapped his steepled fingertips together as I spoke, and I could already see the cogs and wheels turning behind his eyes. "I see. So, a broad overview of Kingshurst at the time, with some insight into how Alasdair MacLeod fit into it all."

I looked at Finn, who nodded encouragingly. "Yes, that sounds like a good place to start."

"Very well," Damien said, rising to his feet. "What years are we talking about? Do we have that much information, at least?"

"We know he was back in Edinburgh by 1756, so we're looking at the handful of years prior to that," I said.

From the corner of my eye, I saw Gareth look up again from his work for the first time since we'd begun talking. He caught my eye and quickly dropped his head again, but something about his abnormally stiff posture told me he was still listening. Aoife returned at that moment, balancing a tea tray in both hands. With a carefully blank expression, she poured out tea and offered around a plate of biscuits. Savvy grabbed half a dozen in a single handful; but then, seeing the expression on Rana's face, she returned all but one sheepishly to the plate, and nibbled at it sullenly. Damien accepted his cup of tea without even acknowledging Aoife, let alone thanking her.

"We can start with student records just to confirm his enrollment," Damien said, taking a hasty sip of tea, and then donning a pair of gloves. He hurried over to a shelf filled with dozens of identical tall beige volumes, and ran his finger along the bottoms, looking for the correct date. Then he pulled one from the shelf and opened it on the table before us. He began muttering to himself as he flipped carefully through the delicate pages.

"Let me see here... hmmm, there doesn't seem to... let's try... ah, yes, here we are!" He jabbed a triumphant pointer finger at the page, a register of the students enrolled at Kingshurst in 1755. There was Alasdair's name, faint but unmistakable, in spidery black script, along with his age, clan, and proposed field of study.

"He was studying history," Rana observed, extending a finger toward the word on the page. Damien made a kind of hissing sound, and she withdrew her hand, startled.

"Please don't touch any of the documents with bare hands," he said. "The oils from the skin can degrade both the paper and the ink."

"Right, sorry," Rana said, returning her hand to her cup of tea instead.

"Where would the history students have spent most of their time?" Finn asked, his eyes still roving over the faded entries.

"This building was Kingshurst's library originally," Damien said, looking around him fondly. "And even when further collections required more space, the oldest and most valuable documents would have been kept here. The building to the north side of the courtyard housed the classrooms he would have attended. Finn glanced out past the courtyard to the building on the other side. He nodded once and returned his attention to Damien.

"What about student societies? Awards? Do you have any records of those things from the same time period?"

"We do." It was Aoife who answered this time, pushing aside her undrunk tea, and rising at once. She opened one of the drawers built into the shelving, and retrieved a very large volume with canvas covers and a spiral binding. It was nearly half as tall as she was, and it was with considerable effort that she managed to set it on the table without tipping over. "Each year has its own archive, just a collection of what we could salvage from records. There are examples of student work, issues of the campus newsletter, announcements of events, correspondence to and from students and faculty, all sorts of things.

Some of it was found and preserved here, but a lot of it has been donated back to Kingshurst from various clan collections, and archives from around the world. I'll get you all some gloves, and you can look through it... carefully."

Rana looked at her watch. "Savvy and I should meet up with Reilly. We're meant to do a thorough sweep of Old Campus. Is that still the plan, Caomhnóir Ca—I mean, uh, Finn?" Rana still had a hard time remembering to call Finn by his first name now that he wasn't technically her instructor anymore.

Finn consulted his watch as well, and then nodded. "I think Jess and I can carry on here."

Savvy and Rana got up from the table, murmuring their thanks to Aoife for the tea. Savvy swiped a clandestine chocolate hobnob and pocketed it with a wink at me as she left.

And so, while Aoife and Damien scuttled around gathering as many resources as they could from the years we had requested, Finn and I set to work scouring the yearly archive volumes. We spotted Alasdair's name in the list of students who placed well in a chess competition, and another mentioned him as a member of the debate society. He was also mentioned in an odd piece of correspondence that seemed to be from a student publication—almost like an editorial. It had been written by an anonymous student who was railing against what he called "radical thinking" and "heretical practices" being encouraged on campus. It read like the 16th-century version of an all-caps social media rant encouraging book burning, and I nearly stopped reading in disgust, when one particular section caught my eye.

Perhaps it would behoove the members of the Council to descend from their ivory tower on occasion and bear witness to the filth spouted by some of their golden sons when out of their hearing. The rot runs deep and cannot be so easily routed if it is left to fester in these hallowed halls of academia where these ideas pose a true danger to impressionable minds. The charismatic Mr. A. M. and his sycophants would not perhaps be so bold if they were made to repeat their blasphemy before the High Priestess.

"Finn, take a look at this," I said, pointing.

Finn read silently, his eyebrows rising with each successive sentence. "Interesting," he said when he'd finished. "Alasdair certainly could have been identified as a 'Mr. A. M.' And of course, as a MacLeod, he belonged to a Council Clan, and a very powerful one at that."

"And his ideas, if he chose to share them, would absolutely fit with this description. 'Rot.' 'Filth.' 'Blasphemy.' Anyone who held traditional Durupinen beliefs would have been appalled."

We both read carefully through the article again, but no more could be gleaned about "Mr. A. M." or what his ideas might have been, other than the fact that they ran contrary to the beliefs of most rule-following clan members.

We continued poring over the volumes for a couple of hours, Aoife and Damien occasionally checking in with us or offering to pull another resource. My neck was starting to ache, and my head to pound from squinting at so many faded and nearly illegible documents—and my stomach was making ungodly rumbling noises even after the biscuits. I stood up to stretch my legs, and my foot nudged into my backpack, knocking it over.

"Wait!" I said. "We actually do have a couple of things we wanted you to look at, Damien, if you wouldn't mind."

"Things?" he repeated, somewhat blankly. "What sort of 'things?'"

"Sorry, uh... artifacts?" I corrected myself. "Well, one of them, anyway. The other is a drawing."

Damien was still frowning, but he joined us at the table, adjusting his glasses in anticipation of an academic examination.

I pulled the items I'd brought out of the bag as I described them. "The first is a dagger. It looks sort of... ceremonial. More decorative than useful, if that makes sense. Apparently, Alasdair brought it with him from Kingshurst when he came back to Edinburgh, where he... uh, I'm assuming you know what he did there, having read his file?"

Damien nodded, giving a spastic swallow that made him look like he might be ill. "Yes, I am aware of his... activities. They called him The Collector if I'm not mistaken."

"That's right," I said, carefully unwrapping the dagger, and laying it on top of its silken wrappings. I slid it across the table so that Damien could get a better look at it.

Damien's face wrinkled in distaste at the rust-colored bloodstains on the blade, but his eyes lit up as he examined the handle. He leaned forward, nose practically touching the ivory as he examined the carvings upon it. He was very still, very silent, for several seconds. Then he said, in a tense, trembling voice, "Gareth, please join us over here. There's something you should see."

Gareth looked supremely annoyed that he was being dragged away from his work again, but shuffled over to us. He leaned over Damien's shoulder, and I watched in surprise as his expression transformed at the sight of the dagger.

"Dear God," he murmured, fingertips hovering over the carving of the woman that adorned the handle. "Where on earth did you find this?"

Finn and I traded a quick, excited look. My heart was beginning to race. "It was in the basement of MacLeod Manor, preserved in a glass case. Danica MacLeod stole it from the case and hid it away in her room when she was trying to eliminate all trace of Alasdair from their records."

"Mind you, the rest of the MacLeods had already done a remarkably thorough job of that," Finn said with a grimace. "They hid, damaged, and outright destroyed every record they could get their hands on, including the ones at Skye."

Damien looked up, affronted to his core by this disrespectful treatment of historical records, but even his indignation couldn't distract him for long. At this moment, Aoife appeared from behind one of the stacks, and peered curiously over Damien's other shoulder. She blanched, and the fingers clutching the back of Damien's chair went white at the knuckles.

"Where did this come from?" she asked, but Damien ignored the question.

"You said there was another artifact?" he asked. He was practically writhing with anticipation, and Gareth beside him looked downright rabid with interest.

"Uh, yeah," I said, pulling my sketchbook out of my bag, and flipping it open to the relevant page. I held it to my chest as I explained. "Before I show this to you, I want to explain that I'm a Seer."

All three pairs of historian eyes stared unblinkingly back at me.

"Most of my visions come to me as dreams," I said. "This particular vision came to me a couple of nights ago while we were still searching for Alasdair in Edinburgh. I'm hoping you might recognize the location."

I placed the sketch on the table, and turned it around so that they could examine it properly. All three bent over it in silence.

"I wouldn't necessarily have connected the vision to the dagger," I said, "except that one of the carvings on the wall matches the carving on the base of the dagger."

In unison, all three of them leaned even closer to where I pointed, their heads practically touching each other.

"I don't believe it," Gareth whispered.

"The carving, are you sure... I can't discern the detail," Damien whispered. He looked flushed, his eyes shining.

"Hang on, I have individual renderings of those," I said, and flipped the top page up to reveal another page, this one with multiple smaller drawings of the individual carvings. Beside me, Finn's leg was bouncing as he tried to channel his tension.

"The wand, the chalice, the throne, the swine... I can't believe it; it's all there," Gareth cried, his voice building to a fever pitch. His head snapped up and he stared at me, eyes wild. "Where is this? What else did you see?!" He was leaning across the table toward me, his expression so eager as to look desperate, and I drew back from him instinctively.

Aoife lay a hand on Gareth's shoulder. "Steady on there, Gareth," she said quietly.

Gareth shook her hand off. "Aoife, don't you understand what this means?"

"Yes, of course, but do try to calm down. They don't—"

"Sod calming down! This is the biggest discovery we've had since—"

"Whoa, whoa, can we back up here, mate? We still don't know what you're talking about," Finn said, trying to retake the reins of the conversation, as it was now spiraling out of control.

But Gareth was too worked up to listen. "What else can you tell us about this place? Do you know where it is? How to get to it? What did the vision show you?"

My heart sank a little. "I... I'm sorry, but I don't know. We were hoping *you* might know where it is."

Gareth cursed under his breath, running his hands through his hair so that it stood up from his scalp like a mad scientist's caricature.

"You'll have to excuse Gareth. He's very... invested in this work. We all are," Aoife said.

"Okay, but what work? We still don't know what you're talking about," I reminded her, trying to keep my frustration from boiling over. It was Damien who responded, lifting his face at last from the sketches in which he had been entirely absorbed.

"We don't know where it is, but we certainly know what it is," Damien said. "Your vision has shown you something we've only ever heard rumors of, something we've been anxious to uncover for a very long time."

He paused, and the tension inside me finally snapped.

"Well, what is it?!" I cried, all patience gone.

It was Gareth who answered. "This is the meeting place of the Brotherhood of Circe."

11

THE BROTHERHOOD OF CIRCE

The words hung in the air, pinned there by a reverent silence.
And then I broke it.

"The Brotherhood of *what* now?" I asked.

"Yeah, sorry, mate, I didn't catch that either," Finn added.

"The Brotherhood of Circe. You've never heard of Circe?" Gareth asked, looking both incredulous and a bit imperious.

"It's ringing a bell, though I'll admit it's a faint one. It's something to do with mythology, isn't it?" Finn offered.

"Bang on," Gareth said, slamming his hand down on the table. "Greek mythology, to be exact." He leaped up from the table with alarming speed and ran over to the desk he'd been working at since we'd arrived. He'd come alive, the very mention of this brotherhood animating him the way nothing thus far had been able to do. He dug out a large book, brought it back to our table, and feverishly began flipping pages.

"I don't get it. What the devil does Greek mythology have to do with the Gateways?" Finn asked.

"Well, nothing if we're talking about the Durupinen collectively, but for this very small society, it has everything to do with it," Gareth said, waving his hand impatiently.

"So, who were they, then?" I asked, prompting what I knew would be a tidal wave of information, and bracing myself to absorb as much of it as possible.

Gareth was still flipping pages, muttering to himself, so it was Aoife who answered. "They were a secret society. Nearly every old and prestigious university in the world has them. Surely you've heard of the Skull and Bones at Yale University or the Bullingdon Club at Oxford, for example?"

"If those are supposed to be secrets, they're pretty poorly kept," I said.

"Well, many of these societies are known to exist, but their activities are highly secret," Aoife amended. "Their members are some of the most powerful people in the world: future presidents, prime ministers, and captains of industry. They are often known as the secret cogs and wheels that turn the world."

"So is that the point of this brotherhood, then?" Finn asked. "Just sounds like a good ol' boys club to me. Get yourself a leg up and mix with 'the right' people. Just a bunch of posh nonsense if you ask me."

"Some of them are just that," Gareth said dismissively. "They maintain their mystery in their activities, not really in their rosters."

"Of course. The members want the bragging rights. It lends them prestige and mystique, not to mention all the doors it opens for them," I said.

"Yes, but there are some societies that are not only exclusive, but manage to keep their very existence a secret; and that's what the Brotherhood of Circe was able to do for centuries, until Damien and I started digging."

I saw Aoife's shoulders stiffen. "Oh, and I did nothing, I suppose," she muttered, loudly enough for me to hear but quietly enough that Gareth could choose to ignore it, which he did.

"There were rumors, of course," Gareth went on, oblivious to his rudeness. "For generations, there had been rumors of a secret society of Caomhnóir on this campus; but never did a single member ever admit to their existence, nor their activities, at least not on the record. It was whispered of, never spoken of out loud. It was said that any member who broke their code of secrecy would be silenced—permanently.

Finn let out a low whistle. "So, a bit more intense than a good ol' boys club, was it, then?"

Damien nodded vigorously. "Certainly so. There are incidents throughout Kingshurst's history, nasty accidents and the like, that were never satisfactorily explained. The students and faculty alike began to believe such incidents to be the work of this rumored organization."

"People will swallow almost anything when they're scared," Finn said dismissively. "Sensationalism and rumor-mongering is a poor foundation for the truth."

"That may be so, but in this instance, truth was even stranger than fiction," Damien said. "But it was one of these incidents that not only exposed the Brotherhood's existence, but also put an end to the Brotherhood for good." He stood up excitedly. "I'm going to fetch the collection."

I stood up suddenly, the bench scraping across the floor. "The what?"

Damien looked startled. "The... collection of artifacts? From the Brotherhood?"

"Oh," I sighed, feeling my heart slow again. "Sorry. That word 'collection' is a bit of a trigger right now."

Damien looked puzzled, but didn't ask me to clarify. He bustled out of the room and started ascending one of the spiral staircases, while I sank back into my seat, trying to calm down. The report from Catriona didn't mention the Collection. I knew that it didn't because it had been my idea to leave it out. As anxious as we were to catch Alasdair, we were equally as anxious that his dangerous experiments didn't become public knowledge. There was no telling what unstable individual he might inspire next with his madness, and we wanted to avoid that at all costs.

Gareth took advantage of Damien's absence to take over the explanation. "The Brotherhood was a secret society that operated differently. It wasn't a haven exclusively for the privileged, as most other secret societies are, although I am certain there were powerful people among their number. It wasn't about how much money one's clan had, or which held the most powerful Council positions. The Brotherhood of Circe was looking for Caomhnóir who shared a certain sense of discontent—a restlessness with how things were. They were looking for rebels, not rule followers. And so, their ranks likely looked quite different from what one might expect in a secret society in higher education."

"Discontent and rebellion? Certainly sounds like Alasdair," Finn said.

"But I still don't understand who they *were*," I prompted. "If it wasn't about money and making connections, then what was it about? What were all of these rebels interested in rebelling against?"

"Well, to understand that, we must first understand who Circe is," Gareth said, practically writhing with enthusiasm. He pointed to an image in his book, a pen-and-ink rendering of a woman with long, flowing hair holding that same familiar chalice and wand. "Circe was known in Greek mythology as a minor goddess, and also an enchantress. She was the daughter of Helios, the sun god, and was adept at what we would now refer to as witchcraft."

"Ugh, I do *not* want to get mixed up in witchcraft again," I groaned, but Gareth was too involved in his own explanations to notice.

"Circe is perhaps most famous for her jealous nature, and her proclivity for turning her enemies into various creatures. For instance, when she fell in love with the sea god Glaucus, and he spurned her advances, she found the nymph he loved, Scylla, and turned her into a dreaded, nine-headed sea monster."

"Sounds like a real charmer," I muttered.

"Typical," Aoife added quietly. "She was a powerful enchantress, but she was remembered as little more than a hysterical female."

Gareth made an impatient noise through his nose as if Aoife's feminist musings had no place in the conversation. "Perhaps the most famous story of Circe appears in Homer's *The Odyssey*. When Odysseus arrives on her island home of Aeaea, she changes all of his men into swine."

"Swine? Like...pigs?" I asked.

"Correct."

"Well, that explains this carving, anyway," I said, pointing down at the sketchbook where a dozen pigs were scattered around what I now realized was an island. The image had completely baffled me when I'd first seen it, so much so that I thought I must have misremembered it from the dream.

"Look, as fascinating as this all is, I'm still failing to see what would convince a bunch of malcontented young Caomhnóir to name their little fraternity after her, nor why someone like Alasdair would be interested in joining it," Finn said.

"Be patient, I haven't gotten to that bit," Gareth said a little huffily. "Odysseus is able to protect himself from Circe's magic. He threatens her, and she, in turn, invites him to share her bed. Odysseus is able to free his men, and he and Circe live together on the island for over a year as lovers."

I let out a snort of amusement. "She turns his men into pigs, so he sleeps with her? Mythology is just a glorified soap opera, isn't it?"

Gareth threw me a contemptuous look as he continued talking. "When Odysseus says he must continue his journey, Circe advises him to visit the underworld. Do you know what the underw—?"

"Yes, yes, the land of the dead. Crack on, mate," Finn said, somewhat impatiently.

"That's right," Gareth said, a bit stiffly. "Circe tells Odysseus he must seek the wisdom of the dead in order to complete his journey home. Odysseus tells her that it is impossible, that no mortal has ever traveled to the land of the dead. But it's Circe who gives him the means to do so. Aided by her magic, Odysseus is able to travel to the underworld, seek the wisdom of the dead, and return once more to the land of the living, armed with that wisdom."

Gareth paused, watching all our faces expectantly.

"And?" I prompted.

"Well, that's it. That's the belief at the heart of the Brotherhood of Circe."

I turned to Finn, ready to trade a confused look, but Finn's expression had darkened with whatever realization he'd already made. Luckily, I didn't have to press Gareth to keep explaining, because he plunged onward with almost indecent enthusiasm.

"The Brotherhood of Circe had one goal in mind: to discover the same path, a path that would allow them to Cross through the Gateways—not just to the Aether, but all the way to whatever lay beyond, and then to return again."

A stunned silence met these words. Gareth seemed to relish the effect he'd had on us.

"That's impossible," Finn said at last.

"That's what Odysseus thought, too, and yet Circe provided him with the means to do the impossible. And that's what the Brotherhood of Circe sought: the means to make the impossible possible, and therefore achieve the ultimate enlightenment."

"Well, at least it now makes sense why Alasdair would be among their number," I said. "After all, that was the ultimate goal of his work as well, using the Gateway as a revolving door to immortality. But this sounds a little absurd, even for him. Was this a question of actually worshipping the goddess? I mean, they didn't seriously think that if they started a club in her name, an actual Greek goddess was going to show up and whip them all up a magic brew to send them across the Aether, did they?"

Gareth rolled his eyes. "Hardly. Circe was merely the symbol of their quest. I rather believe they had their own ideas about how it was to be done, although admittedly, we've been able to uncover very little evidence of what those ideas might have been."

"But why? Why did they want to do it in the first place?" Finn murmured, more to himself than to anyone else.

Gareth gave an incredulous little cough. "Why, for the same reason every explorer, every adventurer, every academic has ever embarked on their journey of discovery: to uncover or see or do something that no other person has ever uncovered or seen or done. To be the first. To answer the unanswered questions." He looked almost feverish at this point, and I began to wonder if his interest in this subject was purely academic. Did he want to uncover the Brotherhood of Circe, or become one of their number?

Aoife took advantage of Gareth's breathless moment of wonder to interject. "The Brotherhood of Circe believed the Durupinen were wasting our gifts. They believed we were granted access to the Gateways so that we could traverse them freely, not just to guard them jealously."

"Jealously? We were guarding them to protect them, not—" I began, and then stopped as I remembered the Reckoning, and the continued efforts of the most powerful Durupinen to return the Gateways to our blood. "Well, at least at first," I amended.

"They sound like budding Necromancers to me," Finn said. "Are you sure this isn't all just a cover for a bunch of Caomhnóir who turned Necromancer?"

"Necromancers have no natural connection to the Gateway," Gareth said loftily. "They have no ability to see spirits, except when they steal and pervert our Castings. They would certainly have no place in the Brotherhood. The entire basis of their philosophy was rooted in our connection to the spirit world."

"How did the Brotherhood of Circe mean to accomplish their goal?" Finn asked. "The Gateways have been contained in Durupinen bloodlines far longer than Kingshurst has existed."

"As to that, we've as yet found no documentation," Gareth admitted grudgingly.

"I have a theory," Aoife piped up.

Gareth threw her a condescending look. "A theory you have no evidence for," he said.

Aoife's cheeks burned, but Finn said quickly, "Nonetheless, I'd like to hear it. Aoife, please go on."

"Well," Aoife said, her voice softer, more tremulous now in the wake of Gareth's criticism, "I think it's possible that the Brotherhood of Circe somehow discovered the long-buried Durupinen secret—that the Gateways were not meant to be in our blood at all. I think they may even have predicated their existence on it."

Gareth snorted dismissively, but Finn looked thoughtful. "That would make a good deal of sense," he murmured. "If they somehow discovered that fact, their ultimate goal would have seemed that much more achievable. And given the danger of possessing that knowledge, their secrecy would have to be absolute."

Gareth looked somewhat crestfallen that we were taking Aoife's theory seriously. He cleared his throat and said, "A possibility, I warrant you, but not one we can substantiate at this time."

I watched Aoife, breathless and flushed from putting her theory before us all, and I couldn't help but think she might be right. It made perfect sense. If the Brotherhood wanted to traverse the Gateways, they had to believe they were, in fact, traversable; and that certainly couldn't be the case for living, breathing people, when the Gateways were contained inside the Durupinen themselves. I thought about the fact that the Necromancers were our enemies, even in the time of Agnes Isherwood—that it was their constant attacks that caused us to sever the Gateways from the Geatgrimas, and put them into our bloodlines in the first place. That meant that, at one point in history, the Necromancers must have known what we did. And if that knowledge survived the centuries of their routing and destruction, if even one person managed to take the secret with them...

And then there was Alasdair. Alasdair, who sought out the Necromancers. Alasdair, who learned all he could from them. Had he learned this greatest of secrets, buried by generations of Durupinen, making us strangers even to ourselves? Yes, it was possible. Alasdair could have known this secret as well, could even have counted on it, as a means to accomplishing his goal. He would certainly have wanted to bring about the Reckoning, not to protect the Gateways, but to ensure his own, unfettered access to them.

Damien reappeared at this point, rubbing his hands together and looking rather excited. "I've unboxed and laid out our collection of artifacts from the Brotherhood. They're on the upper level in Research Room A. Would you care to follow me?"

Finn, Aoife, Gareth, and I followed Damien up the spiral staircase to the second floor gallery. It seemed to be where they kept a great deal of artwork from Kingshurst's history. I lingered as we passed paintings, portraits, photographs and sculptures, my inner artist wishing we had the time to explore them; but I forced myself to catch up with the others. Alasdair was the priority, and my own nerdy predilections would have to wait for another day.

Damien used his ID to swipe us into a room at the far end of the gallery. Inside, he had covered a long wooden table with the artifacts in question, and I stopped short when I saw them laid out.

"They're all... burnt," I said blankly.

"That's right," Damien said. "Every artifact we have from the Brotherhood was obtained at the very same time, and in the very same location. Let me explain. In the spring of 1755, there was a murder on the campus. A scullery maid from the neighboring village was found dead on the grounds. We do not know much about her other than her name, Alice MacLeary. The newspapers at the time did not devote many words to a victim of such lowly status."

"So, not much has changed then," I murmured. All through history, the deaths of lower class women were ignored and minimized. That was why so many serial killers through the ages chose to prey on prostitutes and runaways—society had already proven they didn't care about these women, and so their killers thought they could more easily get away with their crimes.

Damien continued, and I had to drag my thoughts away from unmourned women to focus on what he was saying. "A local vagrant was hanged for the crime in order to draw suspicion away from the students and faculty of the university."

"Wait, you're saying the university had someone framed for it?" I cried. My voice echoed loudly through the rafters, and I winced.

"It was common practice centuries ago," Damien said stiffly. "The Durupinen had to blend in with the rest of society, but we had our own laws, our own prisons, our own halls of justice. We had to keep it all secret, and therefore, sometimes sacrifices had to be made. If we'd been discovered, there would have been a mass routing that would make the witch burnings look like mere child's play."

I opened my mouth again, appalled, but I caught Finn's eye and quickly shut it again. This was no time to dwell on past injustices. We needed to be focused on preventing any more.

"But the fact is that, on the campus itself, there were serious inquiries. Students and faculty members alike were questioned. There was panic and fear, wondering if there would be any more victims. And then, about a week after the murder, approximately a dozen students, all Caomhnóir, were expelled. The official explanation for their expulsion was arson."

I looked down at the items on the table. "And this is what they were burning?"

"That's right," Damien said. "They were found gathered together in the dead of night, in a remote corner of the campus. It seems they meant to burn these things in secret, but there had been a drought that year; and in their haste, the fire spread out of control, and they were caught. When the fire was put out and the damaged contents examined, it was clear that this was no case of student hijinks. The MacLeods sent their own Caomhnóir in to investigate. The boys were all questioned, and though none of them would say a word about what was found in the fire, the investigators were able to glean enough from the ruined scraps to understand that the Brotherhood was a dangerous and subversive group. Whether they connected it to the murder, I cannot tell you. But all the boys involved were expelled, the evidence hidden away, and the whole thing hushed up. It wasn't until about three years ago, during the restoration to an Old Campus building, that these items were unearthed again. We have been interested in uncovering more about the Brotherhood ever since."

"Some might even say obsessed," Aoife muttered, throwing a dark look at Gareth, who was too busy staring, dewy-eyed, at the artifacts to hear her.

Damien gestured for us to move closer, and we did as he bid us, looking more closely at the collection before us. There were remnants of three black cloaks, two of them badly charred, while the third remained almost entirely intact save some scorching around the hem. There were a number of what looked like ceremonial items, including a tarnished silver chalice, several daggers, and even a sword. There were a number of small statues—busts and figurines—blackened with ash, as well as a large number of books, papers, and scrolls in various states of ruin.

"Did they seriously think all this stuff was going to burn?" I asked, pointing to the statues and daggers.

"They were just lads, and scared lads at that. They probably just panicked," Finn said, bent low over the sword, which had an elaborately carved ivory handle, just like the dagger now cradled in my hands. I undid the wrappings and laid it beside the others. There could be no mistaking it—it was one of the set. Each one had a carving that matched the ones I'd seen in that hallway in my vision. Alasdair had been one of the Brotherhood, there was no question. But had he been caught along with the others?

"These boys who were expelled, do you know their names?" I asked.

Damien nodded. "We have the records, but Alasdair MacLeod's name is not listed."

Perhaps I ought to have been disappointed, but I wasn't. I hadn't expected Alasdair's name to be on that list. In fact, I would have been shocked if it had been. He was a MacLeod. If he had been among the wrongdoers, surely his family would have found a way to cover it up—just another blemish on Alasdair's record that someone blotted out so that they could continue ignoring the danger he was becoming. Another excuse made, another misdeed swept under the rug, in the name of keeping up appearances. It made me want to vomit.

"There was also another boy whose name came up in the inquiry, but he had vanished from campus by that time," Damien added. "His name was Andrew Abercromby and, to my knowledge, he was never found."

"Wait, like... never?" I asked. "No one ever heard from him again?"

"That's right, and if you ask me, I think *he* may have been responsible for the murder of Alice MacLeary," Gareth said. "It seems too much of a coincidence that he would disappear at the very time the murder occurred."

I didn't bother pointing out that no one had asked him. I didn't know who Andrew Abercromby was, and I couldn't bring myself to care at the moment. Alasdair was involved in that girl's killing, I just knew it. It was too much of a coincidence. A girl dies on campus, his little fraternity is broken up, and then, just a few months later, he'd be murdering people in the streets of Edinburgh. What if Alice MacLeary had been his first victim? There was no way to know for sure, and yet my gut was telling me it was true. And now he was back here, at the scene of his first crime. But was it possible the Brotherhood itself was still here, too, waiting for him?

"Okay, so we know the Brotherhood existed," I said, dragging myself out of my thoughts to ask the question out loud. "Is it possible they still do?"

Gareth shook his head. "It's not possible. There's been not a whisper of their existence for close to three centuries. The university instituted a policy in the wake of the expulsions. Every student organization needed express permission and approval from the university president, or any student involved would be expelled."

I considered this. Just because they hadn't been caught didn't mean the Brotherhood had vanished for good. Then again, with their members expelled, their organization exposed, and the majority of their artifacts destroyed, perhaps that really had been the end of them.

"I'd like to know more about this place in Jess' vision," Finn said suddenly, straightening up and turning to Damien. "How did you know about it?"

"It's mentioned in some of these documents. The Brotherhood referred to their secret meeting place as the inner sanctum," Damien said, hurrying around the far side of the table to point out a scroll, blackened with soot and charred along the left side. "This particular scroll seems to be a set of rules about the sanctum—who was allowed to enter it, what they could and could not bring into the space. A lot of it is illegible, of course, due to the smoke and fire damage, but—"

"That's all fascinating," Finn said, and it was only because I knew him so well that I could hear the impatience behind the words, "but you said earlier that you've been searching for it. Do these scrolls provide any clues?"

Damien's face fell. "No. Unfortunately, we've been unable to decipher any information that would help us find the place. We know it must be somewhere on Old Campus, of course, because the rest of the campus hadn't yet been built when the Brotherhood was in operation. But other than that, we have no idea where the inner sanctum is."

"Not for lack of trying on Gareth's part," Aoife said, with just a shadow of a smirk. "Remember when you spent an entire weekend pulling on every book in the library to see if one of them would open a secret panel?"

Gareth glared at her, reddening slightly. "I am a researcher. I leave no stone unturned."

"Or book unpulled," was Aoife's quiet rejoinder.

Finn checked his watch. "We ought to meet back up with the rest of our team. Thank you all very much for your time. Mr. Brightwell, would you be so kind as to leave these items where we can access them? I'd like to spend some more time examining them, if I may."

Gareth looked as though he was going to object, but Damien silenced him with a stern look. "Certainly. Access to this gallery is restricted as it is. I'll update your clearances so that you can come and go freely up here. You'll be able to use your ID cards to get in and out of this room," he added, pointing to Finn's ID, which dangled from a lanyard against his chest.

"There are protocols for handling items such as these. They're posted in every research room, so make sure you review them," Gareth said, his tone combative. It seemed he didn't like strangers coming in and poking their noses into his pet research projects.

"I'll be sure to do that," Finn said placatingly. "And as finding the inner sanctum is a priority, I'd like to come back this afternoon, Gareth, to speak to you about your attempts so far. No point in duplicating efforts," Finn added.

Gareth crossed his arms and nodded once, sullenly.

"Excellent. That's settled, then." Finn said.

We left the artifacts behind, Damien making sure to test that the door to the room was secured before we descended to the lower level. I returned my sketches to my backpack and slung it over my shoulder. Gareth watched them disappear into the bag with a covetous expression.

"Once we find Alasdair, I'll gladly let you add these to your collection," I told him, patting my hand against the bag as we turned to go.

We'd made it to the front entrance hall when I heard hurried footsteps behind us. I turned to see Aoife jogging toward us. She skidded to a stop and handed me a card, panting slightly. "Please, if I can be of any assistance, you can reach me here. That's my mobile. Call or text any time. I'm here at all hours."

"Thank you," I said, smiling at her. "I'll probably take you up on that."

And we left, the significance of all we had discovered weighing heavily on our minds.

12

BLOOD TRAITOR

"Well, that was... enlightening," Finn said, as we hurried to join Savvy and the others.

"Secret societies. Greek goddesses. Cover-ups and disappearances. My head's still spinning," I sighed. I could feel a headache coming on, and it was barely noon. This was going to be a long day.

"It's definitely more complicated than I'd imagined," Finn admitted. "But at least we understand now why Alasdair came back here. It wasn't simply that he spent some time here in his youth. If everything the historians have uncovered is true, Kingshurst was the birthplace of Alasdair's twisted experiments. It would be like coming home for him."

"And now we know why we haven't found so much as a trace of him since we've arrived. In fact, it fits his pattern," I said. "In Edinburgh, he knew he had a secret place he could go where no one would find him: MacLeod Close. And here at Kingshurst, he's got another reliable hideout."

"The inner sanctum," Finn said, clearly already thinking along the same lines. "I think you're spot-on there, love. It's the perfect hiding place. Not only has its location never been discovered, but it represents everything he believes in, all his mad ideas about the Gateways."

"Do you think he was like... the ringleader?" I asked. "That he wasn't just a member of this Brotherhood, but maybe even its founder?"

"The thought had crossed my mind," Finn said. "If there's one thing I can confidently say about Alasdair, it's that he definitely wasn't a follower. He was content to work in secret, on his own. Even Danica was little more than a useful pawn to him. I can just picture him gathering impressionable boys around him and indoctrinating them, but it's hard to imagine it the other way around, isn't it?"

I had to agree. I thought about what Danica had told us about the Necromancers, how Alasdair had sought them out, but soon rejected them and their ideas, just as he had rejected those of the Durupinen. He wasn't a man to be easily influenced or persuaded, living or dead.

"Whether that Brotherhood was his own twisted invention or not, I think you're right," Finn said. "We find that inner sanctum, and we find Alasdair."

Savvy, Rana, and Reilly were waiting for us at the gates of Old Campus. I could tell just from the expressions on their faces as we approached, that they'd come up empty-handed in their search.

"Not a bloody trace," Sav grumbled. "I can't understand it. Are we sure he's still here?"

"I don't know how he'd manage to mask that energy," Rana added. "It's just so distinctive."

"If by distinctive you mean foul as a chippie dumpster," Sav said.

"Well, we just got some information that might explain all that," Finn said. "And going forward, it's a place we're going to be looking for, not a ghost."

I felt my phone buzz in my back pocket and pulled it out to see a text from Tia. *Lab is over. Where do you want me to meet you?*

It was later than I'd realized. I texted her back, suggesting we meet back in front of the dining hall, and then pocketed my phone again.

"I've got to go meet Tia," I told Finn. "I want to get a Melding on her so she and Milo can communicate, and I'll fill them in on what we've found out."

"All right, love. I can catch this lot up. Remember, no more than Tia absolutely needs to know to keep her safe," Finn said.

I gave him a quick peck on the cheek. "Trust me, I want her as uninvolved in this as possible."

A light drizzle was starting to fall as I walked back through New Campus to the dining hall. I pulled up my hood and tucked my hair into it. The air was still pleasantly warm, and so it wasn't as miserable as it could have been, trudging through the gentle rain, watching it settle in a sheen over the grass, and cling to the leaves like tiny jewels. I'd lived in the UK long enough now that rain no longer bothered me the way it did when I'd first arrived. There was a certain beauty to the pearly grey sky, to the gentle swirl of the clouds, and the wisps of fog that twirled and snaked around my feet. In fact, I thought as I looked around me, Skye's stunning natural beauty was enhanced by the weather—it lent a haunting, ethereal quality to the rolling hills and craggy cliffs that made them even more enchanting.

Tia and Milo were already standing outside the dining hall as I approached. Milo was drawing some curious looks from the students who could see him. No doubt they didn't see many spirits on New Campus due to the Warding. I smothered a smile as I watched Tia, her eyes darting excitedly around, as she tried to figure out where Milo was.

"Bless her heart. She's been trying to sense me all morning," Milo said as I approached.

"Hi, Jess!" Tia said with a cheery little wave. Then she leaned in and said in something of a stage whisper, "Is Milo still here? Will you tell him hi for me? It was so strange knowing he was with me today, and not being able to talk to him!"

I laughed. "Yeah, he's here, and he can hear you, remember?"

Tia's cheeks flamed pink. "Oh, right. Sorry. Sorry, Milo!"

"God, she's just so cute. Can we keep her?" Milo asked, pouting.

I rolled my eyes. "Let's go up to the apartment so you two can finally catch up."

We trudged up the stairs to the top floor. I was so busy digging around in my disaster of a bag for my key that I didn't notice the door, until Tia's gasp alerted me to the fact that something was wrong.

"Oh my!"

"What the *fuck?*" Milo added.

I looked up and found myself staring at the words "Blood Traitor" written across the door in dripping red letters. I stared at it for a moment, my mind blank with shock, and then suddenly a snort of laughter burst from me.

"Jess? Are you okay?" Tia asked, sounding wary.

"I'm sorry, I'm just having a flashback to my first day at Fairhaven," I said, still chuckling. I noticed a couple of girls standing at the end of the hallway, whispering together as they stared down the hallway at us. One of them looked vaguely familiar, and I recognized Grace Cameron.

"You know, I'm disappointed," I called down to the smirking duo, whose faces dropped into neutral expressions at once. "I expected a little more creativity. This is the same tired shit insecure little Council princesses were writing on my door almost a decade ago. Tell your friends they need to up their game if they want to get a rise out of me."

I didn't wait for them to respond. Instead, I opened the door, ushered Milo and Tia through it, and slammed it behind me.

"What in the world is going on? Why would anyone write that on your door?" Tia asked, as I set my bag down on the counter.

"Hang on," I said, pulling a Sharpie from my backpack, and dragging her over to the couch. "Let me do this Melding first before I explain."

Melding was a very simple Casting we'd discovered years ago in the *Book of Téigh Anonn*. Just by murmuring a simple incantation and drawing three runes on Tia's wrist, I was able to forge a Connection between her and Milo that allowed Tia to both see and hear him. A few seconds later, Tia looked up and grinned.

"Hey, Milo. Long time, no see."

"It's been too long, sweetness," Milo replied, grinning back.

Tia turned back to me, the smile already slipping off her face. "Okay, now seriously. You've been here a day. How can there already be graffiti on your door?"

"Oh, haven't you heard? Jess is back to being public enemy number one after the Reckoning," Milo said.

"I like to think I was always public enemy number one in their hearts," I said, grinning.

"But I don't understand," Tia persisted. "Wasn't the Reckoning a good thing? You told me all the Gateways would have collapsed if you hadn't restored them to the Geatgrimas!"

"They would have. But unfortunately, the most powerful Durupinen families sort of made the Gateways their entire personality. When I restored them, they took it as a personal attack on their power and privilege," I said.

"You mean they're actually mad at you?" Tia gasped.

"Furious. Livid. Every Council meeting is now a Real Housewives Bad Girls Club mashup," Milo confirmed. "It's both terrifying *and* entertaining."

"Well that's just... I can't... they should be thanking you!" Tia sputtered.

"And yet here we are, and I will likely be spending the afternoon scrubbing graffiti off that door," I said with a sigh.

"Can't the Council do something about it?" Tia demanded, scowling.

"Honey, the Council's half the problem," Milo said. "The Council Clans have the most to lose, and half of them can't see past their own egos to accept it.

In fact, all of this nonsense with Alasdair would never even have happened if the MacLeods weren't so desperate to regain their Gateway."

"Well, someone should speak to the dean of students! This is completely unacceptable harassment, not to mention the destruction of Kingshurst property! And those students—whoever they are—should be suspended!" Tia declared.

"Honestly, Ti, while I appreciate the indignation on my behalf, there's like a fifty-fifty chance the dean of students hates me as much as whoever wrote that message on the door," I said, patting her on the shoulder. "Believe me, a stupid prank is the last thing on my mind right now."

"Well, I still think you should say something," Tia sniffed.

"If it happens again, I will. Okay?"

Tia nodded, mollified for the moment. She checked her watch and sighed. "I've got a lecture to get to. Milo, are you coming?"

Milo opened his mouth to reply, but I answered first. "He'll be along in a bit. I've got some Tracker stuff to catch him up on."

Tia paled. "Anything I need to know about?"

"No. Only that the campus is likely a lot safer than we thought," I said, smiling.

"Oh! Well, that's good news!" Tia said, returning the smile. "Well, keep me posted! Maybe we can meet up for dinner tonight?"

"Sounds great," I said as I walked her to the door. She frowned at the dripping red letters again before hurrying off down the hall. I watched her go, thinking how wonderful it was to see her again, and also how much I wished she wasn't here on campus with me. I missed her like crazy, but this was too complicated. The distance life had put between us was hard sometimes, but then I remembered that it had likely kept her safe.

As soon as I'd shut the door again, Milo swooped in, rattling off rapid fire questions. "Where is everyone else? How did the search of the campus go? Did they find anything, any trace of him? What did the historians have to say?"

"Whoa, rein it in there, spirit guide. I'll tell you everything, but let's open the Connection first. I'd love to only have to explain this once because it's... well, it's a lot."

I turned my attention inward and concentrated on the ever-present link that bound Hannah, Milo, and me together. I felt Milo's energy join me and in a few seconds, Hannah's energy sang along it like a familiar chord on a plucked string.

"Jess! Milo! I'm so glad you're checking in! I was getting anxious."

"Getting anxious implies you were never *not* anxious, and I don't believe that for a second," I laughed.

"Ha ha," she said dryly. "So, what's the update?"

As thoroughly as I could, I filled them in about the existence of the Brotherhood and their inner sanctum. It was a quicker process than it would have been if I was telling them in person, because they could absorb the information as quickly as I could think it—a sort of direct infodump from my brain into theirs. I could feel their various emotions popping off like champagne corks as they tried to take in what I was sending them. At last, I came to the end of everything I'd learned in the archive. I felt the last of it drop heavily into the shared headspace, currently buzzing with a combination of shock and awe.

"Oh my God," Hannah finally supplied.

"I know," I agreed.

"Of course he was a cult leader. Like, of fucking *course* he was," Milo said.

"A murder cult, no less, if the theory is correct that the Brotherhood was tied to that girl's death," I reminded them.

"Of course the theory is correct!" Milo's response felt like a gong in my head. "He was killing people in Edinburgh a few months later! The others probably panicked and wanted out, but by then, they were already in too deep."

"That poor girl," Hannah said. "She must have been so scared."

"And Alasdair wasn't caught along with the others. Typical," Milo ground out.

"And that's exactly why I think he was the ringleader," I explained. "The top guy never takes the fall. It's always the people he gathers around him that he throws to the wolves so he can make his getaway. And besides, even if he had been caught, the MacLeods would have covered it up. Anything to protect their own."

"So now what?" Milo asked.

"Finn agrees with me. Our focus has to be on finding this inner sanctum. That's got to be where he's hiding."

Milo's realization shimmered through my head. "Oh, so that's why you told Tia the campus was safer than we thought it was. I thought you were just trying to calm her down after the whole graffiti thing."

"What graffiti thing?" Hannah asked at once.

Though I would have preferred not to, I told her what had been done.

"Oh for goodness' sake," she replied, the thought vibrating like a growl.

"When is this ridiculousness going to end? The Reckoning is over! We can't reverse it! They're just going to have to accept it!"

"Think about women like Clarissa MacLeod and Marion Clark. When have they ever just accepted anything that they thought could be changed by money, influence, or, barring that, intimidation?" I asked. "I think things are going to get a lot uglier before they get better."

"I hope you're wrong," Hannah said.

"So do I."

And sure, we could hope. But as I listened to that hope ring hollowly through the Connection, felt each of us trying to cling to it, I knew we were going to need more than hope.

"What the bloody bollocking hell is this all about?" Savvy shouted.

I turned from my seat on the couch, where I was doing research on my laptop about Circe.

"Ah, spotted my welcome message, I see," I said, smirking.

Rana, Savvy, and Finn were standing in the doorway, staring incredulously at the message still scrawled on the wood paneling.

"Who did it? Was it that Cameron cow? When I find her, I'll take her by the hair and—"

"Easy, Sav," I said calmly. "We don't know if it's her, and I have no intention of finding out. It's just a distraction, and we have no time to get distracted."

"It's more than a distraction," Finn said, frowning as he pulled off his boots. "It's a problem. We're meant to keep a low profile on this campus. We don't want to draw this kind of attention. The more people who are wandering around campus talking about us, the better chance that Alasdair gets wind of the fact that we've followed him here."

"What do you propose we do? Alert the authorities? The Dean? Campus security? There's about a fifty percent chance one of them actually committed the vandalism," I said.

"Well, then, what do you propose we do about it?" Finn asked.

"Nothing," I said. "Clean it off, say nothing, move on. Because you're right, this is drawing unwanted attention, and I don't want to feed the fire. Let's just let it burn out from lack of oxygen."

I suddenly heard Milo in the Connection. "I'm sorry. What's this about not feeding the fire? Didn't you basically tell the teenagers in the hallway to up their harassment game?"

"I know, I know. Not my finest moment. I won't be egging them on anymore," I silently replied.

Milo's chortle of amusement echoed through my head. "Sure, that sounds like you."

He was still laughing as I shoved him out of my head.

Finn collapsed onto the cushion beside me, looking dejected. Their search for the inner sanctum hadn't turned up anything. Though, as Savvy pointed out, this was to be expected.

"Chin up, mate," she said, slapping Finn on the back in a congenial way as she passed the couch on the way to her room. "It's bound to take a bit of time. After all, that Gareth chap has been looking for the sanctum for ages, and still hasn't found a bloody thing."

"Sav, I know you're trying to cheer me up, but reminding me that this might be impossible is not quite the way to do it," Finn said. His voice sounded hollow, and he needed a shave. The stubble on his cheeks, along with the circles under his eyes, made him look almost haggard. I ran my fingers through his hair, and he closed his eyes with a sigh.

"Hang on now, I never said impossible. Do you honestly think that prat could find his way out of a paper bag?" Savvy asked. "Now that we've got our whole team on it, I reckon it'll be the work of a few days. Mark my words, mate, we'll nab that nasty spirit in no time."

Rana took Savvy's hand and squeezed it, a gentle nudge to let the matter drop.

"Don't lose heart, Finn. We won't leave a stone unturned," Rana said, and the two went off to their room to change.

There was a soft knock on the door, and Finn and I both started. Or rather, I started like a normal person, and Finn jumped up off the couch like he'd sat on a lit firecracker.

"It's okay, I don't think murderous ghosts or vandalizing teenagers generally knock," I teased gently. Finn had the good grace to look a little sheepish, but he stayed standing and his posture was much more alert as I opened the door.

Maeve stood on the other side of it, looking almost equally sheepish.

"Hi, Maeve. What's up?" I asked.

Maeve's eyes darted over to the graffiti, and then back to me again. "Just... checking in," she said.

"Yeah, no luck with Alasdair yet," I told her.

"I meant... about..." and she gestured limply to the graffiti.

"Oh. Yeah, no worries. I've had worse."

"I had a feeling something like this might happen, honestly. I'm so sorry," she said.

"Maeve, relax. It's fine. You don't have anything to apologize for."

Her face turned the color of her hair as she picked at the peeling nail polish on one fingernail. "I probably do, actually. I mean, not literally, I didn't do this," she added quickly, gesturing to the door again; "but I was definitely one of the students sitting around bad-mouthing you, before I met you in Edinburgh."

"No offense, Maeve, but I would have expected that," I said. She looked up at me, surprised, and I laughed. "You're from a powerful family. Historically speaking, that means you probably aren't my biggest fan."

Maeve allowed herself a little smile. "The funny thing is, I was secretly glad you restored the Gateways. Is that weird?"

It was my turn to be surprised. "Maybe not weird, but definitely... unexpected."

"My mom is... well, you've seen how she is," Maeve said, her expression darkening. "I remember wishing that somehow, the gift wouldn't get passed down to me—that it would magically skip a generation, or else show up in some distant cousin or something. She always wore that gift like a crown, and I wanted to see someone take it from her. Not the most noble of reasons, I realize, but I remember heaving a sigh of relief, knowing I would never have to carry that expectation."

Maeve paused, working at that nail polish a bit more fiercely, and I waited for her to finish.

"Of course, I couldn't tell my friends that I felt that way, so I played along by bad-mouthing you and your sister. I probably made it worse. So, anyway, I'm sorry."

"It's okay, Maeve. Seriously, it's fine. I'm fine. And if you hear anyone plotting any other juvenile pranks, maybe give me a heads-up? It really would be better if we could draw as little attention to me as possible for the sake of the Trackers mission."

Maeve bit her lip and nodded solemnly. "I will, I promise. And I'll try to talk to some of my friends. Most of them are just repeating what they heard from their clans anyway."

"Great. Thanks. And say hi to Reilly for me," I said, winking.

"I will," she said, her face breaking into a radiant smile, which faltered almost at once. "He just got back. He told me you didn't find anything today."

"We didn't find Alasdair, no, but we found an important lead. I'm certainly not giving up, so tell him not to either."

"Aye, I will," she said, grinning once again like a lovestruck idiot.

"Okay, okay, ew, get out of here before you make me feel real feelings," I said, pushing her back into the hallway. She laughed and waved over her shoulder as I shut the door behind her, catching one last look at the graffiti as I did so. I sighed. I really should do something about it. The longer it was up on the door, the more people would know about it.

"She's a good kid, huh?" Finn remarked, having watched the exchange from the couch.

"Yeah, she is. I think most of them are, deep down. It's the parents we have to worry about," I said darkly.

Crash.

I sat bolt upright, woken from a dream I instantly forgot as my heart hammered like a panicked creature against my ribcage. Beside me, Finn was already turning on the light, and scrambling from the bed.

"What the devil?" he cried out.

We blinked around the room, half-blinded by the sudden brightness, but I couldn't see anything amiss. The clock on the desk read 2:12 AM. Finn hurriedly pulled on a pair of pants over his boxers as I stumbled out of bed, and the two of us rushed out to the common room. Rana and Savvy were peeking their heads out of their own bedroom door.

"Everyone all right? What the bloody hell was that, then?" Savvy slurred, her voice still thick with sleep.

Finn didn't answer, but mashed his palm against the light switch on the wall, flooding the living area with the harsh light from the fluorescent fixture in the ceiling. I squinted against it and looked for the source of the sound. It was the fluttering curtain in the window that caught my attention first.

One of the two windows in the wall opposite the apartment door was shattered. Shards of glass lay all over the windowsill and the carpet below. Also, on the floor amid the wreckage was a large rock. Someone had drawn a triskele on it in red paint, just like the graffiti on the door.

Finn flew to the window, ignoring my shouted warnings about the glass and his bare feet. He yanked the curtain back and stared into the darkness below.

I ducked back into our bedroom, shut out the light, and ran to the window which looked out over the same stretch of the moon-washed grounds. My eyes scanned the courtyard below, but I couldn't see anything—no movement, no figures shrouded in the shadowy recesses. I was turning away when something caught my eye and I pressed my face to the glass, peering into deeper darkness beyond the courtyard, willing my eyes to focus, to make sense of what had snagged my attention.

There was a figure—cloaked, motionless, a sentinel in the dark—at the gates of Old Campus; and somehow, though I couldn't see the face, I knew its eyes were turned on me.

I didn't stop to think. I simply ran.

Finn, Savvy, and Rana were all calling after me, but I ignored them completely. An impulse I could not control was driving me, pulling me forward, a puppet on strings. I wasn't afraid. Never once did my mind scream at me to stop, that it might be dangerous, that it may even be a trap. It was as though I had heard a call, and now I was answering it in the only way I could. I couldn't explain it, and I didn't want to. I just wanted to find that figure. To stand in front of it. To answer what I could only describe as a silent but deafening plea.

I flew down the stairs, shoeless, sleep-mussed hair flying out behind me like a banner signaling the advance. I could hear the others clattering down behind me, still shouting for me, but I couldn't turn. I couldn't even call back to them. I felt like a hound on a scent, and if I interrupted my pursuit or my concentration for even a second, my quarry would give me the slip. The stairwell was deserted the entire way down, and I burst through the door and into the grounds without meeting a soul, living or dead.

I tore across the lawns, damp grass sliding under my feet, and the moonlight bathing everything in an otherworldly glow that sapped the color from the landscape like an old photograph. The shadows fell differently down on the ground, and though I couldn't see the figure anymore, I knew I was running right toward it. I darted around hedges and over benches, a growing fear inside me that I would reach them at last, and they would be gone. My breath burned like fire in my lungs, but I surged onward, my muscles cramping in protest.

As I rounded the path toward the gates to Old Campus, I skidded to a halt. The gates loomed ahead of me, locked up for the night. The little guard house was empty, its windows like empty eyes. My eyes scanned the darkness for the figure as my heart attempted to pound its way directly out of my chest, but there was nothing. No one. Had I imagined it? Was it a lingering dream, a trick of the light?

My eyes dropped lower, and my heart dropped also. I was wrong—there *was* a figure, but it wasn't standing. It was lying in a heap on the ground in the hedges to the left of the gates, motionless. After moving so far and so fast, I suddenly found that I couldn't move at all. Not another inch.

I heard the panting and pounding of feet behind me that announced Finn's arrival.

"Jess?! What in the name of the Aether are you doing?" he gasped as he bent over at the waist, hands on his knees, attempting to catch his breath.

I couldn't answer, not when he repeated himself, not when Savvy and Rana came stumbling up behind him, sputtering their own breathless versions of the same question. I forced one foot forward, and then the other. Something inside me screamed at me to walk away, to close my eyes, to protect myself from the figure on the ground; but I ignored it, as I willed my body another step and then another. The questions behind me died away into the same terrible silence, that same awareness that something was very, very wrong.

The figure was only ten or so feet ahead of me now, and then I felt a hand on my shoulder, steadying me. I stopped and looked up to see Finn beside me. Our eyes met, and he said, hoarsely, "Let me check, okay?"

I nodded, relieved to stay exactly where I was. Finn strode past me, and Savvy and Rana took his place at my side. We all watched in mute horror as Finn walked once around the figure, and then knelt down beside it. I could make out more of the details now—a pair of running shoes, a pair of legs in black leggings, one of them bent at a strange angle, and a hand lying outstretched, like a pale spider in the dark grass.

Finn reached out and pressed two fingers to the milky white wrist. Seconds ticked past with agonizing slowness. And then he looked up, the answer to our silent questions on his face, and yet he spoke it aloud anyway.

"I don't know who she is," he said. "But she's dead."

I could barely hear his words, much less absorb them. Every muscle in my body had just gone into fight or flight mode as I caught just the slightest whisper of energy—an energy we'd been searching for in vain since we arrived.

Alasdair had been here.

13

ATTACK

"Her name is Helen O'Rourke. She's a first-year majoring in English Literature."

The words ring meaninglessly in my ears, as the security Caomhnóir reads them off the student ID that was found on the ground beside the body.

The body. My mind won't let me attach this girl's name, her age, and her love of books to the shape in the grass. It won't let me process the whole, just the little details—the charm bracelet with a cat on it. The wireless earbud lying in the grass. The tiny heart tattoo visible on her hipbone where her purple Kingshurst sweatshirt has been pulled askew. My brain keeps them all carefully separated so that I won't put them together into a truth too terrible to admit.

"A Durupinen?" Finn asks.

The security guard shakes his head and holds up the ID for closer inspection. No special seal denoting Old Campus access, like on the IDs we'd all been given. This girl was just a normal student.

Milo materialized at my side, his expression grim and frustrated. "I can't track him. The energy signature is only here, in this one spot. There's no trail. Nothing. I don't understand it. How could he even have materialized in this spot? He's not supposed to be able to enter New Campus, not with these increased Wards."

Beside me, Savvy shrugged. "It don't make no sense," she muttered.

"Tell me again how you found her?" The security guard asked, eyeing me suspiciously.

"I... someone threw a rock through our window," I heard my voice speaking, though I didn't remember deciding to answer. "It woke us up. I looked out the window and saw a figure near the gates."

"And your room is?"

"Top floor of the senior flats, building next to the dining hall," Finn interjected.

"And you thought that figure was responsible for throwing the rock that broke your window?" the guard asked, almost smirking.

His expression seemed to bring me back to my senses a little more, as anger flared inside of me, burning away a little of the shock. "No, of course not. I'm not a complete idiot. A person couldn't throw a rock that far. But they were the only thing I could see moving on the grounds, and so I... I didn't really think, I just went after them."

"And that figure was Helen O'Rourke?" the guard asked.

I shook my head, partly in aggravation and partly to shake the girl's name from my brain, because it was too awful to think of her as a real person. "No. The figure was wearing a black cloak. By the time I got here, the figure was gone but...but she was..." I gestured to the ground where the body still lay. I fought an impulse to reach down and tug her sweatshirt down to cover her mid-section. All I kept thinking was, "She must be cold." It was a ridiculous thought, but I couldn't stop thinking it. Beside me, Rana sniffed loudly and wiped her eyes on her sleeve. Savvy put an arm around her shoulders.

The campus around us was still sleeping. No one knew yet what had happened, that a life had been snuffed out, that a family would be swallowed up in grief by dawn.

A second Caomhnóir was squatting beside the body—*Helen, her name is Helen,* I forced myself to think—shining a flashlight around her while a third guard took photos. The second guard reached a gloved hand down and lifted something out of the grass between two fingers. He had to untangle it from a tendril of Helen's hair before it would come free, and he could hold it up for us to see.

It was a strip of fabric, narrow and bottle green. Shiny, like silk.

"Cause of death appears to be strangulation," the guard said, more to himself than to the rest of us. "The marks on the neck match the width of this ribbon."

Finn's head snapped up. "A ribbon, did you say? Let's have it here." He snapped his fingers impatiently.

The Caomhnóir with the ribbon seemed to inflate with indignation. "See here, now, this crime falls under our jurisdiction. You can't simply—"

"I am here on dual orders from Clarissa MacLeod and the Trackers from Fairhaven," Finn barked. "And if that ribbon in your hand means what I think it means, this body is directly linked to the case that brought me onto this campus in the first place. If you want to have a pissing contest, do it on your own time, mate. I don't have the time or the patience for that kind of bullshit. You can help me, or I can get you stripped of your badge and your post with one phone call. Your call."

The offending Caomhnóir deflated and dropped the ribbon into Finn's waiting palm with a petulant grumble, to which Finn paid absolutely no attention. Instead, he held the fluttering green scrap carefully between his fingertips, watching it writhe in the breeze like a living thing.

"Can you feel that?" he asked us, and Sav, Rana, Milo, and I all moved forward.

There it was, that trace of Alasdair's energy, pulsating like a diseased organ around the ribbon-like fabric in Finn's hand.

"That's the blighter, all right," Savvy said, lip curling in visceral disgust.

"But how? A spirit can't murder someone," Milo scoffed. "I mean, sure, okay, I suppose they could scare someone to death or even hurl something at them, but this? A prolonged struggle? It's not possible."

Rana, meanwhile, had stepped toward the body and was bent low, examining the ground.

"What's this then? It looks like... wax?"

The Caomhnóir, already sitting on his haunches, trained his light onto the spot Rana was indicating. Sure enough, there were three drops of white wax, cooled and hardened in the damp grass. I stared down at them and a faint memory stirred, a gentle prodding in my mind, but I was too tired and upset to grab hold of it before it sank again below the surface of the tumult.

The Caomhnóir with the camera moved in to snap more photos. Then the other used a pair of delicate scissors to cut the wax out of the grass, before slipping the pieces into a small resealable plastic bag from the box at his feet—a tacklebox-looking thing with lots of drawers and compartments that the first guard had run for when he realized what it was they were dealing with.

"So this figure you saw," the first Caomhnóir continued, after flipping through his notebook one more time. "Do you think it was a spirit?"

This question pulled me up short. I hadn't ever stopped to consider whether the figure was living or dead. I had simply seen it and taken off after it without considering why I was doing so. I tried to reach back into my memories of half an hour ago, to detangle the threads and try to find the one that could answer the question, but it was all a jumbled knot. I sighed in frustration.

"I don't know," I said at last. "I was never close enough to get any sort of energy, so I can't say for sure."

"Which means you weren't close enough to give any sort of description either, I suppose?" the Caomhnóir asked, sounding frustrated.

I didn't blame him. I was frustrated myself. "No, I wasn't," I answered. "I'm sorry I can't be more help. It... it was wearing a long black cloak and..."

The cloak. We'd seen a cloak just like it the previous morning, laid out with the rest of the artifacts in the research room. I opened my mouth to blurt out my realization, but then caught Finn's eye and snapped it shut again.

Maybe it was the way my teeth were slamming together in the chilly pre-dawn air, or maybe it was the way Helen's body kept drawing my eye, or maybe it was the lingering stench of Alasdair's foul energy, but I suddenly couldn't stand to stay there a moment longer.

"I... I really don't feel well," I announced, my voice too shrill, too loud in the deserted grounds. "Do you have more questions for us, or can we go back to the dorm now?"

Finn's eyes were boring into me as though he was trying to read my thoughts. *Please,* I thought. *Please, I can't bear to stay here another second.*

"I can help them finish up here, love, if you want to go back and try to get some sleep. We can continue this questioning later this morning, can't we?" Finn asked the Caomhnóir with the notebook. He didn't look happy about it, but he nodded his consent.

"I'll need a number I can reach you at," he said.

"I registered all our mobile numbers with the security office before we arrived," Finn snapped impatiently. "It's in the file that clearly none of you have read." He turned to me, his voice low and gentle again. "I'll stay here, oversee the removal of the body and the rest of the evidence collection. I'll meet you all back up in the flat, all right?"

"I'd like to stay, too," Rana said, stepping forward and lifting her chin. "I... I want to help."

"Fine by me. The more pairs of eyes, the better, as far as I'm concerned," he said. "Rana, maybe you could start by seeing if any of the Wards over here were tampered with?" Savvy, Milo, would you...?"

"We've got her," Milo assured him.

"Yeah, she's in good hands, mate," Savvy added.

We walked in silence back to the dorm. Savvy and Milo were both on high alert, Savvy walking at my side with an arm around my shoulders, and Milo circling above us like a reconnaissance aircraft. A slight lightening of the sky at the horizon was the only indication of the coming day—the campus had not yet woken to the horror the night had wrought. Within a few short hours a roommate would wake to an empty room and send a text that would never be answered. A professor would look out over their lecture hall, and notice an empty seat. Then the rumors would begin, whispered across breakfast tables, and exaggerated on threads and in comment sections, until the whole campus would be in a panic.

And they should be panicking. *I* was panicking.

Back in the flat, I began to pace the floor, brimming with a jittery kind of energy even my coffee addiction couldn't produce.

"I don't understand," I muttered. "I just don't understand."

"He's supposed to be laying low," Savvy said. "Hiding, like. Why would he draw attention to himself by doing this?"

"Why? Is the fact that he's a remorseless sociopath not enough of a reason?" Milo asked.

"Not when you've got half the Durupinen world hunting you down," Savvy said, shaking her head. "He's up to something. One of his experiments, like."

"Of course he is," Milo said. "I was trapped in his messed up little bat cave for days, remember? He was obsessed with his work. He barely spoke, unless it was to bark an order at Danica or work out an incantation. I'm not even sure he'd know who he was without his experiments."

"But which experiment? What is he up to?" Savvy asked.

"Well, back in Edinburgh, he was using spirit energy from the Collection to strengthen himself. Maybe he's still trying to do the same thing?" Milo suggested.

"Like Leeching, but in spirit form," Savvy said, repressing a shudder. "No wonder his energy is so foul. It's like it's been... corrupted."

I'd never thought about it that way before, but now that Savvy said it, it made perfect sense. It was the Frankenstein's monster of spirit energies, stitched together from the tortured fragments of dozens of victims. My stomach roiled as the memory of it swept over me.

"He thinks if he makes himself powerful enough, he can regain a body somehow," Milo was saying, when I refocused on the conversation. "Because for Alasdair, it's all about the fear. He's terrified to Cross, not unless he can find a way back; and so, in the meantime, he wants a body. But he seemed really frustrated while I was watching him all those hours. I don't think he'd figured it all out yet."

"Honestly, at this point, I'm less interested in the 'why' than I am in the 'how,'" I said. "Is it stupid to basically announce to the entire campus that he's here? Sure. But we all know what he wants, and we also know he wasn't able to complete his work in Edinburgh, so I guess he's pressing on. My question is how? How did he do it?"

Savvy and Milo looked at each other, as stymied as I was.

I ran my hands over my face and into my hair, releasing a shaky breath. "He shouldn't be able to get through the Wards onto New Campus, but he did. He shouldn't be physically capable of murdering someone, and yet he's somehow done that, too."

"Are we sure it was definitely him?" Milo asked.

"Of course we're sure!" I said. "That murder fit his Collector m.o. exactly! Striking in the middle of the night, the piece of silk used to strangle the victim—and I bet we'll find out she had something taken—some piece of jewelry or a trinket that he bound her soul to so she couldn't escape. Not to mention the fact that the silk was all but dripping with his energy."

"Can't you think of another way to phrase that, Jess? I think I just threw up in my mouth a bit," Savvy said, making a face.

"That's all true, but I just don't see how he could—oh."

Savvy and I both turned to Milo, who had gone so still he looked like a floating photo of himself.

"What? What is it?!" I asked impatiently.

"It's just... I think I know how he could have done it," Milo said, staring off into the middle distance, like he was watching it all play out in his mind.

He didn't speak again right away as he worked through his thoughts. Finally, Savvy lost her patience.

"In your own time, then, mate," she snapped.

"Huh?" Milo blinked at us, then shook his head to clear it. "Sorry, didn't mean to leave you hanging. It's just... I was thinking about what we were just talking about, about Alasdair wanting a new body, and it came to me. What if he Habitated?"

He didn't have to explain what he meant to either of us. After all, it was Savvy herself who showed us that Habitating—a spirit entering and sharing a body with a living person—was even possible. In fact, the very reason why she'd done it—why any of us had done it—was to sneak past the Wards without getting caught.

"Oh my God, of course!" I gasped. "Inside a living body, the Wards would have no effect on him. He could come and go as he pleased, in any part of the campus, and no one would ever know! He obviously hasn't acquired one of his own yet; otherwise, he'd have no reason to keep killing people, so maybe you're right. Maybe he's just... borrowing one!"

"Of course, that would mean that he somehow already managed to find an accomplice," Milo pointed out. "Because you can't forcefully Habitate with someone, at least not for long, and definitely not without doing some serious damage."

I shuddered as I thought back to my first-ever paranormal investigation before I even knew I was a Durupinen. A spirit had tried to do just that—enter my body forcibly in an attempt to get through the Gateway he could sense inside me. If Annabelle hadn't been there to help expel him, I might not have lived to tell the tale.

"But I don't understand how he found such a person," I said, as I turned forcibly from the memory. "He's only been here, what? Two weeks?"

"At the very most," Milo confirmed, "and that's assuming he fled Edinburgh and came straight here, the very night you Walked under the city and found him."

"How could he have found and converted a follower so fast and so completely?" I asked. "I mean, finding a sympathetic ear would be one thing, I could maybe see that. After all, that's how Danica started. But bewitching someone so completely that they'd let you use their body to kill an innocent person? I just don't see how... wait."

"What?" Savvy asked.

"The Brotherhood," I whispered. "What if it didn't end all those years ago, like Gareth said? What if it actually survived in secret? What if Alasdair came back to a whole fraternity of sycophants, ready and waiting for him?"

Milo and Savvy stared back at me with the same horror on their faces that I could feel rising like a tide inside me. Had we driven Alasdair from the city of

Edinburgh right into the waiting arms of his own disciples? Alasdair alone was a formidable enough foe, but Alasdair aided and abetted by a secret society, built on the very foundational ideas that fueled his lunacy? I dropped heavily onto the couch, feeling suddenly both faint and nauseous again.

"I think I need to lay down," I said.

"Yeah, I think we could all do with a lie down," Savvy said, looking at her watch. "And I think we'd better do it while we can, because when Finn and Rana get back, I reckon we'll be right back to it."

I heard a strange sound behind me, and jumped up from the couch in a panic, but it was only the curtain flapping in the breeze that was wafting through the gaping hole in the window. In all that had happened since spotting the cloaked figure out on the grounds, I had nearly forgotten why we had been awake in the first place. I guess after finding a dead body, a rock coming through the window wasn't all that memorable. I tip-toed my way carefully around the glass and picked up the rock with its painted red triskele. I stared down at it, frustration and anger welling up inside of me in equal measure.

Why, when things were finally as they should be, when we had at last gotten the spirit world and the living world on the right course again, was everything falling to pieces? All those centuries ago, when Agnes Isherwood had, against her better judgment, relocated the Gateways into Durupinen blood, the threat was clear. The Necromancers were closing in, desperate to take control of the Gateways, and bend them to their own purposes. But now the Gateways were, at last, where they should be, and it felt like they were under attack already. But this time, the threat came not from the Necromancers, but from the Durupinen ourselves. I'd really thought, once they'd had time to come to terms with it, that we would come together somehow, and carry on the work we'd always done: to answer the calling we'd all sworn our lives to. But we weren't coming together. Things were getting worse. With each passing day, it was becoming clearer and clearer to me that many of the Durupinen had lost sight of their true calling a long, long time ago. We'd become possessive of the Gateways, covetous of the power they afforded us. And if we couldn't find a way to move forward, we would be no better than Alasdair and his Brotherhood, or the Necromancers we'd styled into storybook villains.

We would become the villains of our own story.

14

HIDE AND SEEK

I managed a restless couple of hours tossing and turning before Finn and Rana returned. The rest of the day passed in a haze brought on by a powerful cocktail of guilt, fear, and frustration. It was hard to say which part was the worst, but I'd say having to relive the discovery of the body—first to the guards again in their office, then to the dean of students with Clarissa MacLeod on speakerphone, then to Catriona and Hannah, and everyone else we had to fill in—was pretty close to the top of the list.

The dean of students was a tall, square-shouldered Durupinen named Margaret Robertson, a cousin of the MacLeods of course, because nowhere like in the Northern Clans was nepotism thriving so openly. Dean Robertson's reaction to the news that a student was murdered on her watch was predictably protective.

"Clarissa, I really think we ought to shut down the campus and send the students home. If this Alasdair is responsible, the threat to the student population is ongoing," she said, her voice somewhat shrill from the stress.

"Keep your head, Margaret. Of course we're not shutting down the campus. Can you imagine the publicity? The rumors? Absolutely not."

"But Clarissa—"

"But what? Do you really think Kingshurst can withstand the level of public scrutiny we will get if this news spreads? The code of secrecy will not allow us to take such a step."

"But then, what do we do?" Dean Robertson demanded.

"You craft a statement that makes the student's death sound like an accident, and you distribute that to the wider campus. To the clan students and staff, we can likely stand to share some more details, whatever information we think might help to put them on their guard. And in the meantime, we increase security on campus. I've no doubt we can call up some Caomhnóir from Skye Príosún to increase night patrols."

"That sounds an awful lot like you think the code of secrecy is more important than keeping people safe," I ground out.

There was the slightest of pauses on the other end of the line before Clarissa answered me, each word frostier than the last.

"The code of secrecy and protecting people are not mutually exclusive, Miss Ballard. Nothing could be more dangerous than the Durupinen being discovered for what we are, and I will not risk it."

There was nothing we could do. As Finn pointed out, the Trackers and the Council would no doubt back her up. And I knew she had a point, even if I didn't like it. All I could do was be grateful that Tia, at least, had protection; and I was able to tell her enough to ensure she didn't go anywhere on campus alone, and certainly not at night. Of course, what I actually wanted her to do was pack up her shit and leave immediately, if not sooner, but again, I was overruled.

"Jess, I have worked too hard for too long to simply walk away from this opportunity," Tia said, frowning at me in that stern school marm way she sometimes had that she was too adorable to pull off effectively. "I will not so much as answer my door after sunset, and anyway, Milo will be there."

By the next day, the campus was abuzz with rumors. An official email went out to all the students and staff, but it left out so many important details that it stirred up much more fear than it managed to quiet. Despite the insistence that Helen's death was an accident, the university also decided to instate a curfew—no students out on the grounds after 10 PM without alerting campus security for an escort. It was this, more than anything else, that set the students on edge. I could hear it being discussed at every table in the dining hall as I forced myself to eat something, though everything felt and tasted like cardboard in my mouth.

"I heard she was attacked by another student," a girl was telling her rapt circle of friends, as they all picked at salads. "And that's why they're trying to hush it up. Legacy and all that."

"Well, I heard she had a jealous boyfriend back home," another girl offered up. "Apparently, she was trying to break up with him. What's the betting he came up here to win her back, and killed her in a jealous rage when she refused?"

All the girls seemed to agree that the odds were good before steering the conversation to what kind of self-defense items they carried in their purses, and how effective they were likely to be.

I gave up on eating, tossing my nearly untouched lunch in the trash, and setting off for Old Campus, where Finn, Rana, and Savvy were already on shift, managing patrols and searching the buildings for any sign of the Brotherhood's meeting place. As for me, I had another lead to follow.

I arrived at the archive building to find Aoife sitting at the main circulation desk, cataloging the materials that had been returned.

"Hey, Aoife."

She looked up in mild surprise. "Oh, hello, Jessica."

"You can just call me Jess, everyone does," I told her, attempting a friendly smile.

She returned the smile. "Okay, then, Jess." Then she seemed to remember who she was talking to, and the smile drooped at once. "I heard all about last night. It's so terrible what happened to that girl."

"Yeah, I know."

Aoife leaned toward me, dropping her voice to a cautious whisper. "They're saying that ghost you're hunting is involved. Is that true?"

"Yeah, I'm sorry to say it is," I answered. "He has a very distinctive energy signature, and it was present at the crime scene."

"A ghost murdering a living person?" Aoife whispered, shaking her head. "I didn't think that was possible."

"That's just it, Aoife. I don't think he's working alone. Is Damien here? Or Gareth? I was hoping to talk to them some more about the Brotherhood."

Aoife bit her lip. "They're both somewhere in the building, yes, but they've been conscripted into helping with the search for the entrance to the sanctum. But I can help you, I'm sure."

"Can you?" I asked.

"Oh, yes. Gareth and Damien would never admit this, but I've done just as much research on the Brotherhood as they have, and I know the collection of artifacts and documents at least as well as they do," Aoife said, squaring her shoulders. "In fact, I daresay I know it better because they assigned me the thankless job of cataloging it all."

"That would be great," I said with a smile, "if you're sure you're not too busy."

"Nonsense," Aoife said, waving her hand impatiently. She reached under the desk and pulled out a large brass handbell and a framed sign that read, "Please Ring For Service." She placed them both on the desk and pronounced herself at my disposal.

"Can we go up to the research room?" I asked. "I was hoping to get a look at one of the artifacts up there."

I let my gaze dart around as we made our way to the stairs. There were at least a dozen students in the main reading room. Yesterday, no one had a glance to spare for me, but after the events of last night, the vibe was very different. A constant low hiss of conversation had replaced yesterday's austere silence, and now I found that multiple pairs of eyes were following me curiously.

"Some privacy probably wouldn't hurt, either," I muttered to myself.

I followed Aoife up the spiral staircase to the same room Damien had brought us to the previous day. My God, had it really only been one day? I could scarcely believe it when I considered everything that had happened since we'd arrived. Aoife hit the light switch, and the fluorescent bulbs buzzed and blinked fitfully before settling into a steady hum. I walked slowly around the table, coming to a stop in front of the black cloaks in various states of damage. My heart sank just a little to see them all still there.

"Can you tell me anything else about these?" I asked Aoife, pointing to the cloaks.

Her eyebrows went up in surprise, but she nodded. "These two were pulled from the bonfire when it was discovered, hence the significant fire damage. This one," she pointed to the third cloak, which looked to be all but intact, "was confiscated from one of the young men caught around the fire. In all likelihood, it would have been burned as well. It's something of a miracle that anything of them survives at all. All that would have remained, if the fire hadn't been discovered and put out, would likely have been these clasps."

She carefully shifted one of the charred strips of fabric to reveal a large silver clasp in the shape of a bird with its wings outstretched. I leaned over the table to get a closer look.

"Why a bird?" I muttered, more to myself than to Aoife, but she answered all the same.

"Circe's name means "bird" in the original Greek," she explained. "So the clasps on the cloak are a direct reference to the goddess after whom they named their order."

I dug back through the fragmented memories of the night before, blurred with fear and uncertainty, but I couldn't remember seeing a clasp on the shrouded figure's cloak. Then again, I wasn't sure I'd gotten close enough to notice a detail like that. The figure, when it vanished, was still a good twenty feet away from me in the dark. And, of course, once I'd spotted the body, everything else had gone completely from my mind.

"Are these the only surviving cloaks, as far as you know?"

"Yes, almost certainly."

"And who would have access to them here in this room?"

Aoife frowned. "Access? Just me, Gareth, Damien, and your team."

"None of the other students could get in here?"

Aoife shook her head. "No. Their access would have to be updated in the computer system, but only Damien or Gareth could do that. I don't even have that kind of clearance. Out of curiosity, why do you ask?"

I explained to Aoife about the figure I'd seen near the gates, just before Helen's body was found. By the time I'd finished, her mouth was hanging open.

"You think this... this *person*, whoever they were, stole this cloak and wore it out on the grounds last night?" Aoife asked, her voice barely more than a whisper.

"That was the theory I was working under, yes."

"But... why? Why would anyone do that?"

I shrugged. "To conceal their identity, for one thing. Perhaps to send a message as well? The figure didn't flee when it saw me coming. It stayed near the body as though it were... waiting for me." I hadn't really stopped to consider how strange this detail was, but now that I was saying it out loud, it did sound rather odd. A person who committed a murder would surely flee as soon as possible, in order to avoid being caught. So why did this person choose to reveal themself, remaining until the body was found, and then vanishing?

I also hadn't seriously considered that the person might not be a living person at all, but a spirit. I hadn't noticed any spirit energy apart from Alasdair's, but perhaps that was because I hadn't gotten close enough? Or perhaps because Alasdair's energy was strong enough to mask a second spirit's presence? Spirits could be subtle. When I was first learning how to use my gifts, I could have whole interactions with a spirit before realizing they weren't alive. Obviously, I was more skilled at spotting them now; but perhaps the darkness, the distance, and the distraction of a dead body had masked the telltale energy.

"Jess? Are you all right?"

I looked up to see Aoife gazing at me with some concern, as I spiraled down my mental rabbit hole.

"Sorry. Yeah, I'm fine. Just... just trying to make sense of what I saw."

"Well, for what it's worth, I don't think anyone could have gotten in here to steal this cloak, and then put it back. The building was locked after eight o'clock and wasn't opened again until eight o'clock this morning. I was here by eight-fifteen."

"What about last night? Were you here until closing?"

Aoife shook her head. "I left around seven o'clock. Actually, it might have been closer to seven-fifteen. Gareth and Damien were still here, working."

"And who opened up?"

"Gareth usually does, but I'm not sure about this morning. He and Damien were both already here when I arrived, so you'd have to ask them, I suppose."

"Huh. Okay," I said, my mind still spinning.

"Jess, do you... do you think this cloaked person was helping Alasdair MacLeod? Like they're some sort of accomplice or something?"

I shrugged somewhat helplessly. "I just don't know. I don't see how he could have committed the murder without help, but I also don't know how he could have found that help. Aoife, are you sure the Brotherhood isn't still in operation?"

Aoife didn't answer right away. She seemed to be considering the question carefully. Finally, when she did reply, it was slow, deliberate, and careful.

"If I had to base my answer solely on the evidence, then I would say that the Brotherhood disbanded on the night these things were burned." She held a hand out over the table of charred artifacts. "But being a historian has taught me lots of things, and one thing I've learned is that there is nothing harder to kill than an idea. The Brotherhood wasn't just men, and it wasn't just rituals and meetings and silly props like these. They were based on a philosophy—an idea. And that idea was strong enough to bind them together. It was strong enough that at least one of them likely killed for it. Ideas have a way of surviving even when there's almost nothing to sustain them, and they can burn brighter and longer and hotter than any one life. And so yes, I think it's possible the Brotherhood survived in some form, even if it doesn't look the same way now as it did then. Does that make sense?"

I thought about the Necromancers and how they rose and fell, but never quite vanished. I thought about Alasdair himself, formless and friendless, subsisting for hundreds of years underneath the city he terrorized, sustained on a single obsession. Finally, I thought about the Durupinen, torn apart at what should have been our deepest and strongest seams by the warring ideas of what we owed to the spirit world, and what we desired from it.

"Yeah," I answered finally. "Yeah, unfortunately, it makes perfect sense."

Aoife helped me for the next couple of hours, pulling box after box of old disciplinary records to see if we could find any trace of additional Brotherhood activity. We didn't find anything conclusive, although there were definitely some incidents that raised an eyebrow here and there. In 1807, a Caomhnóir was expelled for "Castings unbecoming a clan member in good standing," although the report neglected to provide any truly helpful details. Another box produced notes from a disciplinary hearing for two Caomhnóir who were stripped of their membership in an honor society for "experiments in spirit communication which blatantly disregard the responsibilities of our calling." Here, too, there was an aggravating lack of detail, although one member of the disciplinary committee waxed poetic on the "flagrant disregard of the rightful and protective purposes for which Caging was designed." None of it was enough to establish that the Brotherhood was still formally ongoing, but it felt like there were a few breadcrumbs left behind—possible hints at a rebellious streak in the Caomhnóir at Kingshurst that continued through the decades.

"I can keep searching," Aoife told me, as she carefully filed away the boxes on their appropriate shelves. "I'll pull whatever I can find and put it aside for you to look through when you come back."

"Thanks, Aoife, that would be great. I should probably check in on Finn and the others. I really appreciate all your help."

"Of course." Aoife said, smiling. "That's why we're here. If it's buried in Kingshurst's past, we'll find it."

I texted Tia on the way just to check in, and she confirmed she was fine, currently working in the lab, and that Milo was with her. She then followed with a bunch of medical jargon that I couldn't understand, but which contained lots of exclamation points and smiley face emojis, so I assumed that the project she was working on was at least going well, even if nothing else on this damn campus was.

I found Finn by following one of the cloisters into another of the buildings surrounding the Geatgrima courtyard. He was leaning over a massive set of blueprints, Damien on one side and Reilly on the other.

"...and this wing wasn't added until 1782 when a fire destroyed the south section of the library, so I think we can safely rule out that area," Damien was saying as I joined them. Finn looked up and smiled at me, though the smile was strained and didn't quite reach his eyes.

"How's it going?" I asked.

"Hello, love. I mean, we're certainly making a go of it, but we haven't found it yet," Finn said, rubbing a hand over his jaw. "We've been going stone by stone, it seems, in every corridor and classroom."

"I imagine the fact that classes are ongoing complicates things," I said.

"It sure the devil does," Finn sighed, jotting a few words onto a sticky note, and sticking it to the blueprint. "A lot of our work can't begin until classes are over for the day, and as Clarissa refuses to make any changes to the day-to-day running of the campus, aside from the curfew, we are limited as to what we can accomplish during daylight hours. Still, we've managed to cover quite a lot of ground today, working when classrooms are empty, and in areas not currently used by students. And thanks to Damien here, we've been able to narrow things down a bit."

"Really? How?" I asked.

"There's a collection of campus blueprints and other building records. By tracing the history of each part of Old Campus, we can determine which sections of the structures were here when Alasdair was a student, and which have been added or renovated in the time since. It will help us narrow down the search a good deal."

"Helpful, but time consuming," Reilly said. He was bouncing on the balls of his feet, like he was hoping a fight was going to break out over the stacks of papers and ledgers. Like most of the young Caomhnóir Finn trained, he seemed constantly eager to apply his combat skills—a practice used much more frequently in Novitiate training than it ever was in real life. The day-to-day job of a Caomhnóir was, for the most part, much less action-packed than the training suggested.

"Oi! Finn! Come here! I think we've found something!"

The voice was Savvy's, and it was echoing down the long corridor I'd just walked through. Finn, Damien, Reilly, and I abandoned the blueprints at once, and took off toward the sound of Savvy's voice, though we soon left Damien huffing and puffing behind us as he shuffled along in his leather Oxfords, one hand pressed to his lower back.

We found Savvy and Rana in a room off the hallway which appeared to be a sort of faculty lounge, or a department common area. The room had several sagging, mismatched sofas, a long counter with a coffeemaker and a microwave, and a humming refrigerator, all of which looked absurdly out of place against the ancient stone walls—like someone had badly photoshopped it all in. Rana and Savvy were standing in the far corner beside a yawning wood-paneled fireplace, waving frantically for us to join them.

"What is it?" Finn asked.

"I was examining the walls, like you asked, and I noticed this stone. It's a lighter shade of tan than the surrounding ones, and it stuck out a bit farther as well," Rana said breathlessly. "I pressed down on it, and it shifted a bit, and I heard a faint grinding sound. But now I can't get it to budge any further."

She stepped back to let us get a closer look, just as Damien came gasping into the room behind us, hands on his knees as he struggled to catch his breath. I could see the slight discoloration right away, and as I leaned in, I could just make out the gap between the stone and the mortar that ought to have been holding it in place. Rana had managed to push the stone about half an inch into the wall around it.

"Step back a bit," Finn murmured, and we did, giving him a bit more room. He placed both hands against the stone and pushed, leaning his body weight forward.

Nothing happened.

He tried again, but though his face reddened with the strain, he couldn't move the stone any further. Meanwhile, I began feeling my way along the fireplace itself, fingers probing at the wood paneling and the marble mantelpiece, and finally reaching inside to examine the soot-darkened interior. The same kind of stone that made up the walls had also been used inside the fireplace. I traced along the seam where they met the wood paneling and felt a strange indentation.

"Finn, stop for a second," I said, and he removed his hands from the wall with one last grunt of effort. "There's something here." I stepped all the way into the fireplace, ducking my head to avoid cracking it on the bottom of the mantel. I wedged myself into the front corner and felt again for the indentation in the stone. I pressed the palm of my hand against it, and the stone immediately sank inward. The movement triggered a deep grating sound, like stone against stone.

"Finn, try it again!" I gasped.

Finn pressed his hand to the stone once more and it gave easily, sinking several inches into the wall, and revealing a hole behind the wood paneling. Finn reached his hand in, felt around for a moment, and then, with a cry of triumph, released a hidden latch. I heard the squeak and the "thunk," and then the long panel along the right side of the fireplace swung inward like a little door.

"Hell's bells!" Savvy murmured.

We all stood for a moment in stunned silence. Everyone had gone still, and I thought they must all be doing exactly what I was doing at that moment: wracking their senses for any sign at all, however faint, of Alasdair's energy. Finally, as though to confirm no one had picked up on it, Rana unclipped the flashlight dangling from her belt, and handed it to Finn. He clicked it on and trained the beam through the opening.

"What do you see?" I asked, when I couldn't take the suspense anymore.

"There's a narrow passage in here," Finn said, his voice full of tension. He stepped inside, ducking down and turning sideways to allow for the breadth of his shoulders. Once inside, he straightened up, but his body blocked what little we could see of the space beyond. I moved a few steps forward, and then...

"It's all right. Come see."

Rana and Savvy wriggled through the opening at once. I looked at Damien.

"Ladies first," he said, still looking rather pale and clammy.

I squeezed through the opening, and straightened up inside a narrow passage, just as Finn described, maybe eight or ten feet long and sloping rather steeply downward. I followed it, pressing my hands to the wall on either side of me so that I could navigate the decline. The passage then opened up into a tiny room—I had to step down through an opening to enter it, and the wooden step that had been put there for the purpose nearly gave underneath me. Savvy was there, reaching out a hand to steady me.

"Mind the gap," she said with a wink.

I looked around. It was a circular room, dug cleanly out of the ground like a root cellar. The walls were damp and smelled of earth. There was a lumpy shape on the ground, which brought my heart into my throat, until I realized it was only a straw pallet. The room also contained a tarnished silver candlestick, a three-legged stool, and the moth-eaten remains of a blanket.

"What is this place?" I asked, staring around me.

"It's a priest hole," Damien said, stumbling down into the room after me. "I can't believe it, you've found a priest hole!"

"What the bleedin' hell is a priest hole?" Savvy asked.

"They were common in the 16th century, during the reign of Elizabeth I," Damien said. "There were several plots against her life when she first took the throne, all of them Catholic led, and so priests were actually hunted down and arrested. Priest holes were built into many buildings at the time in order to protect them from being discovered."

"Why would a Durupinen university have a priest hole?" Rana asked.

"To tell you the truth, we weren't aware that there was one here. So, this is a very exciting discovery!" Damien said, rubbing his hands together, and gazing around the room as if the walls were made of gold. "But historically, there is plenty of precedent. Priests were not the only people hunted down and persecuted by the crown over the years. Most every significant Durupinen building in history has some kind of hiding place built into it. After all, we have many secrets to protect, do we not? Oh, this is just a fascinating find!"

"Fascinating, perhaps, but not the hidden chamber we were hoping for," Finn said, speaking for the first time as he ran his hands over the walls of the little room. "No other doors, no more secret panels. No carvings or torches or signs of the Brotherhood. I don't suppose there's a chance this leads anywhere else? To another corridor or larger chamber?"

Damien shook his head. "They were built purely as temporary hiding places."

All the excitement drained out of me. Yet again, another dead end.

"I can't believe we found an actual secret chamber in this building, and it's the *wrong one*," I grumbled as we all clambered back out.

"I was so sure this was it," Rana said despondently.

"Hey, all this means is we're getting better at searching," Sav said. I turned to glare at her, and she shrugged. "I'm choosing to look on the bright side, mate. Damien and Gareth have been looking for that sanctum thing for years, and they never found this place! So I say, it's only a matter of time."

"Yeah, time is what I'm worried about," I muttered. "I'm not sure how much of it we actually have."

"You mean you're worried he's going to kill someone else?" Savvy asked.

"Sav, he's a serial killer! And not only that, he's desperate. If he doesn't already know we're here, he soon will. He's like a cornered animal, and he's going to fight that much harder to escape. We separated him from his

Collection, and so he can't feed off it the way he intended to. He has to find spirit energy another way, and so he's taken to killing again. We forced his hand, and every day that goes by is another opportunity for him to find another victim!"

"Uh, Jess? You want to maybe... keep it down a bit?" Savvy muttered.

I suddenly realized I was shouting, and that Finn, Damien, and Rana were now all staring at me. Out of the corner of my eye, I saw two people in the doorway to the lounge turn on their heels and walk out again.

"Right. Yeah, sorry. I'm just so..."

"Frustrated. Yeah, I get it," Rana said, fists clenched at her sides, as she looked back at the secret passage.

"We all are," Finn said. "But we've got to persevere. Keep calm and carry on, as it were. If we lose our heads now, we'll never find him."

I took a deep breath, pressing my hands to my head. "Okay. Yes. Not something I'm particularly great at, but I'll try."

"If you'll all excuse me, I'm just going to pop down to my office and put in a call to our history department. I can think of several professors who would like to get a look at this priest hole," Damien said, bowing himself out of the room.

"Rana, Savvy, if you could continue on with your search?" Finn asked, once Damien had bustled his way down the hallway.

"On it," Savvy said with a cheeky wink, and pulled Rana out into the corridor in search of the next room to be examined.

"Let's go back to the architectural notes and wait for Damien there," Finn said to me, taking my hand. "It feels like a good use of our time to narrow down the places we need to search."

"Okay," I said. My voice sounded despondent and hollow in my own ears. I allowed myself to be pulled along. My disappointment that the priest hole had been yet another dead end felt like weights around my ankles, slowing me down with every step.

We were passing through the main reading room in the historical center when raised voices caught our attention—well, raised was a relative term in a library building, but nevertheless, they were much louder than they should have been. They were coming from one of the offices behind the main circulation desk.

"—don't understand why you've taken them!"

"Because they pertain to my research! You don't expect me to stop just because that interfering lot showed up, do you?"

The first speaker was Aoife, I was almost sure of it. And the second voice, with its slight lisp, could only be Gareth.

Finn pressed a finger to his lips, and we edged closer to the circulation desk, listening.

"But everyone is looking for the sanctum now! Don't you think you ought to turn them over to—"

"I was the first person to know about the sanctum! I was the one who found these journals, and I'm the only one who's been able to make any sense of them!"

"But they might help!"

"I'm not interested in helping them, all right? This was meant to be *my* discovery!"

Gareth's voice had risen to such a pitch that the few students out in the stacks were starting to stare.

Finn had heard enough. He vaulted right over the desk and opened the door to Gareth's office. Aoife and Gareth jumped in surprise, and Gareth dropped whatever it was he was holding.

"Everything all right in here?" Finn asked in a calm voice.

"No, it is certainly not all right," Gareth said, scrambling for the item he'd dropped—a book—and holding it protectively against his chest. "Ms. O'Malley has been snooping around my office."

"I wasn't snooping!" Aoife cried, her face turning scarlet. "I was just looking for the keys to one of the filing cabinets, and I thought Gareth had it last. But then I found those." She pointed to a small stack of books, each identical to the one now cradled against Gareth's chest. "It's not as though I tore the place apart or anything. They were sitting right there on the desk! And I recognized them. They're part of the collection of Brotherhood artifacts, and so I was going to return them."

Gareth's jaw stiffened. "You have no business removing things from my office. I need them for my work."

"And you have no business removing things from the collection when they're supposed to be at the disposal of the Tracker team!" Aoife shot back.

"All right, let's keep our voices down here," Finn said, glancing back over his shoulder. "No need to cause a scene. There's already been too much attention drawn to our presence here."

Gareth and Aoife glared at each other, but lowered their voices. Gareth's was shaking with anger as he went on.

"I have been working tirelessly on this project for almost three years. Countless hours and late nights, poring over these materials. No one would even know about the sanctum if it wasn't for me!"

"And you wouldn't know what it looks like without me," I said with a jaunty little wave.

Gareth chewed the inside of his cheek, but said nothing.

"Look, Gareth, we're really not here to steal your thunder," Finn said, and though his voice was calm, there was also a chill to it. It was only because I knew him so well that I could tell Finn had run out of patience. "Our only interest in the sanctum is the fact that Alasdair is all but certainly hiding there. You do know that, right?"

"Yes, yes, but—"

"And that he's already murdered someone right on this campus?"

"I realize that—"

"And that we'd very much like to prevent that from happening again?"

Gareth was bright red and sputtering now. "Yes, I... of course, but—"

"Gareth, things have changed," Finn said, his cool tone freezing to ice. "The sanctum is no longer some sealed up, forgotten place. It is the current hideout of the most-evil spirit any of us have ever seen."

"I... there's every chance that..."

"You know what, Finn?" I said loudly. "If Gareth wants to find the sanctum so badly, let's let him."

Finn stared at me. "I beg your pardon?"

"Yeah, I mean, sure there's a serial murdering super-ghost in there, but he can handle it. If he wants to find it, let him. Send him in first, the canary down the mineshaft. Let's see what's left of him when we pull the cage back up."

All of the angry red color was now draining from Gareth's face, making him look quite ill. Beads of sweat appeared on his brow. "I... well, that is, I never..."

"No, seriously, you'll be doing us all a favor. I'm sure he'll let you have a good look around, and maybe take some notes before he strangles you and dismembers your spirit for his own personal consumption."

I couldn't quite be sure, but from out of the corner of my eye, I thought I saw Aoife smother a smile with the back of her hand. I couldn't blame her. Despite the high stakes of the situation, it was rather fun watching Gareth's bravado shrivel before my eyes. In the meantime, Finn had finally caught on to my strategy.

"Right, fair point! We'll just leave you to it then, Gareth, and if you vanish, well... at least we'll know you died in the pursuit of academic discovery," he said, crossing his arms over his chest.

Gareth looked utterly miserable now. Indignation and fear contorted his features in turn, and the hands that held the book to his chest were white at the knuckles.

Seemingly just for fun, Finn pulled the two-way radio off his belt clip and pressed the button. "Hey team, if you find any more secret entrances, don't proceed through. Gareth has just volunteered for that honor."

"Stop, stop!" Gareth shrieked, starting forward like he was going to knock the radio from Finn's hand, but Finn was quicker. He tossed the radio aside, which I fumbled but managed to hold on to, while simultaneously clamping his hand around Gareth's wrist and wrenching the book from his other hand. Gareth cried out, but though Finn probably wanted to hit him as badly as I did, he released Gareth as soon as he had the book.

"You've got two choices, Gareth," Finn said, as Gareth stumbled away from him, knocking into his desk. "You can cooperate with us and help us find the sanctum as part of a team, or you can continue to obstruct us; and I will not hesitate to arrest you for interference with an official Tracker mission. I hear the view from the cells at Skye Príosún are lovely this time of year."

Gareth swallowed hard. "All right! Yes, I'll... I will help."

"Are you hoarding any other resources we should know about?" Finn asked.

"No, I swear," Gareth said. "Just... just these journals."

Finn looked at Aoife, who nodded. "I haven't noticed anything else missing."

"Very well, then. I'll take those," Finn said, holding out his hand while Gareth, his expression still mutinous, picked up the remaining journals and handed them over. "Excellent. Gareth, why don't you come with me, and you can show me exactly what's in these journals that's worth hiding."

Gareth fixed Finn with a look of utmost loathing before stalking from the room. Finn followed him, the journals now tucked under his arm. He tossed a clandestine little wink at me as he passed.

I turned to Aoife. "Thank you for standing up to him."

She shrugged, looking somewhat forlorn. "I hope those journals are worth it, because I think the work environment is going to be quite hostile from now on. Not that it's ever been what you'd call warm and fuzzy."

"Yeah, Gareth doesn't seem like the warm and fuzzy type. I doubt it's personal."

"Oh, it's personal," Aoife said. "He's always been paranoid about his research. He's been convinced from day one that I'm trying to steal his work. Anything I uncover is 'irrelevant' and 'unfounded,' any question or suggestion is 'infantile.' He even told me that a woman couldn't possibly understand an organization like the Brotherhood because I would historically have been excluded from it."

"He sounds like a delight," I said.

Aoife huffed out a laugh. She looked almost as tired as I felt.

"Well, anyway, we appreciate your help," I told her. "And we'll make sure Damien knows what happened. You shouldn't have to put up with that kind of misogynist bullsh—oh." Her face made me stop. "Damien's almost as bad, isn't he?"

Aoife smiled sadly. "He dresses it up in a bit more civility, but yes."

"That sucks. I'm sorry."

"Well, I'll admit, I knew what I was getting into," Aoife said with a sigh, as she opened the drawer of the desk and took out the keys she had come to locate in the first place. "But I also knew that Kingshurst was the right place for me— the only place, really, for the work I wanted to do. Their disdain will only push me to work harder and publish faster." Her face broke into a satisfied little smirk.

I grinned back at her. "'Atta girl."

15

IN THE SHADOWS

We continued searching the buildings of Old Campus until well into the evening. We didn't even take a break to go grab dinner in the dining hall, choosing to just order pizza instead and have it delivered to the gates. We searched room after room, corridor after corridor, with painstaking deliberation, prodding every stone and pushing on every bit of paneling. We opened and closed windows, searching the sills and openings for hidden latches or buttons. It was tedious and mind-numbing, and by the time Finn told us to call it quits, we were all aching with exhaustion and pent-up frustration.

We returned to the dorm to find that maintenance had repainted the door to the flat, and also repaired the window. If it weren't for the sign on the door warning us of the wet paint, there would have been no hint at all that anything out of the ordinary had happened to our living quarters. I knew I should probably shower—I could feel the dried sweat on my skin—but I was too bone tired to do anything but slip out of my jeans into some pj pants, and crawl into our bed. Finn and Rana were only meant to get a few hours of sleep, and then they were taking a half-shift overnight. I tried to talk him out of it, but he refused.

"I'll sleep when this is over," he said stubbornly. "Besides, we're the only ones who've truly come into contact with Alasdair's energy signature. I want to make sure there's at least one member of our team on every shift with the Skye

Caomhnóir. They might not pick up on it as quickly as we would, and we'll lose precious time."

Personally, I didn't think anyone could miss an energy signature that foul, but I was too wiped out to argue. Finn hadn't even finished unlacing his boots before I was out cold, too tired even to dream.

What felt like only minutes later, the night was rent apart by a cacophonous wailing sound. I shouted and flung my hands up over my ears, my heart galloping in my chest, but the confusion only lasted a few seconds. My eye was drawn to the corner of the bedroom near the ceiling, where a red light located on a small red box attached to the wall was flashing like a goddamn strobe at a dance club.

It was the fire alarm. The fire alarm was sounding at one o'clock in the morning.

I groaned as I peeled myself out of bed, hands clamped forcefully over my ears as the alarm blared. I entered the common room just as the door across the room burst open, and Savvy toppled out of it, looking quite mad.

"S'matter?" she mumbled, eyes still half closed, and an auburn curl stuck to her cheek. "S'going on? Are we on fire?"

"Not personally, no. Someone probably just pulled the alarm," I said.

I flung open the door and peered out into the hallway, where students were already vacating their apartments—some grumbling and sleepy-looking, others fully dressed and made-up for a night out that hadn't ended yet. I caught sight of Maeve, who waved feebly as she stifled a yawn, her bubblegum-hued hair a wild mane around her face. No one seemed particularly alarmed about the situation, and I couldn't see or smell any smoke. Suddenly, Milo's voice was loud and anxious inside my head.

"Hello, are you awake? Are you hearing that? It sounds like an alarm, but I can't tell which—"

"Milo, I'm awake. Now take it down a notch before my head explodes," I muttered as I closed our door again.

"Okay, sorry. But do you hear—"

"Yeah, it's the fire alarm in our building. We're evacuating. I'll keep you posted."

"Holy shit, there's a fire?" he gasped.

"Milo, what percentage of college fire alarms are actually because of fire?"

"Oh. Right. Good point. Okay, just let me know when you're back inside."

"Will do."

I sighed and pulled on my sneakers, stuffing my keys, my ID, and my phone into the front pocket of my sweatshirt before joining the mass exodus outside. Savvy shuffled along beside me, slapping her own face repeatedly in an attempt to wake up, while I had a visceral flashback to all the times some drunken asshole had pulled the fire alarm back at St. Matt's. It happened at least two or three times per semester, I kept reminding myself as a creeping feeling of disquiet began inching through me. The nervousness must have shown up on my face, too, because Savvy caught my eye and gave me a reassuring slap on the back.

"Probably just some tosser who had a pint too many," she said.

"Yeah, I know."

My phone buzzed in my pocket, and I pulled it out to see that Finn was calling me.

"Hey."

"What's happening up there? Is that a fire alarm?"

"Yeah, the one in our building went off. Where are you?"

"Patrolling the gates between Old and New Campus. Should I come up there?"

"No, no, don't be silly. It's just a stupid alarm. I'll keep you posted."

"Jess, keep your eyes peeled. You're vulnerable outside in the dark, all of you."

"Will do."

I ended the call, but hearing Finn's voice didn't make me feel any better. If anything, the anxiety in his tone had caused the disquiet inside me to continue spreading like a stain. Outside, on the road that ran in front of the dorms, the students stood around in a large crowd, some grumbling and complaining, others goofing off and laughing loudly. I caught sight of several Caomhnóir campus security guards among the students as well, which took just enough of the edge off my anxiety that I could calm my breathing back down to normal. I glanced up at the building we'd just exited, but I couldn't see any sign of fire from out here either. A car full of more campus security pulled up, a blue light flashing obnoxiously on top of the vehicle. The students jeered a bit as they stepped out, but otherwise stayed out of their way as they began to investigate the matter. A few minutes later, a fire truck showed up, which caused the students to break into rowdy applause.

"Bring out the hoses!" a slurred voice shouted, and there was another outbreak of whooping and clapping. Alas, the drunken masses were not to be appeased, and no hoses were rolled out. Several firefighters disappeared into the building, and within another few minutes, the alarm stopped blaring, which brought on another round of cheers, this one from the sober students eager to be allowed back to their beds. It was another ten or fifteen minutes, however, before the firefighters emerged and declared to everyone that the dorm was clear of hazards, and that we could return to our rooms. Sav and I hovered near the back of the group, waiting for the other students to go in ahead of us. I felt like a mother hen, watching anxiously to see that all her chicks made it across the road. I watched the other guards shuffling the crowd toward the doors. A few kids were moving in the opposite direction, but I watched with relief as each of them disappeared one by one into the other dorm buildings in the row. We had just begun to move forward ourselves, when Savvy caught my arm.

"Is that... did you just get a whiff of...?"

I stared at her, at the tense, wide-eyed expression on her face, feeling the numbing pressure of her fingers as she squeezed my arm.

"I don't..." I began, and then cut myself off. I hadn't been focusing on reading the energy—I was too busy watching the edges of the crowd, hoping no one wandered off. But now, as though the wind was carrying it to us from some far-flung corner of the campus, I sensed it: the rot, the decay, the bone-deep cold. It was only a faint impression, like a snatch of music when you can hum the melody but can't remember the words, but it was there.

"He's here," I gasped.

I fumbled for my phone as we turned on the spot, scanning the surging crowd of students as they milled around us, past us—laughing and grumbling and pushing like a many-headed monster in the disorienting flashing lights from the campus security van and the fire truck. Everyone's face looked distorted and strange, every sound threatening. I nearly jumped out of my skin as some kid beside me whooped with liquor-fueled enthusiasm. Finn picked up on the first ring.

"Jess?"

"He's here."

"You saw him?"

"No, but his energy signature—it's unmistakable, Finn. He's here, or he was."

"I'm on my way. Don't do anything rash. Stick close to Savvy."

Savvy was already trying to shove her way through the crowd to the nearest Caomhnóir. I grabbed onto the back of her shirt so I wouldn't lose her. I tried to push through my panic, to concentrate on the energy, to see if I could pick it up again; but between the noise, the crush of bodies, and the strobing lights, I was in sensory overload as it was. Savvy managed to reach one of the other guards, and I watched as she grabbed him by the collar and talked directly into his ear. I watched as the confusion and skepticism melted off his features, replaced by instant military alertness. I watched Savvy's warning travel down the line of guards like the most unfunny game of telephone ever played. She turned back to me.

"Let's get out of the crowd, see if we can pick him up again," she said.

I nodded, and we began shoving against the tide this time. I spotted a mop of pink hair, and tugged Savvy hard to the right.

"Maeve!"

I was relieved to see her and Reilly in the crowd.

"Jess? What's up?"

"He's here. His energy—we both felt it, Sav and I."

Maeve's green-blue eyes went round like saucers. "Up here? But... but the Wards! I thought he couldn't..."

"He might be using someone else—Habitating. I can't go into all of that right now. There's no time. Listen to me, stick with Reilly, get back inside, and lock your door."

"O-okay, if you... but where's Grace? Have you seen her?" She looked at Reilly, who shrugged, and then at me.

I shook my head. "When did you last see her?"

"I don't know. I saw her in the stairwell, but then it got so crowded out here, and she was talking to someone, and we got separated—"

"Then she's probably somewhere in this crowd. I'm sure she's fine. Just get back inside, okay? That's where she'll be heading, too, if she isn't there already."

Maeve bit her lip, looking worried, but did as I told her.

I couldn't spare a thought for Grace Cameron at the moment, not with Alasdair potentially so close. Sav and I fought our way to the outer edge of the crowd, and there it was again, faint but definitely present: Alasdair's energy, poisoning the air. I gagged on it, eyes watering, as I turned slowly in place, trying to understand which direction it was coming from, or if it was just lingering behind.

"Jess?"

The voice was tinny and faint and made me jump, and then I remembered that I'd never ended the call with Finn. I lifted the phone to my ear.

"Where are you? What's happening?"

"We're still just right outside the dorm. The kids are heading back in, but the energy is lingering."

"Don't wander off anywhere! Stay where you are and on your guard, okay?"

I opened my mouth to agree, but the call dropped. I swore loudly, but before I could even try to reconnect, Savvy let out a whole string of curses and took off across the lawn.

"Sav! Where are you going?"

"I just felt it again. It's stronger over here!" she called over her shoulder.

"Sav, wait, I told Finn I wouldn't... oh, screw it," I cried, and took off after her.

I'd only gone a few steps before it hit me too, the rot and sulfur stench burning my nostrils—still not strongly enough that I thought Alasdair was still there, but strongly enough that I knew we were headed in the right direction. This wasn't a days or weeks-old trail like the one Finn and Milo had picked up on their first visit to Kingshurst. This was fresh. The lawn sloped up across from the dorms toward one of the parking lots, dotted with trees and shrubs, and cloaked in deeper darkness now that we'd moved away from the well-lit walks around the buildings. I fumbled with my phone with shaking fingers, trying to turn on the flashlight feature. The tiny beam of light found Savvy still charging ahead of me, muttering under her breath.

"Where are you, you cocking great git?" she hissed between her teeth. For a moment, I allowed myself to imagine that Alasdair still had a body—oh, how satisfying it would have been to watch Savvy tackle the bastard and beat the stuffing out of him. Finn always said it was one of his favorite things about Caomhnóir instruction, watching overconfident Novitiates fall one by one to Savvy's brawling skills.

"Sav, we're supposed to be waiting for Finn!" I called after her.

"What, and let that murdering prick get away? Not bloody likely," Sav replied, charging ahead recklessly, pushing apart the branches and peering into shrubs. "We came all this way to catch him, and I'm not missing a chance to do it."

There was no reasoning with Savvy when she got like this, but I also didn't *want* to reason with her. I wanted to catch Alasdair as badly as she did. Finn was on his way, I rationalized. There were a dozen or more Caomhnóir within shouting distance, and Savvy had already alerted them to the fact that our quarry might be nearby. If we just stood around waiting for Finn to show up, Alasdair could disappear before we even got the chance to track him—hell, it was probably already too late. It was this thought, more than any other, that spurred me forward in Savvy's wake.

We certainly weren't sneaking up on anyone, that was for damn sure, with the way Savvy was stomping across the grass and crashing through the undergrowth. There were several darting beams of light visible from where we searched, and I knew the other Caomhnóir had joined in as well. Suddenly, Savvy's voice rang out, making me jump.

"Oi! There's a curfew on, you know! Piss off back to your rooms before you get yourselves killed!"

The shrub she'd been inspecting burst apart, and a pair of students scurried out of it, hastily rearranging their clothing, and snorting with laughter. I came to a stop alongside her, panting in an effort to keep up with her.

"What's the point of making rules to keep these kids safe if they're just going to break them all, eh?" she muttered.

The fact that Savannah Todd was asking this question was without a doubt the most ironic thing I had ever witnessed; but before I could open my mouth to tell her that, I was hit with another wave of Alasdair's foul energy, stronger this time than before. Savvy's face contracted in disgust, and I knew she sensed it, too, beating like a pulse somewhere nearby. Without a word, we both took off in the direction it seemed to be coming from, leading us onward like a trail of poisonous breadcrumbs.

We stepped around a small copse of trees, and Savvy stopped short, throwing out an arm to keep me back.

"What? What is it?" I asked her in a whisper.

She didn't reply, only jerked her head in the direction she was looking. I followed her gaze.

There was a shape huddled on the ground.

God, please, no. This couldn't be happening again.

We both moved forward more carefully now, Savvy's head turning like it was on a swivel, senses heightened and alert to the slightest possibility of danger. With every step forward, Alasdair's energy grew stronger, and yet my instincts were telling me he wasn't here. Not anymore.

Because we were already too late.

Our flashlight beams landed on the bottom of a foot, bare and dirty, a slipper cast off beside it. The light slid up a pajama-clad leg, a sweatshirted torso, and a pale, outstretched hand. For one wild moment, I thought the figure had no head; but then my brain caught up with my eyes, and I realized that the head was completely covered in a curtain of sleek black hair, obscuring everything from the neck up.

Everything inside me froze, as panic flooded me. My knees turned to water and I sank to the ground, my phone falling from my hand to lie forgotten in the grass. With desperate grasping thoughts like scrabbling fingers, I pried the Connection open.

"Milo."

"Jess? What's happening? Are you okay?"

"Is Tia with you?"

"What?"

"Tia! Where is she? Please tell me she is with you right now!"

The fear twanged every thread connecting us like a badly tuned guitar so that I winced from the sensation of it.

"Of course, she's here! I haven't taken my eyes off her!"

The fear refused to relinquish its grip.

"Are you sure?"

"Jess, I'm looking at her right now. I promise. What's going on?"

I simply opened myself up to him so that he could see what I was seeing in real time. His fear spiked and blended with mine inside the Connection, a discordant melody of terror.

"I'm coming," he said.

"No! Stay with Tia, I am begging you."

"You're not alone, are you?"

"No. Savvy is here. And other Caomhnóir, too. Finn's on his way. Just please, if you love me, stay with Tia."

There was a moment of twisting indecision, and then, "Okay. But keep the Connection open. I want to know what's going on."

I struggled to pull myself out of the Connection, leaving it propped like a door, and emerged to find Savvy creeping forward toward the figure on the ground.

"Hello? Are you all right? Do you need help?" she was saying in a cracked and hopeless voice that told me she already knew the answer. She knelt and reached for the girl's wrist, as I had seen Finn do when we found Helen O'Rourke. Her expression as she looked back at me a few seconds later was just as grim. She shook her head.

I fought a wave of nausea and staggered to my feet, forcing them forward, step by reluctant step, until I stood beside Savvy, who was getting to her feet and looking as sick as I felt. She clapped a hand on my shoulder, and then started waving and shouting toward the shapes of two Caomhnóir, maybe thirty yards away.

"Oi! We've got something over here!" she was calling as she jogged toward them.

I didn't follow her. I sank back to my knees beside the girl and, pulling my hand inside my sweatshirt to avoid contaminating the crime scene, swept the hair back to reveal her face.

It was Grace Cameron. Her eyes were wide in her purplish face, pupils blown out to the size of coins, her mouth open in a scream no one would ever hear, thanks to the scrap of silk wound tightly around her throat. In the grass near her outstretched hand were three drops of candle wax, each one a perfectly smooth circle. An indentation on her right middle finger showed that a ring usually sat there, but it was now gone.

A hand fell lightly on my shoulder, and I jumped. I hadn't heard anyone approaching.

"It's me, love," came Finn's tentative voice; and I exhaled, the breath whooshing out of me like a popped balloon.

"We're too late," I said, my voice thick with repressed tears. "She's dead."

"Let's move away now," Finn replied softly. "The guards are coming. We should give them space to collect evidence."

I didn't think I could will myself to stand. Everything was numb. But luckily, I didn't have to. Finn took hold of my arm, put me on my feet again, and then pulled me gently away from Grace's cooling body.

"I told you to wait for me," Finn said, but there was no anger or frustration in his voice. Only weariness.

"I tried. Sav took off. She... she didn't want to miss the chance to..." My stomach roiled again, and I staggered away from him before heaving all of my stomach contents out onto the dewy grass. When I had finished, both Savvy and Finn were standing beside Grace's body, along with three other Caomhnóir. I could also see a vehicle moving toward us over the grass, headlights cutting the darkness like knives.

"It was the fire alarm," I said, panting a little and wiping my mouth with the back of my hand. "He must have used it to get everyone outside. And then he lured her away from the crowd somehow. Was anyone else spotted?"

Finn shook his head. "Not that I've heard. It was all quiet down by Old

Campus gates. It was madness for him to do this so close to the crowd, with so many people around. Someone must have seen something."

"Maeve was looking for her," I said, my voice choked. "When they started letting people back into the building, she asked me if I'd seen Grace and I... I told her she'd probably already gone back inside."

"Jess, don't. It was already too late. There's nothing you could have done," Finn said, though I could hear the sharp undertone in his voice—the guilt slicing through him, the knowledge that he was in the wrong place at the wrong time, again, and that Alasdair had once again eluded them.

"Where's Rana?" Savvy asked in a cracked voice.

"She's still patrolling the gates with the rest of the shift," Finn said.

Savvy didn't say another word, simply stalked off in the direction of Old Campus. Finn didn't try to stop her. He just let her go, recognizing, perhaps, that familiar guilty anger in her stride. As for me, I thought of Rana's long black hair and wondered if Savvy had been, for an instant, as terrified as I was about who exactly was lying on the ground.

"Are you all right?" he asked, turning to me.

"Yeah, I just need a minute," I said hoarsely. I suddenly felt worn out and exhausted, like I'd aged a hundred years in the time it took the adrenaline to drain out of my body.

He handed me a flask from his pocket, and I raised an eyebrow.

"Don't be daft. It's water," he said, with just the merest trace of a smile. "Though we could all probably use something a bit stronger right now. I'm going to check in with these other guards, okay?"

I nodded, and he walked away, back toward the body I could no longer bear to look at. I unscrewed the cap on the flask and took a shaky drink, dribbling water down my chin. I closed my eyes, breathing deeply, and opened them again.

A shadow in the nearby trees shifted, solidified, and resolved itself into something more. The flask slipped forgotten from my fingers as I took a single step toward it, squinting into the darkness. Were my eyes playing tricks on me in my distress, or... no. There it was—the figure in the black cloak, watching me.

I couldn't explain why I was so calm as I stared back. I probably should have shouted at the top of my lungs, but I didn't. No one else had noticed—or perhaps no one else could see. I shoved all of my tangled emotions aside and cleared a mental space.

The last time I saw it, I wasn't close enough to take in any details. Now, I let my eyes rake carefully over the cloak itself, undamaged and whole, with a silver bird clasp gleaming at the throat.

He was a member of the Brotherhood then but not a living one, as I had suspected.

The realization was a staggering one, but I didn't allow it to distract me. Now that I knew it was a spirit, I concentrated hard, and it was only then that I began to understand why no one else had sensed it as soon as it appeared. The energy was... there was no other way to explain it... *incomplete.*

There was an edge to it that smacked of spirit energy, but it was as shrouded in mystery as the figure itself was shrouded in that cloak. Something about it was familiar, and I fumbled through my sense memory to try to understand why. Where had I felt this kind of strange signature before? It was a spirit, but not. Human, but not. And, most distressingly of all, it exuded an aura of pain and sadness which, now that I had picked up on it, was almost overwhelming. And then it clicked.

The Collection. The Collection felt like this. Incomplete and painful and... and *wrong.*

I took a single, small step toward the figure, afraid to spook it, but it stayed right where it was, face obscured in the deep nest of shadows inside the hood. I couldn't see its eyes, but I knew they were watching me. I couldn't see a mouth, and yet I felt as sure that this figure was calling out to me as I was sure of my own name. But why couldn't I hear it?

"Who are you?" I whispered.

The figure shifted slightly but did not reply. Or maybe it did, and I couldn't understand. I didn't hear anything, nor did the answer drop into my head, as it had sometimes done with other spirits. Instead, there was a sort of warping of the air around me, a momentary muffling of sound that seemed designed to prevent me from hearing the answer. It made me dizzy, and I was forced to close my eyes again to steady myself. When I opened them a moment later, the figure was still there, unmoving.

I tried again. "Who are you? Do you have a name?"

It happened again. The warping of the air, the bending of sound, preventing the answer from reaching me. This time my head spun so badly I had to reach out and steady myself on the nearest tree trunk. This time, the question tumbled from me before I even decided to ask it.

"What happened to you?"

The figure lifted its head. A hand reached for the hood to pull it back.

Reality bent around me. My eyes rolled into the back of my head. Everything went black.

16

UNANSWERED QUESTIONS

"Jess, I'm so sorry."

I lay in the quiet dark of the bedroom. Morning had broken, but the blinds and curtains had been pulled closed to protect me from it.

The voice was Hannah's, and it came to me through the Connection, defying the boundaries of the sanctuary that had been so carefully constructed around me. To protect me.

As if protection was possible when the real horror was inside my head, waiting for me the moment I woke.

The Wards around the room were so fresh they were practically pulsating with energy. Likely Finn, in a storm of frustration and fear, had re-Cast them. I had no solid memory of getting back to the flat, just the impression of being cradled against Finn's chest as he murmured to me, and a hazy snatch or two of conversation.

"...what caused her to pass out?"

"The shock, I expect. That's the second dead body she's seen in three days."

They'd left me to rest, and instead, I'd dreamed—dreamed so vividly that when at last consciousness seized me, I felt wrung out, limp, and empty. Hannah had been waiting for me in my head, not probing or nudging, just patiently waiting for me to wake.

"I am too," I said silently. I shifted, pulling my pinned arm out from under me, and feeling the dead weight of it start prickling to life again as the blood flowed back through. I groaned. "Who told you?"

"Milo, of course," Hannah replied. "Who else?"

Who, indeed? I was grateful. I really didn't want to recount the night. Living through it once was enough.

"He said you passed out. Are you sure you're okay?"

"Yeah. I mean, I think so. It was just the shock of... oh."

The memory was still caught in the clutches of sleep. I pried it free and pieced it together.

"There was a figure... a ghost, but not a ghost."

"A ghost but not a ghost?" Hannah repeated, and I felt her confusion humming in my aching head. "What does that mean?"

"It means... okay, can you remember what the energy around the Collection feels like?"

Hannah's answer shuddered with horror. "Yes, unfortunately."

"It's spirit energy, and yet it isn't. Right? Like, it's... incomplete."

"It's what he's done to those spirits!" Hannah's anger clanged like a gong, and I winced. "He's mangled them, torn them to pieces! That's why their energy is so... so... hang on. Are you saying this figure has the same kind of energy?"

"Something like it, yeah," I said. "And he's appeared twice now, both times just after someone has been murdered. And that cloak he's wearing? It's identical to the ones the Brotherhood of Circe used to wear."

"So, the ghost was a member of the Brotherhood?"

"Apparently. I don't really know how else to interpret it."

"You've been saying all along that you were worried that Alasdair had an ally, but you were talking about a living person. Do you think this spirit is involved?" she asked.

"If you're asking if I think the figure murdered Grace and Helen, no. I don't. It was more like he was... keeping watch."

"Keeping watch."

"Yeah. Or... standing guard? I don't know. I can't explain it. My head hurts."

"Did you try communicating with him?" Hannah pressed.

It wasn't until Hannah asked me that question that I remembered the very last second or two before I lost consciousness.

"I was trying to, but something was wrong. It was almost..." I frowned, digging through memories, sifting for that glimmer of recognition. "It was almost like he was Caged." I felt relief at the realization. "The responses were getting warped and lost, and then he tried to show me who he was. He pulled back his hood and...and I passed out."

"What was under the hood?" The question reached so tentatively across the space between us that I almost missed it.

"I don't know," I admitted. "If I saw it, I don't remember."

I felt Hannah's disappointment, a sinking feeling pressing down on me.

"I wish I was there with you," she said at last.

"I don't," I said, and I felt the hurt zing through our heads. "Not that I don't want to see you," I amended quickly. "I mean, I don't want anyone here. I'd evacuate the campus if Clarissa would let me."

"No, of course. I understand," Hannah said, the thought like a sigh. "I'd feel better about being here if I felt like we were making any progress."

"What have you been doing?" I asked, grateful for a chance to talk about anything but last night.

"Sifting through accounts of Necromancer magic, mostly, looking for anything that might be related to the Collection. Flavia's been a marvelous help, especially with translating the Traveler Durupinen accounts on the shelf here."

I'd nearly forgotten that Flavia was also at Skye Príosún. "Flavia must be in her glory, finally getting free rein in that archive."

Hannah gave a gentle chuckle. "She is rather enthused, yes. But so far, we've turned up absolutely nothing worth our time. Though, I suppose Polly would disagree."

"Polly?"

"The head Scribe here? You met her when we—"

"Oh, I remember now. Sorry, I totally spaced. What about her?" I asked.

"She's just a bit... intense. You remember she told us she's the official historian for our clan?"

"Oh, right. Yeah, she did seem a little... fangirl-ish?"

"Well, whenever I'm not actively working, she bombards me with questions. She's trying to flesh out her work on the Reckoning. Apparently, she's been desperate to interview us both about it for months, but Celeste told her to back off."

"Celeste? Really? Why?"

"I don't know. I suppose she thought we were being harassed enough over the whole affair."

"Huh. Well, she's not wrong." I suppressed a thought about the rock hurled through the window. I hadn't told Hannah about that particular bit of nastiness, mostly because it felt superfluous to the reason we were here; but also because I didn't want her to worry any more than she already was. It felt like one more distraction to throw us off track.

But now the thought of the harassment brought Grace Cameron right to the forefront of my mind again, and all I could picture was her body curled in the grass—the fear frozen forever in her eyes, wondering what the last thing was that she saw before she saw nothing at all. I pictured it all in detail again, and I felt Hannah gasp as those vivid thoughts transferred seamlessly into her own mind.

"Sorry," I said. "I couldn't help it. I didn't want you to have to see that, but I couldn't stop mys—"

"Jess, what was that on the ground?"

"Huh?"

"Right next to Grace's body, in the grass. There were these three little circles."

It took me a second to remember what she was talking about. "Oh, yeah. It was wax. White candle wax. Three perfect drops. We found them next to Helen's body too, but we never figured out what it—"

"I've got to go!" The thought was twanging with anxiety.

"What is it?"

"I just had an idea, and if it's... oh my goodness... I have to go check something!"

"I... okay. But what is it?"

"It might be nothing. It might be everything. I... I'll be back!"

And with that, the Connection practically slammed shut.

"Ooookay," I muttered. I couldn't think what the significance of the wax might be, but if Hannah had an idea, it was probably a good idea to let her go investigate it. Besides, I'd avoided reality long enough. It was time to face whatever was waiting for me on the other side of the bedroom door.

The absence of Hannah seemed only to make more space in my head for the headache that was now knocking against the inside my skull. I felt hungover. I popped two extra-strength painkillers and chugged most of a bottle of water someone had left by the bed for me, and then eased the door open into the common room.

It was like walking in on a funeral. Savvy, Rana, Finn, Maeve, and Reilly were all sitting in the common room, along with another Caomhnóir whose name I had been told and immediately forgotten, but who I recognized as having been there when we found Helen O'Rourke. Every pair of eyes turned to stare at me as I walked in, and I felt the blood rising to my cheeks.

"Hey, sorry to sleep so long," I mumbled as I crossed to the sofa, where Finn and Rana had shifted to make room for me.

"Don't apologize. You needed rest, love," Finn said, as I nestled into the crook of his arm.

"I think we have all the information we need for now," the Caomhnóir said, standing up even as I sat. "I'll be in touch." We all watched him go in silence before I turned on Finn.

"Did you tell him he'd have to leave when I woke up?"

"It was more of a direct threat of bodily harm, actually," Savvy said, smirking.

"I didn't want him harassing you. I don't like his attitude. He's a MacLeod cousin, so he thinks he's inherently more important than everyone here, when he's really just a jumped-up little git riding his family's coattails," Finn said.

A sniffing sound caught my attention, and I glanced over at Maeve. She looked terrible. Her eyes and nose were red and swollen from crying, and she sat huddled with her knees tucked up inside what I could only assume was Reilly's sweatshirt, because it had basically swallowed her whole. Reilly had an arm around her, and every tear that rolled down her cheek seemed to compound his misery as well. I could tell that he felt helpless watching her cry and knowing he couldn't do anything to help.

"Maeve, I'm so sorry about Grace," I said.

Maeve shook her head, her expression lost and miserable. "It just doesn't make sense. We were separated for... what, half an hour? Forty-five minutes? How could she just be... *gone*?"

Beside me, I watched Finn's hands curl into white-knuckled fists and relax again.

"And she knew better!" Maeve cried, her voice shrill in frustration. "She knew we weren't supposed to wander about alone at night! She knew the dangers, or she should have! What could have possessed her? I'm so angry with her one second, and then angry with myself the next, because how can I blame her for what someone else did to her?"

Maeve dissolved once again into tears.

"I keep trying to convince her to go home, but she won't do it," Reilly mumbled, as Maeve sobbed into his shoulder. "She wants to stay and help."

"What kind of help am I? I couldn't even keep my own roommate safe!" Maeve's voice was muffled and almost unintelligible.

"That wasn't your job," Reilly said. "There are dozens of guards on the scene, and even they couldn't stop what happened last night. You can't keep beating yourself up over this."

"Oh, I certainly can," came Maeve's petulant reply, though she seemed to make an effort to calm herself after that.

"How are you feeling, mate?" Savvy asked, and I noticed that she was looking at me with some concern.

"She's been in a right state over you since last night," Rana added, affectionately rubbing Savvy's arm.

I tried to smile, but I could tell the result was pathetic. "I'm okay, really. More embarrassed than anything else."

"Why would you be embarrassed? You found two dead bodies in three days. That would be enough to make anyone lose consciousness," Rana said.

"Thanks, Rana, but that wasn't actually the reason," I said, and explained about the shrouded spirit I'd seen near Grace's body.

"The same figure from Helen O'Rourke's murder?" Finn asked. He was sitting up straight now, all trace of exhaustion gone.

"I'm pretty sure," I said, nodding. "I didn't get close enough last time to see whether it was a living person or a ghost, but this time I did. It's a spirit, and the cloak was definitely identical to those worn by the Brotherhood."

"The ghost of a Brotherhood member? You're sure?"

"It's the only explanation that makes sense. But... it's not a normal spirit."

Finn's expression crumpled into a frown of concentration. "Define normal."

I explained the figure's strange energy and how the world around him seemed to warp and distort so that I couldn't understand him.

"That sounds a bit like Caging," Finn said. "Do you think he's been Caged?"

I pressed the heels of my hands to my eyeballs, and watched the colors and patterns burst behind my eyelids, forcing myself to dig deeply into my memories. "Yes, and no. On the one hand, it reminds me of the Silent Child's struggles to communicate. The way her attempts to talk to me met these invisible barriers— the way the atmosphere would literally warp around us, preventing the words from reaching me. But even with that barrier, it was always clear that she was a spirit. Her energy, her presence, it was... complete. This spirit... there's something very, very wrong with him. It reminds me of the Collection. It's the same sort of energy—almost... deconstructed."

Rana shuddered. Savvy swore under her breath.

"And the cloak?" Finn asked. "You're sure it's the same?"

I nodded. "I saw the clasp this time. It's silver, shaped like a bird, and identical to the cloak in the collection of artifacts from the Brotherhood."

"So there's a spirit of a member of the Brotherhood lurking on this campus, and he only shows himself at the sites of the murders," Finn said, the agitation propelling him up off the couch and into a pattern of pacing around the room. "What the hell does it *mean*?"

"It felt like he wanted to communicate with me. I could feel the intention, but not the message. Does that make sense?" I asked.

"That certainly sounds like a Caging to me," Rana murmured, and then, when we all looked at her, her face flushed with embarrassment. "I mean, from what I've heard. I've never actually seen one in real life."

"There's only one reason to Cage a spirit, and that's to stop them from interacting with living people," Finn said. "Maybe this spirit knows something, and the Brotherhood Caged him to keep him from talking?"

"Sounds exactly like the kind of thing that tosser Alasdair would do," Savvy said.

"So the question is, is this spirit in league with Alasdair, or is he working against him?" Rana asked.

"Well, if he can't communicate, we aren't likely to find out," Finn said.

"I wonder if he's one of those resident spirits everyone knows about, like the Silent Child was back at Fairhaven," Savvy said thoughtfully. "We could ask around Old Campus, see if anyone knows who he is."

The words "Old Campus" set off alarm bells in my head. "Wait... the Wards!"

"What about them?" Finn asked.

"I thought the whole point of the Wards at Kingshurst was to contain the spirits to Old Campus, where the only students they'd be interacting with are Durupinen and Caomhnóir. So how is this spirit getting onto New Campus at all?" I asked.

My question was met with nothing but blank stares and shrugs, and I couldn't help but feel this realization only proved my point about this spirit. He wasn't a typical ghost—his strange energy, his ability to manifest where he shouldn't, and the disorienting warping of reality when he tried to communicate all supported my theory. Just like the Collection was inherently wrong, this spirit was wrong, too—very, very, wrong.

Finn's phone buzzed, and he fumbled it out of his pocket to answer it. He listened intently for a few moments, threw a bewildered glance to the kitchen area, and then said, "Okay. We'll be right there."

"What's going on?" I asked.

Finn ended the call. "We've been asked to come down to the campus security office. They found out who pulled the fire alarm. Also, they said..." He hesitated, glancing at the kitchen again.

"What, Finn?" I asked, somewhat snappishly. "What did they say?"

"They said, whatever we do, don't open the fridge."

"Tell us about the rats."

We were sitting in the campus security office across from two girls who were sniffing and sobbing into wads of damp tissues clutched in their hands. They looked almost identical to each other, with long, highlighted hair parted in the middle, hanging in gently curled curtains on either side of their faces. Their eye makeup ran in smoky black rivulets down their perfectly contoured faces. They both kept stealing glances at my face, as though petrified to look directly at me for more than a few seconds.

"It was Grace's idea!" the slightly taller girl—Chelsea, I think her name was —wailed. "Right, Caroline?"

"Oh, for God's sake, Chelsea, we can't blame it all on Grace just because she's dead!" Caroline snapped. Chelsea dissolved into tears as Caroline went on, sniffling. "It was my idea. We were all sitting around, like. Trying to come up with something we could do to scare her off."

"Scare who off?" asked the Caomhnóir questioning them. He had a face like a bulldog.

Caroline's eyes darted to me again. "Her. The Ballard girl. We... we were trying to... to freak her out."

"And why would you want to do that?" bulldog-face pressed.

Caroline's face was practically fuscia now. "Well, she... she ruined everything, didn't she? With the Gateways?" She said it with a knowing look, like she expected the Caomhnóir to agree with her wholeheartedly. All he did was glare at her for a moment, and then jot a few words in his notebook. "Go on," he said.

"Well, like I said, we wanted to come up with something really good," Caroline said. "And I'm a biology major, and I made a joke, like... what if we stole a bunch of frozen rats from the lab and... and left them in her flat?"

Finn made a sound of disgust through his nose. Caroline threw him a frightened look.

"I said it as a joke," Caroline insisted. "I didn't think anyone would actually want to do it because...ew. But then Grace said it was a brilliant idea, and everyone got really excited about it."

"So, just to be clear, were you responsible for the graffiti on the door? And also the rock through the window?" I asked.

Caroline flushed again, tears welling up. "Chelsea and her roommate graffitied while Grace and I were the lookouts," she said. Chelsea whipped her head around to glare at her friend, but said nothing. "And Grace painted the rock, but she got one of her Caomhnóir friends to throw it. She... she was afraid she'd hit the wrong window."

The Caomhnóir made a note, and gestured to Caroline to proceed.

"I stole the rats from the lab and brought them back to the dorm," Caroline said. "We didn't want to get caught, though, so Grace came up with the idea of pulling the fire alarm. It was the only way to make sure that their flat was empty, and that no one else would catch us while we were coming in or out. The plan was for Grace to pull the alarm and then—"

"Wait, you're saying that Grace Cameron pulled the fire alarm?" I asked. Finn caught my eye, looking as flummoxed as I felt. I was sure that Alasdair's accomplice—whoever they were—had pulled the alarm to drive students outside and find a victim. But clearly, Grace Cameron couldn't have been the accomplice *and* the victim.

"Yeah," Caroline went on, squirming uncomfortably under all of the questions. "She was supposed to pull it, follow you all out, and text us when you were outside. Then we went in the flat and... and left the rats in the refrigerator."

I turned to Finn. "Our fridge is full of frozen dead lab rats?"

"Oh, they're not frozen anymore," Finn said with a humorless smile. "They've fully defrosted."

"How did you get into the flat?" I asked, turning on the two girls, who looked terrified at the fact that I was speaking to them directly. "I locked the door behind me."

"We... we swiped a master key from the custodial office," Chelsea gulped, before bursting into noisy tears again.

"But we already put it back," Caroline added quickly.

The Caomhnóir sighed and made another scribble in his notebook. "Okay, so you left the rats. Then what?"

"We went down the back staircase into the quad and walked around the front of the building to try to blend in with everyone else. We were supposed to text Grace when we made it out, but she... she never... never responded." Caroline dropped her head into her folded arms and began to cry hysterically again.

The Caomhnóir opened his mouth to ask another question, but Finn held out a hand, his eyes on the top of the girl's head. "Give her a minute," he murmured, and we sat in silence for a few minutes while her torrent of emotion ran its course. When she sat up again, hiccupping and wiping her eyes, Finn took over the questioning.

"Did you look for Grace at all when she didn't reply?"

Chelsea nodded, venturing an answer as Caroline dabbed at her eyes. "We went all through the crowd expecting to see her, but we couldn't find her anywhere."

"We tried to call her, too," Caroline added. "Then, when the guards gave the all-clear, we went back up to her room to wait for her, but she... she never..."

And that was the official end of any coherence from the two girls, who lost all semblance of control at that point, and buried themselves in each other's identical hair as they cried.

"Would you like us to report this harassment incident to the Dean?" the Caomhnóir asked us, as we were walking out of the office.

I shook my head. "Just let it go. They've been through enough. Just... can you send a couple of guys over to get rid of the rats, please?"

The Caomhnóir shrugged as though he had no real intention of following through on the request, and shuffled away as we started walking in the direction of Old Campus.

"What do you reckon, then?" Finn asked as soon as we were out of earshot.

I sighed. "I was so sure Alasdair and his accomplice pulled that fire alarm. I mean, it makes perfect sense. Prepare for the crime, draw the potential victims out into the open, and then strike. But now?" I shook my head. "How is it possible he just happened to be there, ready and waiting in just the right place to murder another victim?"

"Yes, that is strange," Finn said, chewing on his lip as he thought. "And I don't believe for a second that either of those girls have anything to do with Alasdair. They seem too genuinely traumatized to lie."

"Of course they're traumatized. Hell, I'm traumatized, and I only had two social interactions with the girl, both of which were deeply unpleasant." I paused here, a feeling welling up inside me that stopped me in my tracks.

"What's up?" Finn asked, when he realized I wasn't with him anymore.

"I just... when I first saw Grace lying there, all I could see was her hair. It was just this... curtain of black hair, and all I could think was, 'Oh my God, it's Tia. Somehow, someway, he found the one person on this campus whose death would destroy me, and he killed her. And then I... I realized it wasn't her and I... I felt... *grateful.*"

The last word burst out of me on a tidal wave of tears. Finn said nothing. He simply wrapped his arms around me and held me together while I did my damnedest to fall apart.

"Who does that?" I sobbed. "What kind of terrible person looks at a dead body and has a thought like that? Like, literally, what is wrong with me?"

"There is nothing wrong with you," Finn spoke at last. "Of course you were relieved that your best friend was still alive, Jess. That's the most natural thing in the world. It doesn't mean you were happy it was Grace Cameron."

"You're just saying that to make me feel better," I mumbled, my face still buried in his shirt.

Finn chuckled. "You are such a stubborn creature, aren't you? All right then, how's this for a confession? When I made it up to New Campus, I asked one of the Caomhnóir what was happening, and he said, 'Someone said there's another body.' And I said a prayer that it was anyone but you. And I kept praying it, over and over again, until I found you, and even with Grace Cameron lying right there in front of us, all I could think was, 'Thank God.'"

I stilled against his chest, listening to the steady beating of his heart.

"If you're a terrible person, then so am I," he concluded. "So I leave it up to you, my love. Am I a terrible person, or are you being entirely too hard on yourself?"

"This feels like a trap," I said.

"Well good, because that's exactly what it is. You want to find a way to blame yourself in all this, and I'm not going to let you any more than you're going to let me take the blame. We all know who the monster is here. Let's not lose sight of it."

I finally felt calm enough to lift my face up out of his shirt, now stained with the evidence of my meltdown. I looked up at him. "Where did you get so much annoyingly healthy perspective all of a sudden? Just a few days ago, you were beating yourself up about this whole situation."

"I'm not really sure, if I'm honest. I suppose I just realized that I can't lose focus on who the enemy is. Every time we turn those feelings inward, Alasdair claims a tiny victory, and those little victories can take a big toll. So, I refuse to help him win."

I stretched up onto my tiptoes to kiss him, but suddenly—

"Jess! Jess! Are you there!"

"Ow! Yes! Of course I'm here! It's my head!" I cried, as Hannah's voice came crashing through the Connection like the Kool-Aid man.

Finn looked curiously down at me. "Hannah?" he mouthed.

I barely managed to nod as Hannah's excited thoughts tumbled over one another in what felt like a race to get inside my head.

"I figured it out! At least, I think I did. Oh, I hope I did. I guess it's still possible that I... but it makes so much sense!"

"Hannah, please try to calm down. I feel like I'm being assaulted here."

"Sorry, sorry!" I felt the shift in her, how she pulled back a bit, how she tried to get a hold of a whole thought before she let it come through. At last, she had calmed down just enough that I could understand her.

"It was the wax."

"The... wax?"

"That you found near the bodies! When you mentioned it, this lightbulb went off, and I realized... the connection was right there, but I never saw it!"

"You've lost me again. What connection? Between what?"

"Between the Collection and Blind Summoners!"

I felt like I'd been slapped in the face. I had all but forgotten about Blind Summoners, probably because I tried to keep my memories of darker Castings well-repressed, and Blind Summoners were some of the darkest magic I'd ever seen.

"Explain."

"Well, think about it. The Blind Summoner Casting begins by dividing the spirit from itself—driving the essence from the shell, essentially," Hannah said. I can feel the pain behind the words, bleeding through. She had once been manipulated into using that Casting, and the results were nearly catastrophic. Still, she plowed forward. "And then part of the soul is trapped in the flame, and the other part is yours to control."

"Okay, I guess I kind of see how it's similar to the Collection, but—"

"Wait, Jess, there's more. The Blind Summoner Casting wasn't a Durupinen Casting, remember? It was Necromancer magic. Lucida only knew it because she was in league with them."

My mind spiraled back to Edinburgh, when Danica told me about Alasdair and his Necromancer influences. How he had sought them out, learned from them, and then left when he felt their ideas didn't go far enough...

"You think Alasdair learned that same Casting from the Necromancers, and then..."

"And then bastardized it, yes! He reinvented it to suit his own vile purposes! What used to be a Casting that painlessly divided essence from shell became a Casting that sliced through a spirit like a knife, hacking off whatever it could get." Hannah's thoughts were literally vibrating with all of the rage she was trying so hard to contain.

"Look, I think you're probably right, Hannah. But even if you are, how does knowing about this connection help us? He's obviously majorly changed the Casting. How can we combat it if we don't even know how he's changed it?"

"I'm not entirely sure yet, but there are parts of the old Casting there—the three drops of white wax? He's still using a white candle to trap some part of the spirit, although he's not picky about what part. And remember the trinkets he's taking from the bodies?"

"You mean the trophies? Yeah, I'm not likely to forget."

"Okay, so he's got one part of the soul in the candle, which goes out when he consumes it. He has to trap the remaining part of the soul, but the flame is spent. So, he binds the partial soul to a second object, an object they will feel drawn to in their confusion. Then he takes that remaining part back home and adds it to the Collection, like... like he's putting goddamn leftovers in the fridge to save for later."

It was a rare thing indeed for Hannah to swear. Our rage was co-mingling inside my head, buzzing like angry bees trapped in every thought that zipped back and forth between us.

"Okay, assuming you're right—and I think there's every possibility you are —now what?"

"Now I'm going back to Edinburgh," Hannah announced.

"Wait, what? You're leaving?!" I said this out loud, and Finn started.

"Jess, I have to! This is the breakthrough I've been looking for. I'm going to dig up everything I can about the history of Blind Summoners, and then I'm going back to Edinburgh to unmake that Collection."

There was hope in her voice for the first time in weeks. I couldn't bear to dampen it with any of my own doubts or worries. She needed to try, and I had to let her.

"Good luck. Stay in touch with me, please."

I felt Hannah's surprise. "You're just going to let me leave?"

"You think I can stop you?" I asked with an edge of amusement.

"Well, no, but I did have a whole big, long speech planned to convince you it was a good idea," she admitted.

I laughed. "You don't need to convince me. You have to try. You might be the only person alive who's used that Casting. I doubt you'll find anyone who understands it better in practice. So, go. Those spirits need you."

"Okay. I will. And Jess?"

"Yeah?"

"Be careful."

I felt the lump in my throat, but I ignored it. "You, too."

17

DESPERATE

There was no more hiding the fact that there was a killer on campus. The Dean of Students and Clarissa MacLeod could concoct whatever cover story they liked. Still, the fact remained that two female students had been killed in a matter of three days, and no amount of explanations or excuses could convince anyone that it was merely a coincidence. The deaths were all anyone could talk about. They whispered about it across lunch tables. They speculated about it on comment threads. They obsessed about it over forgotten textbooks and neglected assignments. Still, Clarissa stubbornly refused to close the campus or send students home, despite the fact that her own daughter could easily be next.

"I wouldn't leave in any case," Maeve said, arms crossed over her chest, and a truculent expression on her face that made her look every inch her mother's daughter. "If the rest of the kids have to stay, then I'm staying, too; and my mother can lose as much sleep over it as she chooses. I just hope she has to come face to face with Dominique Cameron someday soon."

"I'm more concerned that Grace's death will turn the Council Clans into some kind of vigilante justice mob," Finn had confided, after hearing Maeve's thoughts on the matter.

As for me, I couldn't spare a single thought about what the fallout for Clarissa might be, or whether the Council Clans would find a way to blame this whole situation on me. I was singularly focused on making sure that what happened to Grace and Helen couldn't happen to anyone else. I spent the rest of the day up at the scene of the latest crime, crawling on my hands and knees in the grass and underbrush, looking for any tiny clue the killer might have left behind that could help us identify them. We had to cordon off the area to prevent the crowds of morbidly curious students from trampling all over the crime scene, and they set up a makeshift memorial to Grace along the barrier: a heap of stuffed animals and flowers and candles and signs that drooped and disintegrated under the slow, gray drizzle that fell all day long, turning the ground muddy and washing away our hopes of further clues.

Savvy and Rana spent the day on Old Campus, questioning the living and dead alike about the mysterious, black-robed spirit who had appeared at both murder scenes. But there, too, we came up on a dead end.

"It's like he never existed before three nights ago," Savvy said, as she peeled off her boots and damp socks back in the flat that night. "Not a single spirit knew who we were talking about. Mind you, half of them have gone round the twist."

"They're not crazy, Sav," Rana said, rolling her eyes. "They've just been in spirit form so long they get confused."

"Six of one, half dozen of the other, I say," Sav replied with a shrug. "If you can't remember your own name or even the fact that you're dead, that counts as barmy in my book."

Milo came to check in, looking as drained as the rest of us. "Has anyone heard from Hannah? I've popped into the Connection a few times, but she hasn't left it open."

I'd told everyone about Hannah's plan to return to Edinburgh. Only Savvy, with her natural optimism, seemed to think she'd be successful in her quest to unmake the Collection.

"It's easy to forget it because she's such a meek little slip of a thing, but that girl's the most powerful Durupinen there is. If she thinks she can sort it, then I consider it sorted."

It wasn't possible for the rest of us to feel so confident. The Blind Summoner connection was definitely an interesting lead, but I still wasn't convinced it would be enough to undo a Casting we didn't fully understand.

"She's experimenting with an experiment," Milo said, his manifestation wavering with the power of his anxiety. "There are just so many ways that could go wrong."

"You think I should have stopped her?" I asked.

Milo snorted. "Oh, sweetness. You could have tried, but what would have been the point? Hannah's ideas aren't just ideas. They're inevitabilities. I don't think we've got any choice but to let her try."

Personally, I still thought the best way to deal with Alasdair's litany of offenses was to find him before he could add another to the list. Once we had him in captivity, I thought it might just be possible to get enough information out of him to undo what damage we could. But of course, there were things we could never fix. Helen and Grace, for example, would never be going home again; and we would have to live with that.

All pretense of secrecy was now over. Old Campus was swarming with Caomhnóir in full uniform, combing the grounds and buildings even as students milled in and out of them, brimming with curiosity, but meeting stony silence any time they asked what was going on. Finn, in the meantime, had taken possession of the journals Gareth had tried to squirrel away in his office. Despite Gareth's insistence that they were helpful, Finn could find no real concrete clue about how to find the sanctum within their sooty and largely illegible pages.

"I have to say, from what I can make out, this Brotherhood was little more than performative," he said, rubbing at his neck and shoulders as he took a much-needed break from poring over the journals. "They discuss these elaborate rituals, but none of them are actual Castings, at least as far as I can tell. They are more a series of loyalty tests, and ceremonial displays of commitment to the Brotherhood. Alasdair—if he was indeed the ringleader—seemed much more interested in molding these other boys into his minions than he did in pursuing his actual goals."

"Well, an army of brainwashed minions would have had its advantages, too, I guess," I said, sitting down beside him. "Once he started committing his atrocities, he would have had willing accomplices, boys who had already learned not to question him or his ideas. If they hadn't been discovered and broken apart, Alasdair's subsequent crime spree in Edinburgh could have been even more catastrophic than it was."

"I do keep seeing this, though. Over and over again," Finn said, pointing to a smudged line of text that I had to squint at to make out.

"Hand to the... chalice?" I asked. "Is that what it says?"

"Bang on," Finn confirmed. "At first, I wondered if it might just be a sort of oath, you know? Like, "Hand to God" or something like that. But now, I'm wondering if it might perhaps be more literal than that."

"You mean like placing your hand on an actual chalice?" I asked.

"That, or perhaps even the *image* of a chalice. Remember, Circe is often portrayed in art with a chalice in her hand. What if there's a chalice somewhere in this building—a portrait maybe, or a bust or something—that hides the entrance to the sanctum, and you have to, quite literally, put your hand *to the chalice* to gain access?"

I nodded, considering. "That's a definite possibility. There's a pretty big collection of art up on the second level of the historical center. I remember wishing I had time to look over it the first time we went up there to examine the artifacts."

"Well, why not take a look now?" Finn said. "It certainly can't hurt."

I was glad to have another lead to follow, however vague it might be, so I did as he suggested and scaled the spiral staircase to the second-floor gallery. I walked to the far north corner and began a slow, deliberate study of each piece in the collection. There were niches set into the walls, with shelves built right into them that looked original to the rest of the architecture, but there was no trace of a chalice among the many busts and statues that resided inside them. Just in case they'd been rearranged over the years, I felt around behind and under them, shifting them gingerly on their plinths, and running my hands under and around them, but had to conclude after an hour of this that the niches didn't hold the secret to the sanctum's entrance.

Next, I began to explore the huge collection of paintings on the walls. Any other time, I would have reveled in examining the brushwork and guessing the time periods based on the style, but today I was only looking for one thing: a chalice. I'd worked my way around three quarters of the room and was starting to despair, when I finally found it.

The painting itself was modest—rather dark and unimpressive compared to some of the more colorful and dramatic works around it. It was almost as if it had been painted intentionally to blend in with its surroundings, rather than to draw the eye. It was a simple still life on a dark and gloomy background that showed a table draped in a white cloth, and set with a number of items, including a bowl of pomegranates, a carving knife, a single candle burning in a dull silver candle holder and—I gasped out loud when I saw it—a golden chalice, filled to the brim with blood red wine.

I stepped forward, pulse racing. Could it really be this simple? It went against everything I knew as an artist, to reach out and touch such an old, delicate painting with my bare hands, but I wasn't about to let that stop me. I pressed my fingertips to the canvas, gently at first, then with increasing pressure.

When that produced no result, I flattened my palm against the canvas and pushed harder.

Nothing at all happened.

Okay, I knew it was a long shot, but I wasn't about to give up quite yet. I began feeling my way around the edges of the frame, which was enormous, elaborately carved, and painted in gold leaf. I wiggled my fingers one by one behind it to see if it would come away from the wall, or if it was affixed there. It shifted quite easily.

"Jess? What are you doing up here?"

I yelped and spun on the spot to find Aoife looking at me curiously, her arms full of books.

"Aoife, you scared me! Hey, could you help me for a minute?"

"Of course!" Aoife said. She looked puzzled, but put the books she was holding down in a nearby niche, and came forward to meet me.

Quickly, I explained what Finn had found in the journal, and how it had inspired me to come check the artwork. Aoife's eyes traveled from my face to the painting behind me, and her eyes went wide.

"Oh! I see! A chalice! And you think..."

"I think it's worth investigating."

"Well, then, let's investigate!" she said, rolling up her sleeves.

Together, we took hold of the massive picture frame and lifted it slightly so that the painting came free of its mounting. Then we lowered it carefully to the ground, arms shaking from the weight. I was impressed with Aoife, who was much stronger than she looked. Then we both stepped forward and examined the section of wall beneath the painting, running our hands over the stones, poking and prodding until our fingers were raw, with absolutely no success. I sighed, admitting defeat.

"I guess it was a long shot," I said.

Aoife, however, was looking thoughtful. "You know, these paintings haven't always hung in the same place."

I snapped my head around to look at her. "Really?"

"Oh yes. I'm not sure when this space was converted into a gallery, but I bet it was after Alasdair's time. I might be able to find some records that would tell us the origins of this painting, and maybe even when and where it was hung originally!"

I could have kissed the girl. "Aoife, thank you. That could actually be very helpful."

"Is this the only painting with a chalice that you could find?" she went on.

"It's the only one up here, I think," I said.

"Well, we should tell the rest of the team to pay close attention to the artwork elsewhere in the building. You may be onto something here," Aoife said, with a solemn nod.

"I hope so," I said, "because I'm starting to run out of ideas." I checked my watch and saw how late it was getting. "We really should be heading back to the dorms for the night. And you should be heading home, too."

"Oh no, I want to start researching this artwork idea. But don't worry," she added, when she saw the look on my face. "I'll ask one of the Caomhnóir on the night shift to escort me back to staff and faculty housing. I have no intention of wandering around by myself."

I narrowed my eyes at her. "Do you promise?"

"Cross my heart," she replied, and drew a little "x" on her chest for good measure.

We heard from Hannah only once that evening, when she let us know that she and Kiernan had arrived safely back in Edinburgh, and that she would be heading over to the Collective in the morning with all the resources they had gathered on Necromancer magic.

"The Blind Summoner Casting goes back centuries," she told us, the Connection abuzz with her excitement. "There's every possibility that Alasdair had come into contact with it. I've deconstructed the origins of the Casting, breaking it into its various components to see how they fit together, so that I can figure out which parts Alasdair used and which ones he discarded."

"That's awesome," I told her, more to keep her spirits up than because I really thought this was going to work. I wasn't really sure why I was doubting her so much—maybe because I was so wrapped up in the immediacy of needing to catch Alasdair at all costs. I couldn't think about the Collection when a campus full of living students was in such terrible danger. "More importantly though, how on earth did you convince that Polly woman to let you remove materials from Skye Príosún's archive? I thought that place was locked up tighter than Fort Knox."

I heard the sly smile in Hannah's thoughts. "Let's just say I suddenly became much more open to the idea of a proper interview with her when our mission was complete."

"You sneaky little bugger," I laughed.

"I'm choosing to take that as the compliment it so very obviously is," she replied.

Darkness had fallen like a shroud over the campus again, and with it, our anxiety spiked. Savvy wasn't on the first watch, but she spent it pacing like a caged animal instead of getting any semblance of rest. I had also given up on going to sleep and spent hours at a time in a chair by the windows, staring out over the grounds for any sign of the cloaked spirit. I had begun to think of him as a kind of omen—if I saw him, I would know that something terrible had happened once again.

At a little past midnight, I started pacing as well. I felt useless just sitting here. Shouldn't I be taking shifts with the others? I had certainly volunteered, but Finn had turned me down flat. He insisted it was because I didn't have proper Caomhnóir training, but I knew that was only an excuse. He wanted to keep me out of harm's way, as usual.

And I was starting to get pissed off about it.

So when Savvy emerged from her bedroom, fully dressed in her uniform and ready to join the guard, I had my Doc Martens laced up and my jacket on.

Sav took one blank look at me.

"No."

"Huh?"

"No! You can't join the watch."

"I'm not trying to join the watch!"

Savvy raised an eyebrow. "So what, your feet got cold?"

"I was going to offer to walk down with you. Then I can walk back with Finn."

"Are you trying to trick me?" Savvy asked, narrowing her eyes at me.

"What? No! Why would you think that?"

Savvy pulled out her phone, swiped into her text messages, and read aloud. "From Finn, and I quote: *Do not let her trick you into joining the watch.*"

I tried to look offended, but I couldn't quite manage it. "Sav, look, I'm really not trying to stand out in the cold all night. I just hate not knowing what's happening. Can't I just walk down with you? You know Finn's going to drag me back up here anyway."

Savvy bit her lip. "Well, I have to admit I'd rather walk down with you than with whatever dung-for-brains Caomhnóir they'd send if I requested an escort. All right, fine. But if Finn asks, you held me at gunpoint."

"Seriously? Gunpoint?"

"I said what I said."

Savvy looked me right in the eye without a trace of humor, so I dropped the sarcastic tone at once.

"At gunpoint. Message received."

And so we set off across New Campus, although for all her talk about not wanting to get stuck with a dull Caomhnóir for company, Savvy wasn't much of a talker on the way. She moved at a very measured pace, pausing to assess particularly dark recesses or poorly lit corners, with methodical precision. It was a mark of the strength of her training that she could move so deliberately and carefully through the grounds, while I wanted to sprint as quickly as I could to the other side of it. For the first time, I admired Savvy for her true skill at her job, rather than the tenacity that had enabled her to attain it.

I was a little ashamed at how long it took me to acknowledge it. But now that I had, I would never take it for granted again. My friend wasn't just a badass. She was a competent badass—a next-level badass.

Neither my concern nor Savvy's competence were necessary. The grounds were as deserted as they had appeared from the window of the flat. If I'd been able to see Finn's expression from there, however, I might have reconsidered my plan.

"Really? All the way across campus after midnight?" Finn asked in a flat voice.

Savvy pointed at me. "Tell 'im."

I looked at her and then at Finn. "I... had a... there was a... a gun?"

"Yeah, yeah, okay, let's just get you back up to the dorm," Finn grumbled, waving a relieved-looking Savvy off toward the guardhouse to check in, before turning back to me. "It's been an unsettled night. Reilly thought he caught a hint of Alasdair's energy, but we fanned out through the area he was patrolling, and we couldn't pick up on it, and even he said he couldn't sense it anymore. It shook us all to think he was out here, so close."

"But if he's here, that's a good thing, isn't it? I mean, everyone's housed on New Campus. If he's down here, at least it means he's not attacking people."

The last word was still hanging in the air between us when a scream rang out in the night.

I locked eyes with Finn. "Where did that come from?"

He spun on the spot. "It sounded like it came from the—"

"Help! Someone help, please!"

This time there was no mistaking where the voice came from because, at that moment, the door to the historical center burst open, and a frantic figure appeared in the light, waving their arms frantically.

"Here! Over here! Someone, please, I... oh, Lord, I think he's dead!" the voice shouted again, and suddenly I recognized who it belonged to.

Aoife O'Malley, flagging us down, terrified tears running down her face.

Finn was off like a shot, and I stumbled along behind him, trying to keep up. We tore across the lawns, took a shortcut through a cloister, and skidded to a stop where Aoife was standing, bouncing anxiously on the balls of her feet.

"Aoife, what is it?" Finn gasped.

"It's Gareth! He's been attacked!" she sobbed.

"Bring me to him," Finn said.

Aoife turned and ran back into the building, leading us straight through the main reading room, and behind the circulation desk to the door of Gareth's office. Alasdair's energy hit us like a slap across the face. At first, nothing seemed amiss, aside from the general disarray of the desk, but then we saw the papers on the floor, the chair tipped over on its side, and an Oxford-clad foot sticking out from behind the desk.

Finn skidded across the paper-strewn hardwood, dropped to his knees beside Gareth, and disappeared from view for a moment on the other side of the desk. I couldn't bear to move around the desk, I couldn't bear to see the body of another person we'd failed to save, but then...

"He's alive!" Finn shouted.

"What? Oh my God!" I cried, running around the desk to join them, Aoife right behind me, still crying stormily.

"Really? Is he really still alive? I thought... when I saw the ribbon..." Aoife managed before dissolving into tears again.

Rana, Savvy, Reilly, and about half a dozen other Caomhnóir were now crowding the doorway.

"Reilly, radio for a stretcher please."

Reilly nodded sharply, pulled his radio from his belt, and stepped out into the reading room to make the call.

"Rana, Sav, can you take Aoife somewhere quiet to calm down? Don't question her till she's got a grip on herself," Finn said.

"On it, mate," Savvy said, and then stepped forward, her voice uncharacteristically gentle. "Come on, love. Let's get you a good ol' cuppa, yeah? My mum would say that's just the ticket."

Aoife allowed herself to be led away, still sniffling, and Finn turned his attention to Gareth, who was stirring faintly. He was taking strained, rasping breaths. Finn fumbled with the silk ribbon around his neck before swearing under his breath and turning to me.

"Help me with this, will you? My fingers are too bloody big."

I picked at the knotted ribbon with my fingernails until it started to come loose. At last, we were able to unwind it from Gareth's neck. He began to cough and take deeper breaths, though they still sounded labored and difficult. His eyes fluttered open, and he began to look around him in apparent confusion.

"I... he... someone tried to... to kill me..." His voice didn't sound at all like his own but like it was scraping and clawing its way up through his throat, raw and desperate.

"His windpipe must be damaged," Finn muttered. To Gareth he said, "It's okay, mate, we've got you. Just keep breathing. Are you hurt anywhere else?"

"He... he hit me on the head with... with something... I think I was knocked unconscious." He gave a rasping cough and moaned from the pain of it.

"I'm sorry to make you talk," Finn said, "but this is really important. You keep saying 'he.' Did you see who attacked you?"

Gareth managed to shake his head before breaking into another painful coughing fit. "I... he was strong. I... I remember his hands over my face. They were big... rough, but I... I'm sorry, I don't remember seeing a face." He held his own hands up in front of him, squinting at them as though he could barely believe they belonged to him, like he was absolutely shocked to be alive and breathing.

"It's all right. You've done really well," Finn said, though I could hear the disappointment under his false cheeriness. "We're gonna get you up to the infirmary, all right? Get you fixed up properly. You'll be making jaw-dropping historical discoveries in no time at all, okay, mate?"

Gareth started to reply, but broke off again into another bout of hacking. At that moment, Reilly appeared in the doorway. Finn gave him an inquisitive look, and Reilly nodded.

"Good, send them in," Finn said.

Reilly stepped back to allow two more Caomhnóir, with a stretcher between them, to wedge their way into the office. Given the size of the room, they barely managed it, but with a little creative maneuvering, they were able to get Gareth onto the stretcher. They placed an oxygen mask over his nose and mouth and carried him out of the room. I pressed myself against the wall to give them room to pass.

"I'm going to process this room for any clues," Finn told me, rising to his feet. "Can you go check on how Aoife's doing?"

"Sure," I said, and went back out into the main reading room. I wasn't quite sure where Savvy and Rana had taken Aoife, but I was pretty sure the closest room with a kettle was Damien's office. So, I started across the main reading room toward it.

As I skirted a long table, I caught a movement out of the corner of my eye. It would have startled me right out of my skin, if some part of me hadn't been anticipating that I would see him.

There was another attack. Of course he was here. I turned to face him, knowing what I would see before I had even set eyes on him.

The shrouded figure, standing like some sort of watchman in the upper gallery, his shadowed face turned upon me.

18

SILENCED

W e stared at each other for what felt like an eternity, but it was probably only a few seconds. Now that I had come into contact with his unusual energy twice, I picked up on it more easily—the incompleteness of it.

The wrongness of it.

"You were in the Brotherhood. The Brotherhood of Circe."

I said the words so quietly, and yet I knew he could hear me. The answer was in his stillness, the intensity of his hidden gaze.

"I need to know who you are. Can you speak with me?"

This time, the answer came in that same strange warping of reality: the light and shadow bending, the air turning thick like soup, and the feeling that the ground was shifting under my feet.

"Okay, so that's a no."

The figure continued to watch.

"Can you stay? Can you stay here and wait for me? I want to help you. I want to undo... whatever this is."

I knew he couldn't answer me, but he seemed to understand. Or maybe I just wanted him to.

Suddenly, before I could say another word, the figure vanished on the spot, and a voice sounded behind me, making me jump and whirl around.

Savvy stood behind me, one arm slung around Aoife's shoulders.

"She's feeling a bit better and wants to answer questions now."

"Are you sure, Aoife? If you need a little more time, you can—"

"I'm sure," Aoife said, in a voice still thick with tears.

"Okay. Let's go find a quiet place to sit, and I'll go get Finn," I said.

We settled Aoife into her own office, where there was a sagging but comfortable-looking armchair she could sink into. She curled her legs under her like a small child, clutching her steaming cup of tea in her hands. Finn joined us and sat across from her on the edge of her desk, a notepad in his hand.

"Aoife, can you tell us what happened?" Finn asked. His voice was deep and soothing. I watched as Aoife's shoulders relaxed downward, and she took a deep breath to steady herself.

"I was here doing some research," Aoife began, and she looked over at me, "like I told Jess I was going to."

Finn looked at me. "She was helping me. I told her to go home before dark, but she promised me she would call an escort."

Aoife nodded. "And I would have, I promise. I just never got the... the chance," she said. She swallowed the lump I could hear in her voice. Then she took a cautious sip of tea and went on. "I wasn't worried about being here by myself. I knew Gareth was also here, working late. Damien left around ten o'clock, but I was wrapped up in what I was doing, not at all paying attention to the hour. Finally, I heard the bell in the tower, and I realized I really ought to be going. I packed up and decided to tell Gareth I was leaving. I exited my office into the main reading room, and that's when I noticed a terrible energy. It was so foul with this rotted stench. I'd never come across anything like it. And I remember thinking, it must be him—Alasdair. He must be here somewhere in the building. I was so scared. I ran to Gareth's office to warn him, and... that's when I found him. I... I really thought he was..."

She sniffed again, and Finn didn't press her. He just handed her a tissue from the box on the desk and waited for her to collect herself again.

"Did you hear or see anyone else?"

Aoife shook her head. "I had..." She took a shaky breath like she was fending off tears again. "I had earbuds in while I was working. I was listening to a... a podcast. I'm so sorry. I should have... If I'd just..."

"Aoife, stop. It's okay. He's going to be okay. You didn't do anything wrong, and you mustn't blame yourself."

Aoife made a strange little movement somewhere between a head shake and a shrug and sipped her tea again.

"Rana and Sav, can you walk her back to the faculty housing? Make sure she gets into her flat safely; maybe give it a sweep first, eh?" Finn said. He kept his tone light, but he gave them a significant look, and I knew he was worried. Aoife was a possible witness now, and it may very well have put a target on her back.

Rana put an arm around Aoife and walked her out. Sav leaned into Finn.

"Want me to beef up that faculty housing patrol?" she asked.

"I want someone right outside her door tonight, just in case," Finn muttered back.

Savvy winked. "Sorted," she said, and followed the others out.

"I don't understand," I said, as soon as they were gone. "Why is Gareth still alive? Why would Alasdair strangle him, and then not complete the rest of the ritual?"

"He must have heard something that spooked him. Maybe it was Aoife moving around in her office, or one of the Caomhnóir patrols passing too closely. A few came inside, but I'll have to check in with them all to see if and when they passed through this area."

"Finn, there's something else," I said. "That spirit was back, the one in the black cloak."

Finn straightened up, all alertness. "Truly? Where? When?"

"Up in the gallery over there," I said, pointing through Aoife's open office door to the far side of the gallery. Even now, the shadows there seemed to shift and congeal strangely, although that may have been my eyes playing tricks on my overwrought brain.

"Finn, he's trying to communicate with me. I can feel the answers to my questions getting swallowed up in the distance between us. We've got to try to Uncage him or something. He knows something. Hell, he might know everything."

Finn's eyes became unfocused as he gazed off into the middle distance, thinking. "If he's actually been witnessing these attacks, he might be able to tell us who Alasdair's accomplice is. And if he was a member of the Brotherhood, he would know where the sanctum is." He refocused his eyes on me. "I don't think we've got any choice but to try it."

It was 3 o'clock in the morning, the witching hour. Gareth had been taken off to the infirmary only a couple of hours before and everyone was exhausted, but I refused to wait. The Uncaging had to be done at night, and there was no way I was letting another day slip past, another opportunity for Alasdair to strike again, to snuff out another innocent life.

I had done this only once before, and so I read the instructions in the *Book of Téigh Anonn* very carefully. The Casting had to be performed on hallowed ground, which fortunately was not a problem because Kingshurst had a forgotten little cemetery tucked into the very furthest corner of Old Campus. It was a wild, overgrown little place, with tombstones scrubbed blank with age, and wildflowers running rampant through the tangled grass. It was like a poem, and I had just enough time for a fleeting reflection that I would love to draw this place, before I set my mind to my task again.

I worked quickly and surely. The Casting required five Circles to be drawn, a large central one, and then four smaller ones marking the points of the compass. I didn't have time to dig them into the earth, and so I formed them carefully with string. Savvy, Rana, and Maeve stood by, each clutching a different colored candle. Not one of them had hesitated for even a moment when I asked them to help me. After all, they wanted to catch Alasdair as badly as I did. I would have given almost anything for Hannah to be there to help me. If she'd still been at Skye Príosún, I probably would have called her and begged her to come. But she was back in Edinburgh, and though I could easily reach her inside my head, it wasn't the same as having her beside me, holding my hand.

When the Circles were Cast and complete, I beckoned the others forward, and they took their places in the three of the smaller circles. I took my position in the north Circle, holding the white candle—the Spirit Candle.

"Are we ready?" I asked.

Three faces nodded back at me, each of them wearing a completely different expression. Savvy, no doubt flooded with the memories of having done this once before, looked solemn. Maeve looked nothing short of petrified, her candle shaking like mad in her hand, sending warped shadows rippling over her face. And Rana looked absolutely enthralled at the chance to participate in a ritual she had only ever read about in a textbook.

I turned to where Milo and Finn stood, just outside of the candlelight.

"Ready?" I asked them.

Both nodded, Finn with one hand on his Casting bag in case our mystery ghost turned hostile, and Milo with a furrowed brow as he focused on reading the energy in the graveyard, ready to warn us of the slightest whiff of Alasdair or any other unexpected spirit. He refused to let us do this without him, so we posted two Caomhnóir outside of Tia's door.

I began the incantation, trying not to overthink it, letting the words flow through me. I didn't know the name of our spirit, but then, I hadn't known the Silent Child's name either and we had still managed to summon her to the Circle. So I tried to trust in the process, trust in the power inherent in the Casting. One by one, I pointed to the others to light their candles. At last, I lit my own and placed it at the center of the large Circle. Then I stepped back, closed my eyes, and pictured the spirit I needed so desperately to communicate with.

"Lost Brother," I thought to myself, for that was what he was. "Come to this place. Let me free you."

A cold breeze whipped between the gravestones, and Maeve let out a squeak of fear. I opened my eyes and found myself staring into the shadowed face of the very spirit I had so desperately hoped to find.

Maeve was whimpering. I could hear Finn muttering to her, trying to keep her calm. We needed her to hold her ground, or we'd lose our tenuous grasp on this spirit, and the Uncaging wouldn't work.

I picked up the bundle of sage, smoldering silently in a bowl at my feet. I circled it over my head, continuing with the incantation. Despite my efforts to keep myself calm, I could feel my heartbeat starting to pick up, my pulse pounding in my ears.

"Now."

The other three girls blew out their candles, plunging their own figures into darkness. The only light that remained radiated from the white Spirit candle at the Lost Brother's feet. I cleared my throat. This was it. If the Casting had worked, if he really had been Caged, then he should be free now. Free to give us answers.

"You're safe here," I told him. My voice cracked with fear, and I cleared my throat, trying to control myself. "Tell us your name."

It happened all over again, just as before. The world seemed to warp around us, with sound, vision, and sense all twisting and contorting. My head began to pound, and my eyes rolled back, but I forced myself to cling to consciousness. I looked around the Circle, but everyone else seemed completely unaffected.

"Why isn't he speaking?" Rana whispered.

"I'm not sure," Sav said, looking at the Circle and the candles as though to satisfy herself that everything was as it should be. "I don't understand. It should have worked."

"He's trying," I said a little breathlessly. "But it's still happening. Something is still interfering with his ability to communicate." I pressed a hand to my forehead, wiping away a sheen of cold sweat before trying again. "Who are you?"

Prepared for it this time, I weathered the resulting environmental tumult a bit better. I clutched the top of a nearby gravestone for support, waiting for the unsteadiness to pass. Again, the spirit could not manage an answer.

I tried one last time. "I'm not sure why this isn't working," I told him and everyone else at the same time. "I thought you'd been Caged, but that doesn't seem to be the case. If you can't speak, can you show me who you are?"

The figure before us held perfectly still for a moment, as though considering. Then he reached up and, in one deliberate motion, peeled back his hood.

Maeve and Milo shrieked. Savvy let out a string of cuss words that would have made a sailor blush. Rana simply froze in place, wide-eyed with terror. Only Finn kept enough of a handle on himself to move forward and get a better look at what the spirit had revealed.

His face—or, I suppose, the place where his face ought to be—was simply... blank. Wiped clean of features, just a flat stretch of smooth, unblemished skin. It was utterly horrifying; but my fascination outstripped my horror, and I stepped toward him. I almost expected him to back away, but he didn't. He stayed right where he was and allowed the indignity of my staring.

"What happened to him?" Finn murmured.

"He's incomplete," I said.

"What do you—"

"Look at him, Finn. He's like the Collection. A vital part of him has been stripped away, leaving him wandering the earth without rest and without identity. He's not an accomplice. He's not even just a witness. He's a victim. He's one of Alasdair's victims."

"My God," Finn breathed.

"It's why his energy has felt wrong. He's not Caged. He can't communicate because the part of him that would allow him to do that has been hacked away and consumed by a monster."

Milo floated forward, his expression inscrutable. He drifted in a circle around the faceless spirit, getting much closer than I ever would have dared to myself, but the spirit didn't seem to mind. Milo put his hands out, letting them trace the shape of him in the air. Then he came to a stop right in front of the spirit, and looked into the place where his face should have been. For what felt like a long time, no one spoke—it felt like no one was even daring to breathe. We were all spellbound, watching this entirely new form of paranormal investigation: a ghost investigating another ghost. Finally, Milo sighed and floated backward, disengaging from the spirit, and breaking the spell under which we'd all been held.

"He's in there," Milo said, his voice quiet and tremulous. "There's enough of him left that he knows who he is. But it's as though he's been sealed inside himself. It's almost as though the piece of him Alasdair took was... his voice."

"What can we do?" I asked. I wasn't even sure if I said it out loud. It might have just slipped across the Connection in this moment when we were all so vulnerable, but Milo answered it out loud.

"I have absolutely no idea. I've never seen anything like it."

There was no sleep to be had for the last few remaining hours of the night. Even if I had managed to nod off for more than a few minutes, I was sure I would have been plagued with dreams of faceless spirits and strangled victims, all crying out for something I couldn't yet give them: justice.

I watched the sun rise over the campus, watching as the light slowly trailed its fingers over the buildings, gardens, and deserted paths. I couldn't stop thinking about the spirit we'd tried to Uncage the previous night and how, instead of gaining clues about Alasdair's whereabouts, all we gained was another victim we couldn't help.

Word came around seven o'clock that Gareth was in stable condition in the campus infirmary. I knew he would need to be questioned to see if any other details of his attack had clarified themselves in his head, after the kind of rest only good painkillers and a healthy dose of sedative could produce. Based on what he'd said when we first found him, my hopes weren't terribly high. Finn headed over to see Gareth as soon as he woke up, and when he returned, he was visibly frustrated.

"I can't believe we have a victim who actually survived, and he can't tell us anything about who attacked him," he growled.

"He said something about the hands being big and rough, didn't he?" I asked. "I think he said that last night."

"Yeah, and that's the only detail he's managed to retain."

"Is he okay, at least?"

"Well, he sounds terrible, but having your windpipe crushed will do that to a person," Finn sighed. "And he's worse than Clarissa about being a patient. He's making such a stink about being in the infirmary that I'm not sure they'll have any choice but to let him out today."

"Probably paranoid that someone else is going to find the inner sanctum before he does," I said, "although why he'd want to risk another encounter with the ghost who already tried to kill him, I have no clue."

"Yeah, he's a bit of an intense bloke, isn't he?" Finn agreed, nodding. "But at this point, if he wants to forego a proper rest and keep helping us, I'm not going to complain. We need all the bloody help we can get."

Three attacks, two of them fatal, in a matter of five days. It felt like Alasdair was as desperate as we were. And my biggest fear was that, having failed to kill Gareth, he would strike again as soon as darkness fell.

Ironically, because Gareth wasn't a student and he wasn't actually killed, there was far less commotion on campus that day than I would have expected. More than anything, students just seemed relieved that none among their number had been targeted. It made no sense to me. Didn't this mean that no one was safe? That literally anyone could be next? I had no energy to waste on trying to fathom it. I was too busy frantically trying to prevent the next crime.

When we arrived on Old Campus to continue our search, I found Aoife and Damien already at work. Damien looked more disheveled than usual and seemed to have lost his focus. He would pick up a book, stare at it as though he couldn't remember why he was holding it, and then put it down again. He hovered around the pairs of Caomhnóir, searching the corridors like an insect, muttering suggestions, and snapping at everyone to be careful of everything. By lunchtime, Finn was so aggravated with him that he had two of the Caomhnóir bring him down to the campus security office for an interview, just to get him out of everybody's hair.

Aoife looked as though she'd slept about as much as I had—so, not at all— but she also had a weird kind of manic energy that sometimes comes with sleep deprivation. I stopped by her office to see her feverishly flipping through the pages of an enormous handwritten ledger. She looked up just as I knocked on the door frame.

"Oh, hi. I just found this catalog someone compiled in 1887 of the artwork on campus. I'm hoping there might be some information on where things were hung and stored. Of course, it's more than a hundred years off from when Alasdair and the Brotherhood would have been here, but I still felt it was worth exploring." She said all of this very quickly, her words clipped and tense.

"Aoife, are you okay?" I asked.

"Of course. I'm not the one lying in the infirmary, am I?" she replied.

"Well no, but Gareth wasn't the only person who went through some traumatizing shit last night. It would be perfectly understandable if you needed a little time to recuperate also."

"I'll recuperate when this monster is caught," Aoife snapped. The sound of her own voice seemed to startle her, and she sighed, sagging a little. "I'm sorry. I don't mean to get short with you, of all people. I'm just so..." she trailed off, searching for the word that could possibly encompass all that had occurred. Luckily for her, no words were necessary.

"I know," I told her. "We all are. Let's suppress our trauma together. If everyone's doing it, it must be a healthy coping mechanism, right?"

This elicited a very small smile, and we got to work, burying ourselves in dusty books with nearly illegible text.

By mid-afternoon, my head was pounding again, which was why it was so painful when Hannah burst into my head.

"Ow! Knock first, woman!" I cried out. "Luckily, no one was around to see me apparently yelling at myself. Aoife had wandered off to scrounge up a late lunch, and Gareth hadn't yet returned from the infirmary. The one good thing to come out of Gareth's attack was that the Historical Center was now a crime scene, so we finally had an excuse to keep students away from it.

"Sorry, I'm sorry, I'm just—"

"Excited, I know. I hope that means you've got good news for me."

"Well, yes, as a matter of fact. I think we've managed to create a Casting to undo the Collection."

Our shared mental space rang with the intensity of my surprise. "Wait, are you serious?"

"Of course, I'm serious! Kiernan and I were working through the night at the Collective and found something in Alasdair's notes that filled in some blanks. We modified some incantations, and did a few experiments with some different Casting materials, but I think it's solid. But the real game changer was the Memory Rifting."

"I'm sorry, back up a second, you've lost me. What the hell is Memory Rifting? Do you mean Rifting like... like *Rifting*? Like how I met Agnes Isherwood?"

"Yes! It was Flavia's idea. She made the connection once she had a better understanding of what the Collection actually was. She said there was a modified version of Rifting that the Travelers had developed to try to connect with damaged spirits. It was back when Irina was Walking all the time and wouldn't return. They tried to use it to communicate with her, to understand where she was going and what she was doing, to ensure she wasn't breaking the code of secrecy. But it never really worked with her because she wasn't a willing participant."

"I still don't understand what it does. Are you telling me they tried to Rift through a spirit's mind? Like, her memories?"

"Yes! She didn't want to let them in, so they never had much success with it. But apparently, they used it in a trial once when a spirit had been Caged, and the Casting had been completely mangled. It was the only way to retrieve the memory of what went wrong so they could try to reverse it. Unfortunately, they weren't able to repair the damage to that particular spirit, but the Rifting worked in obtaining the information they needed."

"So, you're saying you actually did this? You Rifted into the memory of the Collection?" My brain could hardly take it in. I thought we'd had the lion's share of the drama in this case, and here was Hannah just casually telling me she'd entered the collective consciousness of the Collection last night.

"I did." And here her excitement faltered as her emotions kicked in. "It's quite similar to normal Rifting, as far as the ritual goes. There are a few key changes in ingredients and the incantation, of course, and the spirit—or in this case, spirits—you're trying to communicate with also have to be inside a Circle with you when you drink the tea. But once we managed that, I was able to see back into their memories."

"What was that like?" The thought was barely a whisper, a question I both wanted and didn't want the answer to.

"It was... awful." The thought shivered, trembled, and shrank away from me. "It was very confusing—I know you've told me before that Rifting is strange and disorientating, but Rifting through fifty disjointed minds at once was almost unbearable. I was only able to keep going because I was focused on what I needed. I did my best to ignore everything else, and keep every sense awake for the snatches of relevant memory. They were hard to get a hold of at first, but I got better at recognizing them. It showed me enough to fill in the blanks of Alasdair's methods. At least, I think it did. I guess we won't really know until I try to undo it all. Oh, I'm so nervous!"

But I couldn't spare another thought for the Collection, important though I knew it was to unmake it. All I could think about was the faceless spirit and the barrier between us, and how Flavia had had the answer to overcoming it all this time.

"Hannah, I love you, and good luck, but I've got to go."

"What? But I haven't even... don't you want to know what the—"

"I do, but there's no time. Be careful and keep me updated."

"What are you going to do?"

"Well, I can't let you have all the weird fun. I've got to call Flavia and get her over here. I'm going Memory Rifting."

19

MEMORY LANE

Flavia was on campus by five o'clock that afternoon. She jumped right out of the car sent to fetch her and threw her arms around me.

"You look like hell, Northern Girl," she said.

"Thanks, it's a new look I'm trying. Trauma chic."

She grinned. "It suits you."

After I explained to Finn what Hannah had told me, attempting the Memory Rifting became the new top priority of the investigation. The rest of the team was still searching every inch of Old Campus, but it was entirely possible that if this Memory Rifting worked, we would find the answer to every pressing question we had.

We set up in a large empty classroom on Old Campus, in one of the buildings that had already been searched from top to bottom. It seemed best to set up where we weren't likely to get interrupted. It reminded me of the classrooms at Fairhaven where I'd taken my Apprentice classes, including the large fireplace that Flavia was now hovering over, building up the powerful blaze she would need to complete the Casting.

"Luckily for us, Skye Príosún has the most extensive stores of Casting supplies I've ever seen," said Flavia. "I worried at first, when Hannah told me what she wanted to do, that we wouldn't be able to get our hands on everything —a few of the ingredients are somewhat obscure. Instead, I found myself looking through drawers of herbs and stones so rare I'd never even seen them used in a Casting before. It was *fascinating*." She seemed to realize she was gushing and sobered up her expression at once. "Sorry. I guess I'm still sort of in awe of the place."

While she worked, I told her everything we already knew about the spirit we were trying to Rift with, including every encounter I'd had with him, and every detail of the previous night's failed Uncaging. When I got to the description of the faceless thing under the hood, Flavia swallowed hard.

"Sounds like a real charmer. I can't wait to meet him," she said, attempting a chuckle, but it came out a bit hysterical.

Finn joined us, eager to assist and even more eager to be the first one to hear whatever I might be able to glean from my journey. He tried to volunteer to actually do the Rifting, but Flavia shut that down at once.

"Very chivalrous of you, I'm sure, but this is a job for Jess," she said firmly. "She's done it before, so she knows what to expect. And besides, she's the one this spirit has been trying to communicate with from the beginning. They already have a connection. That should work to enhance the Rifting, make the memories clearer."

Finn couldn't argue with this kind of logic, however much he may have wanted to. Still, he seemed relatively calm. After all, as Flavia had said, I had done this before... sort of. And Hannah had just done it as well, with successful results. We knew it was safe—well, as safe as anything in the Durupinen world could be.

"Now, Jess, there is an important difference between Memory Rifting and your average, run-of-the-mill Rifting," Flavia said.

I snorted. "Flavia, absolutely nothing about Rifting is average or run-of-the-mill."

Flavia grinned sheepishly. "Fair enough. Anyway, in Memory Rifting, you don't have to look for a door. The spirit controls how and when the Rifting ends because it's his memories you're traversing. Once you enter, you agree to witness all of what he chooses to show you. He'll close the door when he's had enough."

I nodded. Somehow, this made sense. I was about to enter someone's head. He should have the right to decide when to kick me out. It made me a little nervous that he'd do it before I'd found out what I needed to know, but I supposed that was just a risk we'd have to take.

When everything was prepared—the Circle drawn, the herbal brew steeped, and the space cleansed, Flavia gave me permission to summon the spirit.

I closed my eyes and focused on him, reaching out into the liminal space around me. I tried to imagine that I was Hannah, who could pinpoint those bright points of energy that spirits became when she Called them. I tried to envision myself reaching out my hand and drawing him forward, both an invitation and a command.

Come to me. Tell me your story at last.

It was Flavia's gasp that told me I'd been successful. Whether it was my own skill at summoning or his willingness to connect with me, it only took maybe half a minute before I opened my eyes and saw him sitting right across from me. The smooth contours of his featureless face were just visible inside his hood, and his cloak was spread around him in a ragged circle.

"Now what?" I whispered out of the corner of my mouth.

"When I say so, speak the incantation, drink three sips of the tea, and then pour the rest onto the ground between you as an offering. Once you're under, you won't be able to control what he shows you. He won't really be able to completely control it either, any more than any of us can control our subconscious. So just keep your eyes peeled as much as you can."

"Okay," I said. "Should I... explain to him what we're doing?"

Flavia shrugged. "It couldn't hurt. It might help him access the right memories."

I took a deep breath and let it out to try to calm myself before addressing him. "I know you can't tell me what it is you want me to know, so I'm going to look for the answers in your memories. I need you to help me understand who you are and what happened to you, especially with the Brotherhood."

I glanced at Flavia, who nodded encouragingly. "Good!" she whispered. "Now, the incantation."

I repeated the words she'd written down on the paper in front of me and lifted the tea to my lips, drinking once, twice, three times. Then I reached forward and tipped the remaining contents of the cup onto the ground. I watched it spread as my eyelids began to droop. The last thing I felt before I slipped under was Finn's strong hands reaching out to catch me and lower me to the ground.

"Good luck, love," he whispered.

The sensation was peculiar, like trying to open my eyes underwater. The blurred world around me stubbornly refused to resolve itself, the edges bleeding into each other, and the colors mixing and swirling like watercolors on a page. It took nearly a full minute before I blinked and gasped my way to something resembling clarity; and even then, the world in which I found myself had a strange quality to it, like I was watching it all from behind a dusty pane of glass.

I was standing in a small, dark bedroom, lit only by the dying embers of a fire in a stone fireplace, and a guttering candle upon a windowsill. The room had the slightly desperate look of a sick room: piles of white fabric, a pitcher and basin of water, half-empty bottles, and bunches of dried herbs littered a small table under the window. But no one worked feverishly over them. No one hurried back and forth between the bed and the makeshift apothecary, applying poultices or cold cloths or tonics. The room had gone still, devoid of hope. I knew what I would see before I let my eyes focus on the bed.

A young man—barely more than a boy—lay statue-still beneath the thin coverlet. His sunken chest did not rise or fall. His pale purple eyelids lay closed, his mouth half-open in a sigh that no one could hear. Perspiration still glistened on his forehead and in the hollows of his sallow, wasted cheeks.

This was not a sickbed any longer. This was a deathbed. And someone sat beside it, sobbing inconsolably.

The moment I thought of moving closer, I was suddenly there, as though the very impulse had been the action itself. This time I concentrated on the figure bent over next to the bed, sobbing unrestrainedly into the bedclothes, howling with misery and grief. The moment I saw him, I felt the tether of connection between us. This was the young man whose memory I had entered. The knowledge was complete, unquestionable.

A barrel-chested man entered the room and came to stand behind the young man. He hesitated, and then clapped a bear paw of a hand on the boy's shoulder.

"It's time, Andrew. The undertaker's come. You've had your goodbye, and we've got to let him go now. Come on, lad."

Andrew. His name was Andrew. An answer already.

"I can't," Andrew managed through wracking sobs. "I told him I'd stay with him."

"He's not here any longer, lad. He's shed that body at last. It never did serve him very well, did it? But he's free of it now. Free of this world."

"I want to go, too," Andrew gasped.

"Now, now, we'll have none of that. John would want ye to live your life, not chase him into the grave."

"Why didn't he stay with me? I begged him to stay. We could have been together!" Andrew asked, choking on his tears.

"We can't ask that of each other, Andrew, to stay behind. The pull of the Aether is too strong, and what was there for him here any longer?"

"Me! I'm here! Is that not enough?" The cry sent a stab of pain through my chest.

Andrew's father's voice was soft as he answered. "No, lad. No, it's not."

"But where's he gone, Da? What's happened to him?" Andrew asked, his voice sagging with desperation.

"Come on now, you know where he's gone, sure enough. He's Crossed beyond the Aether. That's where we're all bound when it's our time."

"But what's beyond the Aether? Why don't we know? We ought to know!" Andrew's voice was broken and ragged with grief.

"We're not meant to. We're meant only to guide and to protect. Once a spirit's found the Gateway, their journey must be a solitary one."

Andrew's expression as he looked at his father stole the breath from my lungs. It bore no trace of comfort from his father's words. Instead, anger burned in his eyes so intensely that I felt scorched by it. I turned away and the room seemed to swirl around me, resolving again a few breathless seconds later into another memory altogether.

Andrew now faced a Geatgrima, weathered and crumbling with age. He stood before it with his arms outstretched, his face tilted toward the mottled grey sky. Large, fluffy flakes of snow fell around him, clinging to his dark hair and obscuring the outline of the Summoning Circle in which he had enclosed himself.

"The veil is thinnest here," he whispered into the sky. "This is as close as I can get. John, I Summon you. Please, I need to know where you are, that you're all right."

I stood and watched him, my heart breaking for him as he called into the empty night. I knew his brother could not answer him, not now that he had already Crossed, and I think Andrew knew it, too, judging by the edge of desperation in his voice.

"John, I Summon you! I... I don't know how to be without you. I want to follow you, but I'm afraid. I need to know that you're there, waiting for me. Please. Please can you..." his voice shuddered and faded away as a sob wracked him. My view of him was suddenly obscured behind a film of my own tears. My heart ached for him. If I lost Hannah, I wasn't sure I would know how to survive it. If I had the chance to follow her, I'd be tempted to take it, I was sure, just to stop the pain. Even as I pitied him, though, I recognized the anger that had grown in him, the same anger that had been in his eyes as he looked at his father. It was sprouting beneath the surface of his grief, just a tiny seed of darkness amid his pain, and every second his pleas were met with silence, it would unfurl another poisonous tendril. It would soon overtake him, and he would be an easy target for the likes of Alasdair.

Andrew dropped to his knees, and the scene dissolved like sand taken by the wind, only to swirl around us like confetti, and then resolve again. Andrew was still on his knees, but now he was collecting books and papers scattered on the ground around him, as the confetti pieces of the memory formed into buildings and grass and sky. We were on Old Campus of Kingshurst. Andrew appeared older than he had at the Geatgrima, but not by much—perhaps two or three years. His face was more angular, the features rendered sharper by pain, or perhaps it was merely the frustrated expression that made it appear so.

"Bampots," he muttered under his breath, as he worked to pile up his belongings. I turned to see a group of boys walking away from him, throwing gleeful looks back over their shoulders and laughing raucously, and I realized they must have shoved him on purpose. Andrew had by now gathered all but a single textbook which lay further away than the others and was just reaching for it when another hand plucked it from the gravel, dusted it off, and held it out to him.

Andrew looked up in surprise, taking the offered book and muttering his thanks before stuffing it into his teetering pile. We both examined the young man now standing before him, and I let out a gasp that no one could hear. The hair was short and neat, the face clean-shaven, the expression mildly amused, all of which made it nearly impossible to tell that we were looking at a much younger Alasdair MacLeod. Only his eyes, almost impenetrably dark and heavily lidded, gave away that it was the same man who would one day stalk the streets of Edinburgh for prey.

He did not speak—I think I would have been shocked to hear anything come out of him but a growl—he merely nodded his head, gave Andrew a swift, appraising look, and then continued strolling down the path, his hands stuffed casually in his pockets as he whistled a snatch of a tune. Andrew struggled to his feet, staring after Alasdair with a curious expression on his face, before hurrying off to his destination.

The world broke apart, swirled, and reformed yet again, this time inside a classroom with stone walls and a blazing fire on the hearth. It took several seconds to steady myself from the disorientation of hurtling through someone else's memories, and I had to breathe through a wave of nausea before I could focus on what was happening around me. The first thing I noticed was the sanctity line on the floor, just as I had found on my first day of classes at Fairhaven. When it stopped blurring in and out of focus, I looked up to see that every seat on the right side of the line was empty. On the left side sat approximately twenty young men with books and quills. Most of them, including Andrew, whom I spotted in the second row, were writing feverishly. A few, seated toward the back of the classroom, were sagging with boredom, either gazing glassy-eyed out the window or else doodling absentmindedly on their papers and, in one case, scratching letters into the desktop itself. In the very back row sat Alasdair MacLeod, lounging with his feet propped on the windowsill beside his desk. He was the only student who hadn't bothered even to take out his paper or quill. I saw Andrew pause in his task to glance back at him.

Alasdair seemed to be whispering something to the boy sitting beside him, but though I moved closer to him and leaned in, I couldn't hear the words—perhaps because this was Andrew's memory, and Andrew himself couldn't hear them from where he sat several rows ahead. In fact, I noticed that the corners of the room and the faces of the students farthest from him were somewhat indistinct—almost like someone had painted them, and then smeared the paint while it was still wet. There would be limits to what I could glean from these memories, and those limits were based on what Andrew himself had witnessed. I focused my attention on Andrew instead, and just the decision to do so put me directly beside him without taking a step. It reminded me of the sensation of trying to move around while Walking, but it seemed to require less deep focus and concentration.

I let my gaze stray to Andrew's notes. He was not only writing down what the professor was telling them but also furiously circling, underlining, and crossing things out, as well as scribbling questions into the margins. The topic under discussion was the Geatgrimas and their locations around the world.

"They stand as relics and monuments to our strongholds of the past, a sort of map, if you will, of the places where the clans have settled, and sometimes where they have fallen and been forced to move on. A few have even been lost or destroyed."

Andrew raised his hand, and the professor nodded in his direction. "Please, sir, but how could that be allowed to happen?"

The Professor frowned. "I'm afraid I don't follow, Abercromby."

Ah, a complete name now. Andrew Abercromby. And then Damien's words resurfaced in my own memory.

His name was Andrew Abercromby and, to my knowledge, he was never found.

Another piece of the puzzle clicked into place. The spirit who had been haunting me since our arrival was the boy who had gone missing when that local girl, Alice MacLeary, was killed and the Brotherhood was broken up. He'd been on campus all along, a maimed and mangled shade of himself. But what had happened to him?

"What I mean to say, sir, is that the Geatgrimas themselves mark the places where the veil is thinnest between worlds. Why have we not made it a priority to be sure that all of them remain within our protection?"

The professor interrupted my thoughts. "Just because we were drawn to the Geatgrimas in the establishment of clan territories, it does not follow that we must always build our power around them. They are, after all, more symbolic than anything, monuments, as I said. Just as other civilizations have built statues and memorials to their great moments in history, the Geatgrimas stand as ours."

"But they aren't purely symbolic, sir," Andrew said, not bothering to raise his hand this time. "They are powerful! The places they mark, we should be using them, shouldn't we?"

This time the professor's eyebrows floated up into his unkempt hair in surprise. "Using them? Whatever for?"

"To explore! To... to connect with what lies beyond them! Why has so little been attempted to discover what we can from the Aether and even beyond!"

Perhaps it was the feverish excitement in his voice, but several students were looking at Andrew with alarm. The professor, too, had now crossed his arms over his chest, his previously incredulous expression folding and scrunching into a grimace of disapproval.

"Mr. Abercromby seems to be forgetting the fundamental function of his own role as Caomhnóir. We are guardians and protectors, not explorers. We guard the gates, we facilitate safe passage."

"How can we let people go through a door when we don't know where it leads? It's irresponsible! It's madness!" Andrew cried out, as a hush fell over the class. A few students were looking at him with genuine fear, while the professor's face had darkened into a storm cloud of anger. Only Alasdair MacLeod leaned forward, those sharp, cold eyes boring into Andrew with an expression of keen interest as Andrew glanced around him to find everyone either staring avidly at him, or else intensely trying to avoid making eye contact.

"You seem to be suggesting that our entire purpose on this earth is a mistake." The professor's voice was smooth and calm, but I could hear the danger in it. Perhaps Andrew could hear it too, for he swallowed once, convulsively, and licked at his lips as the professor went on. "Not only that, but the way in which we carry out our purpose could even be construed as irresponsible, if not nefarious. Am I understanding your meaning, Mr. Abercromby?"

Andrew's voice trembled, but he raised his chin defiantly as he answered, "I mean only, sir, that we have... have not taken the very obvious opportunity presented to us, and—"

"Your words smack of malcontent at best. At worst, they are tinged with very dangerous influence, indeed. Tell me, Mr. Abercromby, do you think the Necromancers have it right, then? Should we be stripped of our guardianship of the Gateways because we refuse to abuse them—to twist and defile them to fit our own curiosity and vanity?"

The weight of the hostile glares must have been enormous, because Andrew glanced around warily as the class at large seemed to silently turn on him. The last pair of eyes he locked onto was Alasdair's, and he was startled to see Alasdair nod, once, as though in wordless agreement with him. Andrew turned back to the professor who stood tapping his foot impatiently, but though he opened his mouth several times, he could think of no answer to give that would satisfy the man.

"I think perhaps you need a reminder of your duty, Mr. Abercromby. Come up here now and remove your jacket."

I could feel the fear and humiliation rolling off Andrew in great waves as he rose from his desk, hands shaking, and strode to the front of the room. Eyes fixed firmly on the floor, he removed his jacket, turned his back to the professor, and closed his eyes. I realized what was happening just in time to turn away before the caning began. I kept my eyes averted, flinching at the sound of every blow. All I could see were the other students watching. Some, like me, choosing to look away, others unable to do so. And then a handful who watched with a kind of perverse hunger on their faces—an actual appetite for the violence. Andrew looked up only once, and when he did, he glimpsed Alasdair's face, animated with that very hunger. The sight of it turned my stomach just as the room tore into a million pieces, swirled around me like a howling tornado, and reassembled again.

We were in a small, sparse room containing only a desk, a chair, a narrow bed, a tall bookshelf crammed with books, and a washstand with a chipped white porcelain basin and pitcher. It reminded me of the spartan chambers in monasteries and nunneries, but a quick glance at the personal belongings told me this was Andrew's room at Kingshurst. Andrew sat on the edge of his bed, teeth clenched against the pain of trying to clean and bandage his own wounds. His back, which he examined in a mirror, was a bloody mess.

"They really do despise being questioned, don't they?"

The voice came from the doorway, and Andrew sucked in a breath as he turned to see who had spoken. Alasdair leaned casually against the door frame, looking both untidily handsome and slightly bored.

Andrew didn't reply, merely returning to his ministrations with a closed-off expression.

Alasdair evidently took Andrew's silence for an invitation, because he slunk casually into the room, closing the door behind him.

"You'd think an institution of learning would encourage questions, wouldn't you? Deep discussion. Debate, even. But, no. Express a single original thought and—" He made a whip-cracking noise that made Andrew flinch.

"What do you care?" Andrew muttered. "It's not as though they'd dare cane you."

Alasdair smirked. "Well spotted. So, you know who I am, then?"

"Everyone knows who you are. Everyone also knows you'd have been out on your arse in the first week of term if your last name wasn't MacLeod."

Alasdair's smirk broadened into a grin. "I must admit, the name does have its advantages. How are you getting on? Looks a bit... uncomfortable."

"Leave me alone, will you?" Andrew spat. His eyes were full of angry tears, and it was clear to me he wanted nothing more than to be left alone. I found it hard to believe it wasn't clear to Alasdair too, but he didn't seem to care. He ignored the implied warning and took a few steps closer to the bed. Andrew seemed to take it as a threat and jumped up from the bed, wincing.

Alasdair raised his hands in mock surrender. "Easy there, Abercromby. I'm only trying to help."

"Help? When have you ever helped anyone? All you care about is lording it over the rest of us. I suppose you think I ought to be grateful for the day you picked up my book, when I know you were the one to lock me out in the snow in the first term."

Alasdair shrugged. "Just a bit of fun."

"And shredding my uniform?"

"Ah, come on. We always have a bit of a go at the new lads."

"But it's not all the new lads, is it? Just the ones from poorer, less important clans. That's why they don't care; because they, like you, barely know that we exist except as the butt of some cruel joke. But you? I bet you could cane a teacher, and they wouldn't so much as reprimand you."

"Huh. You know, I haven't tried that. I'm much obliged for the suggestion," Alasdair said, with the air of someone seriously considering the matter. "I often wonder what it would take for them to chuck me out of this place."

Andrew blinked in surprise and then narrowed his eyes. "Of course. A chance like this is handed to you, and all you can do is spit on it rather than see it for the opportunity it is."

"You see Kingshurst as an opportunity, do you?" Alasdair asked, looking slightly amused. "What, so they can indoctrinate you and beat you when you resist? I'd hardly call that an opportunity, Abercromby."

"I don't mean them," Andrew said dismissively. "I mean this place! The knowledge gathered here! The archive alone is bursting with history they never share, and ideas they're scared we'll discover! I'm not interested in what they teach us in the classrooms, I'm interested in what they don't teach us. That's why I'm here." He winced again. "I suppose I'll just have to be a bit quieter about it if I want to stay."

Alasdair raised his eyebrows. "You're tougher than you look, aren't you, Abercromby? Perhaps I underestimated you."

"I assure you, I did not come here to be broken by the likes of you or Professor Murphy," Andrew said through clenched teeth. "But I suppose you'll just take that as a challenge, won't you?"

"Oh no, indeed, Abercromby," Alasdair said quietly, looking uncharacteristically serious for a moment. "I think I can be trusted to recognize potential when I see it."

And with that cryptic remark, Alasdair strode from Andrew's room, leaving Andrew looking both defiant and confused.

The world blurred, not quite breaking apart this time, more like it was stretched and then sprang back again, and I realized we were in the same room. Andrew was sitting at his desk, poring over a book. I could see bandages poking out from under the collar of his shirt, and I understood that, while some time had passed, it hadn't been enough for his wounds to heal completely. I'd only just had time to make this observation when an odd scuffling sound caught both of our attention. Andrew twisted around in his seat just in time to see an envelope slide under his door. He stared at it for a moment before rising tentatively from his seat to retrieve it. I followed him and stood over his shoulder as he tore the wax seal with trembling fingers. It had the image of a chalice on it.

The paper inside read: "The same curiosity that gets a lad the strap can also garner him an invitation. Come to the yew tree by the statue of Socrates at midnight, and you will learn much to your advantage. Tell no one."

In that moment I knew what Andrew did not yet know: the Brotherhood had summoned him.

20

FALLEN BROTHER

Andrew stared at the paper for a long time, but his gaze was unfocused, and I knew he was thinking hard. It surely couldn't be an easy decision. He must have known that the sender of the invitation could just as easily wish him harm as good. Was he going to be punished further for his intellectual trespasses? Was he walking into a trap? He couldn't possibly know for sure, but this did not seem to deter him from taking his chances because a whirling moment later, I was walking beside him down a garden path, a swollen full moon nested in some scuttling clouds above our heads and bathing the campus in its blue-white glow. The grounds appeared deserted. The only sound was the faint rustle of the breeze through the budding leaves on the trees.

Andrew was clearly jumpy, constantly glancing over his shoulder and peering suspiciously into dark corners and clumps of bushes, as though determined to sniff out anyone who might be following or watching him; but if anyone lurked nearby, they were concealing themselves well. By the time the statue of Socrates came into view, Andrew's anxiousness had infected me, and I could barely breathe as anticipation for what would happen next expanded in my chest, crowding my lungs. I felt dizzy with fear and thought Andrew must have felt the same as he turned his paper-white face back and forth, looking for the sender of the cryptic invitation.

We didn't have to wait long.

As though materializing from nowhere, two figures shrouded in dark cloaks leaped out from behind a shrubbery and flung themselves at Andrew, the first pinning his arms behind his back, and the second shoving a burlap sack down over his head to blind him and stifle his cries for help. As Andrew's world went dark, so did mine. I could see nothing, feel nothing, only listen in an agony of worry as Andrew struggled against his captors as they dragged him away from their designated meeting place. A few of their words reached my ears between Andrew's muffled shouts.

"It would have been easier to club him."

"Shut up and keep moving."

"Stop yowling, Abercromby, or we'll give you a real reason to shout."

The sounds of their footsteps changed, and I realized we were now inside one of the buildings, though it was impossible to tell which one. Then they stopped. There was some grunting, a grinding sound, like stone on stone, and the temperature around us seemed to drop by at least ten degrees in an instant. The stone floor gave way to stairs, and then a passage that sloped downward. Then there was the creaking and banging of a door, and the muffled thump of Andrew being thrown to the ground. A moment later, the world appeared again, and I let out a gasp that no one around me could hear.

Andrew now knelt in the middle of a circular chamber with stone walls, no windows, and a high, vaulted ceiling. The only light in the room emanated from candles in gold candelabras taller than me and set at intervals around the perimeter of the room. A long stone table rather like an altar dominated the center of the space, but I could see other furniture—desks and bookcases and chairs—shoved up against the wall in the dark shadowy recesses between the candelabras. It smelled like a crypt—the air was heavy with moisture and the tang of mildew and something else—something sweet and rotting that stung my nose even in this strange memory state. I couldn't be sure, but I thought we might be underground, a fact that would help explain why we hadn't yet located this place. I knew it was the inner sanctum, the place we'd been searching for the last five days. With a pang of frustration, I realized that I still didn't know how we'd gotten here. Andrew's makeshift blindfold had prevented me from seeing the route we'd taken.

Andrew was staring wildly around just as I was, and it was almost at the same moment that we both noticed the movement in the shadows—cloaked figures, a dozen in all, moving slowly toward the center of the room. If I hadn't been me, I would have thought they were vengeful spirits, but my vast experience with ghosts assured me these were living specters, not dead ones—

despite wearing the very same cloak that Andrew always wore as he stalked me around the campus.

"W-what's happening? Who are you?" Andrew stammered now as he watched the cloaked figures bear down upon him from all sides. He searched frantically around him for something he could use to defend himself, but there was nothing but a bare floor and foul air within his reach.

"We are the malcontented. The caged. The silenced," called a familiar voice, a voice emanating from the figure on the other side of the altar. I chanced a glance at Andrew to see if he recognized Alasdair's drawl, but he seemed too panicked to make the connection. Upon Alasdair's words, though, the cloaked figures stopped in their tracks, forming a circle with Andrew at its center. "We are the ones who dare. We are the Brotherhood of Circe."

Andrew seemed to be trying to control himself. He took a deep breath before he asked his next question, and his voice sounded much calmer. "And what does this so-called Brotherhood want of me?"

"This is not about what we want. It is about what *you* want."

This pulled Andrew up short. He chewed nervously at his lip, trying to decide how to answer.

"I... I wish to go back to my room?"

A few of the cloaked figures snickered amusedly, but were careful to keep their heads down and their faces obscured.

"And that is all you wish of your time at Kingshurst? To hole up in your room with your nose in a book, swallowing whole the lies they feed you like a good little boy?"

Andrew opened his mouth and closed it again, surely wondering if this was a trick question.

"Very well, then. We were mistaken in you. You may go."

"Wait, no!" Andrew staggered to his feet, his voice ringing out and shattering into echoes that filled the dank chamber. "I... may I speak freely without fear?"

Alasdair seemed to consider. "You may," he said at last.

Andrew swallowed convulsively. "I... I lost my brother. We have the key to the door he walked through, and yet we refuse to open it. To walk through it. To follow so that we can know for sure what awaits us on the other side—what fate he met. I cannot accept that. I will not accept it."

"You reject the idea that we must be ignorant guardians only?" Alasdair asked.

"Yes." Andrew did not hesitate this time.

"You believe our connection to the spirit world necessitates further exploration?"

"Yes, or we forfeit our right to be the gatekeepers."

"Forfeit?"

"Yes, is that not what cowards do?"

There was some quiet mumbling at this, but Andrew stood his ground, glaring around at the other figures as though daring them to contradict him. He seemed to realize this was some sort of test, and his grief had left him with nothing to lose.

"There are no cowards within this chamber," Alasdair said after a drawn-out pause. "Every man here has found his way to this Brotherhood by the sheer power of his determination, and by asking a simple question—a question that the elders, with all their authority and knowledge and bleating about tradition cannot answer: *Why not?*"

Another murmuring rose up around the room. Heads beneath cloaks nodded in agreement. Andrew chanced a glance around at them, and I watched the fear fade from his eyes as he finally started to understand that he was among like-minded people.

Alasdair's voice boomed out, making me jump. "To those who say we cannot walk through the door, we say, 'why not?' To those who say it is not our place to question or to know, we say, 'why not?' To those who accept our limits and demand our loyalty, we say, 'why not?' They have no answer. And so, we seek the answer for ourselves. We are seekers. We are explorers. We are forgers of new paths. We are the restless wanderers, the creative thinkers, the ones who dare to set out for those uncharted shores. Are you one of us, Andrew?"

Andrew's eyes were alight now with a feverish glow, a look I'd seen before and one that never boded well. "I am! Oh, I swear to you, I am!"

"Then welcome, Andrew Abercromby. Welcome to the Brotherhood of Circe."

The memories sped past me now like a film on fast forward. I watched snatches of Andrew's initiation—the lighting of candles and spilling of blood to bind an oath, and the honorary bestowal of one of those long black cloaks—it was as though Andrew knew what I needed to know. He was racing through his own recollections to get to the important bits. It was all so disorienting that, although I was desperate not to miss anything, I had to close my eyes for a moment just to steady myself.

When I opened them again, I was back in a dorm room, though not the same one. This one was larger, with a canopied bed and beautifully carved furniture—it seemed there were very real perks involved in being a wealthy or important clan when it came to accommodations at Kingshurst. Four boys were lolling about the room, passing around a bottle of something that smelled like it could strip paint. It took me a moment to realize that one of those boys was Andrew, so different was his demeanor. Where before he was tense and closed off, now he seemed at his ease. His arm draped casually over the back of a chair, and he was smiling lazily as one of the other boys told a crude joke. When the bottle made it around to him, Andrew took a generous swig, and only winced slightly as the contents burned their way down his throat.

"...knew he'd pass. They'd never have dared to fail him, not a MacLeod," one of the boys was saying, a stout, curly-headed boy with a snub nose and a large gap between his front teeth.

"I heard he threatened the dean," said a lanky boy with hair so blonde it was nearly white. "Just strolled into his office and told him he'd be out of a job if he didn't make bloody well sure Professor Murphy passed him."

"Would be out of a job, too, I've no doubt," the snub-nosed boy insisted. "Clan Rìoghalachd owns damn near every brick of this place. I imagine they'd shut it down before they let one of their own fail out."

"I don't suppose you heard the topic of his term paper?" a third boy, ginger and freckled, asked the room at large.

Andrew and the other boys turned eagerly to him at once, all declaring they had not.

"Well, I was working in the same part of the library," the ginger boy said, his expression dripping with smugness. "And I had a look at it when he got up to go to the loo."

"Never miss an opportunity to cheat off someone cleverer than you, eh Mahoney?" said the snub-nosed boy.

"Aye, and that's everyone," the other said, and they broke off in snorts of laughter.

"Ah, sod off, the pair of you," Mahoney spat, and made to stand up.

"Come on, Mahoney, tell us!" Andrew piped up. "What was the paper about?"

"Not with these two having a go at me!"

"They're sorry, aren't they? Harris? Bates?" Andrew said pointedly, glaring at the other two, who launched into hasty apologies at once.

"Just a bit of fun, Mahoney. Go on, then," the blonde Bates insisted.

Mahoney kept them in suspense a moment longer while he pretended to debate the matter, but anyone could see he was as desperate to tell what he knew as the others were to hear it. At last, he sat back down, and the other boys leaned in, all trace of languor now gone.

"I was only able to read a bit of the first page, but it was a defense of the Necromancers," Mahoney said, dropping his voice dramatically.

"Come off it," Harris scoffed, though his eyes had widened.

"I swear on the Brotherhood. He was making the argument that the Necromancers had it right, and that the clans were shirking their responsibilities. 'Unreliable stewards,' he called them."

"Called us, you mean," Bates corrected him, who seemed to be having a hard time deciding whether to be offended or awestruck.

"It's no more than we say every time the Brotherhood convenes," Harris said with a stab at bravado.

"Yes, but we don't write it down and hand it to a professor, do we?" Andrew said, frowning. "In fact, we've sworn a vow of secrecy about it."

"But I haven't even told you the wildest part," Mahoney said quickly, noticing that he was losing his audience. "In the paper, he claimed to have firsthand knowledge of the Necromancers."

These words were met with such a thoroughly stunned silence that Mahoney basked in smug satisfaction before one of the others could formulate a reply.

"But that's... that's surely not true," Bates managed at last. "I mean... the Necromancers... they've been long disbanded."

"Count on MacLeod to try to cause a stir," Harris added, almost nonchalantly. "He's got about as much experience with Necromancers as you've got with women, Mahoney."

Mahoney punched Harris in the arm, and the latter fell sidewise off his stool, crowing with laughter. But Andrew could not dismiss the information so lightly.

"Did he say when he came into contact with them? Or how?" he asked.

Mahoney shook his head. "He may have done, but I didn't see it, not in the bit I was able to read before he came back, anyway."

"He didn't say because it's all a bunch of codswallop. MacLeod was bored and wanted to get a rise out of old Murphy, that's all," Bates insisted, sounding almost angry.

"Get a rise out of him or not, if he keeps carrying on like this, the

Brotherhood will be uncovered and all of our work will be for nothing!" Andrew cried out, all trace of relaxation and good humor gone.

The others were staring at him. "You take this rather seriously, don't you, Abercromby?" Harris asked.

Andrew looked affronted. "Of course I do! Don't you?"

Harris shrugged, taking another swig from the bottle. "I'm not sure. Sometimes I think I only joined because I know how much my mother would despise it."

Bates and Mahoney laughed at this, but Andrew rose to his feet, his hands shaking.

"But what about our mission?"

There was a growing wariness in how the others looked at him now. "It's... it's all a bit of a lark, isn't it?" Bates said slowly. "I mean to say, nothing we've ever tried has actually worked, has it? We're no closer to taking a holiday beyond the Aether, are we?"

"I don't reckon it's possible," Mahoney said. "Mind you, I don't plan on telling MacLeod that. He'd go off his nut, wouldn't he?"

The others murmured their agreement, but Andrew was positively fuming now. I could practically feel the fury rolling off him.

"We can't just give up because it's hard!" he cried. "We have to continue on... to persevere! Every failure is another step toward success!"

"Hell's bells, Abercromby, you're as mad as MacLeod, aren't you? Calm down, man, and have another drink," Harris said, holding the bottle out toward Andrew.

But Andrew backed away. "No. No, I... I think I've had enough. I'll see you all later." And he fairly fled from the room, leaving the other boys whispering and laughing behind him.

I followed Andrew all the way back to his room in an adjoining building. I watched him as he removed a false bottom from his trunk and pulled out stack upon stack of paper, books, and Casting materials. He paused before he closed the lid, and pulled out a painting of his brother, a simple little cameo portrait. He placed it on his desk and stared at it for a long time. Then, without a word, he got up and left the room.

The world broke apart. The world reformed. Andrew found Alasdair standing on a sharp outcropping of rock, overlooking the waves crashing below. If I hadn't known Alasdair's eventual fate already, I would have been afraid he was about to leap to his death. In light of his many future victims, living and dead, I couldn't help but wish that he had.

"They don't believe in it," Andrew said, as he came to stand beside Alasdair. "The rest of the Brotherhood, I mean. It's all a joke to them."

"Not at first," Alasdair said, his tone thoughtful. "I chose each of them carefully, you know. This one for his resentment, that one for his brains. All of them were a bit... lost. Looking for something to believe in—or maybe just something to rail against. I thought I could shape them... mold them into what I needed them to be. But I misjudged them—or perhaps myself. They will never be what I need them to be. I must carry on without them."

Andrew turned to face Alasdair with desperation in his eyes. "You mustn't give up! It's too important! Please, I'm not like the others. Don't give up on me. I... I can still be of some use, can't I?"

Alasdair turned to look at Andrew now, a long, appraising look that was no less cold than it was calculating. I would have run as far as I could if Alasdair had turned that look on me, but Andrew was too desperate to see what I saw so clearly.

"Yes, Abercromby, I think perhaps you could be of some use after all," Alasdair said, and Andrew had to repress a sob of relief even as I groaned in despair.

There was something uniquely agonizing about watching these memories, knowing that they would end in tragedy for Andrew, although I wasn't yet sure how that tragedy would play out. Having to simply be a bystander was torture. I wanted to step in, to rescue him from mistakes he'd already made, and events that had already come to pass. It was maddening to have to stand by and do nothing, but I had no other choice. I thought for a moment of Finn, and how this experience would probably make his head explode; and then I wondered how he was holding up, watching me Rift through a spirit's memories. Hopefully, he wasn't pulling his hair out with anxiety and anticipation, but it was hard to imagine him doing anything else.

I refocused on Alasdair, who was speaking again. "I have a theory, Abercromby, that I am most anxious to test, involving spirit energy. You are familiar with Leeching, of course."

"Yes," Andrew said eagerly.

"I have done extensive reading on the subject and a great deal of research, and I believe we may be able to harness the power of spirit energy for ourselves.

Not only will it slow aging and promote healing, but it could also very well be the key to immortality, or something like it."

Andrew's euphoric expression slipped a little. "I... didn't know you were interested in immortality."

"Oh, I'm not, in and of itself. It's simply that this work... this great work we are doing, to find a way to reach beyond the Gateways, it is going to take time, perhaps a great deal of it. If we are to succeed, we will need strength and resilience. But it is more than that. I believe that, if we are strengthened with surplus spirit energy, we will be able not only to pass through the Gateways but return as well."

"But how..."

"It's only a theory," Alasdair said, raising a hand. "I don't pretend to have all the answers, Abercromby, no indeed, not even most of them. But I know we must be bold. We must traverse every avenue that the Durupinen establishment has declared off-limits. I've devised a Casting—it wants only real testing now, a chance to see if it will work the way I intend it to. Will you aid me in this?"

"Of course, I—"

Alasdair held up a hand, and Andrew fell silent mid-reply. "I warn you, this path will not be for the faint of heart. We will have to break rules, Abercromby. We will have to work in secret, and sacrifices will need to be made in service of this greatest cause. You must understand that, before you agree. Now I ask you again, will you aid me in this?"

Andrew was twisting his hands together, hesitating. "And you believe this Casting will really and truly help us get beyond the Gateway?"

Alasdair clapped a hand on Andrew's shoulder. "The first step along the path to seeing your brother again," he said.

Those were the magic words and Alasdair knew it. He was able to exploit Andrew's deepest, most painful vulnerability, and suddenly I found that I could hate Alasdair even more than I had a few moments before. I wouldn't have thought it possible, but then Alasdair himself was something of an impossibility —a monster we never imagined we would need to fight.

The cliffside shattered and swirled around us, reconfiguring the pieces of remembered reality into Old Campus once again, although it took me a few moments to realize where I was. The grounds the night Andrew joined the Brotherhood were bathed in moonlight, but now a moonless, starless darkness had swallowed the campus whole. A thick fog swirled around me, further obscuring any details I may have been able to make out. I could barely see my hand in front of my face, and I heard Andrew before I saw him. He was pacing anxiously back and forth behind a hedge, his cloak swinging about his ankles. He was muttering something to himself, and it was only when I got close to him that I was able to hear what it was he was saying.

"Just stay calm. Just stay calm."

He kept looking at the ground as though checking something, and I had to stoop to see the faint outline of a circle on the ground at his feet. It had been gouged into the pathway through the gravel to the dirt underneath. I could see that Andrew carried his Casting bag. It was swinging from his belt beneath the cloak. He also carried something in his hand. He kept winding and twisting it in his hands—a thin rope, maybe, or a ribbon? I couldn't be sure.

Both our heads jerked up at the sound of voices nearby. Andrew froze like an animal scenting its most dangerous predator. The voices grew closer, accompanied by footsteps, and as I peeked around the corner of the hedge, I could see a light wavering up along the path, a disembodied brightness hovering its way closer to us. Slowly, figures began to emerge through the gloom, thrown into relief by the light, which revealed itself to be a lantern. I caught a glimpse of an angular face atop a broad-shouldered body with a distinctive, loping walk—Alasdair, of course—and a second, laughing face—young, apple-cheeked...

Andrew appeared directly beside me, his face drawn and white. As he raised a hand to pull aside a branch, I spotted what he had dangling in his hand: a length of red silk. And I knew who that second face belonged to: Alice MacLeary.

Suddenly, I understood what was about to happen, and my gorge rose. There would be nothing I could do to stop it. I'd read about it, just dispassionate words on a page, but now it was coming to life in front of me, and I was powerless—a silent witness to a crime that had never officially been solved. The figures drew closer. Andrew swallowed back bile. Every muscle in my body tensed with the repressed urge to leap out and tackle Alasdair, or grab the girl by the arm and run with her, run and run and run so fast and so far that we could escape the past. At any moment, they would appear around the hedge.

The world blurred out of focus in a jumble of sound and distorted images, but it did not reform. This was different, somehow, from the way we moved from memory to memory, and I realized this memory was repressed, as though Andrew himself could not bear to remember what happened in those next moments. I held my breath as the memory raged around us like a storm—the echoes of screams, the scuffling of a struggle, a swirling howl of colors and terror and rage and death. I grew dizzy and disoriented as I tried along with Andrew *not* to see, *not* to hear, *not* to understand. The chaos burned a bright, terrible red, and then there was a crash as the lantern smashed to the ground, and everything went black and silent again.

The world stuttered into existence again like a rapidly blinking eye. Sounds were muffled. I took in a jumble of disconnected images.

Blood on a pair of hands.

An eye, staring emptily upward above a mouth, open in surprise.

A frantic boot kicking at the dirt to remove evidence of the Circle.

The bitter, fiery cold of angry spirit energy.

And then we were back in the dorm, in Andrew's room. Andrew was sitting on the edge of his bed, looking utterly catatonic, while Alasdair stood at the basin, scrubbing at his clothes and hands in icy silence. I was panting as though I'd run a marathon.

"You lied to me."

The words were Andrew's, and they dropped like stones to the ground, heavy and hard and cold.

"I didn't lie to you." Alasdair countered.

"You didn't tell me the truth, either."

For a moment there was no sound but the friction of fabric against fabric as Alasdair scrubbed. Then, "I didn't tell you the truth."

"You should have told me."

"You wouldn't have helped me."

"I might have."

"You wouldn't."

Andrew sank both of his hands into his hair, tugging at it as though he would tear it out. "You said we needed spirit energy. I assumed you meant a spirit."

"I did mean a spirit."

"I meant someone already dead! You never... you just..."

Alasdair turned around with a sigh that could only be described as bored. "The spirits on this campus are ancient. They've been dead so long their energy is depleted and weak. And the Wards keep out most newer spirits, except Spirit Guides, and I can hardly attack one of them."

"But—"

"I've gotten what I can from them already. They have outlived their usefulness, if you'll forgive the choice of words. They cannot assist us. We had to look elsewhere."

"But that... that girl was..."

"Was a nobody," Alasdair said flatly. "A local village girl, not a student here, and certainly not one of us."

Alasdair's dismissal of the girl wiped Andrew's face blank like a slate.

"She was alive," he said. "She was... was a person. A human being."

"And now she's part of something much larger," Alasdair said smoothly as he held his cloak up to the candlelight to check his progress. "She was a kitchen maid, Abercromby. What would her existence have amounted to? What mark on the world could she possibly have hoped to make? It's a gift I've given her, really. Her soul will be part of the greatest experiment of the modern age, the success of which will shape the future of humanity forever. Therein lies her worth. All we did was help her achieve it."

Andrew recoiled. "We?! I didn't... I had nothing to do with—"

"You assisted me. Kept the path clear. Stood look out. Prepared the Circle and the Casting I needed to catch her soul upon its release. You had everything to do with it." Alasdair said the words slowly and deliberately, aiming each word to strike in the most direct and painful manner.

Andrew just shook his head wordlessly.

"You told me I could count on you, Abercromby. I hope I have not been misinformed."

There was a dangerous note in that silky voice. I felt the hairs on my arms stand up at the sound of it. Andrew heard it, too, for his head snapped up, his expression panicked.

"You can count on me, but—"

"I told you this work was not for the faint of heart. I told you we would have to break the rules and that sacrifices would have to be made. I did not soften my words to persuade you. I was as honest as I could be."

"I didn't... yes, I know that you said that, but—"

"I'm not sure what else I could have done to make you understand what you were getting yourself into."

"You could have said you were going to murder someone!" Andrew cried out, his voice dropping to a mere whisper on the last two words. "Rather an important detail to leave out!"

Alasdair took a step closer to Andrew, and his expression was curiously blank. "We are breaking down the barriers between the living and the dead. We are forging a path into the afterlife that has heretofore been an impenetrable barrier. Did you expect it to be easy? Tidy? Gentle? I thought you to have more sense than that, Abercromby."

He looked at Andrew with naked disappointment, then reached into his pocket and pulled out a ribbon, blue and a little frayed at the edges. Even in the dim candlelight I could see that it was spattered with blood. Waves of cold energy were rolling off of it, and my stomach turned over as I caught the edge of it, even through the memory. For Andrew, who averted his eyes from it, it must have been overwhelming.

"I've got to get this to the inner sanctum if I am to complete the second half of the Casting. I cannot risk attempting it where someone else may hear us. I'm not sure how... well, how *uncooperative* she might be when I release her," Alasdair said with a slight sneer. He looked up at Andrew. "You look done for Abercromby. Why don't you turn in."

Andrew looked at Alasdair with contempt. "You think I can sleep? After what we've just done?"

Alasdair chuckled as though Andrew had made a joke. "You see? 'We.' That's more like it. Sleep it off. When you've had time to calm down and be logical, I know you'll see that we've done only what needed to be done. Come to the sanctum tomorrow night, and I'll prove it to you."

Alasdair strode from the room, thrusting the ribbon back into his pocket and throwing the hood of his cloak back over his head. Andrew sat for a long time, staring blankly at the wall, hands shaking in his lap. I could hardly begin to imagine what was going through his mind, as mine was reeling just from being a spectator to the events of the night. He'd been made an accessory to murder. For a moment, I considered that he might have suspected the events of the night would take some kind of violent turn, but I dismissed it almost at once. Here in this empty room, I was the only witness to this solitary hour of reflection, and it was clear he never in his wildest dreams imagined that this had been the plan all along, no matter how Alasdair attempted to gaslight him into believing otherwise.

The tide of memory swept us up and deposited us in the bustling dining hall the next day, where the news that a girl had been murdered on the grounds of Kingshurst was being industriously circulated by every single student. Andrew sat with his eyes lowered, forcing down bites of porridge as the words rocketed around over his head.

"A local girl, they say, from the village..."

"...what on earth she was doing here..."

"It was gruesome, I heard. Blood everywhere."

"It's true. Martin saw it, didn't you, Martin? The path is still stained with it, he said."

"Surely, if the victim was from the village, the killer is, too."

"No one here would bother with a village girl. Scullery maid, I heard, quite lowborn."

"Don't be such a snob, Evans. The lowborn ones are just as good for a roll in the hay and better, I dare say. Loose morals and all that."

Andrew cringed as the conversation took a decidedly bawdy turn. At last he shoved his bowl away, unable to look at it anymore. He glanced over his shoulder and froze as he caught Alasdair's eye from where he sat holding court on the other side of the dining hall. He appeared utterly composed, tucking into a large pile of eggs, bacon, and bread and listening with a half-amused expression to the rumors flying all around him. While Andrew looked haggard and disheveled from a sleepless night, Alasdair looked fresh and well-rested, his hair perfectly coiffed and his uniform spotless. He glanced up, caught Andrew's eye, and his smirk stretched into a smile. He nodded once and raised his glass before returning to his conversation. The little color left in Andrew's cheeks drained away, and he abandoned his seat, half-running for the door as he made a beeline for the lavatory, where he expelled what little breakfast he'd managed to swallow.

When next the world reformed around us, it did so with a cold finality, and I had to repress a shudder. Somehow, I knew we were nearing the end of the story. My pulse quickened as I looked around us—we stood in the corridor I recognized. It was long and full of niches holding busts—the place where Finn and Milo had first caught that slightest whiff of Alasdair's energy. Andrew walked to the end of this hallway, turned a corner, and there it was right in front of us: the still life painting containing the image of the chalice.

My heart leaped. I'd been right. The painting had been used to conceal the entrance to the sanctum, but it had hung in a different place in Alasdair's day.

Andrew reached up and pressed the palm of his hand against the image of the chalice. There was a deep grinding sound, and when it had finished, Andrew pulled the side of the frame, and it swung open like a door: the entrance to the Brotherhood's inner sanctum. We stepped through, and the heavy door ground shut behind us. We found ourselves in the hallway from my vision, the one with the carvings along the wall. It sloped steeply downward toward a door. Andrew hesitated only a moment, then pushed it open.

Alasdair was there, as I expected he would be, but his neat and tidy appearance from earlier in the day was quite transformed. His hair was wild, escaping its formerly smooth ponytail and flopping into his eyes. He had abandoned his jacket and had rolled back the sleeves of his shirt, revealing muscled forearms. Perspiration shone on his face and stuck his shirt to his chest in translucent patches. It was like stumbling into Doctor Frankenstein's laboratory, except his creation was one of death, and the only monster he'd managed to bring to life was himself.

Alasdair spotted Andrew, and his face lit up with delighted surprise, an expression so inappropriate to everything that had passed that it made my skin crawl.

"Abercromby! You came! I wasn't at all convinced that... you're just in time!"

Andrew had to clear his throat before he could find voice enough to reply, "Just in time for what?"

"For the unveiling, of course!" Alasdair said, rubbing his hands together. "All's nearly complete!"

He turned and drew a curtain aside, revealing a work table, and above it—I let out a gasp at the sight of it—was a strange, pulsing, glowing orb. It hovered in the air above the tabletop, upon which Alasdair had drawn a circle with a charred stick. It was much smaller and dimmer, but the desperate throbbing and strange cold energy left no doubt: it was a Collection consisting of a single soul: the soul of the scullery maid he had murdered the previous night. The soul writhed within the confines of its orb, and the energy emanating from it was so bleak, so desperate and scared, that I forgot to breathe as I stared at it. Beside me, Andrew moved forward in a trance of horror, his mouth hanging open as he gazed, transfixed, at Alasdair's creation.

Alasdair, meanwhile, was scribbling feverishly in a large book, mumbling to himself. I moved closer to see what I could see on the pages, but he slammed the cover shut and tossed it aside with a grunt of satisfaction.

"What have you done to her?" Andrew managed to ask at last, and I dragged my attention away from the book.

"I've contained her," Alasdair said. "It's akin to a Caging, but it restricts movement as well as communication. It has also worked to separate her."

"Separate her from what?" Andrew asked.

"From herself—her autonomy, her memories, her agency, her very essence has been severed. She is no longer one being but many parts, each with its own unique energy. She has been *distilled*, Abercromby! Imagine that!"

Andrew's expression left no doubt that he was indeed imagining it, and that the very thought had left him sick with horror. He could barely tear his eyes from Alasdair's creation, and when he did, it was only to gaze upon Alasdair with undisguised wariness. Andrew's one-time awe and respect for Alasdair had completed its transformation. He now looked at Alasdair as though the latter was the most dangerous thing he had ever encountered.

And he was, I thought miserably. He was then, and he remained so to this very day, as dangerous in death as he was in life.

Alasdair finally seemed to notice that Andrew was displaying none of the unbridled enthusiasm that he himself was near to bursting with. His smile slipped, and he huffed impatiently. "For Aether's sake, Abercromby, why in the world are you looking at me like that? We're upon the precipice, man! The brink of greatness! I realize it's all a bit much to wrap your head around, but when you see what we can do, I know you'll see it my way. I know you'll see that it's all been worth the cost."

"Who was she?" Andrew asked in little more than a whisper.

Alasdair's smile vanished altogether now. He looked thoroughly aggravated. "I already told you. A nobody. A scullery drudge."

Andrew shook his head violently. "But she had a name. A family. What was her name?"

The words extinguished the last spark of excitement from Alasdair's eyes. His voice when next he spoke was quiet, unconcerned, and icy cold. "I don't know."

"You didn't ask?"

He cocked his head to one side. "I certainly did. But I forgot it the moment she told me."

"Because you didn't care."

"It was immaterial."

Andrew's hands balled into fists at his sides. "I don't think you care about seeing loved ones again. I don't think you've ever cared about it. I can't imagine there's any person you've ever loved enough to want to see them again once they Crossed."

Alasdair didn't even attempt to refute the accusation, but continued to stare with an expression of outright apathy on his face. He looked almost... bored. And somehow, that boredom was the most disturbing thing I'd seen from him so far. It spoke so much to an utter lack of empathy, that I felt my pulse begin to quicken. My primal fight or flight instinct went into overdrive, and I knew.

Whatever had happened to turn Andrew into the faceless, voiceless spirit he had become, I was about to watch it happen.

Too caught up in his emotions to heed the warning signs, Andrew plunged on. "And that means you used me. You used John. What I can't understand is, what is it all for?"

Alasdair let out a sigh and shook his head. "When will I learn," he muttered.

"When will you learn *what*?" Andrew spat.

"I keep making this mistake," Alasdair said in a very thoughtful voice. He was looking at Andrew more closely now, examining him as he spoke. "I witness the passion in another person—their drive, their determination—and I think we understand each other. It truly seems as though we do. But I fail to dig all the way down to the root of that passion. I really ought to dig all the way down and take a closer look at what that passion has grown from—what has fed it, what continues to nurture it. The roots of your passion are your love for your brother, of course. But I fundamentally misunderstood it. Your love runs broadly, growing like mad and spreading just beneath the surface in every direction. I took that to mean it was strong. But the slightest tug, the first challenge, and I can pull it all up, the entire root system, as easily as I could a blade of grass. It doesn't run deep enough to withstand the challenges of this work. It is too... mortal. Too human."

Andrew's face was astonished. "But... but we *are* human. Our mortality is the heart of who we are. Surely you know that."

"Our mortality weakens us, Abercromby. It limits us, cripples us, leaving us screaming into the abyss, and grasping desperately at the minutes as they tick away. It is not the heart of who we are, it is the clock against which we rage. It limits us, and I do not accept limits. I do not accept arbitrary rules, or flawed moral codes that keep us submissive to that ticking clock. I reject them. I mean to become limitless. I thought you understood."

"I thought I did, too. But this..." he gestured at the spirit orb over Alasdair's shoulder. "You've gone too far."

Alasdair sighed again, a little sadly. "And there is our fundamental disagreement, Abercromby. You believe in 'too far.' And I believe in 'whatever is necessary.' I told you that this was not for the faint of heart, and despite all of your promises, that is precisely what you've turned out to be, just like all the others."

"You didn't tell me it would be like this."

"I didn't know what it would be like. These are uncharted waters—

undiscovered frontiers. We cannot know what they are, and how we will traverse them, until we arrive."

"Well, I won't traverse them. Not like this. And I won't let you do it, either."

A silence curdled between them. The temperature in the room seemed to drop, or perhaps that was only my dread sliding like ice through my veins and chilling me from the inside out.

"You won't let me?" Alasdair asked, his voice quietly poisonous.

"No, I... I won't." Andrew stammered, drawing himself up, nonetheless.

"And how do you propose to stop me?"

"I... I hoped I would not have to stop you. I hoped we could come to an understanding, and walk back from the precipice together," Andrew said, his voice colored with a desperate stab at hope.

Alasdair smiled—a vile smirk of amusement. "Oh, I'm afraid not. There is no going back, not for me. Not for either of us, in fact."

Andrew licked his lips. "What do you mean?"

"I mean that I trusted you, Abercromby, and you betrayed that trust. I brought you in, not just to this inner sanctum," he gestured around the room, "but to mine. I confided in you, and now you threaten to betray me."

"As... as long as we can walk away now, as long as this goes no further, I will never breathe a word of what has passed," Andrew said, his voice cracking with fear.

Alasdair cocked a quizzical eyebrow. "And if I press on?"

"You are saying you will do this again?" Andrew asked, pointing a shaking finger at the orb.

"I'm saying I will do it as many times as necessary to accomplish our goal," Alasdair replied.

"Then you leave me no choice," Andrew said, backing a few steps away. "I'm sorry, MacLeod, but I cannot stand by knowing others will die by your hand. It is unconscionable."

"Very well, then," Alasdair said. "You do what you must, Abercromby, and I... I shall do what I must."

Andrew backed away a few more steps, nearly tripping over the hem of his cloak. "I just... I can't... I'm so sorry." He turned to leave, crossed the room...

For one foolish moment, I thought to myself, *He's going to make it.*

The first blow came from behind and sent Andrew sprawling to the ground. He tried to scramble to his feet, but the second blow came too quickly, and he cried out as he rolled over onto his back, arms up to defend himself. Alasdair bore down upon him, a small stone figure of Circe in one hand, smeared in Andrew's blood, and a flat, merciless grimace on his face. His eyes had gone completely unfocused, as though his mind was somewhere else completely, even as his hands cudgeled the life out of another human being. Andrew would not go down without a fight, however. He thrust out his leg, hooked it around the back of Alasdair's knee, and kicked out hard. The move threw Alasdair off his balance, and he toppled to the floor, landing hard and losing his grip on the statue, which rolled away across the room. In the time it took Alasdair to clamber to his feet again, Andrew had likewise stumbled to his, and was desperately staggering his way toward the door. He looked intoxicated as he wove his way toward his only chance of escape, and I knew the blows from Alasdair had severely impaired his balance.

Andrew managed to wrench open the door and started down the hallway—the long, dark hallway full of carvings that I now recognized from my Seer visions. It slanted steeply upward, and Andrew struggled to put one foot in front of the other as he fought to remain conscious. If he could just get outside. If he could just call for help, raise the alarm.

He heard a roar behind him and turned just in time to see Alasdair bear down on him, his face twisted grotesquely with the intensity of his rage, as he raised the statue once more.

The statue came down, and the world went dark.

21

REVELATION

I surfaced as though I had been underwater, sucking in a desperate breath to fill my lungs as I sat upright.

"Jess! Thank God!"

The room was spinning like a tilt-a-whirl, but I managed to make out Flavia's anxious face floating in front of me, before I turned my head and vomited all over the floor.

"Are you all right? It's very disorienting, the reentry process. Here, drink this."

Flavia thrust a small bowl of tea at me. The herbal smell wafting up from it was so strong it made my stomach heave again, and I pushed it away.

"Unless you want to feel like you're spinning in circles for the next twelve hours, I'd try to get some of that down you," she said dryly, thrusting it toward me again.

"Okay, okay," I croaked. "Anything to make this stop."

I forced a scalding sip down my throat and then another, wrestling with my stomach muscles to keep it down. The effect was almost instantaneous. The room righted itself, and my cramping insides relaxed.

"Ugh, you were right, thank you," I said with a sigh of relief.

"I usually am," Flavia said, quirking one corner of her mouth in the suggestion of a smile, before it faded completely. "He's been very... agitated."

I turned to see Andrew, still within the boundaries of his own circle; but where before he had been sitting up straight, now he lay curled in the fetal position, his hands thrown up over his head as though he could hide from the memories we had traversed together. A lump came into my throat, and I reached toward him, but Flavia caught at my hand.

"Wait. I have to close out the Casting first. I'm not sure what would happen if you tried to touch him now. You might even be pulled back in."

I snatched my hand back and nodded. I wanted to comfort him, but I most definitely did not want to wind up falling headfirst back into his trauma.

"Are you sure you're all right?"

"I think so," I said, though it sounded more like a question.

"Do you remember any of what he showed you?" Flavia asked, as she lit a bundle of sage and circled it three times, first around Andrew and then around me.

I retreated into my head, thinking, remembering, catching at details, and it was with relief that I could answer in the affirmative. "I think I'd quite like to forget most of it," I said, "but yes. I remember it."

"I hate to ask, but do you suppose you could fill me in?" she ventured. "I promised Finn I'd get every scrap of information out of you before he left."

For the first time, I realized Finn wasn't there. "Where did he go?"

"I'm not sure. Savvy came in and whispered something to him, and he followed her out."

"Oh." I felt a twist of worry. Had something happened? Another attack?

"I'm sure everything's okay. He'll be back as soon as he can. In the meantime, I'm sorry to make you relive it all," Flavia said, resting a gentle hand on my leg.

"If Andrew can relive it again, then I certainly can," I said.

For the next few minutes, while Flavia worked to close out the Casting, I walked her through the journey I had taken through Andrew's memories. She listened eagerly, clearly just as interested in what the experience had been like as she was in the discoveries I had made. A few times, I had to redirect the conversation, because Flavia kept asking questions about things like sensory perception and movement within the memoryscape.

"Sorry," she said a bit sheepishly, after she interrupted for the third time. "It's just such a fascinating process."

"Flavia, I promise, once we catch Alasdair, we will sit down, and I will give you enough detail to fill a book," I said, smiling at her.

"Yes, of course. Right. Carry on. What happened next?"

I told her about Andrew's brother and how Andrew caught Alasdair's attention at Kingshurst.

"Yes, I'm sure he could smell the vulnerability a mile away, and started circling him like a vulture," Flavia said, her disgust palpable. I looked at her in surprise. "Sorry. I've heard so much about this Alasdair from your sister over the past few days, that I've come to loathe him almost as much as you do. That Collection..." She shook her head, momentarily lost for words. "So Alasdair was the ringleader then, not just a disciple of the Brotherhood?"

I thought hard, trying to remember all the details of the conversations I'd heard. "He was definitely the leader when Andrew was there. Whether he founded it, I can't say for sure, but he certainly had every member of it wrapped around his little finger. You should have seen the way those other boys followed him around like sycophants, hero-worshipping him. No wonder he thought he could get away with whatever he chose."

I explained the incident with the scullery maid, and Flavia groaned.

"Ugh, now I feel like I'm going to be sick. What a monster. Never even bothered to find out her name. How did you know it?"

"It was in the records the historians found for us, the old bulletins and files from Alasdair's time at Kingshurst. They wound up hanging some poor vagrant who lived down in the village. Apparently, he woke after a night of heavy drinking to find a bloody weapon in his hand, and a lock of Alice's hair pulled out by the roots and tucked in the pocket of his jacket. Whether it was Alasdair himself who framed the man, or someone higher up the food chain, we'll probably never know for certain."

I remembered being shocked at the notion of the Northern Clans framing an innocent man for a Caomhnóir's crime, but Flavia didn't look shocked at all. "Go on, then. What happened after they killed that girl?"

I walked her through the rest of the memories, culminating in Andrew's murder. She listened, transfixed. I couldn't tell if Andrew could hear me or not. It had been several minutes since Flavia had closed the Casting, and yet he had not attempted to leave the circle in which he had been contained. He kept his hands pressed over his face and made no movement or reaction as I finished the story.

"Alasdair killed Andrew so he wouldn't turn him in, and then used a Casting to make sure he could never communicate what had happened to him, even in spirit form," Flavia muttered, shaking her head in disgust. "It's sick."

"And that's Alasdair, isn't it?" I ground out. "Of course he'd find something crueler even than murder. I mean, killing Andrew was bad enough, but why didn't he just let him Cross? It would have made things much simpler—after all, Andrew wouldn't be able to betray Alasdair's confidence from beyond the Gateway. But no, that wouldn't have been depraved enough for the likes of Alasdair. Better to tear Andrew's soul apart and use it for his own vile means. With an incomplete soul, Andrew was prevented from the only thing that ever really mattered to him."

"Seeing his brother again," Flavia finished, her voice cracking.

We sat silently, each of us stunned wordless by the sheer evil that human beings were capable of. I'd honestly thought, after all I'd seen, that I'd been hardened to it, but it turned out I could still be shocked. I wasn't sure if that was a good thing or a bad thing, but it was a truth I had to sit with for several seconds before I could find my voice again.

"I wonder where Finn's gone. Do you think I should go and find him?"

"Hang on," Flavia said. "Didn't you say the memories took you into the sanctum?"

The word sanctum felt like a slap in the face. Holy shit, what was I still doing sitting here?

"I have to go! I have to go find Finn and tell him I know how to get into the sanctum!"

"Don't let me hold you up!" Flavia said, shooing me toward the door.

I paused as my eyes fell on Andrew, still curled up on the ground. "Can you—?"

Flavia didn't even need me to finish the question. "I'll take care of him. Don't you worry."

I pulled her into a cursory one-armed hug. "That's a placeholder hug," I told her. "I'm going to hug-tackle you when I get back. Probably kiss you, too."

Flavia grinned. "Looking forward to it. Now go!"

I skidded out into the hallway, trying to get my bearings. I turned on the spot, going through a mental map of the buildings, trying to remember which way I had to go to get to that hallway where the painting used to hang. I sprinted out of the building I was in, and down the cloister that connected it to the Historical Center. I skidded around the corner and...

WHAM.

I slammed into something solid and was launched to the floor, knocking the breath from my lungs. My head spun as I tried to jump to my feet.

"Whoa there! Slow down, mate!"

I had run smack into Savvy, who was running in the opposite direction. I'd gone flying, but she just stood there, solid as a block of granite. She hauled me to my feet.

"Savvy, I'm so sorry, I was—"

"Did someone tell you about Aoife?" she asked.

My heart stuttered to a halt in my chest. "What? No! What about Aoife? Oh God. You don't mean... she isn't..."

"Gone," Savvy said. "From her office."

No. No, no, no.

I tried to keep my response rational. "How do you know she hasn't just stepped out for—"

But Savvy was already shaking her head.

"Blood," she gasped. "So much blood."

"Did you tell Finn?" I asked, realizing at the same moment that yes, of course she had told Finn. That's what she'd come to tell him while I was Rifting. That's why he'd vanished. "Never mind, stupid question. We've got to find her, Sav!"

Savvy bit her lip. "What do you think we've been trying to do? But we may be too late. That room... I don't know if—"

"That's right!" I shouted. "We don't know, which means there's still a chance that she's alive! And now, thanks to Andrew, I know where she might be!"

"Wait, what? Who's Andrew?" Savvy asked, totally bewildered.

"I'll explain later, there's no time," I said. "Here's what I need you to do. Go find Finn. Tell him to meet me where he and Milo first discovered that faint trace of Alasdair. Can you do that?"

"Meet you at... yeah. Yeah, all right," Savvy said, somewhat breathlessly as she tried to take in everything that was happening.

"He needs to bring Caomhnóir reinforcements. As many as he can, okay? This is it. I know where the entrance to the sanctum is."

Savvy's eyes went wide. "I'll get him. I'll... don't do anything on your own, all right?"

"I will wait for you, I promise," I said.

Savvy gave me her trademark roguish wink and took off to find Finn while I bolted in the direction I'd already been heading before I hit her like a runaway train.

I took three wrong turns in my haste to find that damn corridor, but at last, I skidded into it, breathless and wild with adrenaline. I wanted to keep running, but I forced myself to slow down. Now was not the time to be reckless. I had to tread very carefully. Aoife's life might depend on it.

I took the hallway deliberately, one foot in front of the other as quietly as I could manage, straining every sense I possessed. It seemed to be completely deserted, lonely, and cold. I passed all the stern-faced busts of long-dead men and women, unable to shake the feeling that their cold stone eyes were following me. The closer I came to the corner, the harder my heart pounded against my ribcage. The others would be here shortly, I reasoned. I didn't need to go any further by myself. But then I thought of Aoife.

The wall in front of me looked utterly ordinary. The painting that had once hung there now graced another part of the building. Aoife had been helping me find out where else it might have been displayed. I swallowed against a lump in my throat at the thought that she was likely working on that very lead when she was...

I would not think "killed." I would *not* think that word.

I stepped closer to the wall, running my hands gently over the stones, feeling for any inconsistencies or obvious irregularities, but it looked just like every other blank stretch of wall in the place. I closed my eyes, picturing the painting that had once hung there, remembering the way Andrew had simply reached out his hand. I raised my own hand, fingers trembling...

"Miss Ballard?"

I shrieked and whirled around to find Gareth standing in the hallway behind me, carrying a stack of books, and looking utterly bewildered to see me standing in the deserted place all by myself.

"Gareth! You're out of the infirmary!" I managed to gasp. His sudden appearance had so completely terrified me that I'd almost forgotten how to breathe.

"Yes, they let me out a few hours ago. I couldn't stand to be stuck in there, with everyone here searching. But now Aoife..." He shook his head sadly. "I saw the office. It was terrible. I don't see how she can be alive."

"Don't say that!" I shouted, and he took a step back from me, alarmed. "Sorry," I said. "I'm just on edge."

"What are you doing down here?" Gareth asked, and I saw his eyes move curiously to the wall behind me.

"It's a long story, but I found out that the entrance to the sanctum is here, hidden in this wall."

Gareth staggered, his face going white. "You're... you're joking."

"I'm not."

"How did you—?"

"Again, long story. But can you help me? I'm trying to open it."

"Of course!" Gareth said. He hurried forward, dropping his stack of books to the ground without a second thought. He stood beside me, his eyes scanning the stonework eagerly. "How does it work? Do you know how to open it?"

"The mechanism is definitely somewhere on this upper part of the wall." I gave Gareth an appraising look, and determined he was roughly the same height as Andrew. "Just stick your hand straight out in front of you and start pressing stones!"

We set to work pushing and prodding. Without the picture there on the wall to guide me, it was hard to tell how far to the left or right the secret latch might be. At last though, Gareth pressed a long-fingered hand to a particularly flat stone and pushed.

The stone pushed inward and triggered some sort of mechanism. There was a deep grinding noise, and a whole section of the stone wall began to pull away from the whole. It swung slowly inward until a loud clunking sound revealed a dark hole about four feet high and maybe three feet wide. Stale air wafted up out of it, and I wretched and stumbled back a step because I knew that smell.

The stench of crypt and rot and horror. The stench of the abomination that was Alasdair.

Gareth pulled his shirt up over his nose and mouth. "I know that energy," he gasped in his still raspy voice. "That was the energy I felt just before I was attacked! He's in there, or he was! What do we do? Should we go in?"

"No," I said firmly. "Finn and the others will be here any minute. We should wait for them."

Gareth nodded, looking frankly relieved that I hadn't just dragged him on through the opening. He peered into the darkness beyond. "Can you see anything?" he asked, dropping his voice to a whisper.

I narrowed my eyes, but I couldn't make sense of the blackness before me. It was too deep, too impenetrable.

Gareth swallowed hard. "I... I think I see something. Is that... is there a shape huddled on the ground there?" He turned to me with wild eyes. "Do you have a torch we can use?"

I fumbled to extricate my phone from my jeans pocket. I flicked on the flashlight feature and crept forward just a step, training the beam of light directly into the hole, but it barely penetrated more than a couple of feet.

"Damn it. I don't see anything."

I squatted down so that I was perched right on the lip of the opening and thrust my phone out further to illuminate a bit more of what lay beyond.

I had barely a glimpse of a narrow stone passage with a dirt floor when Gareth shoved me roughly between my shoulder blades, and I tumbled ass over tea kettle right into the waiting arms of the darkness.

22

ACCOMPLICE

I tumbled down a short set of steps and landed hard on my back, knocking the breath from my body. I lost my grip on the phone, and it skittered away across the floor, its beam of light trained on the ceiling. Blinded by pain and unable even to pull in a breath, I couldn't even shout when the opening above me began to grind slowly shut again. I just had to lay there in the near-total darkness, waiting for my head to stop spinning and my lungs to reinflate. When they finally did, the opening had sealed up again, and I was alone in the muffled silence of the musty passageway.

My brain felt sluggish as I tried to comprehend what had just happened. Gareth had pushed me. Gareth, whom Alasdair had tried to murder just the day before. Gareth, who had been strangled within an inch of his life. I couldn't take it in.

Groaning, I rolled onto my side and tried to assess what my injuries were. My shoulder was aching like hell, but it didn't feel broken—probably just jammed. My ribs and tailbone were sore, too, but again, not broken. I felt like one giant bruise, and yet all my limbs seemed to be functioning as I struggled first into a seated position and, finally, to my feet. I hobbled over to the corner to retrieve my phone, which had also survived the fall, with the exception of a small crack in the bottom corner of the screen. I flashed the beam of light around me to get a better understanding of where exactly I was.

It was a long hallway, sloping downward into the impenetrable blackness ahead. The interior walls, made of stone like the outer walls, were smoother, and I could just make out the first of the carvings—Circe on her throne, a chalice in one hand, and a wand in the other.

There could be no mistaking it: this was definitely the passageway from my Seer visions and Andrew's memories, which meant that at the end of it was the inner sanctum of the Brotherhood.

There was no sound, no movement to suggest I wasn't alone, but I still hesitated to move forward without knowing what was waiting for me. Gareth could be barricading me in or setting the building on fire right now. I had to warn the others. I held up my phone, but whatever spotty service I'd had aboveground was now nonexistent. I attempted to call Finn, but I knew it was no good before I was even finished dialing. I might as well have fallen through a hole in time.

I climbed painfully back up the stone steps I'd just tumbled down and pressed my ear to the door. I didn't expect Gareth to still be there. I knew that he couldn't linger long near the entrance to this passageway without being caught, either by Finn or the other Caomhnóir that would soon be swarming the area. Savvy had promised to find him and tell him where to meet me, so that meant help was on the way. I banged my hands against the unrelenting stone, but could hardly make a sound.

"Hello?" I shouted. "Finn? Hello? Can anyone hear me?"

I held my breath, listening. No reply.

I tried again. "Help! Can anyone hear me? I'm trapped down here!"

I pressed my ear against the stone, but could hear nothing from the other side, which meant it was unlikely anyone would hear me either. I ran my hands along the sides of the door, feeling again for a secret trigger that would cause it to re-open and release me, but though I searched for what felt like several minutes, I came up empty. Was it possible that the door could only be triggered from the outside? If so, there would have to be another exit somewhere, and if I wanted any chance of getting out of here, I was going to have to find it.

But first, I would have to try to find Aoife, because I was still convinced that if she had been hidden away somewhere on this campus, it was in the Brotherhood's inner sanctum. I hesitated for only a moment longer, thinking. Savvy would give Finn my message. It would lead him right to the door and the passageway. He would be right behind me. And if Savvy's description of Aoife's office was to be believed, I was wasting what little time Aoife might have left. I would have to try to find her, and hope that Finn and the others would find us both.

I descended the steps carefully and started down the passageway, my phone held out in front of me to light the way. I swung it back and forth across the space, illuminating all of the carvings along the way that told the stories of Circe. Had Alasdair himself carved them? Or some of the other boys he had conscripted into his creepy little cult? I supposed I'd never know. But I was so fixated on them that I didn't spot the thing in the middle of the floor ahead of me, until I was almost close enough to trip over it. I let out a shriek, and then immediately slapped my hand over my mouth to stifle the sound.

My first thought was of Aoife, but no. The shape that lay huddled on the floor in front of me was coated in dust and wrapped in the remains of a rotting black cloak. Shaking, I lowered myself into a crouch so that I could examine it more closely. Pale bone peeked through the holes in the cloak, and I swallowed back a gag. Little though I wanted to, I took the edge of the cloak between two of my fingers and peeled it back.

A skull stared blankly up at me, mouth open in an eternal scream. All the flesh had long rotted from the body, leaving it little more than a skeleton draped in scraps of moldering material. And lying on the ground, beside the skeleton's outstretched hand... a small stone statue of a woman, discolored with a rusty, dried substance.

"Oh, dear God. Andrew."

Alasdair had never even bothered to move him from the very place he had murdered him. Perhaps whatever Casting he had used to silence Andrew's ghost required his body to remain within the circle that had been drawn around it. Or perhaps he didn't move it because he simply didn't need to. The body would have a better chance of lying undiscovered here than if he had hidden it somewhere else. After all, the Brotherhood had already been disbanded by that time, and Alasdair himself was mere weeks from leaving Kingshurst for good. By that summer's end, he would be terrorizing Edinburgh under the morbid guise of The Collector.

I stood up and turned away from Andrew's bones. There was nothing I could do for him now, but I might still be able to help Aoife. I had to press on, and hope we'd have the chance to give Andrew a proper burial when this was all over.

I left Andrew behind me, letting the dark swallow him up again, whispering apologies and tingling with rage. It was Alasdair. It all came back to Alasdair. A trail of death and misery spanning centuries was all his doing. He had to be stopped.

I continued down the passage, swinging the light back and forth, now horribly aware that there might be other bodies to step over, other victims strewn with equal cruelty and carelessness. At last, the impenetrable darkness right ahead of me resolved into a heavy wooden door. I hesitated for a moment before it, shining my light around the perimeter. There were symbols carved into it all the way around the door frame, and while I couldn't be entirely sure, I thought they might have been written in ancient Greek, because they looked familiar to the ones in the old versions of the Odyssey that Gareth had shown us. I threw one last look over my shoulder, but there was still no sign of the others. I couldn't afford to wait. I reached out a tentative hand and applied some gentle pressure, wondering if I could ease it open and get a glimpse of the room beyond without alerting anyone to my presence, but it was no use. The door was too heavy. Sucking in a deep breath, I leaned my aching shoulder into the door and shoved as hard as I could.

Even with every ounce of my strength, the door scraped forward only reluctantly, its boards swollen with age and moisture,, and the hinges sealed tightly under a coating of rust. There was no way anyone had come through this way, not in a very long time, and I began to doubt every instinct that had sent me down into this place to begin with. Was it possible I was wrong? Could I be wasting precious time while Aoife's life slipped away somewhere else entirely? The thought made me shove even harder until suddenly, the door gave way, and I fell flat on my face into the room beyond.

It was like falling headfirst back into Andrew's memory. I half expected a ring of cloaked figures to emerge around me. I scrambled to my feet, staring around wildly, but the room appeared to be empty at first glance. I didn't let my guard down, however. Someone had lit candles in several of the towering candelabras, which meant someone had either been down here, or they still were. Alasdair's energy was certainly in the air—it was like tasting death on the tip of my tongue, but there was none of that bone-deep chill that meant he was currently nearby. This realization allowed me to exhale, but the relief was short-lived. As I took a step forward into the inner sanctum, I spotted a figure crouched in the corner against the opposite wall—a slight figure, spattered with blood, a figure that scrambled to its feet the moment it saw me, too.

"Aoife!"

"Jess?!" Her face was pallid with shock, and probably loss of blood.

I hurried forward. "Aoife! There you are! Thank God. Are you all right? How badly are you hurt?"

Aoife was still staring at me as though she couldn't believe I was real. "I... I think I'm... not too badly, I think." Her hand was pressed to her side, where there was a dark stain seeping through her shirt.

"That looks bad," I said, moving toward her, but she stepped away from me, as though trying to protect herself. "Don't worry, I'm not going to touch it. We need to get you to a doctor. Can you walk?"

"I... I can, but... How did you find me? How did you get in?" Aoife asked.

"There was a ghost. He used to be a member of the Brotherhood."

Aoife's eyes went wide. "I don't understand."

"Look, I know this is all really confusing, but we can't just stay here. We can talk about all that later, there's no time to—"

I reached out to grab her hand, but she pulled out of my grip and let it fall to her side. "I need to know how you found me."

I stared at her. Why the hell did it matter how I found her?

"His name was Andrew Abercromby. Alasdair killed him when they were both students here, and he silenced him too. But Flavia had a Traveler Casting that let me experience his memories, and that's how we found this place. Okay? Now let's go!"

"You said 'we.' Who else have you told?"

"What?" What was happening here? Why was she just standing here asking questions when we should be running for our lives?

"Who else knows?" Aoife asked again.

"Savvy went to tell Finn where to meet me, and there are others on the way, but we can't wait for them. We need to go."

"We can't. There isn't a way out."

"Look, I know the passage doesn't open from the inside, but Finn and the others will let us out if we can just get back there without running into Alasdair or... wait."

I stared at Aoife, and she stared calmly back at me.

"Was it Gareth who attacked you?"

"I'm sorry?"

"Tonight. You were attacked in your office. But Alasdair can't attack people, not in his present form, so someone had to be helping him. Was it Gareth?"

"No, Gareth didn't attack me." She almost laughed.

"Look, I know it doesn't make any sense, because he was attacked too, but he shoved me in here, so he's involved in this somehow. But if it wasn't Gareth, then who was it?"

Aoife looked down at her own blood-spattered appearance as though she had only just noticed it. And I looked closer, too. I had been so relieved to see her there alive, I hadn't taken the time to examine her beyond the obvious evidence of gore. But now I looked at her. *Really* looked at her. She didn't look disheveled or dirty or hurt. No signs of struggle, or of trying to escape. And her eyes... there was no fear there, no trepidation.

No. Oh, no. God, I was such an idiot.

"You weren't attacked at all, were you?" The words dropped from me, hollowed out with the horror of my realization, come much too late.

Aoife's lips pressed into a tight little smile. "Gotten there at last, have you? No, no one attacked me. I came here of my own free will, although I tried to make it look like I'd been kidnapped. I didn't think it was enough to simply disappear. I had to make you all think I'd been the next victim, and that required staging." She moved her hand from her side, where the blood was darkest, and I could see now that there was no tear in her shirt, no sign of a wound.

"But... all that blood. How did you—" My head was spinning, trying to catch up to the realizations now raining down on top of me.

"We're quite fortunate that Kingshurst has such a robust medical research program," Aoife said, looking down at all the blood with something like academic interest. "It was a simple thing to break into the refrigerators there and slip a few bags of blood into my purse. No reason to spill my own when there was such a handy alternative at my fingertips."

"I don't understand," I whispered, but that wasn't really it, was it? I didn't *want* to understand. I didn't want it to be true.

Aoife sighed, and for a moment, she looked much older than she was—weary. "It's not been easy keeping everyone off my track, but it ought to have been even harder. That's one good thing about being an outcast, you see. In some ways, it makes you almost invisible—or at least less worthy of notice. You, of all people, must understand that. I've learned a lot about you, you see, since you came here. Like any good academic, I've been doing my research. You know what it is to be an outsider, an outcast in the very world you were born into. We have that in common."

"Is that so?" I asked, my voice still weak with confusion. "Because in my experience, it's brought a lot of attention—and mostly the bad kind."

Aoife smiled a sad little smile that made her look strangely sinister. "That's because you wore your outcast status like a badge of honor, I suppose. I, on the other hand, was just trying to keep my head down. It's my family, you see—my clan. It is not perhaps one of the most powerful, but they have always ached to be. They have always striven, always reached, and scrabbled for the highest bit of purchase they could find. They're fighters. They've had to be. I think I took that into my heart more than any other member of my family, because while they will fight for each other, I've always had to fight for myself."

I bit down on my tongue and tasted blood. If I had to listen to one more person justify their evil just because they were misunderstood or left out or some bullshit, I was going to scream my throat raw. It was Danica all over again. But I let her keep talking because my head was reeling, and I needed time to think and understand.

"I have two older sisters—quite a bit older, in fact. It was apparent that I was a bit of an afterthought—an accident, even, though my mother would never go so far as to admit it to me. Certainly I was... unessential. In Durupinen as in British royalty culture, there is such a concept as an heir and a spare. My sisters were the heirs—the Door and the Key—and I was the spare, the little kid sister running around in their shadow, simply tagging along for the ride. I fear no one ever paid much attention to me. No one cared that I excelled in my studies or earned academic achievements. No one celebrated when I earned my full scholarship to come study here, or the fact that I was the first non-legacy student to do so. None of my accomplishments furthered the family's cause. My family wasn't interested in history—only the future, and what came next, and none of them saw how I could be a part of that. After all, I wasn't the one earning a seat on the Council, as my eldest sister has now done. I wasn't the one who traveled to Havre des Gardiennes to help shape the new laws and policies that would govern our clans after the Reckoning, as my other sister did. I just stayed here, buried in my books. Buried and quite forgotten."

Her voice was exceedingly calm and gentle, and yet there was a coldness underlying it, a hurt and frustration so deep that it merely ran beneath the surface of her words—never ruffling or upsetting them, but coloring them, nonetheless. It was as though the beating back and shoving down of her feelings had simply caused them to run deeper.

Hidden. Darker.

"Well, this is all fascinating, Aoife, but frankly, I'm done with the sob stories. Lots of us have had hard lives, you know. It doesn't give you a pass to—"

"You said you wanted to understand, and so now you will listen!" she cried, pointing a violently trembling finger at me. For the first time, some part of me acknowledged that this tiny mouse of a girl was dangerous. I pressed my lips together and nodded. She lowered her hand by degrees until it dropped to her side, and she seemed to regain her composure.

"Even here, I never managed to draw much attention to myself. Damien was always wrapped up in his own research, and Gareth was his chosen protege. He did not need me, not in an academic sense. I was here to fetch coffee, reshelve books, that sort of thing. They never seemed to have time to look at my contributions or listen to my input. And so, eventually, I stopped giving it to them. I kept it to myself instead." Here she smiled, just a tiny upturn of the lips, but it gave her expression a sly, sinister air I never would have thought her capable of.

I pulled just enough of my attention away to listen for footsteps, but we seemed to be alone. I could hear no sounds coming from the corridor I'd entered, and there seemed to be no other egress in the circular room. And yet, if there wasn't, how had Aoife gotten in? The door I'd come through hadn't been opened in ages. I watched Aoife carefully, letting my eyes dart away to search the room whenever she dropped her gaze.

Aoife toyed with the hem of her blood-soaked shirt as she continued, watching the color come away on her fingers with an almost childlike fascination. "Unlike my family, Jessica, I saw the value in learning about our past, and not just our official past. I wasn't interested in the clean and glamorous version of our rise, because I knew it was just that—a glamour, a sort of spell we'd put on ourselves to hide our flaws and mask our missteps. I was interested in the corners of our history that we'd hidden and forgotten. I wanted to plumb our darkest depths. That's how I found the Brotherhood of Circe."

My heart plummeted as I watched a maniacal light kindle in her eyes. I'd seen that mad sparkle before, in Danica's eyes, in Charlie Parker's, in Neil Caddigan's, and even earlier that very night, in Andrew Abercromby's. It was the spark of something burning out of control, a spark that threatened to consume everything it touched. Aoife had been lost before I'd even met her.

"I stumbled upon it quite by accident when I found one of Gareth's notebooks he'd left behind. I meant simply to pick it up and return it to him, but my eyes found the words, and without consciously deciding to, I found myself reading. Gareth came upon me a few moments later and flew off the handle. It was the intensity of his response that spurred me to keep digging. I began searching his archive use history, tracking down the books he'd checked out and the documents he'd examined. By following in his footsteps, so to speak, I realized that he—and now we—had uncovered one of those deep, dark corners of our history I'd spoken about—a deviation from the accepted path. And that deviation was... a revelation."

"Is that so?" I asked.

"Oh, yes! We had been so weak, so... limited! All this time, we held in our hands the key to a door, and through that door was every answer to every question that has plagued humanity since the dawn of time! What lies beyond this world? Where do we truly spend eternity? What becomes of our souls? As Durupinen, we knew that souls existed, of course, but we knew no more of what becomes of them on the other side of the Aether than any other mortal being. We opened the door, but we had never walked through it!"

"And as a Durupinen, you must also understand why we didn't walk through it," I offered quietly.

Aoife snorted dismissively. "I knew what I'd been told, the feeble bleating of tradition and fear. But now I was discovering what I *hadn't* been told. Tale as old as time—parents withhold certain information from their children because they are afraid of what the children will do with it. If they know about drugs, will they take them? If they know about sex, will they have it? If they read about fascism, witchcraft, or atheism, will they take it up? But no matter the intentions, the outcome is nearly always the same: eventually, the world will find that child, and if that child is not armed with knowledge, the world will destroy them with their own ignorance."

I couldn't disagree with her in the abstract, at least. I'd always thought that more knowledge was far superior to not enough. After all, it was our ignorance of how the Gateways had come into our blood that had nearly destroyed everything. If we'd known the truth, we'd have been able to restore the Gateways long ago and avoided the Reckoning altogether. We were so busy covering up our misdeeds that we never learned from them.

As though she could hear my thoughts, Aoife spoke again. "The Reckoning proved we were unworthy of the power we held. I saw that right away. Throughout our history, the Necromancers had been painted as the villains, but we've been the villains all along."

"That's a bit harsh," I said. "We fucked up, sure, but we started with good and honorable intentions."

"What does that matter?" Aoife asked, cocking her head to one side in a bird-like movement. "Intentions do not erase responsibility. We had power. We abused it. And you are content to leave that power in our hands, knowing that we will only abuse it again?"

"I'll admit it. I'm uneasy," I said, because I didn't see how lying to Aoife would serve any purpose. "Even now, there are powerful forces among the Durupinen who are trying to reverse the Reckoning somehow—hell, that's how we got into this mess with Alasdair in the first place. But there are many of us who are speaking out against those forces, and fighting to ensure that this time, we don't abuse the power and responsibility we've been given."

"They won't give up. Surely you know that," Aoife said. "They've grown too comfortable in their power."

"Maybe not. But it doesn't follow that the only solution is just to hand all that power over to people like the Necromancers instead," I said, and it was only with a Herculean effort that I kept the anger and incredulity out of my voice.

"Perhaps not," Aoife said. "But consider everything you have ever been taught about the Necromancers. Then consider the source of that information. History is written by the victors, and we were able to paint the Necromancers in any colors we chose. How can you be sure they're so evil, when all you know of them is mere fabrication?"

"How can I be sure? Because the Necromancers aren't just some fairy tale villain in a book to me. I've met them," I said, and there was no disguising the venom in my voice now. "I've looked them in the eye, and I've seen their vision of the world. I can't say what Necromancers were when they first came to be, but I know what they are now. I've seen what they would do with that power, and it is worse than you can imagine."

"I have a very good imagination," Aoife countered. "I wouldn't underestimate it. But we're getting off track. The Necromancers aren't even who we're speaking of. The Brotherhood of Circe were not Necromancers, not really. Oh, they may have taken some inspiration from some of the Necromancers' ideas, but then they branched off and became their own organization—with Alasdair at their head."

"I know all of that," I said impatiently. "Thanks to Andrew, I probably know more about what really happened in the days of the Brotherhood than you do. What I don't understand is what's happening now. The Brotherhood of Circe has been defunct for hundreds of years, so why are you here now? Why are you helping him?"

Aoife narrowed her eyes at me as though she was trying to decide whether my question was a genuine one, or whether I was simply trying to keep her talking. I guess there was just enough bewilderment in my voice to convince her, because she answered, "When I discovered the Brotherhood of Circe when I found this place and unraveled their history, I was inspired. They understood that the Durupinen had limited themselves, that they were squandering a precious opportunity to push beyond our living boundaries, and truly understand what lay beyond. What we should have been doing was concentrating our enormous resources on how to make the door swing both ways."

"The door swing both ways? In all your research, I don't suppose you read up on a little thing called The Prophecy?" I asked, my voice dripping with sarcasm I could no longer contain. "Just an itty bitty prediction that shaped centuries of our practices, and finally came to pass a few years ago? Fairhaven in flames, legions of empty spirits, ring any bells?"

Aoife pursed her lips, but did not reply.

"No? Well, I was there. I watched what happens when the door swings both ways, and it was nearly the destruction of everything. Literal apocalyptic shit, okay? I'm sure the Brotherhood of Circe thought themselves very clever, just like the Necromancers did, but no good can come of reversing the Gateways."

"The Necromancers were greedy and foolish," Aoife insisted tartly. Her dark hair was coming down from her top knot, framing her pale, angular face in dark, lank strands. "They were not seeking understanding. They were seeking power, and they didn't care who or what they destroyed to achieve it. The Brotherhood of Circe was not so careless. They were not trying to raise an army of the dead or destroy the Durupinen. They only wanted enlightenment—to travel beyond the veil and to return again, with an understanding of what lay beyond."

I laughed now, though there was no humor in the sound, only incredulity. "I'm sorry, I thought for a moment there you were trying to claim the moral high ground over Necromancers, when even they rejected the depths to which Alasdair was willing to sink to achieve his end. He's a murderer, Aoife, and in following him, other people have become murderers as well. Danica MacLeod nearly killed her sister. And now Gareth has..."

My brain hit a wall as confusion set in. Gareth was obviously in league with Alasdair, but was he a murderer? Had he staged his own attack, like Aoife had staged hers?

"Was it Gareth who murdered the others?" I asked.

Aoife laughed. "Gareth would never have the guts to do something like that.

All his talk about the Brotherhood, all his obsessive research and digging, but it was me who truly brought it back to life."

My heart plummeted like a stone.

"It was you who killed the others then, on Alasdair's orders?"

Aoife's face twitched. "I aided him in his mission. He was not yet strong enough. He needed more spirit energy to regain a body. It was unfortunate, but necessary."

"Unfortunate? Seriously? Murdering two innocent girls in cold blood is unfortunate?"

"You took his Collection from him! You deprived him of the energy he needed! He wouldn't have had to kill anyone if he'd just had—"

"How did you do it? Did he Habitate?"

Aoife nodded. "I didn't have the physical strength to carry out the plan on my own, and he didn't possess the physical form he needed to do it himself. It was... unpleasant to have him inhabit me," she said with a shudder she couldn't repress, "but together we could... could do what needed to be done."

"So, you murdered those girls."

"Alasdair murdered them," she said forcefully. "I was just a tool."

"Bullshit. You were a willing participant."

There was no doubt about it now. Aoife's eyes were filling with tears. "I'm... I regret that they had to die. But—"

"But? You're going to defend this? Wow. Not even Danica MacLeod tried to excuse Alasdair's murder streak, and she's a stark raving lunatic. Awesome, I can't wait to hear this," I said, folding my arms across my chest as I stared expectantly at her.

Aoife resented the challenge. She raised her narrow chin defiantly. "We couldn't use spirits on the campus. It would have given him away, and you would have traced his whereabouts at once."

"So, he made you do his dirty work instead?"

"He didn't *make* me do anything," Aoife spat. "I *wanted* to help him. He's the only one who has ever had enough vision and enough guts to bring us into the future."

"And what does this grand future of yours look like, pray tell?"

There it was—the glint of madness in her eyes. She'd hidden it so well.

"A future where those of the chosen blood can move freely between the worlds of the living and the dead," Aoife whispered reverently. "A future where we can never die because the spirit world and the living world are one and the same."

The chosen blood? For fuck's sake, this girl was a walking red flag. How had we all missed it?

"And remarkably, we have you to thank for it all," Aoife added.

This pulled me up short. "Excuse me? I have nothing to do with your unhinged schemes."

"Oh, but you do! You might think, given that you've been trying to thwart us all this time, that I would hate you, but I don't, truly. In fact, I have to take this opportunity to tell you how grateful I am."

"What the hell are you talking about?" I snapped, dread pooling and churning in my stomach.

"If you hadn't restored the Gateways, all of their power would still be contained in the Durupinen bloodlines, bottled up and confined in bodies that could not be trusted to treat that power with the appropriate reverence, or to wield it with responsibility. My sisters were as bad as the rest of them, lording it over the rest of the family, like they'd been chosen based on some innate superiority rather than what we all know it to be: simple genetic luck. And they abused it, courting favors and Leeching and scrabbling for status. But now, thanks to you, all of that is over. The Gateways are the responsibility of the entire clans, as they were meant to be, and now the Geatgrimas are what they should always have been: the doors that we guard and keep, doors we can traverse through as we choose."

"Are you not listening to yourself? You're just trading one abuse of power for another, and you think it's acceptable because this time you're included among the privileged few who get to abuse it! We didn't restore the Gateways so that you and Alasdair could murder people and dismember their souls."

"We wouldn't have had to murder anyone if you hadn't separated him from his Collection!" Aoife cried, her voice rising to a shriek as she stamped her foot on the stone floor. "He had all the spirit energy he needed! You forced his hand!"

"Maybe, but I didn't force yours," I said. "He was already a murderer—what were a few more victims to a monster like him? But you? Unless you had an undergraduate side gig as a serial killer, I'm guessing you never killed anyone before this. You had a choice. You knew what helping him would mean, and you chose it anyway. I don't know how this is going to end for either of us, but I know at this moment I'm damn glad that's not a choice I have to live with."

Aoife's face had gone still as marble, but for her trembling lower lip.

"I made my choice. I do not regret it," she whispered.

We looked into each other's eyes. We were at an impasse. I wasn't going to convince this girl that she was wrong. She was under Alasdair's spell, and there was no breaking it.

"So, what happens now?" I asked.

A slow smile spread over Aoife's face as footsteps sounded somewhere behind her. A panel opened in the wall over her shoulder and a figure stepped through, coming to stand just behind her.

It was Gareth. He placed a hand on Aoife's shoulder. She seemed to flinch at the touch, but it was a fleeting thing, and then her face was neutral again.

"You've done well," he said. "But we ought to go. The others will no doubt find the hidden passage soon, and we don't want to be here when they do. It's time."

I shook my head, laughing, though nothing had ever been less funny. "The two of you, in league with Alasdair all along. I can't believe it."

Aoife and Gareth looked at each other, trading a knowing smile.

"She hasn't figured it out yet?" Gareth asked. Aoife shook her head.

Gareth stepped out from behind her, closing about half the distance between us. He stared at me as though fascinated. "I admit, I've wished you dead, Walker, but now that the moment has arrived, I'm glad I didn't kill you. I want you to witness my moment of glory."

Every cell in my body seemed to freeze up. We thought Gareth had survived, but we were wrong. Gareth was gone.

It was Alasdair MacLeod who stared back at me out of Gareth's eyes.

23

MOMENT OF TRUTH

"You're Alasdair."

The words were barely a whisper because I could hardly bring myself to admit them.

"I am."

"You did it, then. You regained a body."

A smile stretched over Gareth's face, but it looked wrong. It pulled crookedly at the muscles as if he had forgotten how smiles work.

"I had been so close in Edinburgh. A few more days, and I would have walked away from that place in the first body I could find. But you thwarted me, Walker. You tore me away from my Collection, and I wasn't strong enough yet. But then I found Aoife, and she's been such a good little pet, haven't you?"

Aoife's face twitched a little, but she bobbed her head.

"She enabled me to gain the last bit of strength I needed from the souls of those two girls, and then all that remained was to secure a body for myself. When Aoife suggested Gareth, I knew he was the perfect choice. Always here working late, always a loner, shunning the help and friendship of others in favor of personal academic glory. And by faking his attack, no one would suspect that he was anything but lucky—the one who got away."

"And when we found you, you told us the attacker had large, rough hands, which deflected any suspicion that might have fallen on Aoife," I said.

Alasdair nodded. "All rather neat, I thought. I knew you were closing in, but I did not expect you to find that door. I admit, I thought I had more time."

"Well, you screwed up there," I said. "You left a witness."

Alasdair's face—Gareth's face—twisted in disgust. "What witness? There's no one left who knows of this place, I made sure of that."

"Andrew Abercromby."

The name was like a slap to the face. Alasdair sputtered, angry spit flying.

"I destroyed Abercromby and fed off his soul. He was a shell, an empty vessel."

"There was more of him left than you thought," I said, taking what little pleasure I could from watching his shocked expression. "You let your cruelty get the better of you. If you'd simply let Andrew Cross, he would have gone on to be with his brother, and no one would remain who could unmask you. But you got greedy. You used him the way you used all those other spirits, and then you discarded the scraps. But Andrew remained. And when you returned, he watched over every victim until they were found. And then we gave him his voice back."

"Impossible."

I barked out a laugh. "Listen to you, doubting what's possible. Don't you pride yourself on seeing possibility? Well, we took a page from your book, I guess. We made the impossible possible. I know Andrew Abercromby's story, and that's how I found this place."

Alasdair chewed furiously on the inside of his cheek. "It is of no matter now. You're too late. Andrew is too late. Tonight, I finally achieve the goal I've been working toward for nearly three centuries, and you will be there to witness it. It's time."

He reached around to the back of his belt and drew out a dagger—the very same dagger I had brought with me to Kingshurst. In his other hand, he held a small canvas bag. He turned to Aoife.

"Bring her up to the Geatgrima," he said.

Aoife stepped obediently forward and took my arm. I could easily have broken away from her, but there was no point with Alasdair holding a knife at our backs. She led me toward the door Alasdair had come in through, which led to a narrow stone staircase that wound up into darkness.

I fought back the panic as we climbed. Even if Finn and the others managed to find and open the passage I'd come through, we would already be gone. There had to be another way to...

It hit me so clearly that I couldn't believe I hadn't thought of it before. I didn't need a cell phone, for God's sake! I had my own personal direct Connection. I retreated into that shared mental space, throwing it wide and reaching out for Milo.

"Milo!"

It only took a moment for him to answer my plea. "Jess? What's going—"

I pushed it all into his head—Andrew, the secret entrance, Aoife, Gareth—all of it, one massive infodump. Milo gasped at the force of it.

"Holy shit! Aoife?! And Gareth is... oh my God!" His fear and surprise were popping off like fireworks inside our shared headspace.

"You need to find Finn. Alasdair's taking me to the courtyard with the Geatgrima."

"I'm coming!"

"Don't come alone!" The desperation of the plea clanged like a bell. "Please, Milo, find Finn, find Savvy, find everyone! Get them to the courtyard. I don't know what Alasdair is planning, but whatever makes him look that happy can't possibly be good."

"Okay. Okay, I'm... just hang on, okay?"

"I'm going to leave the Connection open, but I have to pull out. I can't risk being distracted."

"Of course. My God, be careful. Nothing is allowed to happen to you, do you understand me? That is a direct order from your spirit guide."

I surfaced from the Connection just as we reached the top of the staircase. Aoife pushed against the door at the top, and we stumbled out into... her office.

An entrance to the sanctum had been in her office all along.

Aoife couldn't have looked more smug. "How could I not take it as an invitation? A door right into the heart of the Brotherhood, here in my own little office. When I found it, I knew it was all meant to be. My destiny wrapped up in Alasdair's."

I couldn't even speak. This girl was lost before we met her. I couldn't worry about her anymore. I had to concentrate on getting the hell out of this mess.

The historical center was deserted. Everyone had gone to help find the entrance to the sanctum. We walked through the echoing stillness of the main reading room to the far end, where a door led out to a short path and then...

To the Geatgrima itself.

A handful of spirits drifted nearby, but they paid us no attention. They only had eyes for the Gateway that was calling to them, a few looking curious, others wary. Alasdair emerged beside us, his eyes fixed on the Geatgrima with unbridled hunger.

"At last," he whispered.

"Why are we here?" I asked, and though I was trying to sound calm, my voice was sharp with fear.

"Because the moment has arrived to achieve all that I have worked toward," Alasdair said. "I have strengthened myself. I have become more than spirit... more than man. And with this last victory—the regaining of a body—I know I am ready."

"Ready for what?"

He turned to look at me, eyes wild with longing. "Ready to step through the Gateway and back again."

I stared at him. I knew he was mad—no one sane could do what he had done —but this was deranged.

"This will never work," I said.

"You are the one person in this world who knows that isn't true. You've done it, Walker. You've trod that ground and returned again."

"That was different," I said. "I was still tied to my body. I was connected to my sister, a powerful Caller."

"And I am tied here. Now you know the true power of the Collection."

I blinked. Stared.

"I don't understand," I admitted.

"You believed that I gathered all of those spirits to strengthen myself, and that is true. But the true nature of the Collection is so much more than that. It is a tether—a tether that ties me to this world, a tether I can use to find my way back."

I stood there, trying to follow his logic.

Alasdair saw my confusion and snorted in disdain. "Another limited mind. Such a pity. Don't you see? I am no longer just one soul. I am many souls. The pieces of the souls I have consumed are still tied to the Collection. This is why I have divided them from themselves and taken them into myself instead. When I walk through that Gateway, I will still be connected to this side of the veil by a hundred shining points of light. The pieces of soul I contain will still long to be reunited. They will pull against my journey—they will resist it—and it is that pull that will allow me to return. Your sister Called you back. My Collection will do the same for me."

Beside me, still gripping my arm, Aoife gazed at Alasdair with unadulterated wonder. Even in my shock and disgust, I had to marvel at him, too. Because I realized there was every possibility that his plan could work.

Alasdair turned his attention back to the Geatgrima, and I chanced a glance around the courtyard. If anyone had arrived to come to my aid, I couldn't see them. But it would be foolish for them to storm the courtyard while Alasdair was holding me hostage with a knife, and I knew that Finn would never allow a reckless ambush that might get me killed.

Alasdair handed Aoife the bag he was carrying, and then reached out and grabbed me by the arm, sending my panic into a spiral.

"What are you going to do to me?" I asked.

"I'm not about to kill you, if that's what concerns you," Alasdair said, tugging me toward the plinth on which the Geatgrima stood. "I know you think me a monster, but I have only ever done what was necessary, and no more. The murders I committed were not driven by hatred or maliciousness. They were a matter of necessity. Killing you now would serve no purpose for me. But I don't think we'll be lucky enough to remain undiscovered for long, so let's just call you my insurance policy."

It was nauseating to listen to him justify himself, to make himself comfortable with excuses and equivocations. But he was holding a knife about three inches from my chest, so it wasn't exactly the moment to point it out. I seethed silently instead, as we approached the Geatgrima.

The draw of it was so strong, even for a soul safely ensconced in a body. It was a song you longed to sing, a hand you longed to hold. It took all my concentration not to be dazzled by it, to lose my firm grip on the danger of my present situation.

Alasdair was fully in its power, transfixed. His grip on my arm loosened ever so slightly, but I didn't dare try to pull away. Meanwhile, Aoife was hovering at the edge of the plinth, one hand working furiously at the hem of her shirt, while the other still clutched the bag Alasdair had given her.

"We need to hurry. It's only a matter of time before someone sees us. Tell me what to do!"

Alasdair dragged his eyes from the Geatgrima with apparent difficulty, then shook his head, breaking its hold on him. "The Summoning Circle. Cast it here and place the others inside it.

"Others?"

No one answered my question. Aoife set to work swiftly, using a can of white spray paint to create the Circle. She lit candles attached to stakes and shoved them into the ground so they couldn't topple over. Then, she reached into the bag one last time and pulled out three items: a gold ring, an earbud, and a pair of reading glasses. She placed them inside the circle and stepped back. "And now?" she asked.

"Move into the circle and stay there," Alasdair ordered. "If I am gone longer than the agreed upon timeframe, it may mean that the bond with the Collection is not strong enough. If that happens, you are to begin a Summoning, the added strength of which should be enough to call back the fragments of spirit I'm taking with me."

I looked down at the objects in the Circle and finally understood. The ring was Grace's. The earbud was Helen's. The glasses had belonged to Gareth. And just like the victims back in Edinburgh all those years ago, the remaining pieces of their souls had been bound to these objects. He was counting on the souls' longing to reunite themselves to be strong enough to pull him back.

Aoife moved into the Circle and stood there, expectant, and bouncing on the balls of her feet. She had that manic glow in her eyes again, that desperation for something remarkable to happen, and for her to be a part of it.

Alasdair approached the Geatgrima even closer, so that he was standing right on the threshold. For what felt like a long time, he didn't move. I looked down and saw that the knife he was holding was shaking in his hands.

"So now what happens?" I ventured.

Alasdair swallowed hard. It looked painful. "Now I kill this body and Cross through the Aether, further than any man has ever gone. Now I learn the answer to the question that every mortal soul longs for, but that only I can know. And then I will return a god." He raised the knife and positioned the tip of it against his chest.

I braced myself, my mind spinning. Should I try to stop him? Should I let him do it? What if I waited for him to Cross and then destroyed the Summoning Circle? After all, Aoife wasn't armed. I could definitely take her, and then at least one of Alasdair's safeguards would be foiled. But could he still come back without it?

I suddenly realized I'd had entirely too much time to consider these things. I looked at Alasdair again, and he was frozen in place, the knife shaking madly against his shirt, tearing little holes in the fabric.

And that's when I realized: Alasdair was *afraid*.

And of course he was. Hadn't it been his desperate fear of death that had sent him down this horror show of a path to begin with? A fear so deep and so crippling that he turned into a monster just to escape it. Because what did a monster have to fear?

But now all of that was stripped away, and here he stood—bare and defenseless against the one thing he'd never had the courage to face. Now, at the moment everything was within his grasp, he still had to do the one thing he couldn't bear to do. He had to leave this world without knowing what awaited him in the next, just as every other human being has had to do since we began to walk the earth.

And, I realized, he couldn't do it.

"Alasdair?"

It was Aoife's tentative voice that broke the silence. Alasdair's face twisted with rage at the sound of it, but he did not reply.

"Alasdair, is something wrong?"

"Nothing is wrong!" he shouted, spit flying from his lips. "I am preparing myself!"

Aoife stole a frightened glance over her shoulder. "I think I heard something in the cloisters. I think we're running out of t—"

"I know that! Don't you think I know that, you insufferable child?"

Aoife flinched at his words, but asked her next question anyway. "But what are you waiting for?"

Alasdair opened his mouth, but it was a much softer, much calmer voice that answered.

"He is afraid."

We all whirled to the sound of the voice, and I watched with a combination of elation and terror as Hannah—my Hannah—walked calmly into the courtyard carrying a lantern. At the same moment, I felt Milo slide gently into the Connection.

"It's okay. We're all here. The courtyard is surrounded."

"Where the hell did Hannah come from?"

"She flew here from Edinburgh. She was already on her way because she had something to tell us, and she wanted to tell us in person."

"And she couldn't have waited until we dealt with this hostage negotiation?" I asked, my anxiety making the entire Connection buzz like a kicked hive.

"Oh no. This is just the right moment, believe me."

"And is this the plan? To distract Alasdair with Hannah as bait? Because it feels like a shitty one!"

"Of course not. Hannah will tell you what to do."

I disengaged from Milo and focused on Hannah now. She wasn't looking at me. She seemed to have eyes only for Alasdair.

"Stay where you are!" Alasdair shouted. The knife was now pointing vaguely in my direction. "She is only in danger if you interfere."

Hannah stopped where she was. "Oh, I don't mean to interfere at all," she said. "Everything's prepared. You're ready. Go on. Claim your glory, Alasdair. No one will stop you."

Alasdair's eyes were bugging out of his head. He returned the knife point to his own chest, and there it hovered.

Hannah laughed lightly. "Alasdair MacLeod, I can smell your fear. I'll admit I cherished the hope of foiling your schemes, but watching you foil them yourself is so much more satisfying."

Alasdair stiffened, his face contorting. He pressed the knife blade harder against his chest, drawing a thin rivulet of blood; but still, he seemed incapable of plunging it in.

"Alasdair, do it!" Aoife cried out.

"Shut up!" Alasdair shrieked.

I reached into the Connection, a nudge at Hannah. I saw her eyes flicker to me.

"Hannah, what are you doing?"

"Just trust me. And get ready."

"Ready for what?"

She didn't reply. She had focused on Alasdair again. He was staring, not at Hannah, but at the lantern she carried in her hand.

"Oh, I see you've noticed my light. Pretty, isn't it?" Hannah said, raising the lantern and examining the flickering flame within. "But of course, it's so much more than beautiful. You can sense that, can't you?"

What the actual hell was going on? Why were we talking about lanterns? Was she just trying to distract him? Was Finn sneaking up from behind, ready to disarm him? I hadn't caught so much as a glimpse of anyone else, despite Milo's assurances that they had the place surrounded.

"What have you done?" Alasdair asked, his voice strangled.

"I found the Casting—the one you used to sever the souls of your victims and trap them. You see, you aren't the only one drawn in by the Necromancers. You aren't the only one who learned a trick or two from their twisted book. I bet you thought there wasn't a Durupinen alive who knew about Blind Summoners."

Alasdair sounded like he was choking. The knife tilted in his hand, the tip coming away from his skin.

"Once I made that connection, I tried a few little experiments of my own. It took some trial and error, but in the end, I was successful. Your Collection is unmade. And every fragment of soul you maimed is right here."

She swung the lantern gently so that the flame inside leaped and danced even as my heart leaped and danced in my chest. She'd done it. I couldn't believe she'd done it.

That was when the whispering started.

At first, it sounded like the breeze through the trees, but it brought a creeping cold that wasn't of this world. Then I realized it wasn't wind but voices, dozens of them.

And every one of them was whispering Alasdair's name.

Alasdair's face was paper white. He stared at the flame with undisguised fear. Still, he grasped at the slipping threads of his plan.

"What does it matter if you have unmade them?" he asked, with a maniacal titter of laughter. "They still remain here, on this earth, tethered to me. They cannot Cross if they are incomplete. They will draw me back again."

"Are you so sure?" Hannah asked, arching one eyebrow. "Because you've had ample time to carry out your plan, and you still haven't done it. Does that mean you doubt your work?"

"I doubt nothing!" Alasdair shouted.

"Then get on with it!" Hannah shouted back. "If you're the genius you claim to be, you have nothing to fear."

Just then, Hannah's intention dropped into my head. A clear instruction. I watched her eyes flicker to me, a question in them.

"Ready? On my signal."

I swallowed hard and then nodded.

Alasdair placed the knife to his chest again, howling with rage, his fear at war with his ambition. "This is my destiny! You will not stop my return!" he screeched.

"No, I won't," Hannah said softly. "But they will."

Alasdair's face went blank with confusion as Hannah's command echoed in my head.

"NOW!"

Hannah lifted the lantern over her head and brought it down hard on the rock beside her. At the same moment, I grasped the handle of Alasdair's knife and drove it straight into his chest. There was one isolated moment, silent and still like a photograph, when Alasdair's bulging eyes looked into mine, and I saw straight into the heart of his terror.

Then all hell broke loose.

As Alasdair staggered a step and sank to his knees, staring at the hilt of the knife, the fragmented spirits swirled up from the extinguished flame in a torrent of agony and rage and flew toward us. I dove sideways out of the way, rolling over the grass. Aoife cried out and started toward Alasdair, but Finn appeared out of the shadows, tackling her to the ground before she could interfere. At the same time, Savvy dashed into the Circle, splashing something pungent onto the artifacts, and setting them alight with a lighter from her pocket.

The twisted mass of spirits reached Alasdair just as his soul flew free of the body he had stolen, which slumped over, empty and useless. He let out a roar of pure rage and fought against the other spirits as they swarmed him, drawn to the missing parts of themselves inside him. The whole throbbing, thrashing mass was pushing him toward the Geatgrima, but he was powerful, engorged on the energy he had stolen from them, and he fought like a rabid animal against the pull of the portal behind him.

Suddenly three more spirit fragments rose up from the smoldering pile at Savvy's feet, released from their tiny prisons: Helen, Grace, and Gareth. They, too, flew at Alasdair, joining the desperate effort to force him through. But even their added rage didn't seem to be enough to overpower him. For one terrible moment, I thought he would escape them.

And then one final spirit shot like a bullet through the courtyard, a black cloak streaming out behind him. I caught a fleeting glimpse of Andrew Abercromby's featureless face just before he slammed into Alasdair, propelling the whole writhing mass of spirits backward and straight through the Geatgrima into the Aether beyond.

I dropped to my knees, staring at the Geatgrima as though expecting that any moment Alasdair would come bursting back through it again. Maybe it had all been enough. Maybe his mad experiments had worked and he would claw his way back through, a nightmare we could never wake up from. But the seconds ticked by and the Geatgrima was calm, the energy emanating from it unruffled. Could it really be over?

"Jess?"

"Huh?" I heard Finn's voice, but I couldn't tear my eyes from the Geatgrima.

"Are you all right, love?"

"I... is he really... did we do it?" I managed as tears started to well up in my eyes.

Finn tucked a finger under my chin and turned my face to his. "We did it. He's gone."

A ridiculous sound burst out of me—something between a sob and a laugh and a sigh of pure relief. Milo surged forward, circling the Geatgrima once as though he, too, was worried Alasdair would reappear. Then he flung himself at Hannah, who fell backward with a huff at the violence of his hug.

"That was the most badass thing I've ever seen!" he sang.

"Really?" Hannah groaned as she struggled to sit up. "Because I feel like I've pulled off some pretty impressive badassery in my day."

Milo kissed her on the head, making her shiver. "Top five badass moment, for sure."

Savvy was pulling Aoife to her feet and zip-tying her hands behind her back, while Rana stamped out the remains of the fire before it could spread. I watched them share a stolen moment as they reached out to squeeze each other's hands in a silent, "Well done." Then I turned my head, and my gaze fell on Gareth's body, still and empty in a pool of blood. Blood that I'd shed, blood that, I realized, was all over my hands.

"I killed someone," I muttered.

"You did not," Finn snapped at once, and I looked up to see him almost glaring at me. "There will be none of that. That was a ghost in a dead man's body. An abomination, a... a zombie. We will give guilt no corner today. Let it die with Alasdair, where it belongs."

I met his eye, and he smiled at me, gently. "Promise?"

"Promise," I agreed, though I suspected I wouldn't be able to keep that promise until I'd washed every physical trace of the night away in a long, hot shower.

Hannah came and sat beside me, resting her head on my shoulder.

"How are you here right now?" I asked her.

"What, I'm supposed to let you have all the fun?" she teased.

I managed a shaky laugh. "I guess not."

Hannah sighed. She found my hand and threaded her fingers between mine. And even without the Gateway in our blood, I felt the thrumming contentment of our unbreakable bond, the depth and strength of it soothing me like a balm.

And in the calm and silence that followed, Alasdair's twisted legacy was nothing more or less than the pain and devastation he left behind. In the end, despite all his scheming and wild fantasies, that was all he would ever be.

"Cheers, you lot!"

Savvy slammed a tray full of drinks down on the table where we all sat in the local pub.

"I have never needed a drink so badly in my life," Rana admitted, taking a pint from the tray.

"You can keep your pint. This calls for whiskey," Finn said, reaching for his own glass. He leaned back, took a long sip, and sighed before throwing his arm around my shoulders.

"Explain to me again how you just happened to be in that courtyard with the entire Collection crammed into a lantern?" I asked, once Hannah had collected her drink, too.

"Well, I'd already unmade the Collection. By some miracle, the Casting I wrote worked."

"It wasn't a miracle; it was you. You're brilliant," said Kiernan, planting a kiss on her head. Hannah blushed and shooed his words away.

"Anyway, I immediately hurried up above ground so that I could connect with Milo and give him the good news, and that's when he told me what was happening—that you'd all tried to Uncage that spirit—Andrew, was it?—and that Flavia was coming to perform the Memory Rifting. I knew I had to get there, so I called Catriona and told her I needed her to get me to Skye as quickly as possible, and she said, 'is a private jet fast enough?'"

Maeve laughed at this as she sipped her beer. "I knew that fleet of planes would come in handy."

"But what made you think to bring the Collection... uh, that is, the former Collection?" I asked.

"Well, while I was Memory Rifting through the Collection, I accessed a scattering of memories, including Alasdair discussing his plans with Danica. I knew he was counting on the Collection to tether him to this world, and so I thought, well, at some point, he's going to try to Cross, and when he does, we need to find a way to break that tether. I felt like I had to be on-site, just in case. After all, he'd attacked three people in five days;. It sounded like he was getting desperate. And then, by the time I landed, Aoife had disappeared, and then so did Jess. And then Jess used the Connection to tell Milo what was happening, and we realized we were out of time."

"Well, all I can say is, thank God," I said. "If you hadn't been there, Hannah, I don't know what would have happened."

"I bet in all his decades of scheming and murdering, he never once considered the fact that the tether could work in the opposite direction," Milo said, shaking his head. "There's something so delicious about how self-inflicted his own demise was, isn't there?"

It was hard for me to think of any part of the night's events as "delicious," but I couldn't deny that watching those spirits take their revenge on Alasdair was deeply satisfying.

"What do you think will happen to them?" Rana asked. "The fragmented spirits?"

Hannah sighed, her brow furrowing. "I suppose we can't know for sure. But they were able to Cross through the Geatgrima, so I'm hopeful that means that they were able to become whole again. When Jess released Alasdair's spirit from Gareth's body, she released all those spirit fragments he'd stolen along with it. I have to believe they were able to reunite themselves, or else I don't think they could have Crossed."

"Can we maybe try not to talk about the whole stabbing thing?" I asked, shuddering. "I realize he was already dead, and that body was stolen, but I'd still rather not relive the whole 'plunging a knife into another person' thing."

"I'm sorry you had to do that, love," Finn said. "Believe me when I say I tried to volunteer for the job."

"It was too risky," Savvy said, shaking her head. "Too many things could have gone wrong. Jess was right there within reach. It was much easier for her to just grab the—"

"Okay, but how are we still talking about it?" I cried, covering my ears with my hands.

"Oh, yeah. Right. Sorry, mate," Savvy said with a sheepish smile.

"Anyway, the point is, it's over," Milo said. "So, I'd like to raise my imaginary glass to Alasdair's victims. They took their lives back tonight. Let's wish them peace at last."

We all raised our glasses. I thought especially of Andrew, finally reunited with his beloved brother.

"Peace at last."

We stayed on Skye just long enough to ensure that Andrew Abercromby had a decent burial and to attend the funerals of Gareth Cadwalader, Helen O'Rourke, and Grace Cameron. The last one we almost skipped since there was about a fifty-fifty chance the sight of us would start a riot; but in the end, we sat in the very back row, determined to pay our respects. Not a single member of Grace's clan so much as looked at us, but in a moment that shocked me to my core, I heard my name and turned to see Clarissa MacLeod coming toward me, Maeve pushing her in a wheelchair.

"The indignity of this confounded thing," Clarissa grumbled as Maeve struggled to get her down the narrow aisle. "Never mind, Maeve, never mind. That's close enough, for Aether's sake."

Maeve stepped away from the chair to give her mother some privacy.

Clarissa cleared her throat awkwardly. "I wanted to take a moment to thank you for all that you've done in seeing that Alasdair was stopped. Clan Rìoghalachd failed in our most sacred duties. You have righted our wrong, and you did it despite my attempts to ensure you failed. I am... I am grateful to you."

Hannah and I traded one incredulous glance before I said, "Thank you. I'm glad we were able to see our way clear to working together."

"I am a woman set in my ways," Clarissa said. "I have never been content to let things change around me—instead, I learned to mold the world to my vision. But the world is not beholden to my wishes. It has been a hard lesson to learn, but I think I have begun to learn it. I want you to know that I... I will no longer be working against you. The Reckoning restored the world to what it ought to be. I know that now, and I intend to honor it. You are—both of you—welcome back to Edinburgh at any time."

"Thank you," I said, too stunned to say anything else. However, upon further reflection, I thought it would be a long time indeed before I had any desire to be Clarissa MacLeod's house guest.

The only thing left to do before leaving Kingshurst was to say goodbye to Tia, but at least I knew this goodbye would be a short one.

"Hannah told me I'm invited to the wedding!" she gushed, as she pulled me into a hug. "So you're guaranteed to see me in a few months, anyway!"

"Well, that's good, at least," I said. "And I swear I'll get better at checking my emails so I don't descend on your next educational endeavor with a murderous ghost."

Tia rolled her eyes. "Jess Ballard, don't make promises you can't keep."

As we pulled away from Kingshurst for the final time, I felt the last vestiges of dread leave me. It would likely take some time to believe it, but Alasdair's reign of terror really was over. The future stretched in front of us, a blank canvas ready for a new picture.

Well, maybe not completely blank...

"And then there's the second fitting, which will include the veil but NOT the shoes, and then at the third fitting, we add heels, but only for the first dress, because the second one has this..."

Milo prattled on endlessly about lace and trim and accessories as Hannah listened, her expression resigned.

"Karen called me." She told me, "The invitations just went out. The countdown is officially on."

I reached over and squeezed her hand. "And you're sure you're okay with it all?"

Hannah smiled—the first contented smile I'd seen on her face in weeks. She glanced over at Kiernan, his face buried in a book, and the smile broadened.

"I'm getting my happily-ever-after," she said. "Of course I'm okay with it."

I smiled, too. And hey, an unreasonable number of costume changes aside, we could be sure of at least one thing. With Milo in charge, we were all in for one hell of a party.

ABOUT THE AUTHOR

E.E. Holmes is a writer, teacher, and actor living in Massachusetts with her husband and two children. When not writing, she enjoys performing, watching unhealthy amounts of British television, and reading with her children.

To learn more about E.E. Holmes and *The World of the Gateway*, please visit eeholmes.com

Printed in Great Britain
by Amazon

44004782R00169